ALSO BY MAGGIE BARBIERI

Maeve Conlon Novels

Once Upon a Lie

Murder 101 Novels

Extra Credit

Physical Education

Third Degree

Final Exam

Quick Study

Extracurricular Activities

Murder 101

LIES THAT BIND

LIES THAT BIND

MAGGIE BARBIERI

MINOTAUR BOOKS ❅ NEW YORK

LIES THAT BIND. Copyright 2015 by Maggie Barbieri. All rights reserved. Printed in the United States of America. For information, address St. Martin's Press, 175 Fifth Avenue, New York, N.Y. 10010.

www.minotaurbooks.com

Design by Omar Chapa

The Library of Congress Cataloging-in-Publication Data is available upon request.

ISBN 978-1-250-01170-1 (hardcover)
ISBN 978-1-250-01169-5 (e-book)

Minotaur books may be purchased for educational, business, or promotional use. For information on bulk purchases, please contact the Macmillan Corporate and Premium Sales Department at 1-800-221-7945, extension 5442, or write to specialmarkets@macmillan.com.

First Edition: February 2015

10   9   8   7   6   5   4   3   2   1

For Jim, Dea, and Patrick. Thank you for your love and support.

ACKNOWLEDGMENTS

Thank you, as always, to the people at Minotaur, friends and colleagues I have come to think of as family: Elizabeth Lacks, Andy Martin, Sarah Melnyk, Paul Hockman, and my fantastic and ever-supportive editor, Kelley Ragland. Thank you, too, to agent extraordinaire Deborah Schneider and her team at Gelfman Schneider, Cathy Gleason and Victoria Marini, for whom no question is too big or small, not to mention stupid.

Alison Hendrie has been an invaluable sounding board to me over the last decade or so and without her help, my "outlines" of stories would never develop into anything more. Thanks also to Marian Borden and Laura Bradford, fantastic writers and treasured friends, who always have good advice and respond to queries with an alacrity I can only hope to embrace myself one day.

My family is always there and always supportive, and for that, I'm eternally grateful.

LIES THAT BIND

CHAPTER 1

Maeve knew a guy who knew a guy, well, who knew this guy.

What a gorgeous day for a ride, she thought, heading up the Taconic in her sensible Prius. She pulled into a rest stop about forty-five minutes after she left her house, spying her contact immediately. Handsome, with waist-long dreadlocks, he looked exactly as he had been described to her, standing out among the elderly leaf-peepers who stopped to eat their bag lunches, the families on their way to the apple orchard off the highway that Maeve had once taken her girls to a long time ago.

Plus the state trooper idling in his car in the parking lot.

No one looked twice at the petite woman in a hybrid stopping by a rest stop on a beautiful day, one made for the people touring the Hudson Valley. She sat in the car and waited until the trooper drove off, his lights turning lazily as he hit the highway, trolling for speeders on a scenic, twisty road.

The guy she was about to meet had been given a wide berth by the other people there, the area surrounding his shiny sports car devoid of other vehicles. He was young, and if he didn't have the hair, would have looked like any other college kid she knew. Dark-washed jeans, a nice designer polo shirt. Clean shaven. Bright, white smile.

If she didn't know what he did for a living—or maybe it was just a sideline—she would have picked him out for Rebecca, at college and unhappily single. She pulled up two spaces away and looked over at him. He gave her a warm smile and a quick wave.

"Hello," he said when she emerged from the car. In the sunlight, she noticed a wide streak of caked icing on the right thigh of her jeans. What must he think of her, this rumpled little woman with a very particular, peculiar, need?

"Nice to meet you," she said, offering her hand, sliding an envelope into his palm with a polite shake. He didn't look scared to meet her, this guy who was young enough to be her son—or maybe her nephew if she was feeling generous. Why should he?

Maybe he didn't know she was likely more dangerous than he was.

"A beautiful fall day," he said. "Warm." The bag he handed her, the one that he reached into the front seat of his car to get, was a recycled gift bag. He had gone so far as to stuff the top of it with brown tissue paper, tying the handles with some jaunty raffia. It looked as if he were giving her a birthday present.

"A gift?" she said. "For me?"

"A gift," he said, with fake solemnity. "For you." His laughter shook his dreadlocks.

It wasn't really a gift; that's what the envelope stuffed with cash had been for. It was more of a transaction. She held the bag; it was heavy, just like she expected it would be. "So, what are your plans for the rest of the day?"

He pointed to the backseat of the tiny car, where his little boy sat in a booster seat, drowsing peacefully, his thumb hanging from a slack mouth; Maeve hadn't noticed him up until this point. "I'm taking the little guy to the haunted house at a farm up the road. He loves to be scared."

"Don't forget to get some apples," she said. "The Macouns are particularly tasty this time of year." The talk of apples jogged her memory and she opened the back of the Prius. "That reminds me," she said. She pulled out a plain brown box; in it was a freshly baked apple pie. "Named 'Best of Westchester' by a local magazine," she said.

"Is that a pie?" he asked, a little surprised by the gesture.

"It is."

"Our mutual friend told me about your pies. And your cupcakes. He loves those. My granny will be so happy."

She was finding out more than she needed to know, wanted to know. She had to end the conversation. "Have a safe trip home."

"I will."

Good. He didn't seem to know her name. And she didn't know his. Better that way.

"I'll be off," she said.

He reached into his pocket. "Here's my card. In case you need anything else," he said.

But she wouldn't. One was enough for now and probably ever, if she took good care of her purchase. The card had only a number on it, no name. She put it in her jeans pocket, making a mental note to throw it out the window as soon as was acceptable and he was out of sight. She didn't want to offend him on the off chance she needed him again. Her friend would be able to find him again; the card was unnecessary. "Have fun at the haunted house," she said, walking around to her side of the car. He was still standing there as she drove off, heading south on the Taconic, marveling at the beautiful colors of the changing leaves.

It had been a wet end to the summer. That's why the leaves were so brilliant. At least that's what they had said on the news the night before. She drove along the highway, enjoying the time alone, the respite from her busy store. For the first time in a while, she felt free.

And her hands—her palms really—had finally stopped itching. It took her a moment to figure out what felt different.

It was all she could do not to pull over and caress the gun that lay in the bag beside her.

Why did she need a gun? She wasn't sure. But she needed it; she was sure of that and that was all that mattered. Security, a feeling of safety, of never being afraid, had been robbed from her years ago and while she had no immediate—or even future—plans to use this item in the bag, she felt safer having it. No one really would understand that, ever; after all, she was a suburban mom, a business owner. A nice lady, as one of her clients called her. It made sense, but only to her.

She would keep it hidden; no one would ever know.

"Thanks, Rodney Poole," she said, the utterance of his name bringing a smile to her face.

CHAPTER 2

"Two hundred dollars."

The words hung in the air between Maeve and her landlord, an unsavory character who she tolerated, but only because she had to. Given the least bit of provocation—provocation that went beyond raising her rent—she would feel no guilt in blowing his head off; his proclivity for standing just a little too close to her, laying a hand on her arm or shoulder in a way that made her uncomfortable just two reasons for her dislike of him.

Then, there was the garlic.

Sebastian DuClos seemed to bathe in it, his odor making its way into the store before his physical presence. Maeve could smell him coming a mile away even if he didn't always pick up the rent on the same day, the first of the month, twelve times a year.

"Two hundred dollars?" Maeve repeated. "A month?"

"A month," he said, smiling slightly. "Do you have a problem with that?" he asked, leaning forward, his ample belly grazing the edge of the butcher-block island that ran almost the whole length of the kitchen. From a bag, he took out a ripe tomato, something she didn't expect to see in December. "And a little peace offering, Maeve. Something to take the sting out of our conversation," he said.

She took the tomato. "Thank you?" Maeve said. She wasn't quite sure what to do with it, so she placed it on the counter between them.

He usually came alone, but today, he had brought along a helper, a kid he introduced as a local named Billy, who grunted a greeting while pocketing Maeve's envelope of cash. Billy's lack of conversational aptitude aside, he was well dressed in a blue oxford shirt and khakis, low Doc Martens on his feet. He had that well-tended look of a Farringville teen, one who always got a trophy for showing up and whose parents fed him the best locally sourced vegetables, those that looked like DuClos's beautiful tomato. If nothing else, he was polite, addressing Maeve as "ma'am" and keeping his mouth shut while DuClos spoke.

DuClos looked around the kitchen. "Looks clean."

"It has to be. Board of Health and all," Maeve said.

Billy walked over to the pantry door and jiggled the handle.

"Can I help you with something?" Maeve asked, donning a clean apron in the hopes that she would send the message that she had work to do. "That's a pantry." As she did every month, she handed Du-Clos a loaf of bread, fresh from the oven, and a box of cupcakes. "Are we done here?"

DuClos seemed in no hurry to leave, leaning against the counter, settling in for a chat. "You've been here a while, Maeve. Right?" he asked.

She knew where this conversation was going and she didn't like it. She checked her watch, hoping that whatever he had to say would be said quickly and she could get over to Buena del Sol to see her father before it was too late. The longer Jack Conlon was awake, the less cogent he was, and she feared this might be the day she would walk in and he wouldn't know who she was or why she was there.

"Well," DuClos said, clutching the loaf of bread that Maeve had given him between his hands, exhaling a breath that filled the kitchen with the pungent odor of garlic previously consumed. "Time to raise the rent then," he said. "Don't you think?"

She was glad that he wasn't evicting her. She had too much on her plate: an ailing father with Alzheimer's, two teenaged daughters, one college tuition, another one on the way, and a mortgage. The business was finally firmly in the black and she wanted to keep it that way; a move to another location would have been a problem she didn't have the energy to solve.

Two hundred dollars. Ten more loaf breads a month or two big cakes. No sweat.

"You're successful," DuClos said. "I hear things. 'Best of Westchester'?"

"Yes," Maeve said. The accolades hadn't done all that much to increase business.

"Then two hundred a month should be a piece of cake for you," he said. "No pun intended."

Next to him, Billy looked around the kitchen, staring an inordinately long time at the ceiling tiles, the keypad for the security system by the back door, looking anywhere but at her forlorn face. When he caught her looking at him, he smiled in an approximation of sympathy.

"Fine," she said, opening the refrigerator. "When does this begin? First of the year?"

"First of the year," DuClos said, fingering a button right over his ample belly that had come undone during their conversation. "New year. New rent. I hope it won't be a problem."

She shook her head. She didn't want to give him the impression she was happy with just two hundred dollars, nor did she want him to think it was out of her reach. "Fine. First of the month."

"My associate here will be picking up rents in the future," DuClos said, the smell of his garlicky breath filling the small space. "Will you be closed over the holidays as usual?"

Maeve nodded. "As usual." She filled the butcher-block counter with the ingredients for an order she had to fill, a bridal shower cake for sixty people. "Nice to meet you, Billy," she said, though she didn't really mean it. She wanted them out of her store, but couldn't be rude. Time was ticking away. Her father's handle on the present was slowly leaving his mind like the sunlight dwindling outside in the little swath of parking lot that she could see from the open kitchen door.

"Ma'am," Billy said, nodding solemnly. She wondered what Du-Clos would have an "associate" do exactly, besides pick up the rent from the shopkeepers. She decided, just as quickly, that she didn't want to know.

Her landlord and his lackey made no attempt to leave. "I need another loaf of bread, Maeve," DuClos said.

More to sop up the garlic that would likely be in his dinner, Maeve thought. She went into the front of the store where Jo was gazing into the refrigerated case.

"They still in there?" she asked, her pregnant belly at odds with her lanky arms, her long neck. Pregnant now, some smells bothered Jo, and just the idea of being in an enclosed space with Sebastian Du-Clos made her sick to her stomach.

Maeve grabbed a loaf of bread from the counter and nodded. "Yep," she said. "But I think they're on their way. Stay put for now."

Back in the kitchen, there were a few additional moments of awkward silence before the two men drifted out the back door to the noisy car that had transported them to the bakery, the assault on her nose the only thing to let her know that they had been there in the first place, that it hadn't been just a bad dream. Maeve peeked through the small round window in the door that separated the kitchen from the front of the store.

Jo came into the kitchen to check on her friend. "So, now that they're gone, how's it hanging, sister?"

"Low and saggy," Maeve replied, attempting to smile but falling short. She felt like that a lot lately, as if she couldn't really make her mouth do what she wanted. "He's raising my rent."

"Rat bastard," Jo said.

Maeve turned and pointed to a large bin of flour, about half her size. "And someone," she said—and since it was only she and Jo that spent any time in the kitchen, that narrowed the suspects—"didn't close the flour last night. I just noticed it. I have to dump it now." She had been eyeing it the whole time her landlord had been in the store, willing herself to remember that when he and his associate were gone, she and Jo had ingredients to discard, something that pained her.

"Heather was here," Jo said, trying to foist blame onto Maeve's youngest.

Heather had been there, but Maeve knew her youngest daughter well enough to know that she didn't touch any of the baking ingredients if she didn't have to. A face full of flour one day when she tried to make cupcakes by herself had convinced her to let the experts—namely, her mother—do the baking. Jo peered into the bin. "Is that a bug?"

Maeve looked in. It wasn't, but it was a bit of detritus that had likely flown in through the back door when one of them had entered that morning, a piece of a leaf from a tree stripped bare long ago. It wasn't a ton of flour to throw out, but it was enough. She tamped down any feelings of annoyance she may have had and pulled out a big black plastic garbage bag from the box on the shelf and asked Jo to hold it open, tightening the seal around the bin so that flour didn't fly around the work area and get into Jo's sensitive and delicate nasal passages.

"Okay, let's get this done," Maeve said. "I need to see my father before dinner."

"How is my old boyfriend, Jack?" Jo asked. She asked about him every day, and Maeve wasn't sure why, but Jo was one of the people that Jack hadn't forgotten.

"He's good," Maeve lied. He wasn't. He was ornery, the dementia turning him into an angry approximation of his old self, complaining vociferously that he wanted out of Buena del Sol and into her house so that he could live out his final years with his only child. It wasn't going to happen. What was more likely was that he would be moved to the full-care section of the facility and reside in a state of confused unhappiness until his hale and hearty body finally gave out. Rather than focus on the truth of the matter, Maeve turned her full attention to the flour barrel.

The task seemed beyond Jo's capabilities as Maeve struggled to upend the bin into the garbage bag. The struggle continued as she poured the contents of the flour into the bag and Jo attempted not to breathe in a heavy dose of flying particles. By the time they had finished, Jo had a white nose and Maeve was laughing, something she hadn't done in a long time. It felt good.

"That was a lot more work than necessary," Jo said. Maeve tied up the kitchen garbage and put it into the bag with the flour.

"Can you carry that outside for me?" Maeve asked, going into the front of the store to make sure they were ready to close. On the counter, the place where Maeve did most of her work, its surface littered with spatulas, piping bags, and cupcake holders, her phone trilled. It was Angelle, the nurse from Buena del Sol who visited Jack every day in his apartment.

"He's gone, Miss Conlon." There was a hitch in the woman's voice, a small hiccup of grief. "I'm so sorry."

CHAPTER 3

Maeve went through the motions at the wake, the funeral, and the burial, greeting the mourners and, in many cases, consoling them. But she was Irish-American and one thing she knew how to do was make plans to send a loved one to the "great beyond."

And how to throw a mean after party.

When it came to what was eaten after a good, old-fashioned Irish Catholic sendoff, one had to pull out all of the stops for the mourners. To some, it was more important than the actual funeral Mass, though Maeve wasn't one of those people. Still, she felt as if she had to have something nice.

They expected it. It was required. And she was sure that Jack Conlon would haunt her until the day she died if she didn't send him off with a culinary bang.

With that in mind, she booked Mickey's, a watering hole not far from her house where she knew the owner. Mickey guaranteed her that he would kick out the drunks who sat at the bar in the middle of the day and provide a buffet befitting Maeve's father and his appetites.

There was Jack's favorite shepherd's pie, steam rising from atop the layer of mashed potatoes; a pasta dish; and chicken Francaise, a dish that Jack referred to as "fricassee," even though a fricassee was something completely different. Maeve smiled as she put a piece of chicken on her plate, thinking of her father, adding some vegetables and turning to find a seat in the main dining area where Conlon mourners had taken all of the seats. The six tables that she had reserved were filled with friends and family, none looking terribly sad now that the funeral and burial were out of the way; a couple looked like they were well into their second or third Stellas, the DPW guys in particular. That helped the sadness of the morning wither away like the dead leaves that clogged the gutters outside the old village establishment. Who could blame them, these people who had come to pay their respects? Free food and booze. It took an iron will to turn down either, not to mention both.

Jack would have been thrilled at the turnout overall but would have also noted who hadn't shown up, whispering in a voice that everyone would have been able to hear, "Don't let my dying interfere with your bocce game, De Luca!" or "I've only died, but that hair appointment needs to be kept, Bernice!"

Maybe if she kept this running commentary in her head, she'd be able to keep a little piece of him alive and the hole that had opened in her heart would be filled with his memory.

He had died in his sleep, just like he prayed for every day, and Maeve took a bit of comfort, knowing that he had drifted off, never to awaken.

Before she sat down, Mimi Devereaux, Jack's "main squeeze" at the home, as he had referred to her, stopped her. "So sorry for your loss, Maeve." She had on a feather boa and thick orangey-red lipstick that Maeve felt sure had gone out of style around the time of Pearl Harbor.

"Thank you, Mrs. Devereaux," she said, her eyes locked in on the smear of lipstick that adorned the woman's prominent front teeth.

Look away, she cautioned herself, but she couldn't. It was a cosmetics train wreck.

"I just wanted to know, dear. How long do you think it will take to move your father's things out of the apartment?" she asked.

This isn't happening. This woman isn't asking me so that she can have someone else move in, Maeve thought. "Soon," Maeve said. I'll squeeze that in between getting ready for Christmas and the other life events that are sure to come up in the next few weeks, she thought. "Why do you ask?"

"My dear friend, Stanley Cummerbund, is on the waiting list. Next in line for a place!" she said, clapping her hands together excitedly. "And he'd love to move in right away."

"Well, I'll get right on that," Maeve said. "As long as you and Mr. Cummerbund are happy, I'm happy," she said, a smile on her face that belied the anger bubbling beneath her placid surface. She looked up at the ceiling. You hear this, Dad? She's already moved on. I told you she was a hussy, that you'd never find a woman as good as Mom. My mother was a saint.

"Oh, wonderful, dear." Mrs. Devereaux smiled widely and Maeve took in the lipstick on just about every tooth in the woman's mouth. "I won't make any promises but I'll let him know that it will be soon."

Maeve detached herself from the old woman and made her way through the dining room, careful not to stop and talk to anyone who wanted to order a cake, move into her father's recently vacated apartment, or discuss current events. She just didn't have the energy.

Margie Haggerty waved enthusiastically, the underside of her arm flapping with the effort. Maeve made a mental note to wave to herself in the mirror when she got home; if that's what middle age looked like, she had better get on the stick, and fast. "Here! Maeve, come sit here," Maeve's old neighbor from the Bronx beckoned, the chief mourner in her sights.

Mickey's was small and Maeve couldn't pretend that she hadn't seen Margie, which is how she found herself sandwiched between Margie and her older sister, Dolores, who was encased—because, really, that was the only word for it—in a dark blue pantsuit that was surely from the Hillary Clinton collection at Nordstrom. They had been neighbors a long time ago when they were all younger, and while Maeve would have said they were also "more innocent" back then, it wasn't really true.

Dolores, six years older, had never been innocent, and Margie's innocence was still in question. And Maeve's innocence had been stolen early on by the man Dolores eventually married—Maeve's first cousin—but he was dead now and Maeve didn't have to worry about him anymore.

Maeve looked at her plate, piled high with food. She was starving. When had she eaten last? She couldn't remember and it didn't matter. She dove into the shepherd's pie, hoping that by concentrating on eating, she wouldn't have to talk to Margie or Dolores. She looked over and smiled at her daughters, seated with their father and his wife, otherwise known as Mrs. Callahan #2, at a table tucked into a far corner.

"Very nice of you to come," Maeve said, managing to add a smile to the sentiment. There was a sordid history between the two families, though Maeve wasn't sure how much the sisters knew of it. That Dolores's husband, Sean, had abused Maeve. That their father, a drunk, had run Maeve's mother down in a hit-and-run, something that had remained a mystery until recently for Maeve. That Martin Haggerty had left her mother to bleed to death on a Bronx avenue, never telling a soul until he was near death about what he had done.

Margie clasped Maeve's hand in her own freckled one. "We wouldn't have missed it, Maeve. We . . . I . . . loved your father." She even managed to produce a tear or two. "He was a kind man."

"Yes, he was," Maeve said. "Contrary to . . ." But she bit her tongue, remembering their serpent-tongued mother. But then again, Fidelma Haggerty hadn't had a nice word to say about anyone; she hadn't reserved her vitriol for just Jack. "How are things, Margie?" Maeve asked.

"Everything is great," she started, keeping an eye on her sister; Maeve had her back to Dolores and wasn't troubled in the least by not showing good manners in this case. Dolores was well on her way to getting sloshed and Maeve didn't even like her when she was sober, so it was downhill from here.

It was only the feeling of a cold splash on her leg that interrupted Maeve's concentration. Beside her, Dolores had upended her glass of Chardonnay onto Maeve's skirt, soaking it through.

"Sorry," Dolores slurred. Instead of helping Maeve clean it up, she motioned to the waitress busing the tables. "Another wine, please," she called out.

Maeve blotted her skirt the best she could with her napkin and another one, slightly used, from the now-empty space across from her. Nothing like a drunk woman at a somber event to clear a room or diminish her once-ferocious appetite. She pushed her plate away and focused on a wormhole in the knotty pine paneling, a blackboard hanging on it touting the *homemade desserts from The Comfort Zone!* and took a deep breath. Just how long were these things supposed to go? She looked at Margie, the safer and more sober of the two sisters, but it was Dolores who wanted her attention. Her wine had been delivered and the glass was almost empty.

Margie leaned in close to Maeve. "It was Sean's death," she said, her voice so low that Maeve could hardly hear her. "She's been drinking ever since. It's becoming a problem."

Maeve didn't respond. It wasn't becoming a problem; clearly it was already a problem. Dolores had married Sean Donovan; there had to have been massive amounts of alcohol involved, his wealth and success notwithstanding.

Sean's was the last funeral she had attended before her father's. She hadn't expected them to happen so close together but she was starting to figure out that life didn't happen the way you planned it. Mrs. Callahan #2 was a testament to that fact.

Dolores pulled Maeve close, attempting to tell a story about Jack that Maeve wasn't sure cast him in the best light. "So, he got our tree and then lit a cigarette and the whole thing went up in flames," she said, holding Maeve's gaze even though Maeve wasn't really following the story. "My father put it out with his hands. His bare hands."

Maeve tuned out, studied her plate of food.

Dolores shook her head at the memory, at Jack's supposed carelessness. "Almost burned our house down."

"Well, all's well that ends well, right, Dolores?" Maeve said. The Haggerty house remained standing, after all.

Dolores pulled on the sleeve of Maeve's black turtleneck. "Do you know what you should do now?" she asked, her wine-soaked breath wafting up to Maeve's nose.

Next to her, Maeve felt Margie freeze. She couldn't imagine how she could make restitution for a thirty-year-old Christmas tree, but she'd be interested in what Dolores had in mind. "No, Dolores. What should I do?"

"You should find the other one," she said, slurring so that all the words ran into each other.

Maeve was confused. "There was another tree?"

Margie reached out and grabbed Dolores's arm. "We should go."

"The other what?" Maeve asked. The food that she had pushed away looked gray and unappetizing; she put a napkin over it, giving it a peaceful death. Having Dolores Donovan around would be great for the diet she would start immediately following today's feast.

"The other one," Dolores said, finishing off her drink in one long swallow. The outside of the glass was coated with food and greasy fingerprints.

Maeve waited. "The other what, Dolores?" she said, her voice getting louder, her impatience growing.

Margie leaned across Maeve and took her sister's face in her hands. "Enough, Dolores." She turned to Maeve. "We're very sorry for your father's passing. We'll talk soon."

No, we won't, Maeve thought. We won't talk soon and we'll resume the lives that we want to live. Mine is absent of yours, in case you're wondering. She hoped she wasn't wrong about that. This had to be the last time she would see them.

"The other one," Dolores said, not to be deterred. She picked up a glass of beer from the place beside her; Mr. Moriarty, Jack's best friend at Buena del Sol, had been sitting there just seconds earlier but had beaten a hasty departure to parts unknown when it was clear that things were going to unravel. In his place remained an unfinished beverage; Dolores took a noisy slurp.

Margie pulled two coats off the hook behind the table and dropped a Mass card on the table. "We're very sorry for your loss, Maeve," she said. She threw her sister's coat over her shoulders. "Your father was a nice man." She turned to her sister. "Dolores. Now."

Dolores stood on unsteady feet, catching herself with a hand to the edge of the table. "You need to find her."

"Who?" Maeve said, aware that she was yelling. The other guests were staring. Whatever was happening needed to stop; maybe a raised voice was the only way to get Dolores's pickled brain to pay attention. After all, raised voices were the Haggertys' stock-in-trade. Maybe Dolores didn't know how to respond to anything else. Maeve's daughters, Rebecca and Heather, still sitting with their concerned father, turned and looked at her. "Who?"

Dolores smiled. "Your sister."

CHAPTER 4

Maeve raced into the street, stopping on the double yellow line, a car coming so close that her hair whipped in its wake. The Haggertys were out of the parking spot before she had hit the sidewalk, Margie's old Honda speeding away under the threatening storm clouds, her sister in the backseat, her face the last thing Maeve saw before she felt the touch of her oldest daughter's hand on her arm.

Rebecca put an arm around her. "Mom. It's cold. Come inside."

Maeve waited until they were out of sight, standing in a misty rain that should have felt colder when it hit her skin, but her face was hot; she was burning up. The words "your sister" rang in her ears, Dolores's voice not unlike the screeching sound that the neighborhood women's grocery carts—and their voices—made outside the bedroom window of her childhood home on a tree-lined street in the Bronx. "The butcher had pork on sale, Mrs. McDermott. Fifty-nine cents a pound." "Thank you, Mrs. Blaine. Don't forget to get your church raffle tickets." If Maeve closed her eyes, she could imagine she was back there, sitting on her bed, her chenille bedspread lumpy clumps of cotton beneath her, the sound of neighborhood business being attended to, children's voices wafting up as they played in the streets. You could do that then, play in the streets. Those thoughts, jumbled up with the unpleasantness of her encounter with the Haggertys, roiled around in her brain.

She had been an anomaly then, an only child, motherless, the neighborhood women clucking around her, making sure her hair was cut the proper way, her knee socks cuffed at just the right place. Her father adored her and she adored him because it was just the two of them, making them the smallest family on the block. More than one woman had criticized Jack for the way he was raising her, a "ragamuffin" among good, holy little girls, someone for whom baking had become a respite, albeit a solitary one. He never cared about what they said. To him, she was perfect. She was his. He told her so every day.

She wouldn't go back inside. Couldn't. Standing there, frozen to the spot on the street, watching cars pass in front of her, she thought of one memory that would stay with her and resurrect itself every time she heard their names: Dolores and Margie. Margie and Dolores. The Haggerty sisters. Fidelma and Marty's girls.

Her mind went back decades, the world now fading from her consciousness.

"Big step," Jack had said when he handed over the key to the house, a *Partridge Family* key chain holding the key that opened their front door. She was nine. "Now, do you remember what to do?" he had asked.

"Come straight home. Lock the door behind me. Do my homework. Don't use the oven," she had said, having memorized the routine so that she wouldn't let him down. She knew her father worried about her, worried that she wouldn't be able to execute those few steps with any kind of accuracy, and that bugged her. She was smart and responsible. She begged him for the chance to prove that.

That first day when she arrived home, she searched her book bag but the key was missing. Even though she had touched it throughout the day and made sure it was still there, it was gone.

Her heart sank as she pulled every book out of the bag and searched the pages, hoping against hope that it had gotten stuck, that she had really not lost it. It had to be there.

When the rain started to fall, light at first but eventually turning heavy and unrelenting, she went next door to the Haggertys', a place she never wanted to go. Mr. Haggerty drank. Mrs. Haggerty was mean. And the girls? Well, they were their own set of problems. Dolores had answered the door, a sullen teenager with a mouth set in a perpetual sneer.

"I lost my key," Maeve had said, her knee socks ending a few inches below her plaid uniform skirt and not providing any protection against the chill that accompanied the rain. She was so cold that she couldn't get the next sentence—"Can I come in?"—out.

"Too bad," Dolores had said. "What do you want me to do about it?" Her already developed and ample chest strained against a St. Barnabas volleyball sweatshirt, Dolores's heft coming in handy on the court, Maeve imagined years later.

"Who is it?" Maeve heard Fidelma Haggerty call from the kitchen.

"It's no one," Dolores had called back, turning her attention back to Maeve. "No one at all."

Behind her on the table in the front hallway was Maeve's key, the *Partridge Family* key chain a dead giveaway. "That's my key, Dolores," she said as a guilty Margie slithered by, slipping the key and key chain into the pocket of her jeans.

Dolores turned. "I don't see anything," she said before slamming the door shut in Maeve's face.

Jack got home at ten o'clock that night and found her sitting at the picnic table in the backyard, soaked to the skin but not crying. She had cried all afternoon; no tears left. He had carried her inside and dried her off, making her a cup of scalding-hot tea that burned her tongue and singed her throat when she sipped it, but she didn't really feel anything at all at that point.

She never told him about the girls' cruelty. She had gotten good at keep secrets from a young age.

"I'm sorry, Daddy. I lost the key," she said, because she knew that if she did tell what she saw and what she knew, her life would become ten times worse than it already was. He would go to the Haggertys. He would fight with Mr. Haggerty. Dolores would make her life more of a hell than it already was. She was smart enough to figure that out.

When Jack did call his sister-in-law to find out if her cousin Sean was available after school to take care of Maeve, he asked her why she didn't go to the Donovans' first, why she didn't find someone at home so that she could sit in a warm house rather than on a picnic table in the rain.

At nine, her first inclination was to lie. "They weren't home." They were home, and if she had gone there, there would have been more pain from Sean, her abuser, more than she had already endured. So, she lied to her father and she could see on his face that he didn't believe her, the first crack in the trust that was between them.

He had wondered about that; she could see it on his face. He wanted to believe her but couldn't. But one thing he never wondered about later is why his little girl never cried even when she was hurt or sad. That question never came out of his mouth. And she never really cried again, the ability to show fear or sadness something that had been tortured out of her all those years ago.

CHAPTER 5

Eventually, she did go back inside, said good-bye to her guests, put the memories of the Haggerty sisters from her mind, the thing Dolores had said. She and the girls left Mickey's after the last mourners had departed and got into her Prius, Maeve gripping the steering wheel to steady her shaking hands; she willed herself to calm down. She drove to the train station, Rebecca's questions to her going unanswered. Who were those women? What did they say? Would she be all right even after Rebecca left, the few weeks until she came home for Christmas break?

By the time they reached the station, Rebecca was ready to hop out of the car before it even stopped moving. Before they left Mickey's, the girls had been in deep conversation at their table for two, their father and stepmother having left right after the scene with the Haggertys, Heather's head bent in such a way that her long, thick hair covered each side of her face like the curtain Maeve used to pull aside to use the confessional at St. Margaret's. Back then, Maeve confessed the made-up sins of an eight-year-old who had picked up pointers from some magazine called *True Confessions*. Turned out that the magazine had stories that weren't about the kind of sin she was thinking about at her young age but she didn't know that.

"Aren't you forgetting something?" Maeve asked as Rebecca prepared to make her exit.

Rebecca leaned over and kissed her mother's cheek. She threw in a hug for good measure. "Are you okay, Mom?" she asked. "I'll be home on the twenty-first. Not too long from now."

"I'll be fine, honey," she said, pushing Rebecca's hair back from her forehead and holding her hand there. "Are you sick?" she said. "You feel warm." Being a mother was what she knew. Being an orphan, not as much.

Rebecca smiled. "I'm fine," she said. "You worry too much. I love you," she said, and then was out of the car, leaping up the stairs to the station, two at a time, like a lithe gazelle.

I do worry too much, Maeve thought. That's my job. And I love you, too, she thought but didn't say because Rebecca was almost out of sight. She opened the window. "Dad will pick you up at school on the twenty-first!" she called after her, but Rebecca was gone, lost in the throng of afternoon commuters, on their way to see the tree at Rockefeller Center or the decorated windows along Madison Avenue.

Maeve waited until the train pulled out of the station, willing her heart to slow its beating, her hands to stop shaking. In the backseat, Heather was wearing noise-canceling headphones and crying softly, wiping her nose on the sleeve of her pea coat. Two years younger than her sister, she was Maeve's "little gypsy," as her grandfather used to call her, dark, brooding, and prone to long bouts of silence. Maeve caught Heather's eye in the rearview mirror but knew better than to go any further than reach back and squeeze the kid's knee.

She drove back through town, pulling up in front of the house. She wasn't ready to go home and she wasn't ready to go back to work, but she knew that baking would calm her nerves, keep her from thinking about the absence, her deceased father. She gritted her teeth, willing the tears away, and waited until Heather went back into the house before driving off down the street.

Baking had gotten her through many a tough time. It was after her mother died, and after watching a show on public access television, that she had become interested in food, sweets in particular. She had baked for Jack, making him cinnamon buns and coffee cakes that he could eat before he went to work and cookies and brownies that she stuffed inside the bag he carried to the precinct where he worked most of his years on the NYPD. She baked when she was happy and she baked when she wasn't, the bad days outnumbering the good for many years but her prowess growing along with her iron will.

She went into the kitchen and punched the security code into the keypad, taking off her coat and donning a Comfort Zone apron over her soiled funeral clothes. She'd make donuts, even though they were Jack's least favorite of everything she made, a thick, cakelike donut and a cup of coffee all she wanted after the hours spent in church, next to the Haggerty girls. She pulled a big silver mixing bowl from the shelf next to the sink and assembled a few ingredients, going to the locked pantry that Billy, DuClos's "assistant," had tried to get into a few days before, and opening the door with the key on her key ring. She moved a few items around, looking for the new large bottle of vanilla extract that she knew she had bought a week earlier but which now seemed to be missing.

First the flour that needed to be thrown out, and now the missing vanilla. At this rate, replacing ingredients would bankrupt her in no time.

Although she heard the door that led from the front of the store to the kitchen creak ever so slightly, she didn't have time to turn around, down on her knees inside the pantry, before a blow to the back of her head sent her face-first onto the floor. But she did smell something before she blacked out, and although she wasn't sure when she woke up, she was thinking it might be garlic.

CHAPTER 6

Why hadn't she ever noticed that local police detective Chris Larsson's eyes were the deepest blue? Or that when he smiled, the skin around them crinkled in a way that masked the fact that he spent most of his time in serious pursuits, keeping the village safe from crime? From her place on the floor, inside the shallow pantry, she looked up at him, smiling herself.

What a nice sight to wake up to, she thought.

"If I'd known you were coming, I'd have baked a cake," she said, attempting to sit up.

"Whoa, stay there," he said, pressing a gentle hand against her clavicle. "Let's get you checked out before we start moving around too much."

Behind him, Jo was leaning against the butcher-block counter and wringing her hands. "Is she okay?"

"Does she always talk about baking?" Chris asked, standing up and moving away from the pantry.

He was replaced by an EMT, a kid she felt sure was not much older than Heather but who seemed confident in his ministrations. He finally sat Maeve up. "I think we should take her to Northern Westchester for observation."

Maeve put up a hand. "Nope. That's not necessary." She stood, and although she felt a little woozy at first, that feeling was replaced with steadiness and a pounding headache. She put a hand to the back of her head and felt a hard lump. "Who hit me?" she asked, taking a seat at the small desk at which she did her accounting and invoicing. She looked around and took in the concerned faces of another EMT and two uniformed cops. "What happened?"

"I don't know," Jo said, "but I passed a car on the way over here. I came to see if you needed anything from me, if you'd be okay. I found you on the floor of the pantry."

Chris Larsson crouched down in front of her. "Do you remember anything, Maeve? Any sounds?"

"I remember a bad smell." Chris and Jo exchanged a look that told her they thought she had sustained a far more serious head injury than she had. "Garlic?" She went through the papers on her desk and found Sebastian DuClos's card. "Here. Ask him."

Chris took the card and looked it over. "He's your landlord, right?"

Maeve nodded, and just the simple act of moving her head up and down intensified her headache. "Yes. He smells like garlic."

Jo was nodding vigorously. "He does."

"Okay, Maeve, we'll find out where Mr. DuClos was around the time of this incident," Chris said, even though the look on his face told Maeve that he wasn't convinced she would be attacked by her landlord. "Are you behind on your rent?" he asked.

"No," she said. "On time. Every month."

"Are you sure we can't convince you to go to the hospital?" Chris asked.

"I'm sure," she said. She looked over at Jo. "Please put some things together for everyone here. As a thank-you." She motioned to the EMTs. "Go with her to the front of the store and pick out what you want."

The two EMTs followed Jo and left Maeve with Chris. "You, too,

Chris," she said. He was a regular customer on the days he worked, always getting a blueberry muffin, taking his coffee "light and sweet," just like his temperament. "Unless you need to fingerprint?"

"Ah, you've been watching too much television, Maeve," he said, smiling again. "This is Farringville. I'll do some digging around and see what we can find out, but I think you probably interrupted a break-in."

"How did they get in?" she asked.

"Front window was jimmied," he said.

"So they must have come in after I disabled the alarm?" she said, trying to put the pieces together in her head.

"Maybe," he said. "Looks like vandals, Maeve. Got more than they bargained for when you came in, even if they didn't trip the alarm like they probably expected to."

"How can you tell?" she asked, attempting to peek around his massive frame to see the rest of the kitchen. She had never noticed before but he smelled good. Not like cake, like she always did, but clean and fresh. A little like her father once did, but without the heavy hand on the cologne.

"I'm a crack detective," he said, breaking out into a broad smile. "They came for money, I imagine, but they didn't get into the register."

There wasn't anything in there, so it wasn't worth the effort of breaking in.

He jotted some notes on a pad. "Does anyone else have a key to the place? The alarm code?"

"No," she said, shaking her head, the action making little light-ning bolts dance before her eyes. "Just me. The landlord doesn't even have a key. That was our deal when I signed the lease."

"Okay," he said. "Not Jo? Not your husband?"

"Not Jo. And the husband is an ex," she said. She assumed he knew that. Didn't everyone? "Thanks for coming by, Chris," she said, attempting to call an end to the day.

"I heard about your father, Maeve. I'm so sorry," he said, his face sad. "And now this." He buttoned his coat. "I bet someone with a bright idea saw the obit in *The Day Timer* and thought it would be a good idea to break into The Comfort Zone."

"But the garlic," she said, realizing too late that if she kept bringing it up, they'd make her go to the hospital, and that was a jaunt she wasn't in the mood for. "Mr. DuClos," she said. "See where he was." She knew what Chris was thinking: DuClos knew the security code. He could have let himself in any time he wanted. He wouldn't have to break in to the store.

All made sense. Except that his smell followed him everywhere he went.

Chris Larsson wouldn't let her drive home, so she got into the front of his Farringville police car, looking out the window as they passed the usual sights of the small village: the animal hospital, the florist, the place that sold comic books. He would have one of the uniforms deliver the Prius to her house. When she got home, she realized that both emotionally and physically she was drained. She stripped off her clothes, once inside her bedroom, thinking that tomorrow was another day. She had almost forgotten about what had happened prior to her searching for a bottle of vanilla that turned out to be on the bottom shelf of the pantry. This day, the day she had buried her father, was a day she had spent time with people she'd rather forget and been told something about her family that to her mind either amounted to the ravings of an alcoholic whose sole purpose in life was making sure that other people were as miserable as she was, or it was true.

It was hard to know, hard to tell.

CHAPTER 7

Jo was leaning against the counter, her back to the front of the store, her hands on her prodigious belly. It was two days after the funeral, Maeve having taken an extra day off in between. While she lay in her bed the day before, wrapped in her comforter as if it were a cocoon, she focused on the pattern in her bedroom throw rug, the water stain on the ceiling. She didn't think about the fact that her father was gone or that Dolores Haggerty had ruined the funeral luncheon; instead, when she wasn't focused on the rug or the ceiling, she thought about the solace she would have gotten from the kind people who had attended, had Dolores Haggerty not ruined it for her—Mrs. Devereaux and her trolling for Jack's apartment notwithstanding. Jimmy Moriarty. The Department of Public Works guys who loved her and looked out for her like she was their sister.

She had lain in the bed, drifting off every now and again, dreaming of her father. In one dream, she had handed him a loaf of bread and said, "Here, Dad. It's a challah. Your favorite." And he had responded, solemnly, "It's rye."

She had woken up abruptly, wondering if she should have gone to the hospital, just as the EMTs had recommended.

Jo had called, as had Chris Larsson, both checking in on her, both worried that she would never get out of bed, if their voices were any indication. She would get out of bed when she was ready, and two days after the funeral, she was ready.

Now back at the store, once a haven for her, a gullet full of ibuprofen for the pounding at the back of her head, Maeve was already into the throes of the Christmas preparations that she went through every year. This year, though, was tinged with sadness. She wondered if it would always be like that, always a little sad, or if each passing year would bring a little more comfort.

"I'm starting to rethink Jason as the baby's name." Jo picked up a broken cookie from a tray in the case and munched on it thoughtfully.

Maeve cleaned the coffee maker, dumping a large pile of grounds into the garbage can by the kitchen door. "So what are your options?"

Jo traced circles around her belly button with her index finger. On her ring finger glinted a huge solitaire engagement ring and a band alternating with diamonds and sapphires; Doug had chosen well even if Maeve was starting to think he was a bit of an absentee husband. He hadn't attended the wake or the funeral and like always, Jo had made up some excuse about overtime, a big case. "Well, it has to be a 'J' name because Grandma Julia is the last person to have passed. What do you think about Jordan?"

"I like it," Maeve said. This was not the first conversation they had had about the baby's name; in the last seven months, Maeve had lost count of how many times they had discussed it.

"Maybe," Jo said, oblivious to the sound of the bell jingling over the front door of the shop. "We have birth class tonight. Don't forget."

How could she? Jo had only mentioned it every day for the past week, both in conversation and in texts. Maeve thought she might get a pass after having been hit in the head, but apparently, that wasn't the case. She greeted the customer standing at the counter when it was clear that Jo was otherwise occupied, thoughts of baby names and birth class taking precedent over Maeve's business, a money-making venture, as she reminded Jo on a daily basis.

Maeve sold a brown-butter apple tart and a quiche Lorraine, two items that would have landed in the trash bin or Jo's refrigerator had they not been sold; Maeve didn't keep items in the cases more than two days. She ended the day with a fifty-dollar order and felt relieved when she saw that she had had a very good day, retail-wise.

In the kitchen, Jo took her usual seat on a stool next to the counter. "Now that we have some downtime," Jo said, as she watched Maeve wash a sink full of pots, "tell me what happened at the funeral the other day. Something with those old neighbors of yours? I saw you run into the street. I saw what you looked like when you came back. I didn't want to bring it up, you know, with what happened the other day."

Maeve hesitated.

"You know you can trust me," Jo said. "I promise I won't say a thing." She crossed her heart. "I know I haven't been so great about that in the past, but I promise for real this time."

Maeve was wary of saying the words out loud to her friend, to get her reaction; it was going to be overblown and dramatic. History told her that. "Dolores Donovan said that I have a sister."

But there was no meltdown, just Jo's wide-eyed silence. Maeve went back to the pots. "I don't know what that means and I'm not sure I want to know or even if it's true." She looked at her hands in the sink; they were red and raw, wrinkled from the water. Her mother's hands? She would never know.

"The one in the tight blue pantsuit?" Jo asked. "She really needs to go up a size. Just looking at the tight crotch kept reminding me that I'm going to have to push an eight-pound baby out of mine soon."

"That's the one," Maeve said.

Jo busied herself, pulling apart cupcake holders and then putting them back together, thinking. "That is a lot to process."

"That's an understatement."

"Do you believe her?"

Maeve shouldn't, she knew that. But part of her felt as if it were true, that Dolores knew something that had been kept from Maeve. She shrugged in response to Jo's question.

"You need to find out if it's true."

"Again, Jo, I don't know if I want to know."

Jo got up and put her arms out, knowing Maeve wouldn't accept the hug but giving it a try. "I don't know how to say this without sounding insensitive, but you're all alone now. It would be nice to have someone to replace Jack. A new Conlon."

"I'm not all alone," Maeve said, her voice sounding angry. She said it again, but this time, she didn't sound so sure. "I'm not all alone. I have the girls. Well, I've got one of the girls," she said, smiling; the jury was still out on Heather. "I have you," she said, awkwardly taking hold of one of Jo's outstretched arms. "I sort of have Cal, even if he's married to someone else. He's got my back."

"Yeah, well, I don't give that union much longer. You may have him back sooner than you think," Jo said. "The shelf life on that marriage is rapidly coming to past due, I suspect. That Brazilian is a tough one to handle. Gorgeous, but tough."

Maeve wondered how Jo knew that. If it were true, well, served you right, Mr. Charles "Cal" Callahan. Never go for the shiny object; the luster wears off far faster than you would think. The duller models, like Maeve, are always more reliable. "I don't want him back," Maeve said. As for how he felt? She wasn't so sure. There was a time when he admitted to defeat, to not wanting to continue living with the stunning woman in the spectacular house that Maeve lusted after, but Maeve had never mentioned that time and he had never brought it up again. His life. His problems.

Jo took a step back and regarded Maeve, ignoring that. "A sister, huh? Seems like you should be all over that?"

"I'm going to go through my father's things and see what I find. Dolores is a drunk, Jo. I think that's obvious."

"I got that sense."

"And she's cruel. I've known that since we were children."

"So you don't believe her?" Jo asked.

She didn't know what to believe, but she would never confess that.

This time, Jo didn't telegraph the hug that was coming. She grabbed Maeve in an embrace, her belly keeping enough distance between them so that Maeve didn't feel trapped. "He was a good guy, your dad."

"I know."

"He never would have kept something like that from you."

"I hope not."

"Unless he had a good reason."

"There is no good reason."

Maeve broke away and finished the pots in the sink, if only to let Jo know that the conversation was over. As she washed and scrubbed, the front of her shirt becoming wet, she thought about it. Jack Conlon never would have kept something like that from me, she said to herself, agreeing with Jo.

Unless he felt he had to.

CHAPTER 8

The pots done, Maeve and Jo went into the front of the store to finish closing. Jo took out the day's newspapers and put them in the recycling bin by the back door and Maeve locked the front door. Jo found Maeve in the front of the store wiping down the counters, even though Jo professed to have done it earlier.

Jo picked up the ringing store phone. "The Comfort Zone," she said. She handed it to Maeve. "Chris Larsson," she said.

"Chris, hi," Maeve said, handing Jo the paper towels and glass cleaner she had been using and pointing animatedly to the front of the cake case where some kid had generously left the perfect imprint of a small, dirty hand for them.

"Maeve, I just wanted to let you know that Sebastian DuClos has an alibi for the day you were assaulted."

She waited, interested to hear what his alibi might be.

"An AA meeting. He has thirty witnesses to say that he was there."

"Convenient," Maeve said. "Aren't they all supposed to remain anonymous?"

"The leader did come forward and vouch for Mr. DuClos," Chris said. "I probably shouldn't have told you but your number-one suspect has fallen off the list."

"Then look for some kid named Billy," she said.

"Billy?" he asked. "Billy what?"

"Billy, I have no idea," she said. "He's DuClos's assistant or associate or something like that."

"Okay."

"I forgot about him the other day. But I guess garlic can transfer from one person to another, right?"

"Now I have no idea what you're talking about," he said, but she could hear the smile in his voice. "Okay. Billy. Billy who works for DuClos."

"You aren't buying that."

"I just don't know why your landlord or one of his associates might break into your store, hit you, and leave with nothing, but if it helps, I'll track down this Billy kid."

She hung up the phone, stripped off her apron, and hung it by the kitchen door. "I have to go do some work at Dad's apartment and then I'll pick you up," she said. "Six thirty?" she asked.

"Yep," Jo said. "I'll lock up."

In the kitchen, Heather was standing by the sink, her hands on her hips. "Hey!" Maeve said. "To what do I owe this honor?" For a brief moment, she thought that maybe Heather had escaped from the dark thoughts that seemed to feed her perpetual consternation and had decided to help Maeve clean out Jack's apartment. Heather had never remarked on the fact that Maeve hadn't come out of her room for an entire day and Maeve hoped the girl had chalked that up to her mother's grief; she couldn't bear to think that Heather would ignore her otherwise. She processed all of this while she wondered why Heather was holding a long-handled spoon in her hand and staring into space.

She seemed as surprised to see her mother as Maeve was to see her. "Hi. Where are you going?"

"Grandpa's," Maeve said, looking on her desk for her car key. "Do you want to come? And what's with the spoon?"

"It was on the floor," Heather said. "I was just putting it in the sink."

"Do you want a ride home?" Maeve asked. "And why are you here again?" she asked, remembering that she had never gotten an answer.

"I need eighty dollars," she said. "To pay for my yearbook."

Maeve looked at the clock. "Can it wait until I get home tonight?" she asked. "And are yearbooks really eighty dollars?"

"It's fine if you don't want to give me the money," Heather said, walking toward the door.

Here we go. Let the games begin. "I'll give it to you tonight," Maeve said, punching in the alarm numbers before closing the back door and walking into the back parking lot.

By the time she got to her car, Heather was ahead of her, starting for home.

"Could I get even one day, a bereavement day, really, to grieve my father's death?" she called after Heather, whose ubiquitous headphones canceled out the sound of Maeve's voice. "To not be reminded of how I'm failing you as a mother? Please?"

But Heather was gone, around the corner and up the street. Maeve passed her on the way to the assisted-living facility, trudging back to the house with thoughts of murdering her mother on her mind if the expression on her face was any indication. Maeve kept driving. Hopefully whatever punishment Heather meted out to her mother would be swift and painless.

Maeve pulled into a spot as close to the entrance of Jack's former home, Buena del Sol, as she could. Buena del Sol was neither "good" nor "sunny" but it was a lovely facility even if her father had hated it. In his last days, it was clear that his time in the apartment was growing short and that he would have to be moved into the full-care part of the facility; Maeve was glad he died before she had to make that decision. She had put it off for as long as she could.

The apartment still smelled of him. Even with one good hand

and a failing mind, he found time in his morning toilette to put on a half a bottle of cologne—Old Spice—every day. The door handles, the phone receiver, everything he had touched still smelled of the stuff. Maeve stood in the middle of the living room and sniffed deeply. Sure, she could buy a bottle at the CVS and smell it any time she wanted, but smelling it in an environment that he had recently occupied? Those chances were going to disappear as quickly as she could clean out the space, and the sooner the better as far as Mimi Devereaux and Stanley Cummerbund were concerned.

She started in the bedroom, where Jack's double bed was made up as if he were living in an army barracks, Angelle's military precision evident in the tuck of the sheets, the hang of the bedspread. Maeve went through the bedroom slowly. Jo had offered to help clean out the place but would she know to grab the handkerchief that was in his top drawer, the one with the lipstick print—the last surviving link to his wife, Maeve's mother—and give it to Maeve? Would she keep his uniform from the police department, not knowing that Maeve had no interest in retaining that remnant of his professional life in one of her overstuffed closets? His clothes still hung in neat rows in his own closet; a glass of water, half-drunk, sat on the nightstand almost like he would come back to finish it.

She sat on the edge of the bed finally and looked around the room. One deep, shaky breath suppressed the sobs that threatened her handle on her emotions. There was her photo—the one that was taken when she graduated from high school—sitting on his dresser. Next to that was his watch, a memento Maeve wanted to keep, an old Timex that really did survive the years and a lot of carelessness on his part. Maeve picked up the phone on the nightstand and breathed deeply; there it was again, that smell. A pair of socks were folded and sat on the floor next to his shoes, the cordovan leather of his loafers gleaming as usual. Maeve made a mental note to slip Angelle an extra hundred dollars in a heartfelt thank-you note; even though her father had been ill in body and spirit, she had helped him retain his dignity, helping him shave and comb his hair every day and letting himself be seen as the man he still was in his own faulty memory: Jack Conlon, the strongest man in the world, dapper and handsome, a bon vivant who was proud of his daughter and who thought she was perfect.

She missed him already, so deeply; it was like an ache in her gut that resembled a sustained hunger pang.

She got up and pulled some boxes down from the shelf in the closet. In the first one were Jack's high school yearbooks from Cardinal Spellman, photos of the day he was appointed to the New York City police department. A small wedding album, black-and-white photos on every page, their existence speaking to a happier time, one that gave no clue to the pain that was on the way.

The second box was more of the same, though it held more evidence of the trajectory of Maeve's life. Her communion dress, yellowed and brittle, felt odd in her hands, as did the crown and veil that she had apparently worn that day as well. There was another photo album, just her through the years; why *did* she get that perm in 1984? She smiled as she turned some of the photos and relics over in her hands, taking time to remember when things were good and when he knew who she was every minute of every day. When she didn't have to identify herself for fear that he had forgotten who she was.

Little Mavy. The most perfect girl in the world.

There was nothing in his things to suggest that there had ever been another person in their family. "Your sister." Dolores was mistaken. She was drunk. She had been thinking about someone else. Jack Conlon had one girl and he loved her more than anything.

CHAPTER 9

"And breathe . . . ten, nine, eight . . ."

Maeve sat against the wall in the birth class center at the local hospital, Jo positioned with her back to Maeve's front, her eyes closing as the instructor counted down. When she got to "one!" Maeve's eyes flew open, her head smacking against the wall as she was jolted awake.

Jo ceased her rhythmic breathing and turned to Maeve. "Thanks for doing this. We just never know what Doug's schedule is going to be like and I don't want to be caught with my pants down."

"Literally," Maeve said. She knew why she was there; that was another conversation that she and Jo had on a regular basis but that she still didn't truly understand. The baby was Doug and Jo's first and Maeve didn't comprehend why Doug wasn't involved in every single activity related to the impending birth. So far, Maeve had helped Jo pick out the crib, find the birth class, and a host of other baby-related tasks that her husband should have been involved in.

Maeve didn't have a good feeling—about Doug, about his commitment to marriage, his devotion to Jo—but then again, she trusted so few, men in particular, that that wasn't a surprise. It would take some kind of superman to convince her that he wouldn't break her friend's heart. She had been through one long, horrible marriage with Jo, and then a protracted divorce. She didn't want Jo to go through another one, her emotions still fragile, her psyche still being put back together, day by day, piece by piece. This baby was a miracle, Jo having gotten a donor egg, her chances of having a baby after having gone through chemotherapy a few years earlier almost nil.

"Right. Pants. Have to remember to pack them," Jo said, and started her breathing again. When she was done with that set of panting breaths, she turned back to Maeve. "I forgot to tell you." She pointed at her head. "Will I ever get my memory back? It's like a whole piece of my brain is missing."

"Yes, you'll get your memory back," Maeve said, shifting slightly under her friend's weight. "What do you need to tell me?" Maeve prayed it wasn't something to do with a complicated order. As it was, just with the regular inventory demands, she was like the walking dead.

"Margie Haggerty came by the store today."

Maeve felt her back stiffen and then seize up. She pushed Jo off of her. "Get up. I'm having a muscle spasm."

She excused herself and exited the room, stretching her back out before bending over to get a drink at the water fountain. She swallowed as much water as she could stand before her stomach started to revolt; she didn't know what to think about this but something in her suggested she should be angry. Maybe employing the pregnant mother's breathing strategy was the ticket. She stood by the water fountain, panting until the feeling passed.

A thank-you note for the luncheon would have been enough. An apology would have been better. But Margie Haggerty coming back to Farringville was not good.

Jo came out of the room. She was large and extremely pregnant but she was still in her regular jeans, though they sat way below her belly. One of Doug's oxford shirts, the sleeves rolled up, coupled with her usual Doc Martens, completed the look. From the back, she didn't even look pregnant. When Maeve had been with child, she had looked like a beach ball; even her head had been fat, in her memory.

"What's the matter?" Jo asked. Behind her, couples streamed out of the room, the women stretching their legs, the men checking their phones.

"Margie Haggerty. What did she want?" Maeve asked.

"You," Jo said. "I told her that you had left for the day and wouldn't be back until the morning."

"Did you tell her where I went?"

Jo frowned. "You know me better than that." She punched Maeve's shoulder. "I've got your back, girl. You know that."

"Thanks." Maeve leaned against the wall next to the water fountain and closed her eyes.

"What's going on?" Jo said. "You do not like those girls."

"Women. They are women now, Jo."

"Yes, but they were girls once, and I have a feeling that's where all of this started." It finally dawned on Jo. "She was married to Sean Donovan, your dead cousin. The murdered guy."

Maeve looked away.

Jo had a way with words. "The woman in the too-tight blue suit."

"Yes, but that's not it," Maeve said. "It was a long time ago. Our families weren't close. The father was a drunk and the mother was just horrible. I tried to stay far, far away from them."

"Then why did they come to the funeral?" Jo asked.

Maeve shrugged. "That's what you do."

"Your people confuse me," she said. "Sitting shiva is its own kind of dysfunction but at least my people talk about stuff. Try to work it out. Go to therapy."

"Yeah, not the Irish." Maybe therapy would have helped her, but she had been raised to think of it as a sign of weakness. "If you're

Irish and you know someone, even tangentially, and they die, you go to their funeral," Maeve said. "And you especially make sure to hit the after party." She looked around, marveling at the girth of some of the pregnant women around her. Had she looked like that once? How had she remained erect? "My father and I traveled the tri-state area going to wakes and funerals and eating rubber chicken at post-funeral luncheons. I can't explain it. It's just what you . . . we . . . did."

Jo studied her face for any sign that she was joking. "Sounds like fun."

"It's just the way it was," Maeve said. "I don't entirely understand it myself. But I'm breaking the cycle. I'm not dragging my girls to any Haggerty funerals in the near future, that's for sure."

Jo stopped by the refreshment table outside the birth class, and shoved a Girl Scout cookie in her mouth. "And call me crazy, but I could swear she was carrying."

"Carrying?" Maeve asked.

"Yes. There was a bulge in the back of her jacket. Carrying. A gun." Jo put another cookie into her pants pocket. "For later," she said, when Maeve raised an eyebrow.

Maeve didn't comment; she wasn't one to talk. After all, her own gun was tucked safely up into the seat of the Prius, ready to be taken out, if she ever needed it. Yes, she understood that pleasant middle-aged women who looked like her—nice, gentle, a *baker,* for God's sake—didn't carry guns, especially where she lived, a tony suburban county near New York City. A yoga mat? Sure. But a gun? She would put money on the fact that she was the only woman she knew with a gun and who knew how to use it. It was her secret and she kept it close.

She was careful, having carved out a spot under the seat, sure that it wouldn't fall out. She had driven over so many potholes, testing her spot, that when she was done, she had needed a new alignment. No one would ever find that gun. She was sure of that. And if either of the girls ever drove the car, she put it somewhere else, some-where where no one could find it, making sure that she was the only person who ever handled it.

The birth instructor came into the hallway and beckoned the pregnant women and their birth coaches back inside. As they walked the length of the hallway, Maeve looked up at Jo. "Was anyone so mean to you when you were young that you would kill them if you saw them again?"

"Yeah," Jo said without hesitation. "Stacy Morgenthal."

"What did she do?"

"She stole my bat mitzvah date." Jo stopped by the opening to the classroom door. "Mine was supposed to be on my actual birth-day, which was a really big deal when I was a kid, and she knew that but she swooped in with her horrible mother and booked the date. My temple only did one bat mitzvah at a time." Jo rolled her eyes. "Stacy and her mother booked it. Three years in advance."

Stacy Morgenthal wasn't exactly in a league with Margie and Do-lores Haggerty, but Maeve kept that to herself. "You'd kill her for that?"

"You bet," Jo said, taking her place on her yoga mat, lowering herself to the floor with Maeve's help. "My temple was liberal with scheduling, so I had my bat mitzvah on the next available date, which turned out to be one of those 'storms of the centuries.' You know, when you get so much snow that everything is closed down? Well, not Seasons, the catering hall. They were open and wouldn't refund my parents' money. It was me, Rabbi Decker, Cantor Bernard, and my Aunt Sylvia and Uncle Milton from Massapequa. They never missed anything." She shook her head. "Good times."

"DJ?"

"Nope. He never showed. We were eating challah out of the freezer for weeks."

Everyone had their breaking point, Maeve thought. Jo's seemed to require little more than an excess of challah and a thinly attended bat mitzvah, and she thanked the universe for that as she counted Jo's breaths. Not everyone could harbor the sometimes murderous thoughts that ran through her mind.

She dropped Jo off a little after nine, spying Doug's car in the driveway as she rounded the corner. As she drove away, she wondered why he was home and why Maeve was at the birth class for his child. She needed another task to complete, another responsibility, like she needed another hole in her head.

The store was her main responsibility, the girls notwithstanding. She drove by The Comfort Zone just to make sure that everything looked as it should. There was one car in the front parking lot and when she pulled up, the driver drove away. The windows were tinted so she couldn't see inside, couldn't tell how many people were in there. More to the point, she wondered what they were doing there at this time of night, in an empty parking lot in front of a bank of empty stores. She pulled into the back parking lot to make sure that the store was safe, as she left it.

It was, with the exception of one light, the one over the kitchen sink, casting a glow over the back parking lot. She pulled into her usual spot and got out her keys, walking toward the back door.

It was locked.

And when she opened the door and went to the alarm keypad, it was set. She had been preoccupied the last few days; she had left a light on. She couldn't remember doing that. She did remember, though, that the large thumbprint, pressed into a little spray of flour on the butcher-block counter, had not been there earlier. Why hadn't she noticed the make of the car that had been in the front of the store? An approximate year? She was distracted, she knew that. She hoped she wasn't losing her edge.

She riffled through a stack of papers on her desk, finding Sebastian DuClos's card on top of a pile of invoices. Instinctively, she touched the bump at the back of her head. He answered on the first ring, not happy to hear from his tenant. "I'm sorry, Mr. DuClos, but I was wondering if you had been in the store tonight?" she asked. "Or any other night?"

"Why would I come to the store, Maeve?"

Not really an answer, but definitive enough so that she believed he hadn't left the confines of his large Arts and Crafts manse in a woodsy part of town that was home to the richer denizens of Farringville. "I'm just wondering. There was a light on and I . . ."

But she was speaking to dead air, DuClos's interest in the conversation nonexistent. She took one last look at the fingerprint before leaning over and blowing the flour granules into the air.

CHAPTER 10

How many pairs of khakis could one man own?

Seventeen.

That was the number of pairs of pants that Maeve counted in the box that she put together for the local Goodwill store. She didn't know why she felt the need to get rid of everything so quickly, but making sure that Jack's things were inventoried and then sent off to good homes was her number-one priority.

That, and looking through everything to find proof that Dolores Donovan was wrong.

It had been eight days since he had died, and although part of her felt like it was too early to be doing something like this, she did it anyway. Without thinking about what a box of khakis might mean, whose they were, she put the box into the trunk of her Prius and was about to drive away when Heather appeared on the front porch.

"Mom, wait!" she called, in her hands a black jacket that Maeve didn't remember buying or the girls owning.

Maeve rolled down the window. "What's that?"

"It's a jacket. I think it was Grandpa's," she said, stuffing it into the space between Maeve and the steering wheel.

"Where did you find it?" Maeve put it on the seat beside her; in an instant, the car was filled with the scent of Old Spice. Yep; it was Jack's all right.

"Front closet. I was looking for my denim jacket and I found it. You're going to Goodwill, right?" Heather asked.

"Yes. I have to get there and back before Jo leaves."

"Do you know where my denim jacket is?" Heather asked, a hint of accusation in her voice. Maeve had learned that missing items that belonged to her daughters were always a result of something she had done, something she had moved. In actuality, the two of them wouldn't remember their own heads if they weren't sitting at the top of their necks. "I'm going out with Tommy."

"Ugh," was out of Maeve's mouth before she could think. Heather's crestfallen face told her that she had heard it, too.

"He's not that bad," Heather said.

"Well, there's a ringing endorsement."

Maeve had heard some choice words about Tommy Brantley the last few years, "dealer" being the most concerning one. She didn't care if he didn't take Advanced Placement U.S. History or honors physics but she did care that he might be the village's connection to all things hallucinogenic; she just couldn't get the proof she needed, so she had put Jo on the case. "Get your ear to the ground on Tommy Brantley," Maeve had said. "Ask your sources. Check him out."

But Jo hadn't found out anything beyond the fact that Tommy was the only kid the school had to play goalie for the lacrosse team and that made him a valuable asset. Jo said that she had heard that the school turned a blind eye to any kind of transgression when a state championship, purported to be this year's goal, was on the line. So he dealt a little weed? Not an issue when a state championship was at stake.

Was that the way the world worked now? Maeve wasn't sure she really wanted to know.

Maeve was smarter than to be the person who forbade Heather

from seeing him—no better way to make sure that the two eloped before they became seniors in high school—but she was wary and cautious and didn't keep her negative feelings to herself as much as she should.

"My denim jacket?" Heather asked again.

Maeve decided to have a little fun with her daughter. "Look where you'd least expect to find it," she said, enjoying the puzzled look on Heather's face as she drove away. The jacket was on a hook behind the front door, the place where Maeve had hung it yesterday when she found it in a heap on the powder room floor. Never would Heather think to look where the jacket should be, and Maeve envisioned the feverish hunt that would ensue as she drove the short distance to the local strip mall and the donation center.

Her headache was getting better and a small lump on the back of her head was the only thing to remind her that someone had taken the time to break into the store and assault her. Maybe with time, she'd feel more secure and not feel like she had to keep the back door locked all the time, opening it only when she knew who was back there.

Lee Costello was a regular morning customer at The Comfort Zone and the manager of the Goodwill store. She was standing behind the counter, cataloging some muffin tins and a host of assorted unmatched wineglasses when Maeve entered.

"Maeve! Great to see you outside of your store," Lee said, and seeing the box in Maeve's hand, ascertained the reason for her visit. "I'm so sorry about your father's passing," she said.

"Thank you, Lee," Maeve said, and placed the box on the counter. "I have seventeen pairs of khakis, all size 30/34, and a couple of shirts that are practically new. Can you use them?"

"It's Christmastime," Lee said. "We have a lot of customers looking for gently used dress clothes this time of year." She looked through the box, examining the clothes. "Perfect, Maeve. Thank you." She looked up at Maeve and smiled. "They will go to good use. This blazer in particular."

As she walked to her car, Maeve expected to feel sadness, the contents of her father's life rapidly being disbursed or discarded, but she felt happy. His neatly pressed khakis would go to a good home, or several, as would the other things. Lee would be happy to see there was more where those things had come from; Maeve just had to find the time to go through the rest of his belongings.

Baby steps, she thought.

She pointed the key fob at the car and unlocked the doors. Behind her, she heard her name. Lee ran toward her, the blazer in her hand, her short legs propelling her across the lot. She was out of breath by the time she reached Maeve, her sprint from the store having given her some color in her cheeks. Several years of a daily chocolate-chip scone and a full-fat latte wasn't a breakfast routine that lent itself to spontaneous jogs.

"Maeve, I'm glad I caught up to you." Lee held an envelope in her hand. "I found this in the jacket pocket and wanted to make sure I got it back to you. We go through all of our items to make sure that nothing has been left behind."

Maeve took the envelope. "Thanks, Lee. This was hiding in one of my closets so I didn't have a chance to check the pockets."

"I don't know what's in there but wanted to make sure I got it to you. Thanks, again," she said, walking away.

Maeve got into the car and held the envelope in her hands. It was unmarked, the contents stiff.

Photographs.

It was only after she watched Lee enter the store, her mind on the complimentary coffee and scone she would offer her for her kindness the next time she saw her, that she opened the envelope. In it were three photos she had never seen, all black-and-white, all dog-eared and creased, and one holy card, the Blessed Mother surrounded by illuminated stars. She remembered bringing that card home in the second grade right after the May crowning when all of the little girls in her parochial school wore white dresses and processed to the statue of Mary in the church, surrounding her with flowers. One special, chosen girl placed a crown on her head; Maeve had never been holy enough for that task, her socks always falling down, her mouth a little too sharp at times. According to Sister Beatrice, she was "sassy," and her father should be aware of that. Maeve remembered that Jack had been touched that she had given him the card to keep in his wallet; he was a cop and she knew his job was dangerous. Who better to look out for him than the Blessed Mother? He had cried a little bit when he turned it over in his hand and then a little more when he put it in his wallet. She knew now that those kinds of cards were a dime a dozen—you could pick them up at most churches—but she remembered thinking that the rendering of the Blessed Mother on that card was more special and beautiful than any others she had ever seen.

Maeve looked at the card again. She *was* beautiful. She looked how Maeve sometimes pictured her mother, even though she knew what her mother really looked like from her memories of her and the pictures that Jack kept around the house to ensure Maeve never forgot her.

Maeve slid the photos out of the envelope. They were from a time she didn't remember: The 1964 World's Fair, her mother looking chic in capri pants and a crisp white blouse; the Jersey shore or a beach on Long Island, her father making like a muscleman, his arms bent like Popeye's, his head turned to stare at the bulging bicep on his slim arm; her parents with a baby in a christening gown. On the back of that photo was Jack's handwriting: "St. Margaret's, 1960. Our girl. Aibhlinn (Evelyn) Rose Conlon."

CHAPTER 11

So there it was: the proof she hadn't wanted, didn't need. The photograph to prove that there was a sister whom Maeve had never known, who existed somewhere out there, probably not knowing about Maeve's existence either.

The thought of that made her heart hurt just a little bit.

Although she and Jo joked about the secrets kept in families—Jo's mother still swore that she went to Florida in 2004 on vacation, not to recuperate from a tummy tuck—Maeve thought she was the only one who had any in her family. She had kept things from Jack, things he would never want to have known, but she never imagined that he was keeping one from her as well.

There had to be a reason.

The photograph in her hand, she made the decision to drive south. Before she pulled out of her parking spot, she called Jo, who was disappointed to learn that she would be working a longer day than she had originally planned. "It's been a little crazy," Jo said, but that usually meant that three people had come in at once, not that the store had been full of people demanding quiches or scones.

"Crazy is good," Maeve said. "Good register day?"

She heard the bell ring as Jo opened the drawer. "Eh," she said, confirming for Maeve that her crazy and Jo's crazy were two different things. "A hundred and forty-eight bucks."

"Are we good on sugar? Flour?"

"We're good," Jo said. "No flour fairies have visited us recently."

"Good to hear."

"Oh, but some guy came by looking for Heather."

"Guy?" Maeve asked, her antennae going up.

"Yeah. Guy. Kid. Billy something or other?" Jo said. "He said he was looking for Heather."

"DuClos's Billy?" Maeve asked.

"Not a clue what that means," Jo said. "DuClos has a Billy?"

"His new associate," Maeve said. "Remember? Going to be collecting my rent. The guy that came the day my father died. You remember, right?"

But Jo didn't, "pregnancy brain" being the most likely reason.

"He was looking for Heather?"

"That's what he said."

"What did he look like?"

"Kind of cute. Light hair."

Yep. That was DuClos's Billy.

"He was kind of mad, too." She paused. "Said he'd find her."

Maeve felt a frisson of anxiety shoot through her body, something that was quickly replaced by anger. She didn't know who Billy was or what he wanted with her daughter, but if it happened to be something not good, something not on the scale of acceptable, Billy would find himself in very hot water indeed. She had nothing to suggest that his intentions weren't pure toward her daughter except that he worked for DuClos and her relationship to Sebastian was a tenuous one, garlic breath aside. Something about the guy had always given her the creeps. "It's the middle of the day, Jo. Heather would be at school."

"Just reporting what went on here," Jo said. "Now I'm worried."

"Don't worry," Maeve said even though she could feel her own heart pounding. She dug Chris Larsson's card out of her bag and called him, his phone going straight to voicemail. "Now this Billy person is looking for Heather," she said, trying to keep her voice modulated but having no success. "There's another reason to find him and talk to him." She heard how she sounded. "Not that I'm telling you how to do your job." She took a few deep breaths and brought her voice back to a low timbre. "And thank you."

Maeve hung up and started driving, making a mental note to ask Heather who the mysterious Billy was, beyond Sebastian DuClos's henchman. Eventually, she found herself in her old Bronx neighborhood, the place she had been headed all along without really knowing, driving slowly down every street, letting the memories in. Maeve had never called Margie back, not wanting to know what she had to say. But Dolores? She was a different story.

Although Margie had never done anything else to make Maeve not trust her, the memory of her missing key colored her thoughts and opinions of the younger girl always. If she closed her eyes, she could still hear Mrs. Haggerty screaming at her daughters in a way that Maeve hoped she never did to her own. Margie was her usual target. She was stupid and lazy and a host of other unattractive adjectives that Maeve could only imagine had seeped into her brain and made her think that she was actually all of those things. It would take a lot of work, she imagined, to convince yourself otherwise if all you were fed on a daily basis was a steady diet of disparagement.

Maeve had Jack and he thought she walked on water, as he often used to say when he thought she wasn't listening. Dolores and Margie's experience hadn't been the same; she tried to cut the girls some slack for that, going so far as to stick up for Margie once at school when an older boy had knocked her down and stepped on her lunch. Margie had wanted to be Maeve's friend then, and

Maeve suspected now, but that ship had sailed and while she would visit the neighborhood again, she would never revisit the fractured relationship she had with those girls.

Dolores Donovan still lived in the same part of the Bronx, but had moved to an exclusive enclave a few blocks south of where they had all grown up. As Jack used to like to say, "That girl stepped in shit and hit the big time," mixing his metaphors as always. Maeve had known what he meant, though.

Something like that. To Maeve's thinking, she had sold her soul to the devil for a seven-thousand-square-foot home and a Mercedes M-Class. That bargain, it seemed, included marrying Sean Donovan.

She pulled up in front of their old house, hers and Jack's, a semi-detached brick dwelling with a small patch of scrubby grass in front of it that Jack had tried desperately to turn into something approximating a lush green lawn. Not much had changed since she left almost three decades earlier, going off to school, never to return. The front door still held the lion's head knocker and the transom still showed a crack in the glass that had been there for as long as she could remember. Someone had replaced the brass numbers on the front of the house, opting instead for press-and-stick markers to let someone know that they were at Eighty-Five-Twenty-Three. That was an interesting change, Maeve thought; the brass numbers had been there since the house was first built in the twenties. Stolen, was her guess.

It seemed like a hundred years since she had last lived here.

While she sat there, she pulled out her phone and did a search on the Gaelic name "Aibhlinn." A site that was devoted to Gaelic names and their meanings came up immediately. She read the information out loud in the car.

"Aibhlinn, pronounced 'ave-leen,'" she said, "translates to 'the longed-for child.'"

Longed for.

She thought back. Her parents had married in 1959, her father in his mid- to late-twenties, her mother a few years behind that. In that era, if an Irish-American couple who followed Church law weren't pregnant within a few months of marriage, Jack had once told her, something was wrong. People talked. They asked questions. They wondered why there were no children.

Aibhlinn was "longed for." Prayed for. She had come quickly only to go away not long after her arrival. Had she died? Or was it something else, something more sinister? That's why Maeve was here. For answers.

She looked out the window at her old house. Where was Aibhlinn's room? Where did she sleep? Was it the same room that Maeve had occupied years later? Did she brush her teeth on the same stool at the bathroom sink and eat her breakfast at the table under the cuckoo clock that seemed to have gone missing at some point between her living there and Jack moving?

Most importantly, where did she go?

It pained her that the Haggertys knew something she didn't, something that they could hold over her like an emotional cudgel. She could almost hear Dolores Haggerty's voice on that street, making her horrible presence known. "Where'd you get that shirt, Maeve? It's ugly." Or "Who cut your hair? A blind man?" Maeve had turned a deaf ear to her taunts and had remained confident and strong. She wanted nothing to do with Dolores Haggerty, something she didn't feel comfortable saying out loud, even when Dolores asked her to be a bridesmaid at her wedding to Maeve's cousin. "Too good for us?" Dolores had asked when Maeve declined. "You always thought you were. Your father didn't do you any favors telling you how perfect you were."

I *am* better than you, Maeve had thought at the time. I'm better and smarter and kinder; all the things that you'll never be, the qualities that will always elude you.

Maeve tried to find common ground with Dolores but was never entirely successful; Margie had a softer edge and Maeve found it easier to tolerate her. She imagined it had been hard growing up in the house of an alcoholic and his shrill wife, two people who rarely uttered a nice word, even as they were processing toward the head of the communion line, confident in their goodness and religiosity. Maeve had had her own troubles, but instead of dwelling on them and letting them eat her alive, she had made herself become stronger and more loving, because when all was said and done, she believed in good.

In being kind. In love.

Poor Dolores, Maeve thought, as she headed south. She had been "fat" and "stupid" and worst of all, "useless." The words stayed in Maeve's memory in association of that time and place, those girls who were now women and mothers themselves. She wondered if they had learned anything, had carried anything good forward. Or if it was only dysfunction and verbal abuse, something that they had known so well and that was probably embedded in their own moral fiber.

They had never had a chance in hell.

The Donovan manse was as grand and foreboding as Maeve remembered from the last time she had been here, before Sean died, and even with Christmas lights and a perfectly manicured lawn, it still made Maeve think of a house from a horror movie. There were topiaries and professional plantings that were designed to survive winters in the tony part of the Bronx. She pulled into the driveway, right behind Dolores's Mercedes, and walked to the front door, stopping to marvel at the landscaping. Just how much money did these people have? Maeve was lucky if she got one of the girls to cut the grass every two weeks in the summer. Maybe, like Dolores, she should get a team of gardeners.

Nah, the perfection that Dolores was trying to convey just masked the darkness that permeated her life.

A sneak attack was best; Maeve didn't want Dolores to know she was coming so she could prepare her story, be ready with her lies. Although she could have started with Margie she decided to go with Dolores, the original messenger; she seemed so sure of what she had said that Maeve wanted to get her information first. Maeve wasn't sure if Margie would tell her the truth, whereas Dolores would only be delighted to spill it, particularly if the story cast Jack or Maeve in a bad light. Why she had it out for Maeve's family was beyond her. All Maeve could figure was that they were poison, all of them.

When Dolores answered the door, after looking through the peephole, Maeve could tell that cocktail hour had started at lunchtime, a few hours earlier. Or maybe at breakfast. Dolores seemed to be feeling no pain, as Jack used to like to say. Three sheets to the wind. Boxed.

"Maeve," Dolores said, holding open the door. "You're the last person I expected to see."

And you're the last person I *want* to see, Maeve held in, but there you have it. Deaths and funeral revelations make strange bedfellows. Dolores brought Maeve into the kitchen, outfitted with appliances that Maeve could only dream of owning. Instead of her ubiquitous blue suit, Dolores was in a tight velour tracksuit, her short auburn hair uncombed. "You'll have to excuse me. I'm just back from the gym," she said.

If by "gym" you mean "bar," then I believe you, Maeve thought. "Thanks for letting me in, Dolores." She took a seat at the oak table in a sunny alcove in the kitchen. "I've been thinking a lot about what you said last week. At my father's funeral?" she added when it was clear that Dolores had no recollection of what she had said or what the effect might be. "My sister?" The words sounded odd on Maeve's tongue.

"Oh, that," she said, waving a hand. "So, you didn't know?"

Apparently, they were cutting straight to the chase. "Of course

I didn't know, Dolores," Maeve said. "Would I be here otherwise? Would you have told me with such obvious relish?"

Dolores swigged from a water bottle that Maeve was pretty sure didn't hold water. She leaned against the counter and regarded Maeve coolly. "Need to rehydrate first."

The silence was more than uncomfortable; it was unbearable. Maeve looked down at the burnished wood and, using the Lamaze breathing that she now remembered how to do thanks to Jo's class, she waited.

"Retarded," Dolores finally said, slurring. Maeve checked her watch. It was two o'clock on the nose.

"Who?"

"Your sister," Dolores said, drinking some more.

Like father, like daughter, Maeve thought, their language, their words spoken without any art or compassion. "We don't use that word anymore, Dolores. Did she have Down's syndrome? Something else?"

She shrugged, and even that gesture looked off-kilter, blurry. "How should I know?"

"When's the last time you saw her?"

Dolores looked up at the ceiling. "I don't know. I was little. I don't know what year it was."

"Please. Try to remember." Maeve didn't know why it mattered so much but she needed to know, needed the details so she could put the pieces of this puzzle together into one coherent whole.

"I don't know, Maeve," Dolores said, as if Maeve's questions were an incredible inconvenience. "She went away. She never came back." She finished the "water" in the bottle. "I don't know where she went. For all I know, she's dead."

Maeve did her best to remain impassive. In her bag was the gun she had bought, the one that her old friend Rodney Poole had helped her get so that she could feel safe again. In control. In a display of bad judgment, she had retrieved it from its rightful place under the driver's seat in the Prius and put it in her bag, and at that moment, her palms itched with her desire to take it out and use it.

I could take it out and kill her and no one would be the wiser.

Jo would say I had been at the store. She would do that for me.

Not one person would miss her, if I had to guess.

But she didn't act on that impulse, the one she justified in her mind. She held back the question that was on her lips: why hadn't anyone told Maeve? Maeve, more than anyone, should have known the answer to that question, and when she thought about it, it was clear: her people didn't talk about things, particularly ones that were unpleasant and required emotion. They preferred to sweep them away like crumbs on the table after Sunday breakfast, into the garbage, tied up tight, never to be seen or thought of again.

"Dead. Maybe." Dolores rolled over the words, trying them out, seeing if they got to Maeve.

Maeve held her gaze, didn't let her see that the idea of her sister being dead made her sick. "Thank you, Dolores," Maeve said, standing. "It's clear you have nothing else to tell me."

Dolores pointed the empty water bottle at Maeve, her eyes narrowing so that they were almost closed. "See? You're no better than us. You've got your secrets, too. Your perfect family," she said, laughing. "Not so much, huh?"

Maeve started for the front door.

"There was never any difference between us, Maeve," Dolores called after her. "You always thought you were better than us, but you weren't. You with your cupcakes and your doting father. Your perfect life. You were no better than us." Dolores followed her into the hallway.

Maeve put her hand on the door, gripping it until her knuckles turned white. Don't tell her what you did. Don't go to her level.

"You could have been a friend to my sister, but you weren't," Dolores said.

"I *was* a friend to your sister," Maeve said, remembering holding the younger girl's hand—only a grade behind Maeve—and taking her to the school nurse so she could get herself together before class, her squished bagged sandwich in the other hand. Maeve had given her part of her lunch, thinking momentarily that she shouldn't, given what Margie had done. But she wasn't like that, wasn't raised like the Haggerty girls to be sneaky and, worse, mean.

Dolores went in for the kill. "They sent her away, Maeve. What parents do that to their child? A child like that?"

She didn't know. And she didn't want Dolores's theories either. She closed the door behind her, breaking the top off of one of the garden topiaries as she walked by, if only to give a small measure of relief to the vengeance that was like a living, breathing thing pounding through her veins.

CHAPTER 12

Maeve turned onto Broadway, the blood still pounding in her temples, and pulled to the side of the road to take a few deep breaths. God, why did it have to be them, the Haggertys? Why did they have to come back into her life and bring with them all of the memories from a childhood she wanted to forget? She banged on the steering wheel. This wasn't fair.

She picked up her phone, on the seat next to her, and saw three missed calls, all from the same number. A voicemail had been left while she was in Dolores's house, and while she sat there, her car idling, she listened to it. It was the assistant principal at the high school; Heather hadn't shown up that day.

She called the main number at the high school, and the secretary put her right through. "Mr. Jackson? Maeve Conlon. I understand we have a delinquent student?" she said, trying to keep her tone light but thinking that the minute she laid eyes on Heather, she was going to let her have it, although she didn't know exactly what that meant. Corporal punishment was out and grounding was merely a ploy to make Maeve feel more in control. Heather was a second-story man, scaling the trellis in the back and leaving the house in the dead of night more than once. Heather thought that she lived in a gulag, where to her, what she considered rights were mistaken for privileges that were earned and the house rules weren't fair because her older sister was a "loser" who had never had any friends anyway. Not true, Maeve had pointed out on more than one occasion; Rebecca had been an athlete and a scholar and had had plenty of friends from both endeavors. So what if her Friday and Saturday nights included her staying at home or going to a movie with a friend? It didn't mean that she was a loser. And it didn't influence Maeve unduly in following through with the rules and curfews she had set up when she didn't know that Rebecca would be a homebody and Heather would be someone whose expertise at tapping a keg made Maeve's heart sink just a little bit.

Mr. Jackson wasn't as convivial as Maeve would have hoped. "I am very sorry for your loss, Miss Conlon, but I also get the paper and know that your father was buried several days ago. Therefore, unless you send Heather in with a note explaining her absence, the day will be a cut. An illegal absence."

The little shit. "Thank you, Mr. Jackson. I'll discuss this with Heather when I get home."

"And the note?" he asked.

"As you said, the day will be a cut. My father was indeed buried several days ago."

On the ride home, she didn't know what made her angrier: her conversation with Dolores or the fact that Heather had cut school. She called Jo and begged her to do the close by herself; she had things to take care of. She pulled into the driveway with such velocity that she had to stop short before she hit the retaining wall, gravel spraying up and hitting a cat on the neighbor's lawn. She wondered if that was the cat who used her backyard as a litter box. If so, nicely done, Prius.

She stormed in the house, marveling at how much better anger

felt than sadness. Than grief. When she stepped into the front hallway, she heard voices at the top of the stairs, coming from one of
the bedrooms. They were loud. And someone was crying.

She went to the second floor. Heather's door was closed but she
was inside with someone else. Maeve tapped lightly on the door, right
over the Reflektors poster, and called out to Heather. "Heather? Are
you in there?"

Whoever was in the room fell silent and the sound of shuffling
feet and, eventually, murmured tones came through. She knocked
again. "Heather? Open up."

The door opened but it wasn't Heather. Tommy Brantley, his
skull-and-crossbones tattoo on full display on a small but bulging
bicep, opened the door and gave Maeve a hard-eyed stare. "Mrs. Callahan," he said, sounding much older than he was. Maeve was surprised to find that he was only a few inches taller than she was, but
sturdily built; he hadn't looked as imposing those times she had seen
him from the safety of her living room when he sped up and picked
Heather up for a "date." If he wanted to, and it seemed that he might
based on the flush in his cheeks, from where he was standing, he
could have easily pushed her down the steps. She took a step to the
right and looked into Heather's room.

Heather sat on her bed, her head hanging. "Tommy was just leaving, Mom."

Tommy gave her a hard look. "I was just leaving," he said. He
raced down the stairs and to the door in a split second.

She watched him go out the door, the screen slamming behind
him. When she was sure he was gone, she went into Heather's room.
She knelt in front of her. "He didn't hurt you, did he?" she asked.
Heather's face was covered by her lank, dark hair.

"No!" she said. "How could you even think that?"

Maeve stood. "We've been over this, Heather. This does not seem like a good relationship. You never seem happy when he's around, or after you've seen him." She pulled her daughter up off the bed. "Tell me what's going on, why you cut school today."

Heather stood before her, mute.

"And who is Billy? He came by the store today, looking for you," Maeve said.

"He's no one," Heather said.

Maeve stood there, looking at a kid who had sprung from her loins all piss and vinegar, a baby with an attitude. Not much had changed. "I'll be downstairs," Maeve said. "You have ten minutes."

"And then what?" she asked.

"And then . . ." she started, and realized there was no "then." She admitted it to herself, hoping it didn't show on her face, and it felt weak. She had nothing. She couldn't accuse him of anything; she couldn't call the police. He had been in her daughter's bedroom and she had been crying but that was all she had. It was horrible to feel so powerless.

She went down to the kitchen and poured herself some wine in a tumbler; a dainty wineglass wouldn't do. She drank half of it down and slammed the glass onto the table just as Heather appeared in the doorway.

"Am I in trouble?"

"Unless you give me a reasonable excuse as to why you cut school today, then yes." Maeve pushed her wineglass around on the table. "And a reasonable excuse is 'I had malaria' or 'I was so sad about breaking up with my hoodlum boyfriend.'" That had pushed it too far and she knew it, but seeing her daughter cry, because her boyfriend had made her, made Maeve feel a little less than genial toward Tommy. "Is it Grandpa?"

"I can't talk to you," Heather said. "I will go back to school tomorrow."

"Listen, Heather," Maeve said, standing up and going to the refrigerator, "going to class and getting good grades are your ticket out of here. Don't forget that," she said, looking inside to see what she could make for dinner. "And you know our house rules; no one comes over unless I'm home."

"But you're never home," Heather said.

Maeve didn't have an answer for that. "House rules. They are always in effect." She drained her wine. "Now, who's Billy?" she asked, but Heather was already on the move.

"Who's Billy?" she called after Heather, but she was gone. Christmas vacation was coming, and for all of her impotence in dealing with Heather's transgressions, Maeve knew that if it took every ounce of strength she had, Heather would be staring at the four walls of her bedroom for those two weeks. She wouldn't be leaving the house.

Maeve stood in the kitchen for a long time, looking at the closed front door at the end of the hallway. Finally, she opened the refrigerator. It was dinner for one, as it turned out.

CHAPTER 13

She dug through the remaining boxes, Jack's things, for the next few days, whenever she had a free moment. In what was left, Maeve found nothing else to suggest that there was another child in her father's life. Tonight she sat on her bedroom floor, items scattered around her, and scanned the detritus. She would keep the photo albums and some of the holy cards; forgive her if she wanted the one marking Martin Haggerty's death out of her house as soon as possible. Why Jack had kept it was beyond her. She looked at the wallet-sized photos of newly married couples that must have come in thank-you cards throughout the years; she recognized a few of the couples but not the others.

Maeve crossed her legs and took a sip of wine from the glass on the floor next to her. She didn't hear Cal enter the room, his old bedroom, and she looked up only when he cleared his throat.

"Is it okay that I'm in here?" he asked. He had taken to wearing glasses instead of contacts and looked like a "hipster." At least that's what the girls said. They were heavy, black-rimmed frames and made him look a little silly, in her opinion.

"It's okay," she said, patting the bed behind her. He sat down and she moved so that she was facing him. "What's going on?" She hadn't told him about the break-in or that she had been hit over the head; she found that the less Cal knew about unpleasant things, the better. She didn't want news getting out about the break-in because she couldn't have anything jeopardize her business. That, and she couldn't stand the look of pity that would wash over his face, the one that told her that if she just had a man to take care of her, everything would be okay.

I did have a man, she always wanted to yell, and he left me for someone who smelled better and didn't jiggle in all the wrong places when she walked.

He pulled an envelope from his pocket. "Here's a check from one of your dad's insurance policies. I knew someone at the insurance company in town and they pulled a few strings to get it cut quickly." He handed it to her. "It's a little one but it's a nice chunk of change."

She opened the envelope; three thousand dollars. That would come in handy, especially since the oven in the store was making a racket when she turned it up past four hundred degrees. "Thanks." She handed him the glass of wine. "Here. Take this. You look like you've had a long day."

"Thanks," he said, looking around the bedroom. "This room still drafty?"

"Yep," she said. "Maybe I'll use some of this to get new windows." She patted the envelope on her lap.

They sat in companionable silence, a state she couldn't have imagined several years earlier when he had announced he wanted out of the marriage, his love for her now focused on someone else. Someone younger, prettier, and more successful. She hadn't cried then and she wouldn't cry ever because really, it was just a waste of time. It was clear when he told her, and even before that, that he had already moved on. There was no turning back.

But now, they were fine. Friends, even. Maybe they should have never married, staying the good friends that they had become when she was fresh out of the Culinary Institute and he was a lawyer at a firm in Hyde Park, the only job he could get at the time. They co-parented pretty easily these days, even if she thought he was too lenient and he, in turn, thought she was too strict. The girls likely saw them as two people who acted like grown-ups and if they couldn't be together, that had to be good enough.

"Hey, I may need your help," she said, lowering her voice. Heather's bedroom was on the other side of Maeve's bathroom and sound traveled. That's how she knew that Heather had been deep in conversation on the phone with her sister when Maeve had entered her own bedroom an hour earlier, the hunger strike still in effect.

Heather would crack eventually. Maeve's girls couldn't go three hours without eating, never mind skipping dinner altogether.

"With?"

"Heather issue," she said, relaying her conversation with Mr. Jackson, her run-in with Tommy.

"I hate that kid Tommy," Cal said, and for him, those were pretty strong words. This from the man who was perpetually "disappointed" with bad behavior rather than stark, raving mad like his ex-wife. "He's trouble. I thought they broke up?"

"Me, too," Maeve said. "But he was here today even though Heather knows the rule: no visitors unless I'm home."

Cal made a face that indicated how he felt about that rule. "She's a teenager and a cranky one at that. But I think it's okay for them to have people over if you're not here." He brushed his ridiculously long hair out of his eyes. "Face it, Maeve. You're not here a lot. Kid would never have any friends over if you enforced that rule all the time."

She didn't feel like having this argument. "Do you know someone named Billy?" she asked. "He came to the store, looking for Heather. He works for my landlord, I think."

Cal's face grew dark but not because he knew anything. "Billy? No. Did you ask Heather?"

No, Cal, I didn't ask Heather, she thought, but didn't say. I would never ask our daughter the most obvious question to ascertain this guy's identity. She nodded. "Of course I asked Heather. She's not talking."

"Keep me posted on this. If you need me to kill Tommy, I will," Cal said.

Maeve smiled. He was starting to sound like her.

"No. Really," he said. "This is getting on my last nerve."

Finally. She saw a spark in him, something that told her that he was more than a little disappointed in one of his daughters, would back her up when the parenting push came to shove.

"I have a sister," she said suddenly.

He smiled. "I could swear I thought you said you had a sister."

"I do. Aibhlinn. It means 'longed-for child.'"

Cal looked confused, understandably. "I have no idea what you're talking about."

Maeve rehashed her conversation, if it could be called that, with Dolores. By the end, Cal looked as stricken as she had felt that first day, the day of the funeral, when Dolores had first uttered the words.

"How do I find out if someone died?" she asked.

Cal thought for a moment. "Search death records, death certificates, I guess. I've never thought about it really. I was a mergers and acquisitions guy."

"Can you help me with this?" she said.

"You want to find her."

"I do."

"Okay." But he looked uncomfortable at the thought; she wasn't sure why. "Is this how you're going to spend your Christmas vacation?" he asked.

"Probably."

Cal loved corporate law. In his former line of work, although he worked with a large group of lawyers, paralegals, and support staff, his clients, for the most part, were nameless, faceless members of a corporation that he would likely never have to meet. He had chosen it specifically because, as he had once told Maeve, he was a "softie, not a killer." He couldn't look across the table at some cuckolded husband or wife and insist that they—not the adulterer—pay alimony. Or go to bat as a defender, knowing his client was in the wrong. Corporate law, to him, was numbers, facts and figures. So for Maeve to ask that he help her with something as messy as a missing—or possibly dead—developmentally challenged sister and for him to agree was something neither of them ever expected.

She didn't have to wonder if he loved her anymore because she knew that he liked her and that was enough.

She showed him the photo. "That's my sister. In the christening gown."

He studied it for a long time. "She's probably dead, Maeve. I hate to tell you that," he said.

"Why would say that? What makes you so sure?"

He handed the picture back to her. "That you never knew. That Jack, even as his mind was going, never said anything. Don't you think that's weird?"

On the face of it, it was. But Cal grew up in a different environment from her; his was tony, upper class, educated. People went to therapy when they were sad, talked about their emotions when they couldn't get a handle on them. Told each other things and sorted other things out. Didn't wear their anger proudly and unabashedly.

They didn't keep secrets. Unless they were sleeping with your friend and didn't want you to know; then, they were champs at keeping secrets.

That was something he never understood about her and her family, how things happened—"my mother was killed in a hit-and-run" was said with the same emotion as "please buy bread when you go to the store"—and were rarely spoken of again. His people talked about feelings and ran the gamut of emotions, not just from anger to sadness, as her people sometimes did.

"Do you think maybe you're attaching more meaning to this because then you don't have to deal with your loss?" he asked.

Here we go, she thought. Let's take a stroll down Therapy Lane, right at the corner of Feelings and Emotion. "I don't know, Cal. Think about it. You'd be curious. You'd wonder. You'd want to find her, too, if she was all you had."

"You have the girls. You have Jo. You have me," he said automatically, immediately chagrined. "Well, you know what I mean."

"Yes," she said, letting him off the hook. "I know what you mean."

He walked to the bedroom door. "Yes, get some new windows. I don't want you to wake up with pneumonia." He turned back and faced her. "I'll let you know if I find anything out."

"Thanks, Cal. You're a good egg," she said, and meant it.

He chuckled ruefully. "I think the jury's still out on that one."

CHAPTER 14

That night, she was tired but she was also antsy. So after tossing and turning in her bed for the better part of two hours, she got up and decided to do what she did best.

She baked.

In her small kitchen, the old cabinets, original to the house, needing to be replaced, the faucet's drips tuneful against the cast-iron sink, she pulled out a Bundt pan and set about making a German chocolate cake, wondering about her sister. Did she like cake? Wherever she was, did the people she lived with take good care of her, love her like Jack would have, should have?

With Christmas a little less than two weeks away, she thought about where Evelyn might be, who she might open presents with, and decided, after feeling that choking sensation in the back of her throat, the one that preceded a strangled sob, that she would try not to think about that anymore. Maybe Cal was right. Maybe she was dead. And the thought of that, coupled with the loss of her father, filled Maeve with a sadness that was depthless.

After the cake was in the oven, she opened her laptop, going straight to social media to find out who the mysterious Billy was and what he might have to do with Heather.

What no one knew was that Maeve had a fake Facebook profile. A fake Twitter account, too.

She was still figuring out Reddit, otherwise she'd be set up there, too. Pinterest (if only for the home improvement ideas she would never get to), Tumblr, Foursquare. Instagram. Snapchat. She had them all. And none of them bore her real name.

She was the only person who knew that the photo of Veronica Kurtzman really belonged to a model from the winter 2006 J.Crew catalog, that Veronica didn't live in Garrison, that she didn't date Troy Nettles (he was a fake, too, even though he didn't have his own Facebook profile like Veronica), and hadn't seen Beyonce eight times "and counting!" But Veronica knew things that Maeve wouldn't know normally, namely that Rebecca had tried her first beer at Vassar only hours after Maeve had dropped her off for her freshman year and that Heather's boyfriend Tommy was mercurial and constantly breaking up with her daughter and then getting back together with her.

He was trouble, plain and simple, if his recent DUI, as reported in the local paper, was any indication.

Maeve had tried everything to get Heather to stay away from Tommy, but it was no use—the girl "loved" him, she once told Maeve, and he wasn't "as bad as everyone thought." Maeve thought he might be worse. At first, Cal, in his infinite wisdom, told her to keep her opinions to herself, her mouth and thoughts driving the girl straight into Tommy's arms. Maeve knew that that could be true but she was worried, more worried than her ex seemed to be. Shouldering that burden alone weighed on her.

The last few days had been busy and challenging, so she was behind on what was going on in town. Her usual reconnaissance. She caught up on the latest party invite—it was this coming weekend at Alexandra Cortez's place out by the Farringville River—and gossip. Marie Dunworth had broken up with Frankie Alonso. Tyler Banks was "hooking up" with Stacey Trainor.

Jo told her that she had read an article—in *Frou Frou* no less, edited by Gabriela Callahan, the new Mrs. Cal Callahan—that said that Facebook had become the parents' online domain and kids were finding different places to post pictures and thoughts. You'd never know from what Maeve gleaned from her "friends'" posts.

"Huh," Maeve had said at the time, finding the article and reading it herself. She had made sure to read up on the new sites that were cropping up, hoping to stay one step ahead of her daughter and her Internet presence. Fortunately, in the case of Heather Callahan and her "boyfiend," Tommy, as Maeve had taken to thinking of him, the memo hadn't gotten to them yet. Heather's page was up and open, meaning anyone could see her postings and photos, though Tommy's wasn't. But that didn't mean that he and Maeve—um, Veronica—weren't still friends.

Maeve checked Heather's page for a Billy and hit pay dirt on the first try. "Billy," or "Will" as he was known on Facebook, was indeed a local.

Tommy "Boyfiend" Brantley's older brother.

The cake out of the oven, cooling on the top of the stove, she grabbed her keys.

The Brantleys' house was large and beautiful, the kind of old house that Farringville was known for, a colonial with a large wraparound porch and a bank of windows in the back that looked out over the Hudson. She didn't know the family but Jo had told her that Mr. had started a hedge fund that made a ton of "dough" and Mrs. got drunk during the day a lot while playing bunco with other wellheeled Farringville women. The couple hosted epic parties, many of which ended with naked adults diving into the heated swimming pool. Jo had been there once for a party with her former husband, Eric, and it was at the Brantleys where she had first witnessed him kissing someone on the waitstaff of the local catering company and thought that just maybe, marrying him had been an epic mistake.

Maeve didn't know what she expected to see while sitting there on a darkened street, but she wanted an image of the house and the surrounding area in case she ever needed to come here again. Tommy Brantley and his relationship with Heather was something she thought about a lot. It was keeping her awake at night and she was running out of ways to deal with it. While showing up and threatening him at gunpoint wasn't really an option—because really, even for her, it was just unseemly to threaten a teenager—it remained in the arsenal of her imagination and made her feel better, if only for a little while.

A car drove slowly down the street, its headlights blinding her for a minute. When it pulled into the Brantleys' driveway and she could see well enough to ascertain that the driver was Billy, she reached under the seat and pulled the gun out from its hiding spot and tucked it into the back of her jeans. She looked at the car but couldn't tell if it was the same car she had seen in the parking lot that night at the store. She wasn't sure if he was dangerous, but she wanted to be safe.

She approached the front gate, professionally wrapped with fresh garland, and opened it, surprising him on the front lawn. Sensing them, a spotlight came on in a stark blaze, giving both of them a bleached-out look.

"Hey, Billy," she said, a small woman confronting a much larger man, him not knowing that one false move would change both of their lives forever, the gun solidly in the back of her baggy jeans, "we need to talk." She leaned in close and took a deep sniff, looking for telltale signs of garlic, but all she could smell was some cheap cologne with a hint of sweat.

He backed away. "Are you smelling me?" he asked.

Why he looked so afraid was beyond her, but she guessed that in his mind, the thought of seeing a woman, a smear of chocolate across her cheek, standing on his front lawn and smelling him, was disconcerting at best. Or maybe it was that he knew that the last time he had seen her, he had blindsided her, bashing her over the head after breaking into her store. If she weren't so curious about him and his pursuits—not to mention why he had come to find Heather— she would have laughed out loud at the ridiculousness of the situation. "Ma'am?" he said. Although he looked innocent enough, he was related to Tommy Brantley and worked for Sebastian DuClos. In her mind, he had two strikes against him. "Are you sick?"

"Sick?" she asked. "What does that mean?" What did he know about her exactly?

"Nothing, ma'am."

"Call me 'ma'am,' call me Maeve, call me Mrs. Conlon," she said, "but please don't lie when you tell me why you were at my store looking for my daughter. Or if you broke in and hit me over the head."

He tried to walk past her, but she grabbed his arm. "I don't need to talk to you," he said, the polite façade gone. "And I didn't break into your store."

"You actually do," she said. "Or I'll make your life a living hell."

She wished he hadn't laughed in her face.

Strike three.

Her palms itched, the gun in her waistband hot against her skin. "I may look like someone's chubby, middle-aged mother, Billy, but I'm telling you right now: leave Heather alone." She smiled. "It's better that way."

A cloud of concern crossed his handsome features and she wondered what she looked like, if she could replicate whatever it was that showed on her face and made him look repulsed. Frightened.

She waited a few seconds, the two of them in a macabre standoff on a lovely, manicured lawn, and then walked away. In the end, reason overtook insanity and she left. She was no closer to a motive for his behavior and that gave her pause. In addition, the company he kept? That was a major concern.

CHAPTER 15

The next day, Jo's incessant chatter kept Maeve's mind off the one topic she was thinking about.

"You seem tired," Jo said.

You have no idea how much energy it takes to threaten young men in the middle of the night, she thought. "It's been a long week," Maeve said.

Jo went back to her monologue. "So they are working this huge homicide," Jo said, referencing her detective husband as Maeve iced a birthday cake for someone's seventieth birthday. It was gorgeous, if she did say so herself. "Doug says thank you for taking me to class. Honestly, I think the real reason he doesn't want to be at the birth is because of what he might see, not his schedule."

"He's a homicide detective," Maeve said, "and the thought of childbirth disgusts him?" Something pinged in the back of her brain. He's lying, she thought.

Jo shrugged. "Don't ask me. Maybe he just doesn't want to see me like that. You know, splayed out like a turkey on Thanksgiving. There are men out there like that." She dropped her voice to a whisper. "And then there are the vaginas."

"I'm sure there are," Maeve said, crafting a perfect rosette and placing it on the cake. "What makes a homicide 'huge'?" Maeve asked without going to her follow-up questions: And is your husband really that much of a pantywaist? And you still find him attractive?

"More than one body at the scene. Drugs. Execution-style." Jo held her finger to her head. "Pow! One to the front temporal lobe." She looked out the window to the parking lot, tapping the glass. "Can you drop me off at home and on our way can we stop at that Ecuadorian place on Main Street in Prideville? I have a hankering for chorizo. And they got 'Best of Westchester,' just like you."

"Chorizo? That's what you crave?" It was a little out of the way but Maeve rarely said no to Jo's requests for bizarre foods, being as she realized, after the fact, that she craved them, too.

"Yes," she said. "And flautas and arepas and anything salty and anything filled with cheese." She rested her hands on her belly. "My goal, before this baby is born, is to try every food item that was in the magazine and got 'best of.'"

"*That's* your goal?" Maeve asked. Mine is not to not harm anyone before Christmas who is looking for my daughter. To find my sister. Anything less than achieving one of those things would cast an even greater pall over the holiday.

"Doug sometimes brings me home a Cuban sandwich after work." Jo was still working her way through the items on her to-do list, Cuban sandwiches having made their way on there, despite being available only out of county and not a "best of" item.

That's better, Doug, Maeve thought. She knew "after work" sometimes meant the middle of the night, but she wouldn't judge. She remembered making some interesting culinary choices when she was pregnant with Heather; in particular, once finishing off a large tub of hummus for breakfast.

"Oh, I forgot," Jo said, starting some dishes in the sink, uncharacteristically. Maybe her nesting instinct was kicking in; Maeve could only hope. "Doug said that Rodney sends his condolences."

"Rodney?" Maeve asked, although she knew exactly who Jo was talking about.

"Yeah. Rodney Poole? His partner? I know there's no love lost between you two after the whole accusing-Jack-of-murder thing, but he's actually a really nice guy, Maeve."

"I'm sure he is," she said, as if she didn't know. She knew he was a nice guy. They were kindred spirits, but Jo didn't need to know that. She would be lying if she said she hadn't thought about him once or twice, called him to find out how to buy a gun that could never be traced. She wondered if after finding out what she did, endorsing it, and letting her go scot free, if he slept at night.

She suspected he did. Like a baby.

Rodney Poole. Huh, she thought. Now there's someone who might come in handy regarding my sister. He had helped her once. Well, twice. He would probably help her again.

Maeve finished the cake and stood back to admire it. "What do you think?"

Jo turned to her, the shirt stretched over her belly wet from leaning over the sink. "What's going on with your sister? Finding her?" she asked, completely out of the blue.

"Nothing going on with my sister. And her name is Evelyn." She had started thinking of her that way, referring to her by that name because that was what she had been called, she thought. It was easier for everyone if her name was Americanized. She thought about how much to tell Jo and knew that she would have to give her a little information, if only to shut the conversation down. "Cal is going to look into it for me. Research death certificates," she said, her voice catching. "See if she's maybe still alive?"

"You're really going through with this," Jo said. "You're really going to try to find her."

"I am."

"And what if she's dead? What then?"

"Then, that's it," Maeve said, looking down, concentrating on her work. "She'll have died and I will have never known her."

But she knew that wasn't it. She knew that she would carry that death around in her heart just like she carried her mother's and her father's.

Jo turned back to the sink. "I hope she's alive."

"Me, too," Maeve said, opening the refrigerator door and making room for the cake. "Jo, a hand, please?" she asked as the refrigerator door—off-kilter and off-balance like everything else in the old store—started to close, threatening the perfection of the seven-layer cake in her hands. "Clear that shelf," Maeve said, motioning with her head, "and hold the door open for me."

Jo reached in and moved a few items around, a gallon of milk, a container of icing. She pulled a Ziploc baggie out from the way back and held it up, keeping it at arm's length. "Have you started making fondant body parts?" she asked as Maeve slid the cake onto the shelf. "Someone having a *Walking Dead* party?"

Maeve slammed the refrigerator door shut. "No." She peered at the bag and its contents.

"Because that sure looks like a finger to me," Jo said before dropping the bag on the floor.

CHAPTER 16

Chris Larsson had held the baggie up to the light. "Yep, that's a finger." He asked Maeve and Jo to show him their hands. "And it doesn't belong to either one of you," he said, laughing.

"It's someone's finger, Detective Larsson," Jo said, put out. "Is this really a good time for your comedic stylings?"

He grew somber, chagrined. "That's a good point, Jo." He inserted the baggie into an evidence bag and went through the kitchen again, looking for other body parts or any kind of evidence that might help him figure out who the finger might belong to. "So, be on the lookout for any customers who are missing a pinkie," he said, examining the digit in the bag more closely.

"Please, Chris, I'm begging you," Maeve said. "Please, please keep this out of *The Day Timer* and the police blotter." So far, he had done that with the break-in and the assault; she was hoping he could keep up his good track record.

He looked down at her, the big, handsome Swedish guy with the gallows humor, and smiled, understanding her concern. The guy whose nose looked like it had been broken more than once, bringing to mind Jack's friend Jimmy Moriarty and his own damaged proboscis, and the kind blue eyes that belied what he did for a living.

He had a face that looked like it belonged behind an old-time butcher counter in the Bronx, with the giant hands to match, not of a small-town cop who probably had to look stern more than he was comfortable doing. The smile that broke out on his face every time he saw Maeve couldn't just be related to her, she thought, but it did make her wonder.

Jimmy Moriarty coming to mind, Maeve made a mental note to track him down, see what he knew, if anything, about Evelyn. If Jack hadn't told her anything, why would she think he'd tell Jimmy? Worth a shot, though. Those old cops really stuck together. "Blue wall of silence" and all.

"The last thing I need is for The Comfort Zone to become a place where dismembered body parts go to hide," Maeve went on. "And owners get assaulted. If this ends up in the blotter, I'm dead," she said. "And if the Health Department gets wind of it, well, it would be over for sure." Her planned two-week closure for the holidays would be more like a six-month hiatus, and that would be a very bad thing.

"Dead," Jo repeated solemnly. "Over."

"Maeve, I'll do whatever I can," he said, before heading toward the back door. "If I had to go somewhere else for my muffin, I'd be very sad."

"Does this have something to do with the break-in?" Maeve asked.

Chris shrugged. "You've got to give me time to investigate further."

"Can I stay here and bake?" she asked. Out of the corner of her eye, she spied Jo, her hands together in prayer, beseeching Chris to close them down.

He leaned out the back door and consulted with some of the guys he had brought along. "We've got everything we need," he said. "It's not like we do DNA sampling at the station or even do fingerprinting. We're Farringville, Maeve. It's usually small-town stuff," he said.

"I think McCloskey out there is aroused at the thought of what we may get to do in relation to this. Cop-wise, that is."

"TMI, Chris," Maeve said. She knew that the sight of that finger, long and with the nail bitten to the quick, would stay with her for a long time. As would the question of to whom it might belong.

"Sorry," Larsson said, lingering for a moment. He had a habit of saying the wrong thing at the wrong time, making jokes when they weren't required. Still, Maeve found that a little endearing.

Jo shuddered as she left the kitchen, returning to the safety of the front of the store, which Chris had deemed devoid of any additional body parts. Maeve could hear her talking to herself while she cleaned up, muttering about her job, fingers, Ziploc baggies that held things they shouldn't.

"Thanks for coming so quickly, Chris," Maeve said. She handed him a blueberry muffin from a tin on the counter. "These were made pre-finger discovery, so it's up to you as to whether or not to eat it."

"Listen, I know you're busy but I just . . . well, I wanted to ask you a question," he said, changing the subject. "Have you been to the new place in town? Monty's?"

She hadn't, but she knew where he was going with this line of questioning. And she could think of nothing that would set tongues wagging more than the local baker out with a village cop, but being as she had always lectured her daughters on friendship and the right thing to do, she had a hard time thinking of a reason to turn him down completely. He was single, though newly according to Jo, and she had no attachments. Jo knew the whole story: his wife had left abruptly after twenty-two years of marriage. She had moved upstate and was involved with a man who used to be a woman, though Maeve wondered if that was just small-town embellishment for embellishment's sake. Chris had been shocked and heartbroken, though Maeve had never seen evidence to support that. He was always Chris Larsson, blueberry muffin and coffee light and sweet. If she had allowed herself to think about it, let her mind go to places that had been closed off, she would have realized that he had been trying to woo her for a while.

She looked at him, enjoying his blueberry muffin like he was a starving man who had just been handed a steak dinner. If she was really honest with herself, she had to admit that she was lonely and she suspected that he was, too. She remembered what six months into a divorce felt like and it wasn't enjoyable, her "freedom" something she had never wanted.

"I haven't," she said. Before his crestfallen face could really take shape, she added, "But I've always wanted to go back to that Indian place in Irvington. I went there once and it was great." As the words slid out of her mouth, she realized that Chris, a product of Farringville, might not enjoy Indian food, looking more like a meat-and-potatoes guy. He surprised her by brightening right up.

"I love that place," he said. "So what's good for you? I know it's short notice, but how's tonight?" he asked.

She thought about it. Anything to rid herself of the mental stench of this day. "You've got a . . . date," she said, stumbling over "date."

"Really? Tonight is good," he said, getting up.

"I guess I should have played harder to get?" she said, chagrined at the thought that she had said it out loud.

"Nah. I hate hard to get," he said. "I'll pick you up at your house." She started to give him her address. "I know where you live," he said. "And not in a stalkery way. I know where everyone lives."

"More cop humor?" she said.

He smiled. "Thanks for the muffin. And the . . . date. How's eight?"

"Perfect." She watched him go and wondered what exactly she had gotten herself into.

She figured whatever it was, it had to be good, if only for a little while. And that was good enough for now.

CHAPTER 17

That night, after debating for far too long about what she would wear on the date, Maeve settled on the usual: turtleneck. Nice jeans. Boots. Tinted ChapStick. She scrubbed her nails under the bathroom sink, trying desperately to get rid of the red icing that seemed to have taken up residence around her cuticles. It was no use; the icing was staying and Chris Larsson, if he were someone who noticed things like that, would just have to get used to it.

He picked her up at eight, just like he said he would. That was a good sign. Cal was habitually late and that had driven her insane. Just not as insane as some other things he had done, like sleeping with her friends, marrying one of them.

How do I do this? she wondered. Does he know how complicated my life is? How I had accepted that I would be alone for the rest of my life?

And then the thought that she wasn't proud of: I wonder how much experience he has with missing persons.

Maeve realized that she was thinking all of this as she watched the river whiz by, Chris not terribly concerned with the speed limit on Route 9; her father had been the same way when he had had a license. Cops drove fast and rarely, if ever, suffered the consequences.

They darted in and out of traffic, always hurrying to the next thing. "Has that ever happened to you?" he asked.

She hadn't heard a word of what he had said, so preoccupied with her own thoughts that she had tuned out; her mind kept returning, even as she willed it not to, to her father's death. Family secrets. Her sister. Billy Brantley. She turned and rather than try to cover up, admitted that she hadn't been listening. "I'm sorry," she said. "It's been crazy. As you know."

"No problem," he said. "My ex used to accuse me of never listening to her, and you know what? Guilty as charged." They stopped at a light. "I'm working on that," he said.

She fiddled with the charm bracelet on her wrist, the one her father had given her and had added charms to her whole life, the last being a tiny donut with an emerald where the hole should be. She was impressed by how relaxed Chris seemed, much more relaxed than she was. Had he done this before, taken out a woman from the village for Indian food? Was he more experienced when it came to dating after a divorce? Rather than wonder, she asked him outright. "Have you dated since your divorce?"

"Nope," he said. "First time."

She let out a breath. They'd be jumping into the deep end together, and knowing that was a tremendous relief.

"How am I doing so far?" he asked.

"You're doing great," she said and sank back into the passenger seat of his Jeep, a car that existed in direct opposition to Cal's Town & Country minivan, which beeped when it went in reverse and that, to Maeve, always smelled like baby formula and crushed Goldfish. This car, this manly vehicle, smelled like coffee and some indescribable scent of the male species. Man with SUV. Man who wore gun. Man who didn't constantly have a baby strapped to his chest and refer to his flaky wife as "Mommy."

Man who seemed just the slightest bit interested in Maeve, her own scent of flour and butter and her unwillingness to tolerate fools of any kind seeming to be the recipe he was looking for.

The restaurant was just as she remembered it: warm, inviting, and smelling of an exotic blend of spices she knew weren't in her pantry. They were seated upstairs with a table that had a river view, and ordered drinks, a beer for him and a glass of white wine for her. As they perused the menu, they talked easily about what they had eaten in the past, what was good, and what didn't need a second chance. He expressed his sympathy at her father's passing.

"You doing okay with that?" he asked, scanning the menu, not wanting to meet her eye.

"No. Yes. I don't know," she said. "He was old. He was sick. But he was all I had," she said, surprising herself at the admission. "Well, not all. I have the girls. I have Jo."

"I understand what you mean. It kind of thrusts you full on into adulthood, losing a parent," he said, and then seeing she didn't understand what he meant, added, "You're no one's child anymore."

It was honest, direct, and probably not what she needed to hear at that precise moment.

"I'm sorry," he said. "It's how I felt when I lost my mother last year."

"And your father?"

"Died when I was a kid."

They had that in common, losing a parent when they were young. She wondered what else was similar about their backgrounds. For his sake, she hoped it was not much else.

After they ordered, Maeve asked Chris about his job. "So, you're a detective. What kind of detecting do you do in Farringville?" Beyond what you do with me at my store, she thought. She had a pretty good idea of what kind of detecting he did based on how many times he had been at The Comfort Zone in a professional capacity in the last few weeks.

"Mostly drug stuff," he said. "But I'll definitely be looking into fingers that end up in freezers," he said, laughing. "We did have a bit of excitement last year when that Lorenzo guy took a dive off of the dam. Remember that?"

Maeve kept the same expression on her face, wondering if he had detected the slight tic at the corner of her mouth; she couldn't hear Lorenzo's name without that happening. "I remember that. Suicide, right?"

Chris nodded vigorously. "Oh, most definitely. No one just climbs up over the fence for a better look at the water. Unless they're an idiot," he said. "And by all accounts, the guy was a bit of a jerk but definitely not an idiot. You probably saw it in the blotter. A couple of domestic disturbances at their house." He took a sip of his beer. "Wife would never press charges. I warned that guy a dozen times but he never seemed to get the hint." He shook his head. "Domestic disturbances are the worst."

Maeve made some kind of sympathetic noise to indicate she understood. The Haggertys popped into her mind again.

He continued. "I also do some outreach at the high school, a little drug prevention work, things like that."

"D.A.R.E.?" Maeve asked, thinking that the program was a waste of time and money, taught at the wrong time in kids' development— fifth grade—and not supported with anything that helped dissuade certain kids, like Heather, from the "gateway" drugs. But she couldn't really criticize. She hadn't done such a great job herself.

"Not really. We have a uniformed female on that. But since I do most of the drug busts in town and know who's doing what with whom," he said, smiling slightly, "I try to make myself a presence in the school. If the kids aren't going to stay away from drugs for any other reason, I'd like them to know that I'm watching."

"Does it work?"

He crossed his arms on the table and she took in his strong

forearms, the dusting of light brown freckles on his skin. "Hard to tell. Some days, I feel like I'm playing Whack-a-Mole. Lots of pot around these parts, as you know, and now a little heroin creeping in."

"Heroin?" she said, her stomach feeling a little sick.

"Yeah," he said, sitting back as the waiter delivered their appetizer. "Horrible, right? We had an overdose four years ago. Don't know if you remember. Carter Westman?"

She did remember, but the girls were still young enough and still easily monitored so that the news of the overdose hadn't stayed with her. Now, though, with Heather acting the way she was, in love with a kid who Maeve hated, she worried.

He put his hand over hers, an intimate gesture that didn't seem out of place. "Don't worry. We're on it." He broke out in that broad smile again. "And don't base our current lack of investigative ability when it comes to what happens at your store as an indication of how we operate. We're much better than we appear and we'll eventually figure it out."

While eating the appetizer, a cauliflower dish smothered in some kind of sauce Maeve was sure was an aphrodisiac, she wanted to change the subject. "Do you have any experience with missing persons?"

He looked intrigued. "A little. Why do you ask?"

"I have a sister. She's missing."

"A sister?"

"Yes," she said, putting her fork down and scanning the dining room before looking at him again. "Someone from my past came to Dad's funeral and said I have a sister. She may have been . . . she is developmentally challenged. I didn't know about her."

"What are you doing to find her?" he asked.

"My ex, Cal, is helping me search death certificates. Beyond that, I'm not really sure what to do." She had never called Margie Haggerty. Dolores had been the one who had told Maeve, the one Maeve had gone to see. She didn't think Margie had anything to offer but wondered if she had written her off too quickly.

"Did you think about hiring a PI?" he said. "I could give you a name."

"Maybe," she said, but with the house, the store, and Christmas approaching, funds for a private investigator were limited.

"I'll help you in any way I can," he said.

"You will?" she asked. "Why?" To her, it was a logical question.

To him, the answer seemed obvious. "Because I like you." He looked down at his plate of food. "I always have."

"Oh, that's just because you want free muffins," she said, what she had planned on being a joke causing his face to fall. She tried to recover but wasn't sure she knew how. "I like you, too," came out sounding insincere even though she did like him. She had just never noticed that she had before now. She didn't allow herself to have those thoughts and she wasn't sure why.

Maeve was aware she had broken the mood so she went to her best offense—humor—to bring things back into balance. "So we've talked about your job. Is there anything you wanted to know about what goes on at The Comfort Zone? Any secrets I might have that you're interested in?"

"Yeah," he said, softening a bit, willing to play. "The blueberries in the scones. Fresh or frozen?"

"Fresh when I can get them. Frozen when I can't," she said. "That's all you want to know?"

"No," he said, blushing like he had when he asked her out. "There's a lot more I want to know but I don't want to find everything out all at once."

Now it was her turn to blush.

It was after dinner, in the parking lot, the river just a few feet away when he turned to her. "Would it be all right if I kissed you?" he asked. "I don't really know how to do this so I figured I'd ask."

She looked up at him, the blueberry scone and coffee guy who had become a little something more, and savored the moment. She remembered every first kiss she had had but she never thought she would have the opportunity to have another one. That part of her life was over, or so she thought. "It would be just fine," she said, forgetting, when he wrapped his arms around her, about everything that she had been thinking about just hours earlier, storing it all somewhere for later. Somewhere that wouldn't ruin a mood that she had never anticipated.

Chris was the anti-Cal, sure and confident in spite of his asking to give her a kiss. He was tall and fit—but with just enough heft—with that crooked nose, kind and gentle but with just the right amount of softness. He had been in her backyard all these years but she had never taken notice.

But he had and that was all that mattered.

He pulled away and pushed her hair away from her forehead. "I've been wanting to do that for a long time."

"You have?" she said. "Kiss me?" The kiss had taken her breath away and she had a hard time finding words.

"Yeah," he said. "Kiss you. I have." He took her hand and they walked back to the car. "It's okay if I've just been the blueberry muffin and coffee guy to you."

So he knew.

"Maybe I can become more than that?" he asked, leaning her up against the car, pressing his body against her. He kissed her again.

"Maybe," she said, in between the breaths, the tongues, the murmurs.

"Maybe."

CHAPTER 18

She was in a good mood when she got to work in the morning and didn't even get a knot in her stomach when Jo was thirty minutes late. Chris had dropped her off a little after ten the night before, early enough so that she wouldn't feel like a zombie the next day. Although he was a gentleman and didn't press it, she could tell he wanted to come in, but she held firm. First date. Late night. Early morning. A kid upstairs. All of the usual excuses. He had finally driven off, giving a little toot of his horn as he rounded the corner.

For just a minute, she had forgotten about lumps on the head, severed fingers, and missing sisters.

Jo—who after finding out that Maeve had been on a date with Larsson, pronounced Chris "yummy" and said that she herself had always had a bit of a crush on him—was dying for details but Maeve was deliberately sketchy. "Have you been to the Indian place in Irvington?" Maeve asked.

Jo shook her head. She was stacking cookies into the shelf by the front door.

"It's delicious." Maeve slid a large chocolate cake into the case. "We had this wonderful appetizer with cauliflower. I don't even really like cauliflower." She walked around the front of the counter to look at the contents of the cake case. "And my entrée was amazing."

Jo turned. "Enough about the restaurant! I couldn't give a rat's ass about cauliflower. Or your entrée. Details! Did he kiss you? Did you sleep with him?"

Maeve clutched her chest in mock indignation. "No, I did not sleep with him," she said. "I am not sure I even know how to do that anymore."

"Promise me this," Jo said. "If it gets close to that point, if you think you're going to sleep with him, please, please, have a quick consult with me. You probably have tumbleweeds in your vagina or at least in that place in your brain where you think about sex. If you even do that anymore."

"Why do I need to consult you?" Maeve asked. "Do people do it differently now? Have things changed that dramatically since my divorce? Please don't tell me I have to learn anything new. I'm just too tired. And believe me, there are no tumbleweeds in there."

Jo walked over to the counter and laid herself on top of it, swanning dramatically, too exhausted from what Maeve didn't know. "It's the same. It's you who's changed."

"You mean 'older,' right?" Maeve asked, pinching the little roll that hung over the top of her jeans. "You mean because of my appropriately named 'muffin top,' correct? The one I got from making— and eating—too many muffins?"

Jo rose. "Okay, treat it as a joke. It will be to your detriment." She floated off, and went through the kitchen doors, muttering to herself as she did. "I'll get you a vibrator. Practice with that . . ." she said as the door slammed behind her.

Maeve reviewed the list of orders she had for the week, happy with the amount of money that they would bring in but a little nervous about how she would execute everything. She felt that way a lot, delighted with how the business had grown but wondering how she would do everything herself. She leaned against the counter and started thinking dollars and cents. With Jo leaving to have the baby, the time was coming to hire someone new, and the thought of going through that process made her head hurt just a little bit.

She was deep in thought when the back door to the kitchen opened, no knock to indicate that someone had arrived. Margie Haggerty stood there, tentative, her hands clasped in front of her, the look on her face telling Maeve that she was nervous. Maybe a little afraid.

Maeve was glad to see that look, the sight of her former neighbor's tense expression making her feel that maybe, just this once, she had the upper hand. That she'd get the truth. And although she couldn't say she was pleased that Margie had shown up at her place of business, the woman's appearance had saved Maeve a step in this process, allowing her to cross one thing off of her mental to-do list. She had wanted to call Margie first but life had intervened, as it had a habit of doing.

Maeve bypassed any pleasantries. "What are you doing here?"

"I think we should talk."

"Did you know I had a sister?"

"*Have* a sister. You have a sister," Margie said. Maeve didn't understand why the tense was important or why Margie sounded so sure. For all she knew, her sister was gone, but she hoped that wasn't the case. "Yes. She was discussed in my house, your sister. My mother prayed for her. Every day." She stared off at a spot somewhere over Maeve's head. "We were sworn to secrecy. We weren't supposed to tell."

Knowing that didn't thaw the ice Maeve had in her heart toward the late Fidelma Haggerty.

"She prayed for me, too," Margie said, "but didn't get what she hoped for."

Maeve looked confused.

"A nun. Remember? She wanted me to be a nun."

"Right," Maeve said. She looked up at the clock on the wall. She needed information, not a walk down the Haggerty memory lane, a jaunt filled with emotional broken glass and uneven pavement.

Margie looked at her, tears in her eyes. "I'm so sorry. I should have said something sooner."

"This seems like just the kind of information Dolores would have loved to have given me when we were kids," Maeve said. "She's special like that. So, why didn't she?"

Margie stared off into the distance without saying a word, taking in the sights of the kitchen: the piping bags, the cookie sheets, the appliances that needed updating. She never answered.

"And why didn't Sean tell me?" Maeve asked, as if Margie would know why her abusive cousin would have kept something like that from her. It seemed like something that he would have loved to have held over Maeve, like he had held her mother's death over her. She thought about it. "See what happens when you tell?" he would have said. "You get sent away. And then you die." There's no way he could have known and not told her; that kind of information was too good for him to hold in, to keep to himself.

"Maybe he didn't know."

"Then why did you know? How? Your family?" Maeve asked. The Haggertys were neighbors, acquaintances. Maeve wouldn't go so far as to call them "friends" to either herself or Jack.

Margie didn't answer that question. "Listen," Margie said, tapping her finger on the bar, seeming to be mounting a defense of her defenseless sister, "my sister . . ."

"I know," Maeve said, holding up a hand to stop her, her other hand holding on to the counter for support, "she's been through a lot. Spare me." She started toward Margie, making the woman back

up toward the door, looking for escape. "Tell me. Is she dead? Evelyn?"

Margie shrugged. "That, I don't know. But I can help you maybe."

Maeve didn't respond, couldn't bring herself to ask for the help
from Margie. Stubbornness, pride really, wasn't Maeve's most attractive character trait but the one that helped keep her going,
helped her achieve what she had. She wondered if she should re-
lent in this case. She made one last attempt for any information,
trying to keep the ball in her court. "Any idea where she went?"

Margie's answer surprised Maeve and broke her heart just a little
bit. "Mansfield," she said.

Maeve wished she had said anything but that. After that, she
would have preferred hearing that her sister had died.

CHAPTER 19

Maeve had few memories of growing up that weren't related to Sean Donovan or one of the Haggerty girls exacting their brand of justice on an innocent kid with no mother. One other memory was the day her mother left for the store, never to return, and another was the day she saw her father cry the first time.

She had just made her first multilayered cake from scratch; she was eleven. As she put the last bit of icing on the top, careful to make the edges neat and tidy, she heard her father, in the living room, let out a gasp and then a sob. She wasn't sure she wanted to know what he was watching, why he was crying, but she peeked around the corner anyway. He was standing in front of the large Zenith console, his beloved "color TV," his arms crossed tightly across his chest. He swayed a bit, the color draining from his face.

"Those poor souls," was all he said. "God help them."

On the television was a story about the Mansfield Institution, a place that, judging from the news story, was as close to hell on earth as a place could get. Maeve had a few memories of the moving images from the story: bars on the windows of brick buildings, a few haunted souls walking the grounds, overgrown shrubs and weeds growing in front of the main structure. Back then, she knew, people with a variety of issues were sent to places like Mansfield, those with mental illnesses and those who were developmentally challenged. Things that were now understood, treated and addressed in a particular way with medication or therapy, were less understood then. She shuddered at the thought of her sister, her flesh and blood, in a place like Mansfield.

After Margie left the store, Maeve stayed in the kitchen, focusing her attention on piping cannoli cream into the shells that she had left cooling on a rack, while Jo worked in the front of the store. Behind her, the door to the back parking lot opened and Chris Larsson came in, his smile doing nothing to alleviate the physical pain that had settled around her heart. He wrapped his arms around her from behind and she leaned into his chest, willing herself not to let all of the sordid details come spilling out. He was a much more welcome guest than Margie Haggerty, a man who hadn't kept the truth from her, someone who seemed to be as open and transparent as any one person could be. She wasn't sure how she knew that about him, but she felt it.

He turned her around and looked down at her, their height differential not preventing him from giving her a long kiss. The door to the kitchen swung open—its squeaky hinges alerting Maeve to Jo's presence—but just as quickly, it slammed shut and Jo returned to the front of the store. Chris smoothed the hair that had come loose from her ponytail off her forehead. "You look upset," he said. "Is it kissing at work or something else?"

She hadn't told Jo a lot about her talk with Margie because she couldn't go down the emotional road that Jo would take her on. Chris was used to hearing unsavory things and not reacting; it was part of his job. She thought about it for a few seconds and told him the rest of the story. He listened intently, and just as she had hoped and had wanted, didn't react with anything other than concern.

"Mansfield?" he said. "The place upstate, right?"

Maeve nodded. "I remember the news stories," she said, picking up her piping bag and worrying the top, twisting it until the filling oozed from the tip. "I remember some senator talking about the people there. That there were hundreds too many for the space. That the conditions were deplorable." Her hands started to shake so she put the piping bag down and wiped her fingers on her apron.

At the time the news about Mansfield broke, Maeve lived in a nice row house with a nice father and although she endured other horrors, living incapacitated in filth and despair was something she didn't know. It seemed to upset Jack to a far greater extent than it should have, now that she thought about it. It was disturbing and vile but it was far away from them and their lives. Now she understood why he had reacted the way he had.

Chris leaned back against the counter and crossed his arms over his chest. "I don't remember it on television, but for some reason, I do remember hearing about the place."

"I remember my father's words to this day. 'Those poor souls. God help them.'" She didn't remember anything beyond that—no searches, no conversations, no desperate phone calls—just sadness, tears, and a little bit of brokenness that entered his body and stayed for a while.

"What happened to the place?" Chris asked. "The actual location?"

"It's a SUNY," Maeve said, because she had looked it up right after Margie left. "Specializes in the arts. Dance. Music." She had also learned something else while digging around on her computer, the orders that she needed to fill having to wait. "Some people went missing when it closed."

Recognition dawned on Chris's face. "The Mansfield Missing. I remember hearing about them."

A dozen young adults, or maybe more; the twelve had been identified by their families as having never come home once the place closed, but according to reports, there could have been more who disappeared. No one knew. Which left Maeve wondering if her sister was among those who had vanished in the wind once the doors had slammed shut. The record-keeping had been shoddy, the administration mostly uncaring, the workers scattering far and wide to avoid questioning and maybe prosecution. Some thought a fire in one of the outbuildings was responsible for the missing persons, but others thought a more sinister plot was at work. It all added up to finding a needle in a haystack, years later.

Maeve answered the questions before he asked. "I don't know if she was one of them. I also don't know why my parents would have sent her there." Lacking anything else to say or do, she handed Chris a cannoli. "Try this for me."

He took a bite. "Only if I have to," he said, closing his eyes at the taste of the luscious cream, the crispy shell. "Amazing."

"I've got to find her, Chris. I remember my father's reaction that day and I don't remember much," she said, lying about her memories. "He was crying. I wonder if she went missing."

"I'll help in any way I can," he said.

Maeve could tell by the way he said it that he thought she needed protecting. She didn't have the heart to tell him, standing there with a hint of ricotta cream on his lips, that now that she was grown, she could take very good care of herself. And she didn't need protecting.

"Did you find Billy Brantley?" she asked, changing from one sordid subject to another. It was worth a try.

His face clouded over a little bit but he tried not to give anything else away. "Um, yes."

"Spill it, Larsson," she said.

"Nothing to spill," he said. "Tommy Brantley's brother. A little pot in the house. Crazy parents." He finished off his cannoli. "Last I heard, he was trying to go straight after a few high school dust-ups. Get his GED."

"He never graduated?"

He shook his head. "Nope. Why do you ask?"

"No reason. So did he have an alibi for the afternoon of the break-in?" she asked.

"I'm almost embarrassed to tell you," he said. "He was at a meeting, too. Again, confidential."

She started laughing, but there was no merriment in it. "Am I the only person in town who isn't in a twelve-step program?"

"Maybe?" he said. "I'm not either, by the way." He paused. "And in case you were wondering," he said, "we've got nothing on the finger yet."

"What does one do with a severed finger?" Maeve asked.

"The only thing a small-town detective could do," he said. "I turned it over to the county crime lab." He stood, ready to go. "Well, that and look at every pair of hands in town for the one that has only nine fingers. You'd be amazed at how many people are missing a finger or part of a finger."

"Really?" she asked.

"No," he said, laughing out loud, the sound of it breaking the tense mood that had stayed after Margie's departure.

She wondered about his self-deprecation, if it masked a really sharp investigative mind. Only time would tell, she thought. She wasn't sure which answer she wanted when it came to him. His ignorance of her—of what she had done, of what she was capable of doing—was bliss. He just didn't know it.

She had worn a mask most of her life—loving daughter, devoted wife—the one that let the world believe she didn't have any scars. She could never let him see who she really was, and wondered if he had the ability to find out on his own.

CHAPTER 20

Chris went back to work, two cannolis in a bag for later, and Maeve went to her desk to review the orders that she'd need to fill before the holidays began in earnest. But her discussion with Margie was still on her mind, her quest for more information like a hunger she couldn't sate, so she pushed the stack of orders aside and went to her computer, Jo still in the front of the store to deal with the light foot traffic that the midmorning usually brought.

The Mansfield Missing. She went back to them. A dozen young adults, different ages, sexes, and ethnic backgrounds, were never located once the facility was closed. Was the fire to blame? Did they wander off before it closed? Or had something more sinister happened? The institution's administration were at a loss to explain what had happened. One of them had even gone to jail, dying there years before.

There was a lot more information in various places but Maeve didn't have time to search them all. Some people had shared the names of their missing loved ones, but others, citing privacy, did not, leaving Maeve to wonder if Aibhlinn "Evelyn" Conlon was on the list.

She thought back to her conversation with Margie. Could Maeve trust her? Was Margie as altruistic, as helpful, as she seemed to be? Wanted to be? Maeve couldn't be sure. She typed her name into the search engine and waited to see what she would get in response. Maybe the information that turned up would give Maeve the answer she was looking for.

"Disgraced cop."

"Mishandled evidence."

"Discharged from duty."

It wasn't a huge story; it couldn't have been, because Maeve didn't remember reading about it. It had happened over a decade ago but even then, if she had read about it, Margie's name would have rung a bell in Maeve's overtaxed mind. The story was simple: after searching an apartment and confiscating drugs, Margie having been on a drug task force at the time, she took a detour and had a drink with a colleague, one Ramona Ortiz, at a bar in Washington Heights. She got drunk. She hit a telephone pole. And when her colleagues were called to get her out of the jam she had gotten herself in, it became clear that the chain of custody had been broken and any work that had been done on the case thus far—with the help of the FBI and DEA—had gone to crap, leaving her holding the bag, as it were. Or not.

And now? With the law degree that she had gotten after she had been discharged of her duties, according to a later article, she had opened up a little office, specializing in workman's comp cases, but that information didn't shine any light on Maeve's real questions about her former neighbor. Was she good? Was she bad? Or was it a combination of the two, like it was for so many people, Maeve included?

She was going to tread lightly.

Cal walked in as she was closing the computer; he had just finished a stint at the gym, judging from the sweaty T-shirt peeking out from under his hooded sweatshirt. He knew his way around and poured them each a large cup of coffee before taking a seat at the butcher-block counter, his usual spot when he dropped in for a chat. He had grabbed a muffin as well, taking a large bite. Maeve started a cake batter, pulling a container of ganache out of the refrigerator, suppressing a shudder when she thought about the finger in the baggie.

"Where's Devon?" Maeve asked. Maeve was unused to seeing Cal without his latest progeny.

"Sitter," Cal said. "I needed to get to the gym," he said, patting his trim midsection.

You wanted the younger wife, Maeve thought. That kind of decision comes with a hefty price tag, namely daily spin classes and dead lifts.

He looked up at the ceiling, changing the subject. "Listen, I did a search. No death certificate for Aibhlinn . . ."

He mangled the pronunciation. "Aveleen," she said, saying the name phonetically. "Or Evelyn, if you want to Americanize it."

"Right. I searched both. I searched by middle name as well." He balled up the wrapper and held it in his hand. "There's always the chance her name was changed. There's always the chance she's dead."

Why he could not understand that it pained her to hear that her sister might be dead—after all, she had just learned about her—was a mystery to Maeve. She held her tongue, pursing her lips tight. She didn't want to say anything that might push Cal away, make him not want to help her more.

"Is there anything else we can do?" Maeve asked. "To try to find her?"

Cal considered that. "Yes. Lots of things. But anything you undertake will take time and money," he said, adding, "two things you don't have a lot of."

"You sound like you're talking to a client," she said.

"Maeve, your dad would have told you about her if she were alive," he said. "I think she's dead."

"Stop saying that," she said, and the catch in her throat caught him by surprise.

"I'm sorry," he said. "I just don't know why . . ."

"I'd be invested? Want to find her?" she asked. "Take one minute, Cal, and think it through." She had never thought him to be lacking compassion, but in this instance, his lack of understanding spoke to its absence in his personality.

"You're just hurting right now," he said.

True. It was an old wound, one she didn't know she had.

"I don't want you to hurt anymore."

"Then help me." She told him about her conversation with Margie. "Mansfield. Do you remember that place? The investigation?"

"Yes," he said. "It was horrible there."

"She was there. I don't know where she might have gone after it closed." "If she was still alive" went unsaid. She looked at him. "Help me."

He didn't answer but in that silence was his complete assent.

"One last thing," she said, "and you can't tell a soul."

"Shoot."

"Jo found a finger in the refrigerator the other night."

He spit the last of his muffin into a napkin and let out a little gag.

"Don't worry," she said. "I cleaned everything. Everything has been sanitized. And it was in a baggie."

"Oh, I feel so much better," he said, throwing out the napkin. "I've got to ask you, Maeve? Are you in the Mob?" He smiled but he looked a little wary of her.

"No," she said. "Does this sound like a Mob thing?"

"Definitely," he said. "What about your landlord? Is he mobbed up?"

"How would I know that?" she asked.

He went to the back door. "See if he has nine fingers next time you see him. That ought to let you know."

CHAPTER 21

Good advice, Cal, she thought, as she sat on a darkened street in a wealthier part of town, watching cars drop by Sebastian DuClos's stately home, stay for a brief moment, and then speed away into the night. She had left after dinner, whipping up something easy when she got home and eating with Heather, all in silence as usual, still no closer to figuring out what Billy Brantley had to do with any of this or where things stood with Tommy.

Heather was sticking close to home and that worried Maeve more than when she wanted to break free and explore the nighttime world of Farringville, like usual. She was in her room when Maeve got home from the store, and stayed there until dinner. After dinner she returned to her room, shutting the door, closing off the world outside.

Maeve called Jimmy Moriarty at Buena del Sol before she left, getting his answering machine. She tried to sound casual, light. But what she wanted from him was any information he may have had about Evelyn, any indication that Jack had told him something about the sister Maeve didn't know she had.

Tired of sitting in the car, she tucked her gun into her pants, thinking again of why she felt the need to carry. Sean Donovan, she decided. He had stripped away the vestiges of security that she felt growing up around her wonderful father, leaving her paranoid, nervous. Afraid some of the time. Having a gun made her feel in control and like she could handle anything, even if it were totally at odds with how she felt about firearms in general.

She was different. He had made her so.

She backed the Prius up to the end of the street and, keeping to the side where there were no streetlights, walked along the road, the people in cars passing her not seeming to pay any mind to the small woman wandering alone on an otherwise deserted street. Was this middle age now? Did you become invisible to the general public? She wondered about that.

Sebastian DuClos's house sat kitty-corner to the road, at an odd angle. Sideways, really. She waited until there was a break in the action and walked up the driveway, snaking around his car, the one with the noisy engine—a Jaguar, she could now see—and going to the back of the house, staying as far away as she could, and at the edge of the property, the Brantleys' motion detector reminding her that when it came to security, most Farringville residents had her beat in spades. Her own house boasted a busted front porch light and a powder room window that anyone could enter if they had the desire.

The deck was raised off the ground and beyond it was a brightly illuminated kitchen where Maeve could make out DuClos and no one else. She wondered who was manning the front door, answering when the people driving the cars that were buzzing in and out of the street stopped to check in.

Or to buy, she thought.

There was no other explanation for the beehive of activity that was Wendell Lane, a street where there were only two other houses, both up the street and closer to the main road than the DuClos manse. He was perfectly situated; cars could drive up and not disturb the other residents, their houses tucked away in wooded areas far up the street. Maeve stood in the backyard, inching closer to the house to see if she could get a look.

She ducked under the deck. Beneath it was a weirdly lit basement, and as she crept closer, she wondered exactly what was happening down there. Tanning? Tomato growing? She couldn't tell but, her body on alert, she heard the sliding glass doors to the kitchen open above her and footsteps on the deck just a few feet from her head. Was that garlic she smelled? She couldn't tell. She held her breath, not daring to make a sound, plotting her getaway in case she was detected.

She pressed herself against the house's brick foundation and waited, hearing the jingle of a dog's collar and the click of nails on the wood above. She heard labored breathing, the hallmark of a bigger dog, as well as a gate opening on the stairs above, and the dog making its way to the grass below.

Oh, Jesus, she thought, hearing the heavy footfall and the jingling getting closer. She sprinted from beneath the deck, across the backyard toward the street, hearing the dog bark and begin its pursuit of her, the collar's jangle, a warning to her, getting faster as the dog ran behind her.

"Bruno!" she heard DuClos call out, whether to silence the dog, call him back, or sic him on her, she wasn't sure. But she ran like her life depended on it, hoping that even with her short legs, she could outrun the hound.

She crawled through a hedge, feeling the nip of teeth on the hem of her jeans, getting to the other side. She ran across the street, deep into the woods on the other side of the house, finally coming to rest against a fallen tree stump.

This is stupid, she thought, almost saying it aloud. In her head, she heard her father's voice say the same thing. "You're right, Maeve. This is stupid. Go home."

She reached the car a half hour later, after she was sure no one would be looking for her, and drove away. When she was a safe distance from Wendell Lane, she did a search on her phone.

Huh, she thought. So that's what they were. Hydroponic grow lights.

She'd learned a lot about her landlord tonight. Garlic lover. Dog owner. Tomato gifter. Pot grower?

CHAPTER 22

There was one pay phone left in town and it was next to one of the many nail salons in Farringville. Maeve pulled the car over and dialed 911, disguising her voice, adding a little accent for good measure, letting the police know that there was a tremendous amount of activity on Wendell Lane at the DuClos house, hanging up before the officer could ask any more questions.

When she got home, Maeve threw together a cookie batter, scooped them onto a sheet and put them in the oven, the smell of which wafted up to Heather's room, making her emerge from her bedroom and break her silence. "Want a cookie?" Maeve asked when Heather entered the kitchen, handing the girl a warm cookie. She expected Heather to drift off after she got a few cookies, to continue her silent treatment.

Hmmm, Maeve thought, when Heather sat down at the table. Playing it safe. Being the good girl. All fine offensive strategies after the last few days. She looked for any sign that the girl was lovelorn, missing her boyfriend, but she seemed on an even keel, dare Maeve say happy?

No, she wouldn't go that far.

"What happened to your pants?" Heather asked.

Maeve looked down. Bruno had taken a wide swath of denim with him after chasing her. She was just thankful it hadn't included any flesh. "I don't know."

"You look tired," Heather said.

The kid was right. Maeve was exhausted, but she wouldn't tell Heather that part of the reason was because she had been running away from a dog down a deserted street. "Oh, I'm okay," she said, picking the remaining cookies off the sheet and putting them on a plate. Ever since the day she cut school, Heather had lain low, giving her mother a wide berth, even as she stayed cloistered in her room. To Heather, Maeve was just crazy enough to do something supremely embarrassing, something that would require her to move to another school district, or worse, transfer to Catholic school. The girl had learned the hard way; don't push her mother too far or she would find out exactly what she was capable of. Maeve tried not to think about a possible connection between Billy, Tommy, and Heather. Oh, and Sebastian DuClos.

"Where's Tommy been?" Maeve said, ignoring Heather's observation about her physical state.

"Not around," Heather said.

"Where is he?"

"Lacrosse camp," Heather said, looking down at the table, the cookie on a plate in front of her, anywhere but at her mother.

"Before school ends?" Maeve said. "Before Christmas vacation starts?"

"He wants to get a scholarship to Duke so he's going to lacrosse camp," Heather said.

Case closed. But to Maeve, it sounded like a lie. The school had a liberal policy when it came to student athletes, but letting a student go away on school time seemed out of character even for the Farringville school board. But if he was gone, Maeve was happy. Merry Christmas and all that. She couldn't think of a better present.

"And why was Billy looking for you?" Maeve asked.

Heather shrugged. "Maybe to see if I was okay with that? I don't know."

Lies. Every single thing that came out of her mouth was a lie. "Do you have homework?"

"Do you have a sister?"

Maeve tried not to react. It was jarring to her to think that she did but it was also up to her to try to make it seem as commonplace as possible, even if it wasn't, to her daughter. "I might." She put the cookie sheet in the sink, running water over it. "How did you know?"

"I heard you and Dad talking."

Damn those thin walls and drafty windows. Maeve had been right to lower her voice when she had spoken to Cal about Heather but should have been more careful about discussing Evelyn. It wasn't that she didn't want the girls to know; it's just that she needed to find the right way to tell them, to explain that although people didn't send their children away now, at one time, they did. Implicit in Heather's statement was that she was angry that she hadn't been told. "I didn't want to say anything until I was completely sure."

"And now you are?"

Maeve pulled out a chair across from her at the kitchen table. "No. Not entirely."

Heather picked at the cookie. "Do you think she's still alive?"

Maeve thought for a moment, tracing some letters in a pile of spilled sugar on the top of the table. "Yes," she said finally. "I do."

"You would know something like that, Mom," Heather said. "Siblings know stuff. Sisters, especially."

"They do?"

"Yeah. Like I know when Rebecca is missing home and not just because it says it on Facebook." This was the longest conversation Maeve and Heather had had in months; Maeve stayed quiet while

the girl talked. "So, I'll text her and ask what's up and she'll tell me. Siblings know. Gabriela agrees with me."

"She does?" Maeve said, hiding the aggravation that accompanied the utterance of Cal's wife's name.

"Yes," Heather said. "Dad told her the whole story and she agrees with me."

"You sound sure. About siblings knowing." Her daughters were obviously closer than Maeve knew; that was the good news amongst all of the other revelations she had heard lately.

"I am sure," Heather said. "It's not telepathic or anything. Just feelings." She finished eating the cookie and gave her mother her full attention, something Maeve was unaccustomed to. "Tell me the whole story. What you know."

When she was finished with the telling, Maeve wasn't sure how she felt. Heather had remained impassive during the entire monologue—which was admittedly short; Maeve didn't know a lot—but unlike her adult counterparts, those who had already heard the story, Heather didn't offer an opinion. Maeve appreciated that. She just stared at Maeve with those deep brown eyes and listened. Maeve got up and went upstairs to the bedroom, returning with the only photo she had of her sister.

"That's her," she said, handing the photo to Heather, who treated it with the care and gentleness that it required and deserved.

Heather turned the photo over in her hand. "Another Gaelic name?"

Maeve smiled. "Grandpa was very tied to his Irish roots."

"I'll say," Heather said, trying to sound out the name.

"Ave-leen. It's Evelyn, if you Americanize it."

"She would have had a tough time in school. No one would have been able to say it or spell it," Heather said. She pushed her plate away from her and finished her milk.

"She wouldn't have gone to school. Apparently she was . . . is . . . developmentally challenged."

Maeve got up and took Heather's plate to the dishwasher. When she turned back around, Heather had pulled out her computer and had begun work on what Maeve figured was the mountain of home-work that she tackled each night with the steady focus and precision of a surgeon, cutting her way through French before tackling His-tory and then going on to Literature, giving everything the least amount of effort she could muster to complete each task. Heather had her troubles with Maeve, often ending up grounded after one transgression or another, but had started embracing the idea—her mother's idea, really—that her ticket out of Farringville was a col-lege far, far away. The University of Washington. Oregon State. Berke-ley. Anywhere that was far from the little village that Maeve mostly loved—except when she didn't—and, Maeve assumed, her mother. That realization, coupled with urgings from her sister, Maeve hoped, would transform her almost–juvenile delinquent daughter into some-thing of a scholar, the recent cut day notwithstanding. Nothing like a small town and the prospect of escape to turn one recalcitrant snot bag into a reasonable student and person. Was it possible? Maeve hoped so.

"Mom, look," Heather said, turning the computer toward Maeve.

Maeve looked at the computer screen; on it was a Web site whose entire home page was taken up by a beautifully drawn tree, one with branches that hung down and had links to other pages on the site. "Mansfield Support Center," it said, and it took a few minutes for Maeve to read through the paragraph of description and understand what it meant.

"It's a support group," Heather said, before Maeve finished read-ing. "For people who had family members who went to Mansfield."

The mere term—"support group"—made Maeve's skin prickle uncomfortably; her "people," as Jack always referred to them, weren't

open sharers. In fact, they didn't share at all, which is one reason why she found herself in her current state—with a sister, without a sister. She leaned in over Heather's shoulder and read the site more closely. The group was located equidistant from both Mansfield and Farringville, about an hour away from each, in a YMCA that Maeve had passed a few times on her jaunts north of the village. Their weekly meeting was the next night.

"I'll go with you, if you want," Heather said. She scribbled down the address, day, and time of the next meeting on a Post-it, and handed it to her mother.

Maeve slid the paper into her pocket and put her other hand on Heather's shoulder. "Thank you. Let me think about it."

Heather, at that moment, reminded her of Jack, her sensitivity to her mother and her pain something that didn't show itself very often. There were times when Jack was that way, but they were few and far between. There were times when he was completely lucid and normal, asking her about her day, remembering the conversation. And then there were other times, especially near the end, when it was almost as if he didn't know who she was.

She looked at Heather, marveling at the moment, at what they were sharing.

Heather looked back at her. "Can I have ten dollars?" She held out her hand. "And you never gave me the eighty dollars for the yearbook."

And just like that—as was often the case with Jack—the spell was broken.

As she lay in bed that night, she did what she said she would. She thought about it. How much would she need to reveal, if she went to the support group? There really wasn't that much to tell.

But maybe someone there had something to tell her.

CHAPTER 23

The next night, after locking up the store, Maeve drove north and found the YMCA easily, her excellent sense of direction and memory of places visited not failing her. She pulled into the lot under a blinking streetlight, a habit undertaken long ago at Jack's instruction.

"And if someone comes after you, Mavy, give them everything. Your purse, your wallet, whatever they want. Better to be safe than sorry. Things can be replaced," he used to say. "But you can't."

She knew that and had absorbed most of his commonsense rules about safety, even if she didn't follow every single one of them every single day. Sometimes she crossed against the light and one or two times, she hadn't worn her seat belt for the short trip home from the store.

She hadn't always listened, but she had been a good daughter and that had to count for something.

And she always had a gun. That counted for a lot.

The fake Christmas tree in the lobby of the Y struck her as both joyful-looking and depressing at the same time, multicolored lights blinking furiously, tacky glitter and garland on every strand. Maeve hurried past it, feeling guilty that she hadn't bought her tree yet from the local Lions' Club who sold trees in the grocery store parking lot. Inevitably, it was always dead and losing needles from the moment it was attached to the top of her car and by the time Christmas was over, was basically just a trunk with some brown branches. She tried to buy a tree that fit the size of the living room but usually came home with something too big and too fat; out in the parking lot, all of the trees looked smaller than they really were.

There was a community room in the building where the support group was held; Maeve found it after making a few wrong turns, the strong smell of chlorine and the sound of echoing shrieks announcing that she was getting closer to the pool but likely farther away from the room where she needed to be. When she did find it, she was surprised to find thirty chairs in a large circle already set up, most of them filled. She took a place next to a young woman who looked like she had been crying long before Maeve had arrived. On the other side of Maeve was an older lady who smelled like talcum powder and tea, a comforting combination.

The elderly woman, white-haired and frail, had a walker by her side. Maeve wondered how she had gotten herself there, as she seemed to be alone even though she also seemed to know everyone in the room. She introduced herself and the woman smiled.

"I'm Francine Alderson," she said. "Nice to meet you, Maeve. That's a lovely name."

"It's Gaelic," Maeve said. "It means 'warrior queen,'" she told her, blushing slightly. Saying that always embarrassed her but she had found that it was always the next question after inquiring about the name's origins. The name Alderson rang a bell; the woman's son was one of the missing. It was one of the few names Maeve had turned up, remembering it from the Web research she had done.

"Irish, dear?"

Maeve smiled. "With this face? Was there any doubt?" she asked, pointing to the dusting of freckles across her nose. "And you?"

"From north London, originally." She smiled at Maeve. "I haven't had an Irish friend in a long time. Isn't that hard to believe?"

The leader, a young woman who looked as if she had just gotten her social work degree, brought the group to order. "Welcome. I see we have some new members tonight. Let's introduce ourselves."

Maeve froze involuntarily. This part was always hard for her, any kind of public speaking. That's why she baked. It was solitary; she could be alone with her thoughts. No one expected a soliloquy on the finer points of making muffin batter. When it was her turn, she stood and faced the crowd of friendly faces, people all willing to listen to her story, to hear it spoken aloud as only she could speak it.

She had listened to some of the other new members talk about themselves, their relatives. Some were siblings or a generation removed, now more knowledgeable and informed about developmental challenges and what they meant. For most of the people who spoke, it was hard for them to understand why parents or grandparents sent their children away and why they let them live in such dire conditions.

But Maeve couldn't judge because she didn't know.

And she had a few questionable decisions in her past as well.

"I had a sister. Her name was Aibhlinn." Her voice sounded raspy, like it didn't really belong to her. "Evelyn, translated. It means 'longed-for child.'" She told the group that she had just learned of Evelyn's existence but didn't go into detail as to why. The sympathetic looks on the other attendees' faces nearly made her crack but she managed to hold it together.

When she sat down, she found Mrs. Alderson's hand on her own, her fingers intertwining with hers, the papery skin warm and comforting. Maeve looked down and watched a tear, for someone she had never met but who she was now desperate to find, land on the old woman's thumb. She heard the crowd welcome her, all saying her name. She didn't realize it when she was driving up or when she had entered the building, but she had a link to this group that could never be broken.

Mrs. Alderson was the one who suggested that Maeve join a small group for coffee at a local diner before she went home. She checked her watch; it was eight thirty and she was exhausted from her workday as well as the group session. She hadn't gone into too much detail about her sister mainly because she couldn't. She didn't have a lot of details. But she listened and learned from the others who were there, wondering the whole time if Heather was right.

If siblings knew.

At the diner, spread across two booths, the people, predominantly women, mostly her age or a bit younger with the exception of Mrs. Alderson, chatted about a variety of things unrelated to Mansfield or their relatives. Maeve wondered why but figured if she kept attending, she'd find out. Was it because they left their pain at the YMCA? Was that all they could do to keep going in the face of such disturbing knowledge? She didn't know, but she realized she had been starved for this kind of camaraderie, an interest in her beyond what she baked and when she baked it, what was for dinner, when she would drop Heather off at Cal's. The fact that she owned The Comfort Zone brought smiles to many of the faces surrounding her. Did she make quiche? And was she the one who had the amazing cinnamon buns that one woman's sister had told her about? Yes and yes. Maeve smiled, drinking enough coffee that she swore it would keep her going for several days or more.

After a few minutes, a story or two about a relative did emerge, and she found out that of the eight people there, all had had siblings at the institution, with the exception of Francine Alderson.

The old woman pulled out an old photo. In it, a young man in black pants and a starched white dress shirt was standing in front of the building, his mother by his side. Mrs. Alderson hadn't changed all that much since then; her face was lined but she still retained a youthful sprightliness that Maeve had never possessed, despite her elfin size. "That's my Winston," she said. "I named him after my favorite prime minister." He was handsome. Tall. Strapping, even.

The group fell silent. This was a conversation, a recitation, the rest of them had heard before.

"He's still alive," she said. "I know it."

Maeve could tell by the interest the others gave their food or the way they stared into their coffee cups that not many agreed with her. Maeve looked closely at the photo; Winston would likely be in his fifties, if not early sixties, by now. She handed the photo back to the older woman. "Thank you for sharing that with me," Maeve said, because that's all she could think to say. She couldn't, in good conscience, assure the woman that her son was alive; she couldn't assure her that they would be together again. She now knew how Cal and Jo and her girls felt about the revelation about Evelyn; who could swear to Maeve that she was still alive? She couldn't do that for Francine Alderson. But she could let her know that she appreciated being introduced to Francine's son via the photo. Winston mattered to her.

The group broke up shortly thereafter. Maeve learned nothing from the women about what may have happened to anyone who had lived at Mansfield, least of all Evelyn, but she was happy she went. Of the remaining seven people, none had found their siblings. All were looking.

All had hope.

She would go to the support group again. And again. Maybe she would learn something eventually. And if not, maybe she would learn where to put the feelings that now were layered over her usual feelings of love for her daughters, dedication to her store and her craft, loyalty to Jo.

She had thought that the feeling of duty to someone other than herself was gone, that it had died with her father. She was glad to find out that it hadn't.

CHAPTER 24

Maeve drove home along darkened Farringville streets, wired from the coffee and the experience. She drove down Wendell Lane again but the street was quiet that night, the DuClos house dark and closed up. The same was true of the Brantleys'. Did everyone go on vacation all of a sudden, all at once? Maeve envied the lives of people who could pick up and go whenever they wanted.

When she got to the house, it was after eleven and she was surprised to find the porch light on and Heather in the living room, a gorgeous, fresh tree upright in the stand.

Maeve stripped off her gloves and coat and hung them on the hook behind the door. "Hey. What's going on?" she asked.

Heather was stringing lights around the tree; a box of ornaments, some from Maeve's childhood home, were at her feet. "It's a Fraser fir. Dad said it's your favorite."

"Dad's right," Maeve said, approaching the tree. She reached out and fingered one of the branches, the smell of a freshly cut tree hitting her nose. "It's beautiful. When did you get it?"

"Earlier," Heather said. "We wanted to get it for you so that you didn't have to put it on your list."

Maeve was a list-maker. The task "get the tree" was on several lists that she had created in the past week, and was likely to have made it onto several more before it actually was crossed off. "Thanks. It's beautiful," she repeated, still in awe that it was in her house, in the stand, and being decorated. She had checked Facebook on her phone while waiting for the group to start and knew that there was a party at Andy Broder's house that night, his parents having left for the Napa Valley to celebrate Mr. Broder's fiftieth. Andy was planning a party complete with multiple kegs, a band, and "all night partying, dudes!" something Maeve had intimated to Heather wasn't an option for her.

She was surprised that the girl had obeyed. Something was afoot and Maeve wasn't sure what it was.

"So, you stayed in tonight?" she asked, fingering one of the tree's supple branches.

Heather continued to stare at the tree. "Yeah. Nothing going on. Nobody's around."

"Really?" Maeve asked.

"Really," said Heather, a kid who hadn't missed a Farringville party since her freshman year, despite Maeve's vigilance. "How was the group?" Heather asked, her attention focused on a strand of tangled lights, anything but look at her mother.

Maeve was glad that Heather's back was to her. "It was good," she said, swiping a hand across her eyes. "Lots of very nice people. Lots of sad stories."

"And all the people there? Their relatives are missing?" Heather asked.

"It seems that way," Maeve said, flashing on Mrs. Alderson and her never-ending stash of hope. "I didn't hear everyone's stories."

"Did you tell yours?" Heather asked, untangling the lights and burying them deep into the tree for a multi-hued effect that Maeve had never attempted.

"I did," Maeve said, settling on the couch. "At least what I know."

Heather continued stringing the lights and when they were done, she turned to her mother. "Rebecca says hi."

"She called?"

"Yes. I told her Daddy was picking her up when she finished her finals."

Before she went upstairs, Heather asked about the store. "Have you heard anything from the police about who broke in? You know, the day of Grandpa's funeral?"

She hadn't heard a thing on that, or the finger investigation. "No. Not a big deal," she said. "Lost some flour but it could have been worse." Maeve walked around the tree, surveying the ornaments that Heather had hung. "Why? Have you heard anything? Anyone at school say anything that would help the police maybe?" Anyone down a finger suddenly?

Any goodwill that resided between them evaporated. "God, you are so suspicious. Why would you even say that?" She hung her last ornament and stormed off.

"Good night!" Maeve called after her, right before the bedroom door slammed shut, effectively ending the conversation. Maeve didn't let it dampen her mood, though; the tree was beautiful and it was straight, so she had that.

She went up to her bedroom and stripped off her clothes, sitting on the edge of her bed and making a list of things to do the next day:

Go through the last boxes from Jack's apartment.
Wash Rebecca's sheets.
Go to the grocery store.
Deposit insurance check in the bank.

She picked up the envelope on her nightstand and opened it, needing to sign the check before she deposited it first thing in the morning when the bank opened.

There was one problem: the envelope was empty.

CHAPTER 25

"How many *bûches de Nöel* have you taken orders for?" Maeve asked.

Jo looked at the slip in her hand. "Five." She arched her back, pressing a hand into the bottom of her spine. "Is that really how you say it?"

"What have you been saying?" Maeve asked, rearranging the cookie packages in the shelf by the door.

"Bucks day knoll. I always forget how to say it. I do it phonetically."

That was one way to handle it.

Maeve didn't have time to worry about Jo's pronunciation of store inventory. She walked around the front of the store rearranging the tables and pushing the chairs in, thinking about the empty envelope on her nightstand at home. The night before, when she discovered the check from Jack's insurance missing, she had torn her bedroom apart, even wondering if the draft from the window next to her bed had picked the check up and blown it to a far corner of the house. Would she ever find it? She had enlisted Heather's help but she had proven to be not much help at all, bowing out after five minutes of searching the dust-bunny-riddled underside of Maeve's bed and helping to pull the nightstand away from the wall.

It was gone. Maeve called Cal and left him a message, asking if they could put a stop on it, even though she was sure that it was somewhere in the house. It had to be.

It was times like these she started to worry. Was she destined for the same fate as her father, though far earlier in her life? She shuddered to think that and shook it off, that feeling that she was losing her mind, one insurance check at a time.

She went behind the counter and rearranged some cakes in the case, turning one so that the design on top of the cake was in better view, repositioning another so that it caught someone's eye immediately when they walked in.

In the kitchen, she put the finishing touches on a cookie platter, tying the ribbon around the cellophane and displaying it prominently on top of the cake case. She hoped it would attract a buyer, someone who had forgotten to buy the baked goods they had promised to bring to the office Christmas party maybe, and she would be rid of it before long, pocketing the forty bucks that it would bring. She hung her apron by the back door and went through the process of locking up; Jo had left earlier to get a few holiday gifts, promising Maeve that she would "love!" what Jo had picked out for her.

Maeve could only imagine what that might be. Last time she checked, they didn't sell units of sleep at the local Brookstone, and really, that's all she needed.

To sleep. To rest. But not to dream. Her dreams were not pleasant and filled with candy-coated clouds and unicorns; they were darker and deeper and defied interpretation.

She turned the OPEN sign to CLOSED, set the alarm, and went into the back parking lot. The car was cold, the windshield covered with a film that would take a few minutes to defrost. It had been a nice December, high forties mostly, unseasonably warm, but cold as the sun went down. Maeve thought about Jack and his dismissal of any facts having to do with global warming; the nice weather would be all the proof he needed that climate change was made up by the Democrats, something he protested often and loudly.

Maeve blew on her hands while she waited, scrolling through the messages on her phone. There was a text from Chris Larsson, something that warmed her more than the air blowing from the vents in the car. He missed her. He didn't know if he could wait until after the holidays to see her. Maeve wasn't used to this; this kind of attention, this care for her and her feelings, was new. She liked it.

She smiled. This one was a keeper.

Eventually, as it always did, her mind drifted to her father and their relationship. She sat there, watching frost disintegrate from the windshield and revealing a small envelope tucked under the passenger-side wiper blade. She jumped out and grabbed it, the outside a little damp from the moisture on the glass, opening it under the light of the streetlight that sat at the edge of the parking lot. Inside was a short note from Margie Haggerty. An address. And a name: Hartwell.

She didn't have Margie's phone number, didn't want it, even though it would have come in handy at that moment. She stared at the name and the note, and wondered if Margie was telling the truth. If this person knew something about her sister. If, as Margie claimed, they had worked at Mansfield around the same time that Evelyn Conlon had been a resident.

If this was true, then Maeve didn't need Margie Haggerty anymore. She would get the answers herself.

Her focus had shifted. While the back of her head still bore a small lump, a reminder of the break-in at the store and all of its attendant nastiness, her mind was centered on finding Evelyn Conlon. She could be single-minded like this, her attention taken up by one thing, one task. It was what made her a good baker, a smart businessperson.

But she had to keep herself in check, because one slip and that single-mindedness could get her into trouble, sending her down roads she didn't want to explore. She knew that from experience

CHAPTER 26

It was Senior Citizen Day at the grocery store, something Maeve forgot every week. It wasn't until she spied the idling Buena del Sol minivan parked in front and found the produce section packed with seniors that she remembered. The store was very good to their senior population, giving them a 10 percent discount on their entire purchase every week, but maneuvering through the aisles on that day proved difficult for the younger set.

By the seafood case, she spotted Mr. Moriarty, picking out some salmon for his dinner. Jimmy Moriarty, for all of his bluster, was a soft touch and wasn't beyond bursting into tears at the sight of his old friend's daughter. She didn't want to catch him by surprise so she wheeled her cart around the prepackaged seafood and approached him at the case after he had spied her in the distance.

"Hi, Mr. Moriarty," she said as she went in for a hug. "I've been wanting to talk to you. Did you get my message?"

He didn't respond directly to her question. "How many times do I need to tell you to call me Jimmy, Maeve?" he said. "How are you?"

"I'm fine," she said. That was a lie. She could barely hold it together in front of this physical reminder of her father. The happiness she had felt earlier had melted away, this gruff guy making her remember why inside, deep down, she felt so sad. She smiled and the effort almost made her wince instead. "How are you? Ready for the holidays?"

"I am," he said. "Going to the daughter's house in New Jersey. Infernal place, that state, what with all the tolls and the traffic."

"Well, please stop by the store before you go and let me give you something to take with you," she said. "You were such a good friend to my father. It's the least I can do."

A shadow crossed his face, an emotional darkening. "Why, thanks, Maeve. That would be nice," he said softly, a bit of his bluster making a hasty exit.

Maeve didn't know when she would see him again, so she went for broke. "Mr.— I mean, Jimmy, this is going to sound strange, but did my father ever mention anyone named Evelyn? Another daughter he may have had?"

The man turned quickly at the sound of the seafood counter guy asking him to pick out the salmon steak that he wanted. He studied the case intently, Maeve unable to see his face. "What about the third from the top?" he said. "Love salmon," he said, when he turned back to Maeve. "I think it's part of our makeup, you know? Irish? Salmon?"

She didn't know what that meant. She waited to hear an answer to her question.

"No, Maeve. He never mentioned anyone." Moriarty took the plastic-wrapped salmon from the guy behind the counter. "Talked about your mother a lot. Always talked about you. 'The most perfect girl in the world,' he used to say." He smiled sadly. "Wasn't a lot going on up here the last few years," he said, pointing to his own head, "but we were still great friends. Never in my wildest dreams did I think I'd find another brother from the Job in Buena del Sol. Especially someone I hadn't seen . . ." He stopped, reaching out and grabbing Maeve's shoulder, giving it a gentle squeeze. "Bye, honey. Be good."

"I try," she said.

She watched him walk away, only coming out of her funk when an elderly lady hit her from behind with her cart. Maeve stumbled into the case that held bags of clams, sticking her hand deep into a pile of shaved ice. She pulled it out, shaking ice chips to the ground.

"Be careful, dear," the old woman said. "Someone could get hurt."

Maeve kept her eyes trained on the old cop, her dad's dear friend. Someone could get hurt. And someone was lying.

CHAPTER 27

"Hakuna matata!" Jo said brightly as she handed a large stack of cake boxes, all tied together, to a well-dressed woman Maeve had never seen in the store before.

After the woman left, and Maeve watched her drive away from her perch on a stool by the window, she turned to Jo. "Hakuna matata?" she asked, placing a stack of orders in a neat pile beside her calculator. "'Happy holidays' would suffice, you know."

"I guess," Jo said, sliding the door of the refrigerated case shut. "It's just so boring."

"Boring is fine," Maeve said, jumping off the stool. "Boring is good. We like boring."

"*You* like boring."

Maeve did. She had had enough excitement to last a lifetime. "Let's start the close," she said, picking up the orders and bringing them into the kitchen. Like every year, she wondered how she would get it done, and she knew from experience not to sweat it too much. It always got done. There might be a few sleepless nights and a few solitary evenings of baking after Jo left the store, but she always got it done.

The back door opened, letting in a gust of frigid air, and Cal walked in, his hipster glasses fogging up in the warm kitchen. He took them off and rubbed them against his shirt. "Hey, baker lady," he said, using a name he used to call her but had stopped using after the divorce. "How are things in cupcake world?"

"Is that your indication that you're looking for a freebie?" Maeve asked. Jo walked in with a tray of cupcakes, as if on cue. "Take your pick."

"You look good, Jo," he said. "Feeling good?" he asked, looking over the tray to pick the one he wanted. Marble with chocolate icing was the winner.

"Feel great," she said. "Missing some of my less honorable pursuits," she said, holding two fingers up to her lips and pretending to inhale, "but there's time for that after the baby's born." She exited the kitchen and went back to the front of the store.

"What brings you here?" Maeve asked as she organized the mess on her little desk in the corner.

"Well, first, a question, and then some bad news."

"Bad news?" she said, her mind going to his search for death certificates.

He shook his head, reading her mind. "No. Not that. I haven't found anything."

She exhaled. "Good. Then ask the question."

"What are you doing for Christmas?" Cal asked, breaking off a huge piece of cupcake and shoving it in his mouth. There were more where that one came from and he wasn't averse to having two or three at a time. Maeve recollected that his record was six, unbroken by anyone she knew.

She thought about it. The girls were set to spend the day with him after opening presents at her house; a bottle of crisp Sancerre and a plate of cheese followed by a viewing of *Love, Actually* was likely on her menu for the day. She didn't tell him—it didn't need to be said—that she'd be alone. That was a given. "Oh, you know. Catching up on television. Relaxing. Sleeping."

"Would you come to dinner? At my house?" he asked, giving the plate of cupcakes his undivided attention, all the better to hide his discomfort in articulating a really unusual plan. "We're having filet and some kind of potato that Gabriela swears is an old family recipe and that she knows how to make by heart." He chuckled. "Being as I've never seen her cook anything, I'm getting a backup tray of potatoes from Leonardo's," he said, referencing an Italian deli a few towns over.

"It won't be awkward?" she asked.

"It will be totally awkward," he said, smiling, "but I'd, well, we'd, love it if you were there."

She wasn't so sure about the "we" part of loving the plan, but she accepted it. She thought about it. If she went, she'd be with the girls. She wouldn't be alone. Maybe she wouldn't think about Jack, about Evelyn. About just how alone she really was.

"I accept," she said.

"You do?" Cal asked, surprised.

"I do," she said. "Just tell me what you want for dessert and I'll bring it."

"Cupcakes," he said, biting into his second. "Lemon bars. A pecan pie."

"Anything else?" she asked.

"Nothing," he said. "Nothing at all." He finished his cupcake while she washed some dishes in the sink. "This is going to be great."

"And the bad news?" she asked.

He grimaced. "The insurance check has been cashed so we can't put a stop on it."

Her mind went back to Tommy Brantley's visit to her house.

"Are you locking your doors?" Cal asked, bringing up a topic that had been a sore subject when they were married. She never locked the doors, her memory of sitting in the rain in the backyard always in the back of her mind. Her kids would be able to let themselves in always, even if they had forgotten their own keys; that's the way she wanted it and that's the way it would stay.

"Most of the time," she said.

He knew she was lying but fortunately didn't go into full-on guilt mode. "Well, there are people out there who are desperate and do things like look at the obituaries to find out when people are going to be out of the house at funerals."

"You gave me the check after the funeral," she said.

"You know what I mean," he said testily.

She really didn't but she didn't let on.

"Can we find out who cashed it? Where?" she asked.

"I'm working on that," he said, showing an initiative that she found refreshing.

"Okay. And one more thing," she said, Cal cutting her off.

"Yes. Rebecca. I'm leaving this afternoon. I didn't forget," he said, his tone petulant, as if his track record was impeccable where it came to the girls.

After he left, she ran through the possibilities for where the check had gone, and kept coming back to Heather's grungy boyfriend. They had a lot to discuss when she got home, even though delving into the topic would be painful. Maybe Heather would see now why Maeve wasn't so enthusiastic about her choice in men. While scrolling through a funny text from Chris Larsson she thought about the latest developments in her life.

Christmas at Cal and Gabriela's.

Three grand gone missing.

A sister who may or may not still be alive.

A boyfriend?

She wasn't sure what order to put that list in.

One day, one thing, at a time, she concluded.

CHAPTER 28

Maeve drove up to the mall later that night to pick up a few Christmas presents for the girls. There were the special socks that you could only get at the Gap for Heather and an iPad case that Rebecca "had to have!" or else she would die, or something equally dire. She was bone tired but she wanted to get this errand out of the way and crossed off her list.

Rebecca had come home earlier and gone straight to her room after a brief conversation with her mother. Maeve tried to fill her in on Evelyn and how she was doing her best to find her but Rebecca was only half listening, seeming to have swapped her gentler personality with the more difficult one of her younger sister. She was "exhausted," school having used up every ounce of energy she had. She was too tired to empty the dishwasher, even, something that Maeve wondered about. Just how much energy did it take to put dishes from the appliance into the cabinets?

A lot, apparently. Rebecca was still in her room when Maeve left.

Washing some pots at the sink after Rebecca had disappeared, she watched Heather out of the corner of her eye, devouring the meatloaf that Maeve had made at the store and brought home.

"How was school?" Maeve had asked.

"Great," Heather said, more cheerful about the subject than was necessary.

"Really?"

Heather had known where this was going. "I was there, I went to class, I have finished my homework. I haven't left the house in days." And with that, she had eaten the last of the meatloaf.

"Why is that? Why don't you leave the house anymore, except to go to school?" Maeve asked.

"Homework," she said. "Any more questions?"

Just one. Maeve didn't push it by asking about Tommy specifically. "You know I had a check in my room and now it's gone. Do you happen to know where it went?" She would give her one more chance. She watched Heather's face for any sign that she knew, didn't know, or was lying. The girl's expression gave nothing away. She looked her mother dead in the eye. If she was lying, she was damn good at it.

"I don't. How much was it for?" Heather asked.

"Three thousand dollars," Maeve said, looking away. She had lost this staring contest, Heather never breaking eye contact.

Cal had called earlier to say he had nothing to report on the case of the missing check, not who cashed it, not where it had been cashed, and Maeve had had no opportunity—or inclination, really—to have the conversation with Heather about why Tommy may have taken it. She had called the bank and confirmed that it hadn't been cashed through her personal accounts nor any of the store's accounts.

On the way back from the mall, Maeve rehashed the conversation, thinking of any verbal or physical tic that might have indicated that Heather had had something to do with the check's disappearance, but there had been none. As she drove through the village, taking in the lights in the store windows and the greenery that lined the streets in large pots, the thought that her father wouldn't be with her this year deflated her completely. She hadn't done anything this year to get the store ready for the holidays; it was all she could do to keep the cases filled with the treats that people came to expect from her and The Comfort Zone, to keep ample stock of Jo's old linguistic nemesis, the *bûches de Nöel*. She passed the local restaurant that Chris Larsson had originally suggested for their first date, its large windows revealing happy diners at every table, a warm glow coming from inside the main dining room, twinkling lights visible in the bar. She headed down toward the river and hung a right, on her way home finally after an inordinately long day, the only kind she seemed to have anymore, her energy gone, her spirit for anything having vanished.

The power of positive thinking. Or just complete denial. Maeve wasn't sure which it was when it came to Jo's passionate devotion to Doug and the choices he made.

Maeve hadn't had a hankering for wings and a glass of wine in a long time but when she saw a very familiar Ford Taurus sitting outside of Mickey's, the local tavern around the corner from her house, her mouth suddenly watered for the taste of hot sauce and cheap Chardonnay.

Jo's husband Doug drove a very specific kind of car, the kind of car that no self-respecting middle-aged guy would drive: a bottle-green Ford Taurus station wagon. Maeve gave Jo unrelenting grief about the car, the polar opposite of something that Jo would consider "cool," but Jo defended her husband's choice of vehicle, saying that it was "practical" and would be "helpful once the baby was born."

She found Doug sitting at the bar, chatting amiably with a blonde whose black roots were evidence of a delay in getting to CVS for a box of hair dye. The tenor of their chat also spoke to his familiarity with a local denizen that Maeve wouldn't have expected Doug—he of the self-described "crazy work schedule"—to have. There was a seat on his right, putting him in the middle of his friend on the left and Maeve on the right, once she sat down. Really, she looked like more than a friend and the thought of that made Maeve see red.

"Doug! Hi," she said, sliding onto the stool at the corner of the bar. Maeve wondered how he survived as a detective; one look at her and his cheeks turned red, his eyes wide at her appearance. Guilty as charged, she thought. She couldn't imagine him interviewing anyone, trying to deceive a suspect into telling the truth. He could barely hold her gaze as she alternately stared at him and then at the woman, who she recognized as the manager of the local Dunkin' Donuts. "Tammy, is it?" she said, leaning across Doug and extending her hand.

"Tamara," the woman said, staying put.

Maeve glared at her. "Nice to see you, Tamara." She looked at Doug. "And you? How are you?" she asked.

He stared into his beer.

"Could you excuse us, Tamara?" Maeve said. "Doug and I have some important business to discuss."

Tamara looked as if she were searching her pickled brain for a snappy retort but when she couldn't come up with anything better than "Bitch, please," she sidled off in a haze of cheap perfume and misplaced indignation.

The bartender, someone Maeve had known for years, took her order, leaving her to think about what she wanted to say to Jo's husband. The guilt was written all over his face, but guilt for what, she wasn't sure. Being out? Chatting up Tamara? Something worse? She cut to the chase. "Tell me you're not stupid enough to be carrying on with someone who a) hangs out here and b) lives in your own town?" Maeve asked. There was a "c"; she just didn't know it, her mind clouded with an angry film. "Who works at Dunkin' Donuts?" Oh, there it was: c.

He looked at the Brooklyn Lager sign hanging above the bar for far longer than was necessary. "No, I'm not that stupid," he said, but he wasn't very convincing. He reached down and smoothed the front of his ubiquitous Dockers khakis, the only kind of pants that Maeve had ever seen him wear. He and Jo had honeymooned in Bermuda; had he worn Dockers there the whole time as well? Her guess was that he had.

"Then what are you doing here? And why am I taking your wife to birth class, and to buy cribs and diapers and onesies? What exactly are you doing?"

He continued to stare at the sign. "I don't know what I'm doing."

Maeve's drink arrived and she drank half of it before she spoke again. "This is a fine time for a midlife crisis, Doug."

"It's not a midlife crisis, Maeve," he said.

"Then what is it?" she asked, downing the rest of her wine and signaling for another. She lived around the corner; if she had to, she'd leave the car, walk down the hill, and get it in the morning.

He finally turned and looked at her, leaning in close. "I'm not sure I can go through with this." He sighed, and in that sigh lay a thousand indications of his dissatisfaction and woe.

It was all she could do not to reach out and grab him by the neck, strangling the life from his body while everyone in Mickey's watched. She hadn't meant to telegraph her intent, but it must have been clear; he backed away from her, his eyes growing wide.

"I wouldn't expect you to understand," he said.

"Oh, you wouldn't?"

"No," he said.

"A whining man is not attractive, Doug," Maeve said. "Tamara would have let you know that if I didn't have the opportunity to first."

"It all happened so fast," he said. "I was married and having a baby before I really even thought about it."

"And you were powerless to stop it?"

He looked at her, his eyebrows arched. "Have you met Jo?" He stared back into his beer. "She's like a whirlwind."

But in a good way, Maeve thought. She's the best thing that ever happened to you, you ungrateful snot. Maeve asked the bartender for the wings to go; the girls would find them in the refrigerator and eat them, regardless of the hour.

"Don't tell Jo," he said. He hung his head. "It's just a phase. I think."

Maeve thought about that. "Okay," she said. "But on two conditions."

"What?"

"First, you get involved. You go to birth class. You set up that goddamned crib and make the nursery all pretty."

"I can do that."

"And if I call you and say I need your help, you'll help me."

He looked suitably alarmed. "What kind of help?"

Had she just blackmailed a cop? Or just an immature man-baby who didn't realize what his responsibilities were? Whichever, she felt not a whit of guilt. "Any kind of help," she said, realizing that being able to have him do some of the things she couldn't, from an investigative standpoint, would be most helpful. She didn't know if she'd ever need his help, but wasn't it nice to have him in her own back pocket? "Now settle up and get home to your wife. You have birth class tomorrow tonight," she said. "Seven o'clock."

He nodded, perking up when he remembered he had something to ask her. "Heard you had a finger in your refrigerator."

She clasped a hand across his mouth. "Not one more word."

"Okay!" he said when she finally removed her hand. "I just wanted to tell you that finger removal," he said, dropping his voice to a whisper when she shot him a threatening look, "is very specific to certain kinds of pursuits." She waited while he drank his beer. "Drugs. Mob stuff. We see that a lot in certain types of cases." He raised an eyebrow. "If you know what I mean."

"I know what you mean," she said. "But I don't know what it has to do with me. The store."

He turned his body so that no one in the vicinity could hear what he was saying. "Your landlord? Sebastian DuClos?"

"Yes?"

"Let me put it this way," he said, pulling out his wallet. "Pay your rent on time."

"I always do."

"Good," he said, turning back around.

"How do you know so much about him?"

"I know stuff, Maeve. I get around," he said cryptically. When she didn't buy that explanation, he elaborated. "I did some research at work. He's connected. Just saying." He asked for his check. "Why do you think I've been going to Dunkin' Donuts?" he asked.

"Lame excuse, Doug. Very lame." But interesting development. She wasn't surprised. Now that she knew that DuClos was growing pot in his basement, nothing would surprise her about his pursuits.

She and Doug had nothing left to discuss so she left him holding the tab for her wine and her wings, leaving almost a full glass of white on the bar. She hadn't said the one thing that she really wanted to say: if you leave her, I will kill you.

Poor guy looked scared enough as it was when she threatened him one last time before she left. No need to push him over the edge.

CHAPTER 29

Maeve had been told at the first meeting that the support group held a Christmas party every year, and she'd volunteered to bring the desserts. It was planned for the Monday before Christmas so that the group had a chance to be together one last time before the holiday. Before Maeve went to the Y, she put the address that Margie had given her into her GPS and took a detour, leaving Jo to close the store.

The address that Margie had given her was in Rhineview, due south and west of Mansfield and a bit closer to the support group at the YMCA. The town of Rhineview, where the house was located, had neither a view of the Rhine nor any view at all, for that matter. Maeve drove through the town, finding that the village looked like an artist's colony and a place where rich New York City dwellers bought cut-rate "character homes," as they were now called, from down-on-their-heels locals and either tore them down to build a new, brilliant McMansion, or subjected them to a six-figure restoration complete with professional kitchen. She had looked at a Web site for the town prior to making the trip and found that it boasted a lively bar scene and great restaurants.

Maeve didn't know what she was expecting to find once she got to the exact address; it seemed too easy to think that she would knock at the door and find her sister. She had nothing but her gut to go on, her gut telling her that whoever lived in the ramshackle farmhouse with the dilapidated barn in the back would hold the key to finding Evelyn. The house was depressing-looking, scary even. It had not had the benefit of either a teardown or a wholesale renovation, though, and its owners likely didn't partake of the fancy bars or the expensive entrees at Chez Marie, the place she passed in town and that looked like it was fully booked on this Monday night in the holiday season.

At one time, this house in front of her had probably been beautiful, but now it was in need of a paint job, some new risers on the porch steps, and some structural work, if the slight tilt of the roof was any indication. There was no nameplate to let her know who lived there, but her online search of the yellow pages indicated that the landline was registered in the name of J. Hartwell, the same name that Margie had given her. Before she left that evening, she had taken a chance and called the number.

The phone in the Hartwell house rang fifteen times before someone picked up; there was no answering machine, obviously, and Maeve was ready to hang up when she heard the raspy voice of what seemed to be a two-pack-a-day smoker, at least.

"Mr. Hartwell?"

"Dead."

Maeve had rehearsed what she would say to whoever answered the phone, but nothing prepared her for the gruffness of this person, someone proclaiming Mr. Hartwell's status in a single, hoarse word. "Dead." Maeve steeled herself. "Is this Mrs. Hartwell?"

"Who is this?"

"This is Maeve Conlon. I was given your name by a friend who thinks you may know what happened to my sister, Evelyn Conlon. Margie Haggerty? My sister would be . . ."

Nothing implicated the woman more in the story than her abrupt hang-up.

Maeve was determined to speak to Mrs. Hartwell, if that was even who she was. No one answered the door after Maeve knocked three separate times, each successive rap on the window getting a little more forceful. After standing there in the dark and the cold for longer than she would have liked, a bit of fear creeping up her spine like icy tendrils, she walked the property, trespassing as it were but in her mind daring the woman to call the cops.

Nothing to see here; show's over, Jack used to say.

She was drawn to the barn at the far right side of the house and, keeping in the darkest parts of the yard, some trees covering her progress, she made her way over there and peeked inside. She spied the outline of some boxes, a tractor in one corner, a loft that had probably been used to store hay back in the day. It smelled. It was falling down. In the dark, it looked like a structure that, if she had been watching herself on a large movie screen, would have made Maeve yell, "Don't go in there!"

So she didn't, making her way back to the car, planning to mark time until the support group started.

This entire place scared her. She didn't know why.

She got back in the car and locked the doors, watching the house from a spot across the street, thinking of all the things she had to do to get ready for the holiday, all the baking that would need to happen. She tried to calm her mind. Her thoughts drifted from one mental list to another, her eyes trained on the house. It was a few miles from town and there wasn't another house in sight. It was remote, off the beaten path. Desolate.

Occupied.

Maeve sat up straighter as she saw a light in an upstairs window, not previously illuminated, and a curtain move, as if ruffling in a nonexistent breeze. Someone was in the house, someone who wouldn't—or couldn't—answer the door. She pulled her purse closer to her side and waited.

Behind her, a kaleidoscope of light burst into her consciousness through the rearview mirror.

Shit, she thought. Cops.

CHAPTER 30

Her heart stopped pounding about five miles from the YMCA. A quick story about being lost, and the cops had sent her on her way, even escorting her to the highway so that she wouldn't get lost again, never knowing that the petite blonde with the platter of cookies in the trunk had a handgun stuffed under the seat that she knew how to use.

In the parking lot, she ran into a few of the women she had met that first week: Lorraine Mackin, Judy McDermott, Ann Marie Cardona. The three women peered into the hatch of Maeve's Prius and marveled at the assortment of miniature baked goods, all displayed on gold rounds and covered with red and green cellophane, waiting to be brought into the Y.

Lorraine stepped back. "You're the real deal, huh?" she said admiringly.

"I'd like to think so," Maeve said, handing each woman a tray of desserts. In the lobby, the Christmas tree greeted them, some of its lights now burned out, the garland hanging limply. Ann Marie stayed behind to fix it, giving the tray she was carrying to Maeve.

It was a potluck supper, something that Maeve found a little offputting and actually struck a little fear in her heart. She was bound by Health Department rules at The Comfort Zone but every home kitchen was a complete free-for-all in terms of cleanliness; she had learned that the hard way after seeing a friend open a can of tuna with the same opener she had used to open a can of cat food. There had also been the Great Stomach Flu the previous Thanksgiving that had felled her and Heather, sparing Jo, thankfully, after she had drunk some way-past-its-prime eggnog at a Christmas party in town. She eyed the buffet table warily, spying the requisite Swedish meatballs, old school but making a comeback; a crock of something that appeared to be short ribs; a frozen pizza cut up into bite-sized triangles. She made a move toward the basket of crackers next to the cheese platter and took a few in a napkin. They would have to do. She wasn't going anywhere near the rest of the fare.

Mrs. Alderson wheeled over and took a spot by the punch bowl. "Hello, Maeve, my fair Irish lass."

Maeve gave the older woman a kiss on the cheek. "Hello, Francine. How are you today?"

"I'm good," she said, pushing her walker toward Maeve. "This time of year makes me sad but I'm trying hard not to let it get me down." She smiled sadly. "Really, how many Christmases do I have left? Might as well make them happy ones."

"Do you have other children?" Maeve asked. "Family?"

"Just my dog, Prince Philip," she said. "He's enough, though." She pulled a photo album out of the pocket of her sweater and handed it to Maeve. "Here he is in all of his Labrador glory."

Maeve politely flipped through the photo album and remarked on Prince Philip's handsome face and physique. She handed the photo album back to Francine. "He's beautiful."

"Best dog I've ever had. And I'm old. I've had more than a few," she said, laughing. "Winston will love him when they get to meet."

"If it's not too personal, Francine, can I ask you what you're doing to find Winston?" Maeve asked.

"I go to the support group," she said. "People have very good ideas about finding our loved ones. And I am working with a private investigation group, but so far, there hasn't been too much to report."

"Really?"

"Yes. I find that the comfort I get here, as well as the information about what has worked and what hasn't, is far more helpful than anything else," she said.

Maeve pondered that. She wondered what kind of PI firm was taking this woman's money and for how long but didn't think it right to ask.

Maeve watched Francine make her way along the buffet table, the tennis balls on the bottom of her walker wheels making her journey a silent one. She wondered how a woman so old, and with a search for her son the only thing she really had left beside an old dog with a graying face, could be so happy. So lighthearted.

She wondered. Could that be her someday, too?

Lorraine approached her. "Hmmm. Frozen pizza. I'm not going to judge but that doesn't seem like it took a lot of effort."

Maeve leaned in conspiratorially. "I already went there in my mind but didn't want to say it out loud."

Lorraine picked up a square of cheese and examined it on all four sides before popping it into her mouth. "Any new developments on your sister?" she asked. "Finding her?"

Maeve decided to keep Margie's information to herself. Many people at the support group had been on a search, and with only two members finding their loved one—one dead and one in a group home in Canada—she didn't want to gloat that she had a little information. "Not really. I'm closed for two weeks after Christmas so I'm going to pick up the search in earnest then. You?"

Lorraine, her piercing blue eyes looking at a spot over Maeve's head, shook her head. "I stopped a long time ago," she said, which surprised Maeve; she thought everyone here who was missing someone was still actively searching, hunting. "Every clue led to a dead end. Every private investigator who could help me ended up being a zero." She reached out and grabbed Maeve's hand, the one not holding a napkin full of crackers. "Don't get your hopes up, Maeve. I hate to say that, but it's true. It's like some of these people just vanished into thin air. And those who didn't probably wished they had. I just come here to find out if anyone has had any luck. Found their family member."

Maeve felt a steely resolve creep up her spine. No one told her something was a lost cause, ever. Jack had always said that if he wanted to get her to do something, he just had to tell her that she couldn't. That was all it took. "Thanks," she said. "I'll keep that in mind."

"I just don't want you to get your heart broken," Lorraine said. "Like I did."

I won't, Maeve thought but didn't say. First of all, my heart is already broken.

And second, if she's out there, I'll find her.

Back home, in her bedroom, she took off her clothes and put on a pair of pajama pants and a T-shirt, leaning over to set her alarm, even though she awoke at the same time every morning, alarm or not. Her fingers brushed across the various items on her nightstand, coming into contact with a manila envelope that hadn't been there before. She was almost too tired to comprehend what was in there but handling money every day made her fingers fly through the bills.

The stack totaled three thousand dollars, all in twenties.

CHAPTER 31

Christmas dawned bright and cold. Before she went to the store, giving herself a late open—nine o'clock—she and the girls opened presents and had breakfast. She watched both of them carefully for any signs of guilt or discomfort that might accompany their having stolen, cashed, and then replaced the money from a check that had been on her nightstand, but there was nothing. Before she went downstairs to begin the present opening, she tucked the wad of cash between her mattress and the box spring, as far into the middle as she could reach, smoothing down the comforter when she was done.

This incident would make an interesting blotter entry in the Farringville paper:

Parker Avenue resident reported that some time while she was at work, someone absconded from her house with a check in the amount of three thousand dollars. Check was subsequently cashed and the money was returned to her. The police are not investigating.

Oh, but did we mention the severed finger that they found in the Parker Avenue resident's place of business?

She watched the girls open their presents. Rebecca was delighted with the new down vest that she had wanted as well as the earrings that Jo had picked out at one of the girls' favorite sites and told Maeve to buy. Heather was her usual quiet self, opening each present as if it were the last one she would ever receive, gasping when she saw that her sister had bought her a beautiful chunky necklace, the kind that were all the rage.

After she sold her last pie at the store—a gorgeous apple crumb, if she did say so herself—she and Jo exchanged gifts. Jo was so excited, clapping her hands together gleefully, as Maeve stripped off the shiny Christmas paper from a long, rectangular box.

"A shovel?" she said. She couldn't help it. It was the last thing she expected to open.

"Yes!" Jo said. "I couldn't believe when I found it in T.J. Maxx. It is lightweight and has a pink handle, so it's perfect for you."

Maeve turned the box over in her hands. "A shovel," she said, more definitively this time. "We haven't had any snow yet, but when we do, I'll use it."

"Remember that time you got stuck in the snow out back and you had to call Cal to dig you out?" Jo said, so pleased with herself that her cheeks had flushed a deep red. "And you were complaining that you couldn't do it yourself? And your Triple A membership had lapsed? You were mad," she said, grimacing at the memory.

It was one time, Maeve thought, and there were a million other things that would have been more helpful to her at that exact moment: a new piping bag, a cast-iron skillet, other sundry baking items. That new stove that she coveted, but couldn't afford. She looked at the box in her hands. "I love it, Jo. Thank you. Never again will I need a man's help to get me out of the snow."

Jo gave her a hug. "Next year will be better," she said.

Maeve wasn't sure if she meant it in terms of gift giving or in general. Next year had to be better because any gift was better than a shovel and she was running low on people left to lose.

"It will go nicely with the headlamp you gave me last year," Maeve said.

"Oh, the headlamp! That was the best gift ever," Jo said, proud of herself. "Hakuna matata. See you soon."

Maeve went into the kitchen to box up the items she was going to bring to Cal's, surprised and happy to see Chris Larsson looking through the window of the back door, tapping lightly to get her attention. She was still holding the shovel when she let him in.

"Doing some bulb planting?" he asked, pointing at the shovel. "You're lucky it's been so warm."

"Christmas present. From Jo," she said.

He took it from her, turning it over in his hands. "And the reason?"

Maeve shrugged. "She thinks I need a shovel." She pointed to the counter, strewn with an assortment of items that would end up in the trash if he didn't take them. "Everything except the pecan pie, lemon bars, and a few cupcakes are yours for the taking."

"If I take them, does that mean I have to sleep with you?" he asked. "I'm not that easy, Maeve. I'm not that kind of guy."

She put a pie in a box, followed by some cookies and a cranberry tart, tying all of the boxes together and handing them to him.

"You didn't answer my question," he said, leaning over and giving her a kiss.

"We'll see about that," she said. She wrapped her arms around him. "Merry Christmas, Chris. I'm looking forward to seeing you again." She sounded stilted. She didn't know how to do this. Jo was right; she had said it many times in the past few days and it was becoming clear to Maeve that she was out of practice.

"I'll call you," he said, looping his fingers through the red and white string that held the boxes together.

She stood by the back door and watched him go, wondering if she would ever get any "game," as Jo called it, if she would ever find out just exactly how this was supposed to go.

An hour later, she pulled up in front of Cal and Gabriela's, checking her makeup in the rearview mirror. It would have to do. She used to think about what to wear in front of the flawless Gabriela, but that had stopped a long time ago. She was old enough now that she knew what looked good on her and that her uniform of black turtleneck and jeans covered most social engagements. She wasn't surprised to find Gabriela in a tight wrap dress that accentuated the one curve she had, the one that started at her hips and ended at her perfectly round ass. On her feet were impossibly high heels, and around her waist an apron that said *Kiss the cook!* on it. Maeve obliged.

"I'm so glad you could come, Maeve," Gabriela said. Clearly, she was on her meds this day.

Maeve handed over her down coat, the one with the ripped sleeve, quickly swiping at the flour that ringed the collar. "Thanks for having me," she said.

Devon toddled toward her on the slate floor and Maeve held her breath until he reached her safely. That floor, in addition to most of the design choices in the old stone Tudor, was a hazard to the baby and Maeve wondered how he had escaped injury thus far.

After the girls and Gabriela left the foyer, Maeve grabbed Cal's arm. "The check? It was cashed. Or someone gave me the money. The entire amount, all three grand, was on my nightstand." She looked up at him, illuminated by the large chandelier hanging over his head. She didn't have the heart to tell him that at this angle, it was clear that his hairline was receding. He would be crushed to learn that if he didn't already know. "I feel like I'm going crazy."

"Well, case closed, then?" he said, looking as happy as if he had solved the mystery of the missing check all by himself.

"Not really, Cal," she said. "Someone was in my bedroom,

took something that belonged to me, and while they did return it, the whole thing just seems odd." She stripped off her sweater; with the fireplace ablaze and the oven going in the nearby kitchen, the house seemed as if it were a thousand degrees.

"But you got the money back, right?"

"Do you hear me? Someone took the check, cashed it, and then replaced the money." She looked at him, studying his face for recognition of how odd that was. "Do you get it now?"

He pursed his lips. "I get it now. But you got the money back, right?"

She ignored that; that wasn't the point. "I've got to ask you: Do you think Heather took it?" It was a thought that had floated through her mind a few times over the past few days. Yes, there was the Tommy Brantley angle, but the only other person who had ready access to her bedroom, and who was in the house a lot, was her second-born. The unflappable, inscrutable, sometime liar.

Cal and Heather had a special bond that Maeve didn't understand and which she thought clouded her ex's judgment. He wasn't quite as lenient when it came to Rebecca, even though that girl hadn't given him cause for even one drop of sweat crossing his brow. "God, Maeve, you are so hard on that kid. Why on earth would she steal something from you? We give her everything she wants. You're probably right. It was Tommy. We don't know why, but you've got the money back. Let's put an end to all of this." He sighed, tired of her suspicions, her thoughts always going to the dark side. "You got the money back," he repeated. "Are you really going to take this further, possibly ruin that kid's life?"

"I thought you hated him," Maeve said, recalling their earlier conversation.

"I was angry," he said. "It's over. You've got your money."

Gabriela called out for them, putting an end to the conversation and stopping what would have turned into a full-blown argument.

Cocktails were being served in the great room behind the kitchen. Maeve noted, with interest, that Rebecca, her college freshman, was nursing a glass of white wine. And here we are again, letting the inmates run the asylum, or at the very least, letting the underage members of the family drink. In her mind, Rebecca should still be drinking apple juice from a sippy cup. To Cal, she was old enough to partake with the adults. Rebecca avoided her eye as she took a sip from her crystal goblet. When Maeve accepted the glass of wine that Cal brought her, she made Rebecca's glass her first clink of "cheers."

Gabriela took time out of cooking what smelled like a delicious dinner to sit on the arm of Cal's leather recliner and join them for a drink. Cal was right: it was awkward, at least at the beginning, all of them unaccustomed to being together in the same room, pretending that the joining together of a divorced set of parents, his new wife and baby, and the two daughters from the original union was a completely normal occurrence. Maeve focused her attention on the baby, hoping against hope that today wouldn't mark his first trip to the hospital. In his hands, he held a box of fireplace matches, the head of one making its way toward his wet mouth. Maeve snatched the box away just as Gabriela turned her attention to her husband's ex-wife.

"So, Maeve, Cal tells me that you have a sister," she said, swinging one long leg, the heel of her shoe dangling from one dainty ankle. "Tell me everything. The whole story."

Cal looked away. For some reason, this topic made him more uncomfortable than Maeve had ever seen him look; he hadn't been this unnerved the day he moved out of the house. On that day, even, he had asked for help with one of his boxes. That takes some nerve.

The sun streaming through the almost floor-to-ceiling windows made her feel hot, but suddenly, Maeve was happy to tell the story again. Telling it again, saying the words, made it more real and gave her the strength she needed to continue her search. She caught Gabriela up on the story. "So, she was apparently at this horrible place. I'm not sure why. I can't imagine my father doing that unless he had a good reason."

"He had a good reason," Gabriela said. "He loved her but he didn't think he could take care of her."

In that short retelling, Gabriela had hit on the answer to that one, major loose end that was keeping Maeve up at night. It was the one thing that no one had articulated so succinctly, and although this was what Maeve hoped was the reason for her sister's departure, she didn't know.

"Your father was a very good man, Maeve," Gabriela said, wiping her hands on her silly apron. "There wasn't a bad bone in that man's body. He wanted to take care of her. Make sure she was safe." She paused and looked out the window. "Maybe he got her out of there before it was too late."

Maeve sat in stunned silence. Here she had spent all of this time— the time since Cal had left—thinking that this woman was her enemy, even though they were once friends. Hearing Gabriela speak those words reminded Maeve that she had once liked her, had trusted her opinion on matters large and small. "Then why didn't he tell me?"

Gabriela shrugged. "Things were different then, Maeve. People like your sister went away to places we would never dream of sending our children to now," she said.

And this from a woman who Maeve had never seen hold her own child.

"It was different then, Maeve." She got up. "Remember that. He was a good man."

Maeve watched her as she ascended the few steps to the kitchen. Maybe she had misjudged Gabriela. Maybe she was more astute than Maeve had given her credit for being. Could it be that she was the only one who really understood what Jack had been thinking all those years ago?

In the kitchen, Maeve heard something large and metal clang to the floor and the sound of the baby crying. She held her breath until the baby appeared, unharmed but supremely pissed off, Gabriela holding him at arms' length toward Cal. "Here. He keeps getting into trouble." She went back to the kitchen. "And his diaper stinks!"

Maeve hadn't misjudged her that much. Gabriela did not enjoy being the mother of a toddler, or being a mother at all. But her words, "remember, he was a good man," rang in Maeve's ears, and in her heart, she forgave her former friend just a little bit for upending the life that Maeve had so carefully constructed.

CHAPTER 32

It was dark and she would be back before the girls even knew she was gone so the plan was perfect. Years of owning her own business, of running on little sleep, had prepared her for this not-quite-daybreak visit to Rhineview the day after Christmas and back to the house that she felt certain held the answer to the questions she had. As she pulled on her clothes in her dark, drafty bedroom, feeling cold air seep through the old window jambs, she resisted the urge to shiver. The voice of the woman who had answered the phone that day she had called stayed with her. In it were years of knowing and not telling, of smoking in solitude, of crafting lies.

Maeve wasn't sure how she knew that, but she did.

In her dreams the night before, her sleep fitful and troubled, Jack had met her at the gazebo near the river and instead of saying what she hoped he would say—"your sister is here"—or something to that effect, he handed her a loaf of bread, a challah. And told her that her donuts stunk.

Thanks, Jack.

Back to the challah dreams. In this one, the bread was a day-old challah from a Kosher bakery near her childhood home and she remembered its sweet goodness melting in her mouth as she walked home from school on Fridays, a warm loaf wrapped in paper and in her small hands, half of it gone by the time she entered the house. They weren't Jewish, but she and Jack did buy a challah every Friday if only to have warm French toast the next morning.

When the bread was day-old.

In her dream, Jack handed her the bread and she thanked him. "It's rye, not challah," he said portentously.

She wasn't sure what difference it made. Looked like a challah to her.

Maybe her subconscious was trying to tell her something. She wasn't sure what, but it was leading her back to a time that maybe wasn't so great in reality but for which she had one or two fond memories. Whenever she thought of her father, the memories were good. The smell of butter melting into a pan, the sound of bread drenched in beaten egg and cinnamon hitting the heat, the taste of toasted goodness hitting her tongue. Jack's smile while she ate, refilling her cup of milk as many times as she wanted.

"You are a good girl, Mavy," he said then and in her dream.

Not really, she thought, but I try.

As for her stinky donuts, she had no idea. Jack often complained about them, how they didn't have enough sugar or they were too fancy, but she ignored him. She never left Buena del Sol without him finishing every last one she brought so he wasn't that dissatisfied of a customer. In the dream, he handed her a bag and gave her a Bronx cheer to underscore just how much he didn't like them.

She drove up the dark highway, careful to maintain the speed limit. The first thing she had done when she got in the car was to touch the gun up into the gap underneath the seat; she had no reason to suspect the husky-voiced woman was trouble, but she wanted to be safe. Next, she pulled her hair back into a tight ponytail, tucking it into the North Face hat that she had taken from the top of the closet and was sure belonged to Rebecca at one point before Maeve had made it her own. She zipped her coat up to her neck, in an attempt to ward off the chill that took a long time to leave the interior of the car, despite the heat being turned up to the maximum temperature.

One thing she loved about the Prius was how little noise it made, so as she slid into position, a hundred feet or so before the house, she knew that she hadn't made a sound. When idling, the car was virtually silent and that made for some excellent clandestine snooping, the likes of which she was about to partake in shortly.

Maeve looked down at the headlamp in her hands. When Jo had given it to her, Maeve had stared at it incredulously, kind of like how she had stared at the shovel; apparently, in Jo's mind, it would be helpful if the lights went out and Maeve needed to ice a cake in the dark, something that had never happened and was likely never to be an issue, people not really requiring cakes when the power went out. They usually had other concerns, and if they were like Maeve, they began with how they were going to keep their wine chilled. Maeve had left the lamp in the glove compartment of the Prius, wondering if there would ever come a time when it would be needed, and now she decided that this morning was the day. She pulled it on over her hat and switched it on after getting out of the car, casting a glow on the dirt road that went farther than she'd imagined it would.

She grabbed her gun from under her seat. She wasn't sure if she really needed it, but she took it anyway. It made her feel safer, more secure, and those were feelings she needed to embrace right now in the dark and cold.

She was trespassing. She knew that. But another thing she knew is that she wouldn't rest until she found Evelyn, or figured out what had happened to her. She was like that, making sure that all of the loose ends were tied up and that anything that needed to be known was discovered. Other people would have been more concerned about the finger and its owner but Maeve had other things on her mind now and finding a nine-fingered denizen of her sleepy village wasn't one of them. She hadn't seen Sebastian DuClos—she kept their meetings to a minimum—but she was sure that he had something to do with the finger and its placement.

She reached the edge of the property and looked at the house, set back from the dirt road, its ramshackle structure looking forbidding and eerie in the early hours of the morning. A car, the same one that had been there the first day she had come by before the support group, sat in the driveway. A Rambler so old, it was a wonder it was still drivable.

She hadn't reminisced this much in years but every step she took and everything she passed—a tree here, a low shrub there—reminded her of something from her childhood. The flora and fauna of my mind, she thought. Maybe she wasn't getting enough sleep after all. She wondered if her subconscious was in overdrive, hoping to remember something from her childhood that would lead her to Evelyn Conlon, the longed-for child, her long-lost sister. There was nothing there, though; she was sure of it. Anything that was there would have come to the forefront of her brain by now and taken her down a different path than the one she was on.

The house was dark. She headed toward the barn off to the side and behind the house, nestled in among a copse of trees that had long ago lost their leaves, which now crunched beneath Maeve's snow boots. She was drawn to the barn; she wasn't sure why.

Siblings know.

Did they? Did she?

In the still, early-morning air, her feet made more noise than her car did and she took care to step gingerly through the deep piles of dead leaves that had fallen and collected around a structure more dilapidated than the house itself. The door to the barn was heavy and off-kilter, making it hard to open. Maeve did her best not to make too much noise opening it just slightly; it was times like these when she was glad she was small and could sneak through an opening that wouldn't fit a larger woman.

Inside the barn, she trained her headlamp on various items contained within its drafty walls. Large gaps existed between the ancient slats that held the building together, and the wind whipped through, throwing up a fine silt of dust and dirt. She walked through, keeping the light of her headlamp low so as not to be seen by any passersby—as unlikely as they would be at this hour—through the gaps in the wall boards.

A large wooden table sat in the middle of the room and there were various items on it, some that Maeve didn't recognize, others that were perfectly at home in a barn: small rakes, shovels, and other items one might use to dig a garden. Some twine. An electronic de-icer for a car. A gas can. Nothing sinister, nothing valuable, nothing that would give her pause.

A noise outside, however, made her stop in her tracks. She knew better than to jump immediately to the conclusion that it was a car backfiring.

Shotgun blasts made a sound all their own.

CHAPTER 33

One way in, one way out.

She wished she had scoped this out a bit more, had used her head.
But she could be impulsive, she knew that about herself, and not having a plan had gotten her in hot water before. It looked like it had
again. She switched off the headlamp and stayed low to the ground.
Outside, the sound of boots crunching on the dead, frozen leaves
made her take cover behind a large tractor in one corner of the barn,
moving along the ground slowly and carefully, cautious of making
even one sound. She knelt beside the massive front wheel of the
tractor.

She slowed her breathing, telling herself to get comfortable because she would likely be there a long time. It was still dark out, but
black was turning to gray, meaning that dawn was close at hand.
She hoped that she wouldn't have to stay so long that daylight would
break and take away any cover she might have had.

The door to the barn was still ajar and Maeve could tell by the
movement of dust motes in the air that someone had entered. That,
and the sound of raspy breathing, the hoarse inhales and exhales
reminding her of the voice of the woman she spoke to a few days
earlier when she called to inquire about Evelyn. She stayed perfectly

still and waited, thinking that the person might call out to her or give some indication that she was in the barn. There was nothing, though; just some movement at the opening to the barn, a quick movement of some items on the long wooden table, and then an almost silent exit. The person left, sliding the barn door closed, leaving Maeve inside, her bones rattling inside her skin with fear.

Whoever this was, whoever resided in this house, wasn't very curious. Maeve would have searched through every inch of the barn if she suspected someone was in there. And then, when she found them and ascertained that they were up to no good, which was the only conclusion to draw of someone hiding behind a tractor, she would likely shoot them. That was her way. Fortunately, the person with the shotgun didn't share Maeve's curiosity or bloodlust, two good things for her.

Outside, the Rambler came to life, its noisy muffler indicating that it likely hadn't been changed in several decades. It drove off in a noisy clatter, down the street, past Maeve's car, and to parts unknown. She looked at her watch and waited five full minutes before standing up, creeping out from behind the tractor, and then breaking into the fastest sprint she could away from the barn, down the road, taking care to run behind the first layer of trees that flanked the roads so that she wouldn't be seen by a passing car, unlikely as it seemed one would come by at this hour in this deserted part of town.

Using her hands to bat away errant tree branches and still-attached dead leaves before they could hit her in the face, she reached the car in record time. Tomorrow, or maybe even later today, that sprint was going to cost her. She couldn't run like that anymore, not that she ever could, and if she had to predict, her night was going to consist of a bottle of Brunello, two Aleve, and the heating pad. When she thought about it, though, there were worse ways to spend the night.

She reached the car and started it immediately, hanging a quick

U-turn on the dirt road and speeding away from the house, not looking in her rearview, not taking the time to stop fully at the one stop sign she hit at the far end of the road, not admiring the Christmas lights in the main village. It was pedal to the metal until she hit the highway, and once out of the jurisdiction of Rhineview and away from any cops who thought it interesting that a woman in a Prius was back for a second time and might need to be followed, she slowed down and watched the sunrise, hoping her breathing would return to normal by the time she got home.

It returned faster than that. But with it came the realization that something in the barn had left its olfactory mark on her.

It took some time to enter her brain but she knew what it was, just not why it had taken her so long to realize that the smell permeated the car. Fear? Was it possible that her body and mind, in this case, could only focus on survival, on getting out of Rhineview as soon as possible? Maybe.

She thought about where she had been standing, her place next to the tractor, the long, arced mound of dirt where she had planted herself.

It had been a small grave, and whatever was beneath it had likely been dead for a while.

CHAPTER 34

After that early-morning excursion, she needed a shower and sleep, in exactly that order.

She went upstairs and into the cold of her bedroom, thinking about the insurance money beneath her mattress and vowing to make the call to get the windows replaced. Maybe Cal was right, she thought as she showered for longer than usual, the smell of the grave having invaded her nose; maybe she shouldn't care that the money had been returned but she knew she would never be comfortable with that. After drying off, afraid that the draft would bring with it pneumonia if her hair wasn't completely dry, she got into bed, climbing under the down comforter and falling into a deep and dreamless sleep. It seemed like only seconds later when she awoke to find Rebecca standing over her with the portable phone, but a misty-eyed glance at the phone told her it was nearly one o'clock in the afternoon.

"Mrs. Harrison from Buena del Sol," she said, handing her mother the phone and leaving.

Maeve propped herself up on the pillows; her back was already tightening up after her run through the woods. "Good afternoon, Mrs. Harrison. Did I forget something in my father's apartment?" she asked.

"No, not the apartment," the woman said, terse as ever. "Just the storage unit."

"Storage unit." Maeve had no idea that one existed on the grounds of the facility.

"Yes. Every resident has a small storage unit. Your father had one. In it were three boxes and a bicycle."

A bike. Okay, Maeve thought; that's definitely something I don't need. "I'll be right over."

"Take your time. Mr. Moriarty graciously volunteered to take the items and put them in his apartment until you could get them. But I just wanted to let you know that you owe us an additional one hundred and three dollars for the extra days that the items sat in our facility's unit."

Of course she did. Buena del Sol got you coming and going, and in this case, Jack was long gone. They had one last pound of flesh to extract from her and her father—even in death—and they were determined to collect the sum. She had already gotten a bill for the extra days she had taken to clean out his apartment, having broken a Buena del Sol rule of which she was unaware. She got up and took another shower, taking care to wash her hair thoroughly to get rid of any residual barn odors, and when she was dressed, headed over to the facility in a baggy Vassar sweatshirt that Rebecca had given her on visiting day that fall.

She asked for Mr. Moriarty at the front desk. She pretended to linger casually while waiting, but while the woman was calling the old guy to tell him he had a visitor, she eyed the list of residents on the computer screen and noted that Jack's room was now inhabited by Stanley Cummerbund, just as Mimi Devereaux had desired. Jack would be howling if he heard that one, and knowing that brought a smile to her face.

She pulled out her checkbook and wrote a check for the cost of the overage on the storage unit and handed it to the woman at the desk, someone she had never seen before, while she waited for Moriarty. He ambled down the hall a few minutes later, three boxes on a rolling cart, the bike wheeling along beside it.

The bike was pink. And it had been hers. She didn't remember moving it into the facility and wondered what had possessed her father to bring it along, but there it was, streamers coming out of both handles, a large "sissy bar," as they were called when she was a kid, at the back of the seat. She barely had room for the things she currently had in her own house; where was she going to put an old bike? And it wasn't like she could foist it off on Cal; Devon was a boy and what self-respecting boy rode a bike with pink streamers? Never mind that everything that Devon rode, wore, ate, and played with was top of the line and made from all-natural, organic products. For all she knew, he already had a tricycle made from kale.

Her mind went back to her childhood once again, the one place and time she was trying to put behind her, the bike sparking a memory that she had long repressed. She had gotten the bike for her birthday—she didn't remember which one—and had locked it up in the backyard, the tiny garage at the end of the driveway holding Jack's car, a lawnmower, and a host of other scary, cobweb-adorned things that Maeve couldn't identify and didn't want to. The morning after, when she had gone out to ride it, the tires were flat, slashed all the way around, exposing the rims. Across the fence and beyond the driveway that separated the two houses, she had spied Margie Haggerty assiduously avoiding her gaze.

Moriarty gave her a quick hug. "Hope you don't mind, Maeve, but that old battleax Harrison was setting up a howl about getting Jack's stuff out of storage and she said she couldn't reach you."

Maeve had not one message from her before today's phone call.

"So, there are these three boxes and the bike," he said.

She pulled the lid off the top box and peered in. It was a mishmash of papers and bills, not the orderly pile of items that had been found in the boxes in his apartment. She would go through everything when she got home, not while she was here in the lobby of a place she never wanted to return to. "Thanks, Mr. Moriarty."

"Jimmy. Please."

She gave him a quick hug. "Jimmy."

"Hey, Maeve. Can I ask you something?"

"Sure."

He pointed to the bike. "Will you be keeping that?"

She shook her head. "Nah. Will probably drop it off at the Goodwill on my way home. Why? Do you want it?"

He smiled. "I'd love it. I have a seven-year-old granddaughter who would think it was the best thing ever."

She handed over the bike. "It's all yours."

"I figured your girls were big now and wouldn't want it."

"You figured right," she said. "What do I do with this cart when I'm finished?" she asked.

"Pull up in front and I'll load up your car," he said. "Then, I'll return it. I don't want you to have to write another check for 'use of services' or something like that."

She started a slow jog to the car, gave up and walked slowly. At this rate, she might need a steady IV of Aleve or some kind of muscle relaxer. She wondered how much Buena del Sol would charge for that and then decided that she needed to be done with the place, once and for all.

Moriarty, as promised, loaded the boxes into the back of the Prius and gave her one of his patented rough bear hugs. "Bye, Maeve. Good luck with everything."

"This is more like a 'see you soon' hug," she said, not ready to let go of the one friend her father had, and who had stayed true to the old man in his infirmity.

He didn't look convinced. "Hey, thanks for the bike," he said. "My granddaughter will love it."

"I tore up the North Bronx on that bike. I know it's got a lot of good years left in it." She got in the car. "Happy new year, Jimmy."

"Yes, Maeve. You, too," he said, his eyes filling with tears. "Happy new year," he managed to croak out.

"My sister, Jimmy," she said, holding his gaze. "Nothing? Jack never said anything?"

"Nothing, Maeve," he said, a tear running down his cheek. He wiped it away. "I miss the old coot," he said. "He was my best friend."

She knew that. And she didn't want to linger. Seeing a tough old hooligan like Jimmy Moriarty standing by the entrance of the place he lived in and would die in as well, tears streaming down his face, was more than she could bear today. She focused instead on the memory of the pink streamers flying past her hands as she careened down 262nd Street, braking hard as she hit Broadway, her nose running from both the force of the wind and a little bit of fear.

It had been a good feeling, that, the feeling of the wind in her face, the freedom, the prospect of a little bit of danger. She wondered if she would ever recapture it.

CHAPTER 35

The girls had left her high and dry again, no surprise there, except for the fact that Heather was now wandering a little more freely. Maeve took note of that, noticing that she went on little excursions with her sister and wondering why that was, putting a discussion of this new development aside for a time when she could think. She tended the chicken she had put in the oven, wondering who she could call to help her eat it.

She invited Jo over but she and Doug were having "date night" so that left them out. They'd better be; she didn't want to have to maim Doug in order to get him to commit to her friend, whose emotional wounds had finally closed after all this time. She stared into the oven and at the perfectly browned chicken, juices flowing into the roaster that would make delicious gravy, slamming it shut when she realized she'd be eating by herself. Jack would have loved this meal, and then, when he had forgotten he had eaten, would have a complete second helping that didn't remind him in the least of his first.

She settled on Chris Larsson, who sounded more than happy to help her eat a six-pound Oven Stuffer roaster. He asked if she had wine.

"Is the Pope Catholic?" she asked, channeling her father and one of his favorite tropes.

"I don't know. I'm a Lutheran," he said, before hanging up.

While waiting for him to show up, she focused on the morning, which seemed like days, not hours, earlier. She knew she would be going back to Rhineview; it was just a matter of when. There was something not right about the whole thing, about how Margie gave her the information but not much else, how the woman on the phone wouldn't talk to her, how a warning shot was fired but how she wasn't really looked for in the barn, even though the shooter had to know someone was in the vicinity. None of it made sense, but she had learned a long time ago that by relying on herself, her smarts, she would be in good stead.

She didn't need any of them. She didn't need anyone. She had herself, and for most of her life, that had been enough.

She hemmed and hawed a few minutes—the few she had before Chris came by—before picking up the phone again. Although she relied on herself entirely for most things, she did have a question or two about Margie Haggerty that she couldn't answer, and her lack of trust in the woman niggled at the back of her mind. She had been on the police force as recently as ten years ago and Rodney Poole—someone she had seen recently but hadn't spoken to in over a year—was closing in on retirement. Surely he remembered Margie's case and the details surrounding it even if he hadn't had any direct involvement with it.

She knew he would have an opinion about this, look at it from a different angle. Maybe it would help illuminate what was troubling her and what, if anything, she should do with respect to Margie.

His card was on her dresser; it had been for the last year. She turned it over in her fingers before sitting down on the edge of her bed and dialing his cell. She would go directly to him, not to Doug;

Doug, in her mind, was never going to be a reliable narrator ever again. Finding him in Mickey's solidified that suspicion for her.

"Poole."

"Um, hello. This is Maeve. Maeve Conlon?"

There was a pause followed by a throat clearing. "Maeve Conlon."

"Yes."

"I was sorry to learn of your father's passing." He paused. "I thought about coming to his funeral, paying my respects to a brother officer, but then thought better of it."

She smiled. She understood why. "Is this a good time to talk?"

In the background, she heard voices, and then the sliding of a door followed by silence. "Sure."

Before she got to the real reason she was calling, she asked about Doug. "A new baby, huh?"

"Yes," he said, his voice giving nothing away, positive or negative. "Doug is ecstatic. Over the moon."

Good boy, Maeve thought. Keep it up and then I won't have to hunt you down like a dog. "That's good to hear. Same with Jo." They made a little more chitchat about the holiday, her store, talking like old friends instead of what they really were: unlikely allies. "I'll make this rather long story as short as possible," she said, moving on to the things she really needed to know. She did her best to give him an abbreviated version of the story, leaving out the part where she visited Rhineview and the address that Margie provided. "Do you know her? Margie Haggerty?"

"I do," he said, his tone measured.

"And?"

"Not well," he said. "Let's just put it this way: Margie Haggerty got off easy for what she did. Losing the Job was the best-case scenario for her."

"And should that have any bearing on how much I can trust her or any additional information she gives me?" she asked.

"Yes, Maeve. I think it should."

"Why?"

"Let's just say that she tried to take a few people down with her. Lives were ruined. Not many of us appreciated that." He chuckled. "She has a law office now. Deals with workman's comp cases. How's that for irony?"

"What's it called? Do you know?"

"I don't," he said. "But it's on Two thirty-eighth and Broadway over a bodega. Under the El. Very swank."

She continued to flip the card over in her hands. "Well, thank you. I appreciate the information."

"What are you doing, Maeve?"

"What do you mean?"

"What are you doing with regard to finding your sister?"

"Everything I can."

"I'd expect nothing less from you, my warrior queen."

"I'm going to try to keep my darker thoughts and pursuits out of this one."

He knew what she meant. "Please do."

"But I can't promise anything."

"I wouldn't expect you to." He dropped his voice. "Sometimes you gotta do what you gotta do."

"I'm glad you understand."

"You need my help?"

She thought about that; she already had Doug on the line for that but he lacked such backbone. "I might. Again, I can't promise anything. But I need to find her. Make sure she's okay."

"Alive."

"Yes. Alive." She placed the card on her nightstand. "I'll let you go. Thank you."

"Be well, Maeve Conlon. Be careful," he said before hanging up.

"You, too," she said to the dead air.

CHAPTER 36

The girls were home by midnight and Maeve was out the door by three after making sure they were both in their beds, secure in the knowledge that they were going to sleep and not waiting for her to fall asleep so that they could go back out. That was one thing about her daughters and something that had been true since they were little: once they were asleep, they were out for the count. She had done something right in the sleep-training department. Cal was still regaling her with stories of walking the floor with Devon at all hours, and if she didn't admit to a small measure of satisfaction in hearing that—her rules about bedtime and behavior having met with his ridicule more than once during their marriage—she would be lying.

She knew the way to Rhineview by heart now and even in the inky darkness, found a space to stick the car that was closer to the house but hidden by a copse of dense evergreens. Her headlamp in place, she trudged under the stars to the barn, the place she was convinced held some kind of clue to her sister's whereabouts.

Siblings know. That's what Heather had said. Maeve hoped that even siblings who had never met—or who had never remembered meeting—had the same telepathic bond.

In one pocket, she had her gun. In her opposite hand, she held the shovel that Jo had given her for Christmas, marveling at her friend's foresight. She had been right: Maeve needed a shovel. She just hadn't known it at the time.

The barn door was still ajar, just wide enough for Maeve to wriggle through. This time, the smell hit her head on, becoming more pungent as Maeve made her way farther into the space. Maeve gave thanks for what had been the warm start to winter, using all of her strength to break up the dirt. A quick sweep of the headlamp revealed that the tractor had been moved and was now at the other side of the barn; Maeve wondered why it had been moved, the plow on the front of it not needed.

She went back to the spot that she had been in the day before, where fresh dirt had been mounded in a pile. Today, it was packed down more, the outline of fresh dirt suggesting that the grave, if that's what it was, was really only the size of a small box. She continued to plunge the sharp end of the surprisingly sturdy tool into the ground, using her foot to push it farther beneath the ground. She was perspiring with the effort by the time she hit the box that was buried under a shallow layer of dirt, a plain brown box that you could buy anywhere, store anything in, looking not unlike the boxes in her living room that held the rest of Jack's belongings. The stench grew stronger.

Maeve dug a trench around the box and knelt beside it. Although her goal all along had been to unearth the box and find out what was inside, now that she was close to achieving that, she was hesitating. She had just spent the better part of fifteen minutes digging up a box that held something dead, clearly not a person, probably the grave of an animal who had once lived in the falling-down house beside the barn and had expired recently. Why not bury it in the woods where it would decompose naturally and not leave a scent?

She lifted the lid. The smell was overpowering and her clothes would need to be washed again, if not disposed of completely. She shone the headlamp into the box and found a full-grown cat, hardly decomposed, so fairly freshly dead, and a kitten beside it. Their necks were broken.

Maeve gagged at both the smell and the sight of the dead animals, but her headlamp caught on something tucked under the head of the larger cat. She was thankful she was wearing gloves but even so, the courage it took to move the cat's head and extract the item beneath it was almost more than she could handle.

You're losing your cool, Maeve, she thought, gingerly lifting the animal's head and pulling out a laminated card. It was a holy card, the Blessed Mother surrounded by illuminated stars, her outstretched hands protecting and blessing all who believed in her goodness and love.

It was the same rendering, the same sort of card, that Maeve had found among her father's things.

A dime a dozen, she told herself. Every vestibule of every Catholic church she had ever been in had a stack, along with daily devotions, the way to say the Rosary, the church's bulletin of news and events. It looked just like the one she had brought home all those years ago for Jack, the one that she wanted him to carry so that he would be safe at work, believing when she was a child that that was the talisman, the lucky charm that had kept him from getting shot or worse.

He used to tell her that he wore his bulletproof vest every day but she knew that he was lying most of the time. They were bulky and restricted movement, but at the time, she tried to believe him because it made her feel better to think that he was protected.

One of them needed to be.

She walked back to the car in the dark and when she was buckled in, silently drove away.

I think I might be crazy, she thought, and not for the first time.

Maybe I should stop right now.

But she knew she wouldn't.

CHAPTER 37

Maeve was home before daybreak, well before the girls decided to arise. They had no idea that she hadn't been home, had been driving around an area miles upstate from where they lived, and touching dead cats. The holy card was tucked into the pocket of her jeans and when she got home, she extracted it from her pants and laid it carefully on her nightstand, right next to Rodney Poole's card.

After she slept a bit, she would spend time with the girls, take them to the mall, the equivalent of a consumer cathedral for them, holy and special and the only place in which they didn't fight with each other for extended periods of time. Maeve hated the mall but she wouldn't complain. Her quality time with her father had been going to shooting ranges and then to the local Knights of Columbus for a beer with his cop friends before returning home. She wanted to make sure her girls had a more "normal" upbringing, whatever that was. She was sure it didn't include shooting ranges; that much was clear.

In her bed, the down comforter wrapped around her body, she drifted off to sleep thinking about her father and his religious devotions that didn't extend to him actually going to church. Prayerful and often espousing the teachings, he didn't have much use for organized religion but a lot for the rituals that he had learned as a child himself. As she settled into a deep sleep, Jack returning to her at the gazebo with the day-old loaf of challah bread in his hands once again, she wondered if he was at peace.

"It's rye," he said again, admonishing her for her mistake.

It was after one when she woke up, feeling more refreshed than she would have thought, given her schedule. She realized, with a start, that she hadn't thought of the store once in the past few days, and to not think of it was refreshing. Only passing thoughts of her land-lord and Billy Brantley. Not a care about Tommy, playing lacrosse somewhere like his life depended on it. It meant, despite driving up north and finding dead things, that she was relaxing, if in her own demented way. She got up and got dressed, once again taking extra time to wash the stench of Rhineview out of her skin and hair.

The significance of the card, whether there was any or not, stayed with her as she towel-dried her hair. Downstairs, she could hear voices and a little commotion that could only mean one thing: Jo had arrived.

She was in the kitchen with the girls, where some kind of extrava-gant meal preparation was in the works. Maeve held her breath. These undertakings usually involved something burned and a pot that had seen its last use. They always required Maeve having to clean up a spilled marinara or exploding pea soup. She tried to keep her cool as she saw Jo open a package containing large salmon, raw, and instruct the girls how to bake it.

"Hey," Maeve said, entering the kitchen. "I'm the only profes-sional cook around. Want me to do it?"

"Had a hankering for the saltiest fish I could find," Jo said, turn-ing to face Maeve. "So Doug picked one up at the fish store that won 'Best of Westchester' for their salmon." Behind her, the girls looked relieved that their mother was up and in their presence finally; they weren't used to her not being awake in the afternoon. If she was still in bed, something was terribly wrong. "How complicated is it to cook salmon?" Jo threw herself into a chair, grasping at her belly. "Doug said I couldn't cook it in the cottage because we would never get rid of the smell."

Was it worse than the smell that two dead cats produced? Maeve wondered. If so, Doug had a point. Maeve was thankful to have the fish to prepare, if only to get her nose accustomed to something that would inevitably taste and smell delicious once she was finished with it. "And how is Doug?" she asked, her voice pleasant, not giving away the murderous rage she felt every time she thought of him sitting with Tamara from Dunkin' Donuts.

"Great!" Jo said. "Loving birth class. He's promised that no matter where he is or what he's doing, he'll make sure to get home for the birth."

"First births usually don't go that quickly, Jo." Maeve pulled some greens out of the refrigerator and started to assemble a salad. "I'm sure he'll make it to you if he's not home already."

"That's what the birth class lady said," Jo said, reaching over and plucking a cherry tomato from the container on the counter. "It's weird. It's like he woke up and decided that he really wanted to be a part of this."

Like he woke up. That was one way to put it.

The girls poured drinks for everyone and gathered around the kitchen table, waiting for their mother's attention to be moved from the food preparation to them. When Maeve was finished with her ministrations to the large salmon, she slid it into the oven and took her place at the table where she noticed a slim box, wrapped in brown paper, sitting in the middle of the table.

"What's that?"

Jo shrugged. "Found it on the porch when I came up." She pushed it toward Maeve. "How long for the salmon? And do you have any pumpernickel? Dill sauce?"

Maeve picked up the package. It had some heft. "Jo, as of fifteen minutes ago, I didn't even have a salmon. Why would I have the things that should accompany it?"

Jo was disappointed. "Because you're a cook and cooks have things like dill and pumpernickel around all the time?"

"Not this cook," Maeve said. "I can do fifty things with canned tuna that will make your head spin but salmon is a different story, especially if you want particular sides."

Jo took a napkin out of the ceramic holder on the kitchen table and pulled a pen from her messenger bag. "Heather, Rebecca. I'm giving you a list. A very specific list. And you must get these items and get them back here before this salmon is served." She looked at Maeve. "How do you make dill sauce?"

Maeve took the napkin and jotted down a few items, pulling ten dollars out of her purse. "This should cover it. Hit the gourmet market. There will be less of a line and you're more likely to find what you need quickly."

"Don't forget those pickles that I like!" Jo called after them.

"What kind?" Heather called back from her spot in the front hall.

"Cornichons," Maeve said. Once she heard the car pull out of the driveway, its wheels making a sound on the gravel, she looked more closely at the package. There was nothing to indicate where it had come from. All it said, in black marker across the front, was her name.

The handwriting didn't look familiar. She slid her finger under the tape holding the package closed, opening up the entire seal. "Did you see who left this, Jo?" Maeve asked.

Jo shook her head. "It was on the porch. No one around. Where do you think it came from?"

"Not a clue," Maeve said, pulling the large book out.

Jo traced a finger on the quilted cover, cracked a little from age. "It's a scrapbook," she said.

But it wasn't. It was a photo album. And in it were pictures that Maeve had never seen before, pictures of her mother when she was young, beautiful, and single, if the male suitors who surrounded her in the first few pages were any indication. Photos of Jack as a baby, his proud Irish-born parents holding their son up in front of other relatives for all to see. Photos of her parents when they were dating, darkly tinted lips on her mother, her ubiquitous red lipstick appearing almost black, Jack's hair swept back in a slick-looking pompadour, something that Maeve never would have touched for fear of getting her hands dirty; it looked crisp and sticky but in style for the times. Jo remarked on every photo, noting how beautiful Claire Conlon had been, how a young skinny Jack looked surprisingly the same as an old man.

Maeve touched each page with care. The photos were held in place by little black triangles whose stickiness had long since worn off; some photos listed to one side or threatened to fall from their individual pages. One page held a group of articles, all clipped together with a rusty paper clip, all about the Mansfield Missing, the dozen who were gone and never found.

Maeve hastily turned the page, not ready to go there in her mind, not ready to explain to Jo and the girls what she had been thinking all along. Her sister had been one of the dozen missing teens and young adults, and seeing the articles that Jack had kept all these years solidified in her mind something she had thought but which she couldn't give voice to.

Jo was oblivious to Maeve's quick turn of the page. "Your parents' wedding photo is gorgeous. They look like movie stars," Jo said, tracing the line of Claire's lace dress.

"I know," Maeve said. "I've seen this photo." She turned the page.

"And there's your sister," Jo whispered, the last words she said as she and her best friend flipped slowly through the first five or so years of a life neither knew had existed before a few weeks earlier. "She has your features."

She looks like me, Maeve thought. That's my sister.

CHAPTER 38

Jo and the girls went to worship at the altar of all things retail, leaving Maeve home alone. She pulled a photo from the album—the most recent one of Evelyn—and held it in her hands. She left another message for Doug. "Time to pay the piper," she said. "Call me when you get a chance."

She was restless, far more than she had been before, but the photo album had awakened her desire to get to the truth as quickly as possible. Looking through those pictures made her feel like time was running out, though she wasn't sure why. A sense of urgency replaced a feeling of exhaustion, and before she had time to think, she had unearthed an old coat of Heather's that no longer fit her and sat at the bottom of the closet—pink with a furry collar—donned it, and warmed up the car. Her own coat had lost far too many down feathers to be useful anymore.

Jo texted her and said that they were having such a good time that they were going to have dinner at the mall, a development that gave Maeve time to do what she had been mulling over since they left.

In Rhineview, she didn't hide today, pulling right into the parking space next to the old Rambler in front of the house. Before she got out of her car, she jotted down the license plate number. Might as well give Doug a full list of items to check out rather than just one thing at a time.

She hoped that whoever was inside didn't have easy access to the shotgun that she had heard let out a loud report two days earlier. In the pocket of Heather's childhood down coat was her own gun, locked and loaded. With the photo of Evelyn in her pocket, she mounted the front steps of the house and rapped on the front door with one gloved hand, her other hand in her pocket and fondling the cold steel of her gun.

"Mrs. Hartwell?" she called, peering in the windows that lined the porch. Inside, the house was as unkempt as the outside, piles of newspapers and magazines strewn about what would have been called a "parlor room" when the house was built but which was now where a giant television sat atop a cheap entertainment cabinet. Maeve brushed some frost off the window to get a better look when she caught movement from inside the house. She stepped back and waited in front of the door.

An old lady, her face looking much like those of the women Maeve had grown up around, weathered and Irish, looked back at her from inside the house, her shaking hand parting the curtain that gave a small measure of privacy to the inside of the house.

"Mrs. Hartwell?" Maeve asked.

The hand holding the curtain, shaking wildly now, disappeared and Maeve heard the bolt on the door turning. The woman opened the door a crack.

"My name is Maeve Conlon and someone named Margie Haggerty gave me your name. I'm looking for my sister." Maeve stepped closer to the door but not close enough to be threatening to the old woman, who obviously didn't welcome Maeve's arrival on her front porch. "Please. Her name is Evelyn Conlon. She lived at Mansfield in the 1970s."

The woman stared back at Maeve, her blue, rheumy eyes giving nothing away but stoic, silent determination.

"Please. You're the only link I have," Maeve said.

"I don't know anything," the woman finally said, and Maeve recognized her voice as the woman she had spoken to a few days before when she had called the number Margie had given her.

"Margie Haggerty. I don't know how you know her, but she said you worked at Mansfield. I think," she said aloud for the first time, "that my sister might be one of the Mansfield Missing."

The woman let out a lengthy cough, one that rattled from deep within her, sounding like something was terribly wrong inside her large, soft body. The resolve that Maeve had when she had driven up here—to get into this house and get answers—slowly drifted away as the woman's face hardened with her own steely determination. "I know nothing. Go away."

But that wasn't the truth and Maeve knew it. She tried once more. "Evelyn Conlon. She would be in her fifties now. Probably blond, maybe gray." Maeve didn't know, so she had to guess. "Blue eyes? I don't know for sure." Maeve pleaded with the woman. "That's what she would look like, I think."

The print on the woman's blue housecoat was a cheery pattern with cherries on the collar, belying the hostility of the wearer. "Get off my property."

Maeve stood firm.

"I'll call the cops."

"And tell them what?" Maeve asked.

"That you're trespassing. That you've been harassing me." She let out another cough. "That you've been here before." She pointed out toward the road. "Out there. In my barn?" she said as if to remind Maeve.

One last try. "My father is dead. My mother died a long time ago. My sister is the only living person from my immediate family,"

Maeve lied. No reason for this woman to know about her girls. "Please."

"I know nothing," the woman said, slamming the door in Maeve's face.

"You're lying," Maeve said to the closed door. "You're a liar." But there was nothing else to do but leave.

The woman's face stayed with her all the way home, the hardness and the meanness around her eyes—blue like her own—reminding her of someone she had chosen to forget.

She wondered why she couldn't stop thinking about Dolores Donovan.

CHAPTER 39

Maeve had no interest in Sebastian DuClos dropping by the store, and with the first of the year approaching, she drove over to Wendell Lane, dropped her rent check off at his house, and beat a hasty getaway. He wasn't home, thank God, so she stuffed the check into his mailbox, which was overrun with catalogs, bills, and other things that had been delivered.

Looked like Sebastian hadn't been home in a few days. No sign of Bruno either, or the people who had been driving in and out of the street, hastily getting what they needed and taking off for parts unknown.

Later that evening, she met Doug at Mickey's, after he got off work but before he went home.

"How are you feeling about things?" she asked, truly interested. "Better, I hope?"

He pushed a black-and-white photo toward her. "This helped."

She had already seen it. It was a photo from Jo's latest sonogram, their baby boy front and center, his thumb in his mouth. "What? The other ones weren't good enough?" Maeve asked, knowing that Jo had had several sonograms prior to this one; this latest one was just to gauge how her amniotic fluid, which had decreased a bit over the last few weeks, was holding up. Maeve was preparing herself for the inevitable "bed rest" edict that was sure to come from Jo's doctor and which would leave Maeve shorthanded at the bakery.

"He has her profile," Doug said. "Jo's."

He did. The donor egg was from Jo's cousin and showed that the boy was going to favor his mother's side of the family, at least in the short term and before he truly grew into his features. "Well, look at that," Maeve said. "I hadn't noticed before."

"Maeve, you're not going to tell, right?" he asked.

"No," she said. "Even though I'm not entirely sure what there is to tell." She spotted a customer from the store at the front door and gave her a wave. "What did you do, Doug?"

"Nothing happened," he said, but she wasn't sure she believed him. "It was just . . ."

"A distraction?" she asked.

He nodded, glum. "Yes. A distraction. From all of this."

"Here's the thing, Doug: most people would find the prospect of a beautiful wife and a healthy baby on the way something of a . . ." She searched for the word that Jo often used to describe her good fortune. "Is it *mitzvah*?" She didn't think that was right.

"Don't look at me," he said. "I was a Hebrew school dropout."

She decided that, Yiddish words aside, she needed to be clear with him. "I'm not sure how I'll do it, or what I'll do, but I will hurt you if you do anything to upset this new life that Jo has created. She loves you. She has always wanted a child. She has always wanted a devoted husband." She waved to another customer from the store, keeping a smile on her face as she threatened her best friend's wayward husband. "Got it?"

He knew he was caught but he tried to hang tough in the conversation. "You're threatening an officer of the law," he said, his inner Barney Fife making an appearance.

"You bet I am," she said. She wondered why he didn't tell her to take a hike in more pointed terms, to mind her own business, but something in her tone and on her face told him that she wasn't really prone to hyperbole. She would hurt him if this didn't work out, if he didn't work out. He nodded, if only to get her to stop talking.

He tried to throw her off, not really knowing who he was dealing with. "Anything about the finger?"

"Not one more word," Maeve said as she eyed the bartender drifting toward them. "That's between me, God, and the Farringville police department." When he looked suitably chagrined, she slid the photo she had brought along toward him. "So, here's the story," she said, even though she knew Jo had shared most of it with him. He knew about the finger; why not give him all of the details on her sister? "I have a sister. I don't know where she is. This is the last photo I have of her. She looks to be around six or seven. Is there someone at the precinct who could do some kind of drawing of her, letting us know what she looks like now?"

Finally, Maeve saw a scintilla of excitement pass across his face, something she hadn't seen when he and Jo had gotten engaged, when they had announced to Maeve that they were having a baby. Deep in his heart, Maeve thought, he's a detective; he likes to figure things out. She was expecting to have to cajole him, or worse, remind him of their deal, not taking into account that he was nosy, a byproduct of the Job.

He studied the photo. "I can do that." He finished off his beer and ordered another round for both of them even though Maeve had barely touched her wine. "Tell me more." He already had the basics from Jo and needed her to fill in any missing details, anything she had discovered in her own search and investigation.

"There's nothing to tell, really. I don't know why she was sent away and I don't know where she is."

"Is she alive?" he asked.

"Don't know that either."

He shook his head sadly. "Went through this with my partner a few years back." He threw a couple of twenties on the bar and asked the bartender for change. Maeve was surprised. In their relationship, Jo was the spender and Doug was the saver, something that annoyed his wife. "Poole?" he asked. "You remember him, I guess."

Maeve nodded. "I do."

"Lost a brother in the foster system," he said. "The kids were split up after the mother went to rehab in the sixties."

Maeve waited for the happy ending but there was none.

"Found him in Sing Sing. He's still there." He took in her crushed expression. "Sorry," he said. "I shouldn't have told you that. But your sister isn't in Sing Sing. It's an all-male prison," he said, as if that would take away the sting of what he had said.

God, you are a complete dope, she thought, and in that moment wondered if he was a little challenged himself.

"It's fine," Maeve said, starting on her first glass of wine. The kitchen door swung open behind her and loud salsa music burst forth, breaking the pall that had settled in between them. She pulled a piece of paper out of her purse. "And here's a license plate number. I'm pretty sure I know who it belongs to, but just want to make sure I know the name exactly."

Doug smiled. "That's an easy one."

She almost apologized for blackmailing him into service but then didn't; the thought of him happily seated on a bar stool not two miles from his home with a blonde with a home dye job still made her boil, if only a little bit now that some time had passed. She wasn't going to be able to do this without somebody's help; might as well be his. Cal had proven to be incapable of any critical thinking on his own in terms of finding a missing person, so she might as well use Doug.

"Don't tell Jo," Maeve said.

"I won't," he promised. He stood, smoothing down the front of his pants.

"New Dockers?" Maeve asked. The shade of his pants was a little less khaki and a little more stone-colored. They looked familiar.

"Yeah," he said, a smile breaking out on his face. "Got them at Goodwill. Two bucks. I bought a whole bunch. Must have been seventeen of the same kind."

CHAPTER 40

"Happy new year!"

Maeve was surprised that Jo seemed the least tired of all of them that night and had made it to midnight full of energy. She went into the kitchen and got some champagne glasses down from the cabinet, pulling out some sparkling cider for the girls and her pregnant friend, and a split of champagne for her and Doug, who was sound asleep in a chair by the fireplace.

Rebecca looked disappointed with her sparkling cider.

Chris Larsson showed up a minute after midnight, work having called him in at the last minute. He gave her a chaste kiss on her cheek, her daughters watching his every move toward their mother with an intensity that was making him nervous, if his stiff posture and demeanor were any indication.

"Happy new year," he whispered in her ear, his lips brushing her hair.

"Happy new year to you," she said, grasping his fingers lightly. "Dinner? The girls cooked."

He put his hand on his stomach. "Went to the diner on my dinner break." He followed her into the kitchen. "Thanks, though."

In the kitchen, away from the prying eyes of the girls, Maeve allowed him to kiss her, the two of them pressed up against the back door. She kept one eye on the opening to the kitchen, not really prepared to tell her daughters about Chris or why she might be in a clench with the town's lead detective. She pulled away, smoothing down her hair. "I'm glad you came," she said. "I wasn't sure . . ."

"If I would?" he said, finishing her sentence. He pulled out a chair and sat at the kitchen table, watching her open champagne and pour it into glasses, not a drop spilling over the tops. "I thought about it, Maeve: with the investigation going on, I thought it might not be a good idea to continue with this."

She turned her back on him, concentrating on the champagne. She didn't like where this was going.

"But I decided that it's okay to be happy. It's okay to have fun." He stood and wrapped his arms around her waist. "It's okay to do what we're doing."

"Are you sure?" she asked, leaning back into his broad chest.

"Hold up your hands," he said, and when she did, examined them closely. "You have ten fingers. Five on each hand. That rules you out." He nuzzled her neck. "And I just don't see you as the kind of person who would exact that kind of revenge on someone, no matter what they did to you."

She stayed silent. He was wrong about that.

"You're a baker. You're soft. You're gentle," he said, his whispers sending a tingle up her spine. "You'd never hurt anyone."

He didn't know. And he never would.

After one last kiss, Maeve put the filled glasses on a tray and entered the living room, passing out cider and champagne. Jo nudged Doug awake and gave him a long, passionate kiss to ring in the new year. Maeve introduced him to Chris. After everyone clinked glasses and took a sip, Jo held her glass up. "I hope this year brings you everything you ever wanted, Maeve Conlon," she said.

"Thanks, Jo," Maeve said, clinking her friend's glass again. "You, too."

Jo rubbed her belly. "It's going to be exciting."

It was. For Jo and Doug. For Maeve, it was still an open question.

The girls and Jo were singing along to some boy band on the television, causing Doug, Maeve, and Chris to vacate the room, going back into the kitchen. Doug pulled a folded-up piece of paper from the back of his Dockers. *Jack's* Dockers. She still didn't have the heart to tell him that he was wearing her dead father's khakis, opting instead to compliment him on their fit every chance she got. He smoothed the piece of paper out on the table, Evelyn Conlon's adult image floating into place in spite of Maeve's tears.

"That's her," he said. "To the best of the artist's ability to go so many years into the future like this." He handed Maeve an envelope with the original photo in it. He didn't look at her when he said, "She looks like you."

Maeve nodded, wiping a tear away before it dripped onto the paper, marring the perfect image. She looked at Chris, who was staring at the drawing, and then back at her sister's face, noticing the resemblance. In it, her sister's hair was short, as it had been in the original photo, and her mouth was set in a grim line. But her eyes were lively, happy.

"I'll make her smile," Maeve whispered.

"Sorry?" Doug asked.

"Nothing. Thank you, Doug." Maeve turned and started to put some washed silverware away. She bagged up the garbage, asking Chris if he would bring it out back to the cans behind the house. When he was gone, she asked, "And the license plate, Doug?"

"Regina H. Hartwell."

"Anything on her?"

"Like what?" he asked.

"Any moving violations? Arrests? Outstanding parking tickets?"

It was clear from the chagrined look on his face that he hadn't gone much further with his investigating.

"Can you check?" she asked. She looked at him pointedly, reminding him with her eyes that they had a deal.

"Okay," he said.

"Anything. I want to know anything you can find out about this woman," she said. "Or, I start making trips to Dunkin' Donuts to make sure you're not there."

"I don't go to Dunkin' Donuts anymore," he hissed back at her. "I get my coffee from you even though you keep fingers in your refrigerator."

He left the kitchen in a huff in his dead man's Dockers. She wasn't sure why he didn't understand the terms of their deal; she hadn't set any parameters and he hadn't agreed to any. It was open-ended and that's the way it would stay.

In the living room, the girls continued to carry on, screaming the lyrics of some song that Maeve was sure she wouldn't be able to get out of her head for a long time, the chorus being that combination of catchy and annoying that was the hallmark of all the latest pop hits. She sat at the counter and stared at the picture for a long time, noticing that Evelyn's nose had to belong to some distant relative and the shape of her eyes probably resembled Claire's more than her father's. There were certain things that made them look like sisters and others that suggested some recessive genes at work.

"Happy new year, wherever you are," Maeve said quietly before folding the picture up again and tucking it between two of her favorite cookbooks on the shelf above the kitchen table.

CHAPTER 41

Regina H. Hartwell.

Maeve lay in bed the next morning and typed the name into her computer, after looking at old, grainy footage of the day that Mansfield officially closed. She hadn't been able to do it until now, the thought of the remembered images from that time in her head and not pleasant to think about. The grounds were flooded with people, and school buses and cars could be seen in the background, some idling, most with passengers, their faces looking out at the cameras detailing their exit. Where were they going? It seemed disorganized, a hasty departure. No wonder some people had gone missing. It was also a wonder how something that happened in her lifetime could look so outdated, so ancient. Digital photography and film had really changed the landscape of documenting life's important—and infamous—moments.

There was nothing to suggest that Regina Hartwell had worked at Mansfield, nothing to give Maeve any indication that the woman even existed. The endless possibilities of the Internet suggested that one could find out anything, but most of the time, the reverse was true; what you were really looking for wasn't available online. Maeve had gone through several links but they all led to a dead end; it was like the woman didn't exist. She closed her computer and stared into space, the images of people leaving the institution on the buses seared in her mind. Many very young, most barely adults. She said a silent prayer that something had happened that had made it so her sister was somewhere else, somewhere safe.

Downstairs, there was a knock at the door, and knowing that nothing short of a nuclear blast would get the girls out of their beds, Maeve struggled into a pair of jeans and pulled a Vassar sweatshirt over her head—sixty grand a year and all I got was this lousy sweatshirt, she always thought—padding down the stairs barefoot as she pulled her hair into a loose ponytail. Getting a haircut had been on her list of things to do over the holiday break, along with getting a facial, a pedicure, and a host of other grooming-related services that it seemed wouldn't get done. Rhineview and Evelyn Conlon were starting to inhabit her every thought, her every action. The haircut would have to wait.

Cal was peering in the front window, having made his way along the porch to investigate if they were all awake inside the house. He should have known better; the girls didn't appear until after the clock struck noon or in the event of impending starvation. She opened the front door, allowing him and a blast of cold air into the front hallway.

"Morning," she said. In his hands were two cups of coffee from Dunkin' Donuts.

"Did I wake you?" Cal asked, mistaking Maeve's flight of homicidal fancy for a lack of consciousness.

"No," she said. "I was in bed. Reading."

"I'm so glad you take these two weeks off," he said, stripping off his down coat and hanging it on the banister, something he had done years ago when he had lived here, despite the fact that there was a closet just steps from the stairs. He walked into the kitchen, Maeve trailing behind him. "Otherwise, you'd probably collapse from exhaustion."

She leaned against the counter, peeled the lid off her coffee, and took a tentative sip. Lukewarm. Just what had brought Doug to the lesser Dunkin' Donuts in the first place? Tamara's wily charms? Surely it wasn't the coffee. Now that he knew about the finger, he'd never come back to The Comfort Zone, destined for a life of crappy coffee and mediocre donuts. "What brings you here on this lovely day?" she asked, attempting a smile.

He reached into his pocket before sitting down at the kitchen table. "Here." He handed her a folded-up piece of paper. "It's a list of group homes in the tri-state area, but goes up as far as Ulster County."

She took it and stared at, incredulous. The names and addresses of each home, along with the organization that ran it, were listed in neat type on the unlined piece of paper. "Who did this?"

He smiled. "Well, you might find this hard to believe, but Gabriela had her assistant do it. As a freelance project. She paid her to stay late and put the list together after work."

Maeve chewed on her thumbnail while looking at the list. "She did?"

"Yes," Cal said, jiggling the handle on the powder room door, just inches from where he sat at the kitchen table. "This still broken?"

"Yes," Maeve said distractedly, scanning the list. It represented a lot of legwork. Time. She couldn't do this by herself.

It was like he read her mind. "We can help you."

"How?" she said, seeing several places in Westchester that she didn't know existed.

"We can call them." He jiggled the handle. "This has been broken since I left," he said, the blame in his voice directed at her, not at the fact that he left before fixing it and a host of other items in the old Colonial. "I don't think they'll tell us anything so we have to figure out how to do this. How to cut through the red tape." The handle fell off in his hand. "That wasn't what I wanted to happen."

What he wanted to happen and what actually happened rarely

aligned. She scanned the list and felt overwhelmed by both Gabriela's gesture and the enormity of the task of calling every place, inquiring after Evelyn, if they could even do that. He was right: there were likely laws in place to protect people like her sister.

If she was still alive.

That question entered her thoughts more and more and she didn't like it. But visiting that barn and seeing Regina Hartwell had taken the wind out of her emotional sails a bit. She had to admit to the fact that she felt a little discouraged, "weirded out," as the girls would say. She couldn't shake the feeling that something sinister happened in Rhineview, in that house, and that her sister was a part of it.

"What do you think?" Cal asked.

"About what?" she said, looking at him, forgetting that he was even there. She could feel the cold counter pressing into her sore back and she stood up straighter, putting a hand to her spine where a depression had formed from the hard countertop.

"The same knob or something more antique-looking?" He shook the doorknob in front of her. "I think we should go with something more of a crystal cut. Let me know and I'll go to Home Depot."

"Whatever you think," she said, taking another sip of coffee. "Lots of places on this list." She looked at him, seeing him. "Gabriela, huh?"

"Yep." He wanted to say something else, probably something like "See? She's not all bad" or something like that, but he held back. "All her. Her idea."

"I'll call her. I'll thank her."

"Like I said, I don't know what we need to do to find out if your sister is there, or even if there is anything we can do, but I'm working on it." He juggled the doorknob parts, one hand catching the knob, the other catching the guts of the lockset.

She rubbed the spot on her back, exhaustion pressing down on her. "Thank you."

The moment was strange between them. She wasn't used to be

him being selfless, and he wasn't used to her accepting his help. He stopped juggling. "So, crystal cut?"

"Sure, Cal," she said. "Anything so long as Heather doesn't get stuck in there again. The last time, she had to climb out the window over the toilet and into the backyard. Scarred her for life, she said."

"Yeah, I could see how that could scar you," he said, their easy banter returning. "I've kept a copy of the list, so as soon as I figure out some of the finer points of looking for someone in a group home and you have some time to spend on this, we'll get to work."

She walked him to the front door and he slipped on his coat. "I have to say, Maeve, that I'll never know why Jack didn't tell you about her. About Evelyn," he added, as if there were any doubt as to who he meant.

"I don't know, Cal," she said.

"He wore everything on his sleeve." He shrugged. "Never took him for a secret-keeper."

She didn't want him to know that she was the biggest secret-keeper of all.

And apparently, she had learned from the best.

CHAPTER 42

Maeve napped before heading out to the support group the next night, the first meeting of the new year, and felt rested and calm when she got there. The list that Cal had given her sat on her nightstand with the growing stack of items related to her investigations: the piece of paper that Margie had given her, Rodney Poole's card, a couple of notes she had jotted to herself. Directly below her, in the kitchen, it was Rebecca who was now stuck in the bathroom, calling for her sister to rescue her, a plea that went unanswered. But Maeve was too tired to get out of bed, too spent to unwrap herself from the down comforter that she had bought at that Pottery Barn sale all those years ago. Rebecca went to a good college and had gotten almost a perfect score on her SAT exam; surely she could figure out a way to get out of a small powder room without needing her mother's assistance?

She listened to the conflict brewing in the kitchen while in that in-between state of sleep and wakefulness. Heather arrived on the scene and, noticing that part of the doorknob was gone, something her sister hadn't noticed, tortured her sister for a few minutes, saying that the fire department would need to be called and hadn't Rebecca dated one of the volunteers in high school? Didn't the breakup go badly? Would he really be willing to save the imperiled Rebecca from the confines of the powder room? Maeve smiled as she listened to the drama play out below her, wondering if she and her sister would have had a similar relationship had they grown up together. Would they have joked and played pranks on each other? Would Jack have had to break them up from arguing, or joined in with them when they laughed hysterically at the other's puns? She was starting to feel like she would never know, and that took the smile off her face.

The sounds of roughhousing emanated from the kitchen and shouts of "Mom!" rang out. She pulled the comforter over her head and tried to go back to sleep. The best thing she could do in situations like this was to let them work things out on their own.

She didn't want them solving problems in the ways that she once had, but the shouting and screaming got to be too much for her to ignore. She got out of bed and went downstairs in bare feet, standing in the doorway to the kitchen, her arms folded. They were on the floor, the taller Rebecca on top of Heather, who had a few pounds on her sister but seemed to be incapable of fighting back. Maybe that was because Rebecca had her sister's arms pinned above her head. Maeve walked over and pulled Rebecca up by the belt in her jeans.

"Stop it. Now," she said, taking a small measure of satisfaction when she saw that both girls now looked scared instead of angry. Waking their mother, they knew, was like waking a sleeping ogre, and the fear in their eyes was a testament to what had happened when they had tested her limits. Her own strength surprised her. Was there some kind of law of nature that supported the fact that no matter how old your children got, you could still toss them around like you could when they were toddlers, picking them up and removing them from dangerous—and annoying—situations? She pushed Rebecca back toward the stove and hoisted Heather from the ground. "I expect more from you," she said, handing Heather a napkin to wipe her running nose. "You are sisters. And while you don't have to like each other, you have to love each other."

Protests and angry accusations began but Maeve shut them both down. She sat at the table. "You disappoint me," she said, bringing out the big guilt guns.

Nothing like an irate mother to bring two siblings closer together. Heather joined Rebecca by the stove.

"Do you know how lucky you both are?" Maeve asked. "To have each other?" Suddenly, it wasn't about them but about her, her only-child status, her lack of an extended family. "You need to be kind to each other and take care of each other."

Heather began to cry in earnest. "You'll find her, Mom," she said, blowing her nose.

"It's not about that," Maeve said, although she knew it was. "Be nice to each other. That's all I ask."

The girls skulked off, leaving her to stew about other things, other mysteries besides why two seemingly incompatible human beings had become sisters. Why they couldn't get along. She had to recharge her batteries, find the energy necessary to start this search again. She called Cal before leaving for the support group.

"Cal, one more thing," she said.

He knew what it was about and didn't sound all that enthusiastic.

"Can you do a search of the name 'Winston Alderson' and see if a death certificate comes up?" She figured he knew his way around some of the more legal documents and sites that might be on the Internet and that he could do this while she was attending the support group, which she filled him in on. "There are a lot of people looking for their relatives. This one woman, Winston's mother, has really stayed with me," she said. "She's very sweet."

"Okay," he said. "Devon! Be careful!" he called to the baby inevitably toddling to his death. "I've got to go," he said.

At the support group, all of her friends were in attendance; she took a seat next to Francine Alderson, who was her usual cheerful self, full of life and good will despite the fact that her closest and only living relative had disappeared and never been found.

The meeting started with a short talk by a man named Michael Donner, someone who worked in the county's social services department and who came every year, apparently, to review any findings on missing adults and what steps a family member could take to find a loved one who had gone missing. Frankly, he didn't have a lot to say. There were so many laws in place to protect the privacy of those who had lived at Mansfield and who were now in group homes that legally, the process was long and protracted. Maeve noticed the faces of those around her fall a little bit, as they probably did every year when he came and gave his same talk.

After he sat down and everyone started to share again, like they did every week, one woman, Jessica, reported good news: her cousin, Emily, had been found living in a group home in Buffalo. Maeve sat up a little straighter in her chair.

Jessica was about Maeve's age but weathered in a way that Maeve hoped she could stave off for at least a few more years. "She's a ward of the state. I have to get an informational subpoena and ask the state for information."

Maeve raised her hand tentatively. "How did you find her?"

Jessica looked at her, her eyes red. "I hired a private investigator." She laughed, a little strangled chuckle emitting from her throat. "I don't know how she did it or who she had to pay off, but we found her. I'm completely out of money now, but it was worth it." She looked around the room. Her voice dropped to a whisper. "We found her."

When it was Maeve's turn to talk, she didn't really have a lot to say. "Hello. I'm Maeve Conlon, as you know. I'm looking for my sister, Evelyn Conlon. I don't have anything to report further on my search for her."

The people in the group knew how to react to that news without tipping the emotional apple cart in one direction or another. Most smiled sadly at Maeve while others murmured encouragement, telling her to keep looking.

She looked back at the group and mustered up some inner strength. "I'm going to keep going. I'm going to find her," she said, looking at Michael Donner, who nodded enthusiastically. Maeve wasn't sure if he was behind her in the search or thought she was completely insane, but she didn't care.

After the group disbanded, Maeve tried to find Jessica but she had left. She wandered the halls of the Y looking for a restroom—the one closest to the community room had been locked when she tried to enter—and found one at the opposite end of the pool, which was uncharacteristically quiet that night. School had started and this was a school night; swimming after dinner was a thing of the past, relegated to the next break in the academic year.

Outside, it seemed darker than usual for the hour, but maybe it was just her mood; she noticed that one of the streetlights in the parking lot, the one she had parked under when she had come to her first meeting here, was out. Across the empty parking lot, Francine Alderson was struggling with her walker, attempting to lift it into the old beater that she drove, a Dodge Dart from the 1970s, from the looks of it. Maeve rushed over, careful to avoid the potholes that dotted the surface of the macadam. The parking lot was empty. It was as if Jessica's news had created a mass exodus of the people at the Y; either they were excited and wanted to get home and share the news or newly depressed. It was hard to tell for sure.

"Francine. Wait," she said, putting her purse on the ground and peering into the trunk of the old car. The interior was spotless and held only one tennis ball, an item that probably had fallen off the walker some time earlier.

"You're a dear, Maeve," Francine said, leaning against the passenger side of the car.

Maeve struggled with the walker but finally wrestled it into the trunk. "That was some story tonight, huh?" she said. "Jessica's cousin?"

A look crossed the old woman's face and Maeve could tell that behind her sunny exterior lay the sadness that she, too, felt. "It was wonderful," she said.

Maeve pulled the list from her pocket. "I have a list of all of the residential facilities in the tri-state area and some of the upstate counties as well," she said, wanting to do anything—say anything—to restore Francine's sunny disposition. "I'm going to start calling and find out if my sister lives in any of these. I'll ask about Winston, too."

"If they are still alive, dear," Francine said. Taking in Maeve's crushed face, her smile gone, the older woman recanted. "I mean, that's wonderful." She looked off into the distance. "It will be hard, though. If your sister has a guardian, you'd have to get permission from that person to get information. To renew contact."

She hadn't said much, but implicit in that statement was the truth: if Evelyn had a guardian, that person would have already let Maeve know about her sister because surely it was someone Maeve knew. Who Jack trusted. Who they had known all of their lives. What kind of cruel person would let her continue the search, knowing that her sister was dead? The weight of that realization left Maeve a little breathless. She swallowed hard. "You're right. There are laws," she said simply. "To protect them."

Francine turned to Maeve. "I'm sorry," she said. Her mouth contorted just a little bit. "He's dead, Maeve. I know that. Or I hope so. The thought that he had lived without me for all these years . . ." She stood a little straighter, composed herself, the emotional moment having passed as quickly as it had begun. "Now. Help me get into my car, please?"

"How do you get out when you get home?" Maeve asked.

She snapped her fingers. "I've got this down to a science. Don't worry, dear."

Maeve took her arm and led her around the car.

"Don't forget your bag, Maeve," Francine said, and made her way around a patch of ice that had formed at the back of the car from on earlier shower. Maeve knelt to pick up her bag, which had fallen on its side, the usual personal detritus that resided in her purse—tissues, change, two single dollar bills, a few loose mints—threatening to blow away in the stiff breeze that had kicked up. As she leaned forward, she slipped on the ice, finding herself half under Francine's car, a nasty pain radiating up her leg that took up her complete attention and prevented her from hearing the sound of a car that appeared out of nowhere, at her back. It careered toward Mrs. Alderson, who was making her slow but steady way to the driver's side door.

Maeve stood, ignoring the searing heat in her hip, but was too late. She was knocked to the ground again, this time by the woman's body, hurtling high over her head and then coming to earth astride Maeve's bag, the contents that once seemed important enough to chase in the wind now seeming like what they were: pieces of trash that just got in the way.

Francine didn't make a sound as the life slipped from her body, her kindly eyes fading into some kind of opaque nothingness. Maeve knew better than to try to sit her up or rearrange her on the pavement, the blood leaking from her head letting Maeve know that this situation was hopeless. Instead, she took off her coat and placed it over the woman's body, pulling her purse from beneath her weight and finding her phone. Somewhere in the distance she heard a keening sound, sobs cutting the stillness of the night air. It was only after a few stunned minutes, the shock settling into her bones and making her incapable of thoughtful clarity, that she realized the sounds were coming from her.

She knew in her heart that Francine was dead but that didn't prevent her from sitting next to the old woman and begging her to open her eyes, get up from the pavement. It had only been a short time and they had only seen each other a total of a few hours but the loss of this gentle soul wounded her. She willed herself to get off the ground and ran to the door of the Y, banging so hard on the glass that her hands ached, hoping that there was a security guard or someone inside who could help her. She couldn't dial her phone; her hands were shaking too hard, her fingers uncooperative. In the distance, she heard the car turn a corner and race off.

She also heard someone screaming "Don't leave!" over and over and realized it was her. Her voice, her panic. Whether she was talking to the driver of the car or Mrs. Alderson, she wasn't sure and never would be, even when she thought of the moment days later, its details sneaking up on her like a naughty child who wants to frighten their mother, only to hear her scream in terror.

Finally, a man appeared in the lobby of the Y, taking in her tear-stained and frantic face and getting a look on his own face that let her know that he wasn't sure he wanted to open the door. She looked like a raving lunatic, she was sure of it. She pounded harder and screamed for his help.

He was Hispanic and didn't speak much English. Maeve did nothing more than point to the old woman lying on the pavement, a pool of blood around her, making a shape just like her body. An outline really. He used a key from the large cluster on his belt and opened the door. She asked him to call 911—screamed it over and over until he did what she wanted—and then went back to Mrs. Alderson's body to keep it company while she waited for help.

She held the old woman's hand. In her own warm hand, Francine's turned colder as more blood was lost, the longer she was dead. When the police finally arrived, it took one strong, kind officer to convince Maeve to let go.

CHAPTER 43

From her perch on the cold curb, Maeve noticed for the first time that the moon was full. Had it been any other night, watching lacy clouds float in front of the light that was cast from above would have fascinated her, but tonight, it only served to illuminate the scene unfolding in the parking lot.

The police had wrapped her in what looked to be a large piece of tin foil but which she knew was an insulated blanket designed to keep her warm and help her from going into shock. Marathon runners wore these after races, she knew. She wasn't going into shock; she was acutely aware of everything that was going on, what had happened to Francine Alderson. The shock had passed and in its place was a hollowed-out feeling, a place where only emptiness lived.

Maeve stared at the officers in the parking lot, the EMS workers taking care to load the body into the ambulance, tightening the straps around her slim and aged body before they slanted the gurney and slid it into place, the lights on top of their vehicles turning lazily.

She was the only witness, the janitor having been at the back of the Y building doing his nightly work and not having heard a thing. Although people had passed by on the road adjacent to where the support group met, no one had made a 911 call or had reported seeing an old woman thrown sky-high before landing hard on the pavement.

There was one massive police officer, a big country boy type, who spent some time with Maeve. She told him what she knew and remembered.

"It was a car."

"Color?"

"I didn't see," she said, putting a hand to her hip, which felt raw and bruised. "I didn't see the color or the make or model," she said, almost hearing Jack's admonishments from wherever he was now. "Notice your surroundings, Maeve! Pay attention!" he would have said. "It happened so fast," she said, to herself and to him, absolving herself from the guilt she would inevitably feel when she was less in shock and more cognizant of what happened. When it all became real. She wiped her nose on her sleeve. "I never used to cry."

The cop, a big guy with the look of someone who spent a great deal of time outdoors, snapped his notebook shut. "You have any travel plans, Miss Conlon?"

"No," she said. "I'm going back to Farringville and will be at the number I gave you." She zipped the top of her purse, holding in all of the garbage that had seemed so important less than an hour earlier. "I'm going back to Farringville," she said, more definitively this time. "I'm going home." She was going home, but she was also going back to Rhineview as soon as she woke up the next morning.

Before she went back to her car, she turned to the police officer. "There's a dog. Prince Phillip," she said. "He's in Mrs. Alderson's house. Could someone go get him?"

The cop looked confused. "There's a dog named Prince Phillip? Is this a joke?" he asked, eyeing her suspiciously. "You may be in shock, Miss Conlon."

"No," she said. "There is a dog. A Labrador. Mrs. Alderson called him Prince Phillip. That's his name." She stared the cop in the eye,

tried to make him understand. Was she making sense or like her father, addled and confused? She shook her head. "No. Yes. The dog.
Prince Phillip. Please get him and take care of him."

She waited while the officer called animal control. "He'll go to
a no-kill shelter here in town," the officer said, but implicit in his tone
was the idea that he still couldn't believe that someone had named
their dog after a British monarch. "Don't worry."

Maeve felt better about that, but shaken to the core over Francine's death. She sat in her car for a few minutes, staring out at the
diner across the parking lot until she heard a tap on her window. It
was Officer Beglin, his name tag now visible under the light over
her car.

"I just wanted to check on you. Are you sure you don't need to
be seen by the EMS crew?" he asked, his eyes kind. If she stared at
them any longer, she might start to cry and that wouldn't support
her contention that not only could she drive home, she wanted to
drive home, to do something normal and routine.

He finally let her go. As she drove away, she thought about what
the police had said to each other. It was a hit-and-run, they had murmured, low enough so she couldn't hear them, but she did. She heard
every word they said. The old woman had never stood a chance. She
was gone before she hit the pavement. It was too bad Maeve hadn't
seen anything that would help them find out who did this because
with only one witness and nothing to go on, it was unlikely they
would ever solve this case. Unless the person felt so guilty that they
had to turn themselves in.

It wasn't an accidental hit-and-run, she wanted to say. The car
hadn't been there and then it was. Someone had been driving with
a singular purpose.

She started to think, some time after she crossed the Newburgh-
Beacon bridge, that it was her the killer had wanted.

There was only one thing to think: she was getting closer to the truth.

Maeve knew that Chris Larsson lived in the center of the village, directly across from the high school, his Jeep visible when she picked Heather up, the decal for Boston University—his son's college—on the back windshield. After texting the girls not to wait up, she drove there, parking her car on a side street and walking the block to his house, ringing the bell. Although she wanted to apologize for showing up so late, he didn't give her a chance, taking in her tear-stained face, her shaking hands. He brought her into the warm and cozy house, where a fire burned in the fireplace, and a glass of wine sat on a coffee table next to a variety of sections from the previous week's *Sunday Times*. He took her hand and led her to the couch, and while she wanted to tell him everything, she responded by pulling off her coat, and then the fleece underneath it, the T-shirt beneath that finding its way to the floor.

He was confused but not so confused as to resist her. He stretched out on top of her, distributing his weight, and pushed her hair away from her face. "What happened to you?" he asked, taking his thumb and wiping her tears away.

"If I told you, you'd never believe me," she said, referring to other things, things he would never find out about her. She kept it simple. "I don't want to be alone tonight." Or anymore, she thought, but didn't say. "Does that sound desperate? Predictable?"

"I don't want to be alone tonight either," he said, searching her face. "Should we not be alone together?"

She grabbed him and held on tight, never wanting to let go.

CHAPTER 44

She left a few hours later, after she told him everything, after she promised him that if her hip still hurt in the morning, she would call the doctor, a promise she knew she would never keep.

"I can help you," he said, not for the first time. "I don't know how, but I can help you."

"I will let you know if I think of anything," she said, thinking that his help would consist of comforting her when she was scared, soothing her jangled nerves when she was losing it. He seemed more concerned about her sister than the finger in her refrigerator, and something about that made her like him even more.

On her way home, she wondered how Jo would feel if she knew that Maeve, scared and alone, had gone on a booty call.

She'd never believe it.

Before she left him, while she was picking up her clothes from around the room, she asked him about the break-in, Sebastian Du-Clos, breaking the mood that had been established by her drop-in. There was nothing to report on any front, DuClos having gone on some extended holiday; Billy's whereabouts known but not a cause for concern, according to Chris; the break-in still unsolved.

"I'm sorry," he said. "Do you think I'm the worst detective in Farringville? Or beyond?"

She was so focused on finding Evelyn that she didn't really care anymore, and told him so.

The next morning at home, after a few hours of restless sleep, she got up, the queasy feeling in her gut and the pain behind her eyes not deterring her from getting ready to get back in her car and head north. She knew if she asked, Chris would go with her, but this was a solo job. She worked alone.

In Heather's room, she could hear the girls talking to each other, deep in conversation, their voices low, the subject of their conversation unknown to her. She leaned against the wall of her bathroom, the one that divided the two rooms, but she couldn't hear what they were saying. Why they weren't texting each other from the comfort of their respective bedrooms, like they usually did, she didn't know. All she knew was that they weren't fighting. After the night she had had, she didn't think she could take much more of that.

After going to Dunkin' Donuts and being served by the delicious Tamara—don't think she didn't watch every single item that was put in her coffee—Maeve settled in for the drive to Rhineview.

"So if she's alive, she has a guardian?" Maeve said as she pulled onto 9 North, thankful for the Bluetooth that Cal had insisted she install in the car when she bought it. Little did he know at the time that her chat with him now about lost sisters, guardianship, and the law would be facilitated by the device. She knew the answer but wanted confirmation from a professional, a onetime lawyer. She merged onto the highway just as Doug exited in all of his Taurean glory, his overnight shift completed. She watched in her rearview as he drove straight past the strip mall that housed the Dunkin' Donuts and toward his home.

That's right, Doug. Keep going. Your wife will make you some coffee at home.

"Correct," Cal said, interrupting her reverie about Doug, his old-man car, and his adoring wife, the one who needed him now more than ever.

And here we go again, she thought. In his voice, she heard what she had been thinking but didn't want confirmation on: now that Jack was dead, Evelyn's guardian—unless it was the state—would likely come forward and let Maeve know about her sister. Where she was. How she lived. If she was happy.

"Well, then how do we find out if she's a ward of the state?" she asked.

"I don't know," Cal said. "Petition the state?"

"Can we do that?"

"You're going to need a law guardian, someone who specializes in stuff like this." The sigh was barely perceptible on the other end but she heard it. Apparently, his patience with this search was wearing thin. He had organic, pureed baby food to make and eco-friendly chemicals that needed to be sprayed on the glistening marble countertops in the Tudor. He didn't have a lot of extra time to help Maeve.

As with most things, the time had come when Cal had lost interest in this particular venture, even though it had only been a day before when he had shown enthusiasm for this missing persons case. Why the change? It could have been a host of factors, issues that had shown themselves during their marriage and then after. Interest in something else, like a new piece of technology. An admonishment from his new wife that he was focusing too much on his old one. An ailing baby. A home-improvement project that he didn't have the chops to start, let alone finish. She didn't know and she didn't care. He had promised his help and she was going to get it, one way or another.

"One more thing," she said. "Winston Alderson?"

"No death certificate," he said. "Not that I could find online, anyway."

She tried to keep her voice steady. "His mother passed away last night."

"What? How?"

"Hit-and-run accident," Maeve said, not believing the words she was saying; it had been no accident, "in the parking lot of the Y. She died pretty much instantly."

"How did you find out?"

"I was there."

"Oh, Maeve." In his voice was the sympathy she had been looking for, letting her know that he was back with her on this and would help her until the truth was revealed. "This might take a while," he said, "but we'll figure it out."

But Maeve only had a few days left until the store opened and more to do when it came to finding her sister. She was going back to the house in Rhineview to talk to Regina Hartwell, getting the information she needed if it was the last thing she ever did. She had texted Margie a few times to see if she could cajole her into revealing the rest of what she knew—Maeve was certain she did know more than she was letting on—but the radio silence from her former neighbor was deafening. Margie was done helping, too, it would seem, and Maeve hadn't had the time to hunt her down in person.

Jack had always said she was stubborn, "just like your mother, God rest her soul." Maeve preferred to think of it as "tenacious." The word "stubborn" held so many negative connotations, and her tenacity, she felt, was what let her be successful at the things she excelled at—culinary school and motherhood, specifically—although the latter provided many opportunities for self-doubt.

She found the little cutout at the side of the road and waited. She didn't know if Regina Hartwell was home but she did know that she needed to collect her thoughts, think about what else she could do or say to compel the woman to talk. All of her efforts so far had been met with a stone wall.

Stubbornness.

She sank in her car seat, her warm sigh misting over the cold windshield.

A car raced past her on the road, not the Rambler, going very fast and kicking up a spray of rocks as it rounded the bend not far from where she sat. Maeve sat up a little straighter. She had driven this road from end to end and there was but one house—the falling-down house where Regina Hartwell lived—so anyone who passed her would be going there. Or was hopelessly lost. Maeve started the Prius and, keeping a safe distance, trailed the car directly to the Hartwell house.

The car pulled into the driveway; the Rambler was absent from its usual little parking pad. The man who got out of the car wasn't hesitant at all; he had been here before. He was tall and thin, on the older side, wearing an overcoat over creased suit pants. A tie peeked out where the coat was unbuttoned. He looked surprised to see her, and behind his smile, Maeve could see the wheels turning inside his head.

It was Michael Donner, the man who had been at the support group the night before.

"Hi." She stuck out her hand, acting more confident than she felt. "Maeve Conlon. You were at the support group last night."

He took her hand in his gloved one, hesitating with his introduction and greeting. Turns out the latter didn't exist. "Michael Donner."

"I'm looking for Mrs. Hartwell. Are you a relative?"

He was smiling but it wasn't quite right. "Yes. Brother-in-law. By marriage."

"Right." She pulled her hood over her head. Unseasonably warm, it was starting to rain. "So you knew her husband?"

"Yes. James."

"He died, yes?" Maeve asked.

He nodded, his eyes narrowing. "And who are you, Miss . . . ?"

"Conlon. Maeve Conlon. From the support group last night," she said, looking at his face to see if the name rang a bell, if there was any recognition. Did he know the name? His craggy, lined face gave nothing away if he did. She had nothing to lose and everything to gain. She told him her story. "I'm looking for my sister. She lived at Mansfield. I was told that Mrs. Hartwell might have some information with regard to my search." She sounded stilted, not herself. How many times had she told this story? It was hard to remember. For something she had only learned a few weeks earlier, it was now part of her history, even if the words sounded unnatural coming out of her mouth.

"Well, I don't know if we . . . she . . . can help you. It's been a long time since Regina worked at Mansfield." He turned toward the house. "Now, if you'll excuse me?"

"She's not home," Maeve said. "Her car's not here."

"I know," he said. "I can see that."

"Social visit?" Maeve asked.

"Pardon me?"

"Social visit or work?" Maeve asked, keeping a smile plastered on her face. See? I'm not threatening at all. Not nosy. Couldn't care less as to why you're here but hope you'll tell me. "I think my sister is one of the Mansfield Missing. I want to find her."

"Well, I'm sorry, but I can't help you. I doubt Regina can either."

"Really? Nothing? Any suggestions as to where I start? Please?" she said, sounding a bit more plaintive than she intended. It was clear he had no intention of helping her, even if he could.

But he didn't respond, bidding her a hasty good-bye and signaling that their conversation was over.

It was clear that he wasn't going to move until she left, so she got in her car and drove away slowly, keeping an eye on him in her rearview mirror. He stayed right where he was on the driveway, watching her drive down the road.

At home, she went straight to her computer and searched the name "Michael Donner," finding that he was exactly who he said he was: a worker in the social services department of the county to the north. Then she tried "James Hartwell." She hit pay dirt when she got to his obituary from three years prior.

James Hartwell died peacefully at his home in Rhineview on May 13, 2002. Devoted husband of Regina Hartwell (née Haggerty) . . .

Maeve slammed the computer shut and banged her head on her desk, wondering how she had been so stupid. Why hadn't she looked up Regina Hartwell before? She picked up her phone, dialing the one person she was now sure would always help her, always be there for her.

Her own personal secret-keeper.

CHAPTER 45

Poole answered her call on the first ring.

"Maeve Conlon," he said as he always did. Her first name. Her last. Together.

"Rodney." She was out of breath, the air having been sucked from her lungs at the discovery. "What's the name of Margie Haggerty's company?"

He was at work. In the background was the din that accompanied working in a busy squad with too many open cases. Cursing. Yelling. Protests of innocence. Proof of guilt. The odd breakfast order. Bacon and egg on a roll. "I don't remember," he said. "Why?"

"It's too long a story to go into. I need to see her. Where did you say it was?"

"Hold on," he said. He put the phone down and rummaged around on his desk. "Two thirty-eighth and Broadway, if my knowledge of addresses in that area is correct. Somewhere under the El. Over a bodega." He dropped his voice to a conspiratorial tone. "What are you going to do, Maeve Conlon? The warrior queen isn't making a reappearance, is she?"

He knew what she was capable of, so he was right to be concerned. She slowed her breathing; she couldn't be this keyed up for an extended period of time. Gather your thoughts, calm down. That's what she needed to do. "I need to see her," she said again. "That's it. We need to talk." She wasn't going to call her, give Margie time to make up another story.

Heather wandered into the kitchen and opened the refrigerator, Maeve getting a view of her pajama-clad backside as she pushed items around on the shelves, looking for that one thing that would appeal to her as the first thing she put in her mouth that day. She'd never get used to the sleeping habits of teens. How they could sleep so late was beyond her, her internal clock waking her up before dawn. She bent over farther to pull out the bread drawer and knocked the phone from Maeve's hand.

"Hello?" Maeve said, picking it up. "You still there?"

"Yes." Someone was screaming the name "Juanita!" over and over, the man's shrill voice coming through loud and clear. Someone told him to shut it and the place quieted down for a moment. "Be careful, Maeve. You may be a little out of your league here."

She watched Heather bumble around with the toaster, changing the settings, leaving a knife dangling off the side of the counter. She moved it and gently pushed her daughter out of the way before she hurt herself and burned the house down. "What do you mean?"

"She was a bad cop. Hear she's a lawyer now. And we know that most of them are bad, too." He paused, thinking better of adding something. "I don't know. It just sounds as if you should be done with her."

"A cop? A lawyer? Last I heard, she went into the Peace Corps," Maeve said. "She's had quite a life since I left the neighborhood."

"She gets around. Recently left her marriage to a very nice woman, too, from what I hear."

"It's not like you to gossip, Poole," she said.

"Just want you to have all of the facts, Maeve Conlon."

She pushed the handle down on the toaster. Heather went into the powder room and got stuck. "Listen, I've got to go. Thank you."

She jiggled the handle on the powder room door and released her daughter. "I need new boots," Heather said when she emerged. "Can we go shopping today?"

Maeve's hesitation gave Heather the opening for a speech she had obviously rehearsed.

"You're never here. We don't know where you go and what you do, but we know you leave in the morning and don't come back for hours. We want to spend time with you," Heather said.

Maeve wasn't so sure about that last part but she'd take it. It was more likely that they wanted new boots.

"You're never here," Heather said again. "Where do you go?"

Where did she go? How would she explain it without sounding like a complete lunatic? She kept it simple because, in reality, it was. "I'm looking for my sister."

"But what about us?" Heather asked.

Maeve thought it was less about her looking for her sister, less about them wanting to spend time with her, and more about the fact that she was gone when they needed her. They were grieving, too. She had forgotten about that.

As if to confirm her thoughts, Heather started crying. "I miss Grandpa."

The toast started smoking in the appliance. Maeve popped it up before wrapping Heather in a hug. She felt her own tears come but wasn't sure if it was because she missed her father or because she missed her sister. A sister she had never known. On the face of it, it did sound crazy, but she was stubborn like that.

Or tenacious.

Depended how you looked at it.

Heather's outburst gave her a chance to calm down, to step out of herself and the bottomless well of anger that had built, if only for a minute. She had been mad at Heather for being the kind of girl who went for the Tommy Brantley kind of guy and she had to let that go. She grabbed some tissues from the powder room and handed them to Heather. "How about this? I need to run an errand in the Bronx"—Well, she thought, that was one way to put it—"and then we'll hit the big mall on the Thruway on the way home. We'll go out to eat."

Heather let out a shaky breath, the kind that came after an extended bout of crying. "Cheesecake Factory?"

Maeve pushed her daughter's dark hair off her face. "Sure. Cheesecake Factory." She reached over and closed the photo album on the table. "Go tell your sister."

The element of surprise was her best and closest ally; she wouldn't call Margie Haggerty and tell her she was on her way. She waited while the girls got ready and plotted what she would say to the woman, someone who she had forgotten many years ago and who she hoped to forget again soon.

She responded to a text from Chris Larsson asking if he could see her that night, telling him that she was spending time with the girls. He would understand, she hoped. He had a son. The kid might not be as needy as her own progeny but that was to be seen. Maeve hadn't met him yet, the boy spending time with his mother.

Before they left town, Maeve stopped to get cash. Sliding her ATM card into the machine, she watched as all of her accounts came up: her savings, her checking, Rebecca's savings, Rebecca's checking. Cal had insisted that one of them be on Rebecca's accounts so that if they wanted to deposit money while she was at school, they didn't have to bother sending a check; they could just transfer money for books, necessities, or even food when she couldn't take the dining hall anymore. Maeve hadn't checked the accounts in a long time but glanced at them now just in case Rebecca needed money before she went back to school, something she would never tell her mother, preferring to suffer the indignities of generic shampoo and cafeteria turkey tetrazzini instead, parceling her money out with Scrooge-like frugality.

Maeve hit "Savings." There wasn't a dime in the account. Behind her, the door to the bank opened and someone smelling heavily of grease and oil came in. She went to "Checking."

Nothing.

When Rebecca had left for school, she had had just shy of twenty-five hundred dollars total in her savings account, the money she had saved from birthdays, graduations, and working. Her checking held only a few hundred dollars, something Maeve considered her "walking-around money," the funds she would use for coffee and lip gloss and anything else she might have a hankering for at school.

Maeve rechecked both accounts. The man who had entered the bank cleared his throat noisily. "You refinancing your house, lady?" he asked. "On the ATM?"

Maeve turned; it was the head of the DPW, Marc Foster. "Hi, Marc. I'll just be a second." She noticed that his hand was damaged but resisted the urge to ask him if he had lost a finger.

"I'm sorry, Maeve," he said, seeing his future of free coffee and scones ruined with one cranky comment, "take your time."

While she wanted to stare at the screen and see if the numbers that she expected would magically appear, she couldn't; someone else entered the bank. She quickly withdrew a few hundred in cash for the boots and dinner and went back to the car.

The girls sat in silence, Rebecca in the front, Heather in the back. She looked at both of them but their faces gave nothing away.

She opened the passenger-side door. "You're driving," she said to Rebecca.

"In the Bronx?" Rebecca said, whining. The sound of it got under Maeve's skin in a way it wouldn't have before the discovery of the missing money.

Just what had she done at school? Was it something horrible, something shocking? Did she have a drug habit? As Maeve settled in as a passenger, she tried to think of what would make her daughter spend her entire life savings in one semester.

Beside her, Rebecca was still protesting being pressed into service as a driver but Maeve ignored her, her thoughts on childish spending sprees and just what exactly she would say to Margie Haggerty, trying to keep her more murderous thoughts at bay.

CHAPTER 46

Rebecca had come late to the driving thing and had gotten her license only a month before going to college, and that newness of skill showed when Maeve directed her into the IHOP parking lot on Broadway, right across from the funeral home where she had been several times as a child, Jack's devotion to wake-going with his young daughter being something of an oddity, she had learned years later. She thought everyone went to wakes every week with their father, paying respects to people she barely knew but who seemed grateful at the Conlon family's attendance at whatever "viewing" was taking place that particular day.

Rebecca eased the car, with a great deal of moaning and gasping, into a tight space between a minivan and a brand-new Lexus.

"Good job!" Maeve said. "See? That wasn't hard." *At least it's not as hard as I'm going to come down on you when you finally tell me what happened to all of your money.*

Rebecca brushed her dark hair off her face. "It was really hard." She handed the keys to her mother. "I'm not driving home."

In the backseat, Heather was listening to music, oblivious to her sister's attempts at navigating city streets. "You want pancakes?"

Maeve asked. "I'm not sure how long I'm going to be but you can get pancakes if you want."

Heather pulled her earbuds from her ears, suddenly able to hear what was being said. "I could go for some pancakes," she said.

That was Rebecca's cue to take the opposite stance. What had just seconds ago seemed like a great idea had lost its luster in the wake of her sister's wishes. "I don't want pancakes."

Yes, siblings know . . . how to drive each other crazy. She needed no further proof than her own spawn, packed tight into the little Prius with her.

Maeve shoved twenty dollars into her older daughter's hand. "Have coffee then."

Something in her tone alerted Rebecca to the fact that this conversation was over, the great pancake debate done for the day. She eyed her mother warily. If siblings knew, daughters knew even more, and were especially aware of when their mothers had been pushed to the limit.

Maeve pointed to a spot across the street. "I'll be right there, in that building next to the funeral home. If you need me, call me." She opened the car door. "I won't be long."

Maeve wiggled out from between her car and the Lexus, careful not to let her door hit the other car, and walked across the street to a storefront next to the funeral home. Margie's business was on the second floor, over a bodega, just like Poole had said. Maeve wasn't sure what she was expecting, but the small office with the glass-fronted door looked like it hadn't seen much traffic in a while. It was cluttered and small. The sign on the door said MARGARET HAGGERTY, ATTORNEY, and below that *Hablamos Español!*

Inside, a desk for a receptionist sat empty, a thin film of dust on the top indicating that it hadn't been used in a while. Behind a partition, Maeve could hear Margie discussing a case with someone in fluent Spanish. Maeve's Spanish wasn't halting but whatever Margie was discussing with her client seemed to have to do with a fall from a ladder. Maeve looked at the out-of-date magazines on an Ikea coffee table in the waiting area; she had had the same one until the bolts fell out and the top almost broke one of her toes. She wondered if the string of expletives she had used at the time would sound as dramatic in Swedish as it had in English and decided that it probably wouldn't.

The client brushed past Maeve in the tight office; she was a compact Hispanic lady who appeared to have been crying vigorously, a wad of paper towels pressed to her eyes. Margie peered from around the corner of the partition and blanched when she saw Maeve, quite a feat considering her pale, Irish complexion. She had looked the same way—guilty—the day Maeve had "lost" her key.

"Maeve." She gripped the side of the partition, white-knuckled.

"Margie." Maeve didn't have time for pleasantries. "So Regina Hartwell is your aunt. On your father's side, is it?" She walked back to the door to the office and turned the deadbolt above the doorknob. "Why didn't you tell me that? And what else aren't you telling me?"

Margie backed up until she was at her desk. Maeve came around the partition and surveyed the workspace, which she found dark, messy, and completely unprofessional. No wonder Margie was helping workers with comp cases in a down-on-its-heels neighborhood. Maeve couldn't imagine anyone less desperate than a day laborer in this area would want Margie's services. This was no high-level law firm with lots of cases. This was one woman trying to scratch out a living after being disgraced in her former career. "Is it just you here? Really fancy, Margie," Maeve said. It looked like a one-woman operation, but Maeve wanted to make sure some partner wasn't out to lunch or getting pancakes for themselves across the street.

"Just me," Margie said, unable to hold Maeve's gaze. Had she had a brain in her head, she should have lied and said that there was someone else, someone who would be back soon, but it was clear to Maeve that Margie didn't find her nearly as threatening as she should.

Maeve sat down on an old thrift-store chair. "So, Regina Hartwell. Spill it."

When it was clear to Margie that Maeve wasn't going anywhere, she started to talk. "Yes. Regina Hartwell is my aunt. My father's sister. She lives in Rhineview. Always has."

"And worked at Mansfield."

Margie swallowed. "Yes."

Jesus, that was easy. Maeve wondered what else she could ask. Just where was Jimmy Hoffa? And did Lee Harvey Oswald act alone? Who was Deep Throat? "What happened after the place closed?" Maeve asked. Someone was knocking on the glass in the front door, the pane sounding as if it were going to shatter.

"I'll be right there!" Margie called. She looked back at Maeve. "She lived in Rhineview. We rarely saw her. She was a foster mother to some kids. Developmentally challenged."

"Legally?" Maeve asked. "As in, she adopted them? There were records?"

Margie looked confused. "Of course," she said definitively. She thought for a moment. "I think so," she added, now not so sure.

Maeve thought about the children who went missing after the place closed, of her friends at the support group. "How many?"

"I don't know. I was young the last time we went up there," Margie said. "Maeve, I really don't remember. I was little. My father and Regina stopped talking before he died. I didn't see her very much."

"I've been up there. She won't talk to me."

"Did you tell her I sent you?" Margie asked.

"Yes. Yes, I did. Should I not have?" Maeve said, getting a little tingle of pleasure when she saw Margie's concerned expression, her fear.

Margie shook her head. "No. There's no love lost between our families."

The Haggertys had a way like that. "What else aren't you telling me, Margie? And why didn't you tell me that Regina Hartwell was your aunt?"

"I've told you everything." Margie pushed a coffee cup out of the way and pulled a sheet of paper off a pile on the desk. "And I didn't tell you because I figured you would find out eventually. I didn't actually think it was relevant."

"Are you an idiot?" Maeve asked. She was starting to think that that might be the case. "It is entirely relevant."

"You don't like me. I know that."

"And why would that be, Margie?" Maeve asked. "What could you have possibly done to make me not like you?" The knocking at the door was in time to the beating of Maeve's heart.

"I don't know, Maeve." She looked terrified. "I have no idea."

"No idea."

Margie held firm, something, a memory, giving her more resolve than she had had when Maeve walked in. "Nothing."

The frustration that Maeve felt at getting nowhere with Margie was growing exponentially until it felt like another entity in the room.

Margie handed Maeve the piece of paper. "I can help you, if you want. Find other things out. Here's my fee sheet," she said, "which lists my hourly rates and expenses. I can help you on the legal side of things, if you need me to."

Maeve held the sheet of paper in her hand, a buzzing beginning in her ears that made her head hurt. "You want me to hire you?" she said.

"I can help you."

The knocking, which had paused to give the knocker a chance to rub his or her sore knuckles, started again. Combined with the buzzing in her head, it made Maeve feel as if she were going to punch a hole in the wall. Instead, to release some of the rage that felt as if it were bubbling just beneath her skin, she swept her arm across the desk and watched in wonder as everything crashed to the floor, a cup of cold coffee splattering all over the far wall.

Better that than taking out a gun and shooting Margie in the face or wrapping her hands around her throat, which was her initial inclination. "Margie," she said slowly. "I've got a kid in the car downstairs who probably spent a few grand on shoes and Starbucks, so I'm in no mood for this little dance you seem to want to do today." Maeve's mind went to the Frye boots that Rebecca had worn to her grandfather's funeral, brand new but with that broken-in look that cost a lot of money to achieve.

"Maeve," Margie started in protest, but stopped when she saw Maeve's face. "Okay, fine. You're scaring me a little bit." Finally, Margie could tell that what she saw in Maeve's eyes was pure, unadulterated hatred and it was completely terrifying. The bigger woman leaned back, trying to get away.

"I am?" Maeve asked. "I'm scaring you? The Peace Corps volunteer? The former cop?" She pushed the last remaining items off the desk, those that hadn't tumbled to the floor in the first go-round. "I'm going to be completely honest with you, Margie. I have no one left in the world with the last name Conlon. I have lost my mother, my father, and now a sister I didn't know I had. You," she said, putting her finger in the larger woman's chest, "are toying with me. And," she started, stopping herself. She wanted to say, "I hurt people who do that," but instead, she fell silent. The less said, the better.

She had so many questions she wanted to ask Margie, but her judgment was clouded and she couldn't think straight. Maeve fell silent for a moment, something that seemed to make Margie even more nervous. She fidgeted behind the desk, her clasped hands shaking a bit. The knocking at the office door persisted, punctuating Maeve's anger in rapid staccato raps.

She tried another tack. "Your sister was the mean girl, Margie. I thought better of you," she said. "For a while, anyway. But then you stole my key."

Realization dawned on Margie's face. She hadn't thought that Maeve had anything against her, her memories not as indelible as Maeve's.

Maeve walked away, opening the deadbolt and letting in a frantic black man who took in her wild-eyed expression, the angry flush of her cheeks, and stepped aside. It was only when she was in the stairwell, the pungent smell of bodega food wafting up to greet her, that she realized the black man had been Rodney Poole.

She took a minute to collect her thoughts, settling heavily onto a step in the stairwell. She didn't like this feeling. It felt portentous, like she had to do something to release what was building inside of her. Something dangerous. Something bad.

She didn't know how he got out of the building before her or how he did it without passing her on the stairwell, but Poole was waiting for her on the sidewalk, staring blankly at a group of very distressed and vociferous mourners going into the funeral home. The late Tia Blanca was well loved; that was evident. When Maeve burst through the front door onto the street, he waited until a very loud 1 train passed overhead before talking.

"You threaten her?" he asked.

"Yep," Maeve said. "And I messed up her office." She laughed; that sounded ridiculous, as if messing up Margie's office was just retribution for her lies. She looked at the IHOP parking lot across the street and saw that her car was empty, the girls inside the restaurant, most likely diving into the plate of pancakes she had hoped they would, even though they had talked about having dinner later. She took a few deep breaths. "She knows more than she's telling me, Poole. And it's pissing me off."

"You getting that feeling again, Maeve?"

She looked up at him. "That feeling?"

"The one where you want to kill someone?" he asked.

She calmed herself, bringing her breathing back to normal, her heart rate to a reasonable pace. "I don't know," she said, which was the truth.

"Be careful," he said. "Margie Haggerty knows how to use a gun and her way around the streets. I was afraid you'd lose your head. That's why I came."

"How did you know I was here?" she asked.

He hooked a thumb toward the bodega. "I told the owner to give me a holler when an angry little white woman showed up. Best ten bucks I ever spent." He shoved his hands into the pocket of his baggy coat. "And you are one little angry white woman." He reached out and fingered the arm of her parka. "Pink coat is a nice touch, though." He smiled. "Sounds to me as if she's not going to be much help to you, so just leave her alone. You can do this on your own."

"I can?" she said, letting the self-doubt that she didn't exhibit in front of anyone else out in front of him. "Hey. Cutting off someone's finger?"

"That's what you're planning?" he asked.

She shook her head, laughed a little. "No. Who cuts people's fingers off? To send them a message?" she asked, thinking of that little finger in her refrigerator. If anyone would know, it would be him. Chris Larsson, for his attentive wooing of her and his light and sweet personality, didn't seem to have the chops to figure out its owner, where it had come from.

"Sounds Mob to me. Drugs." He looked at her. "People who want to send a message without going too deep."

She knew all of that but had hoped he would know more.

"You got a finger that's missing, Maeve Conlon?" he asked.

"Found one."

His face darkened. "Be careful. I don't like the sound of that."

"I will," she said. "I always am."

He smiled, giving her a little nod. "I want you to be careful always. To use your head." He changed the subject back to the missing woman. "That's how you'll find her." He looked around, seeing who was on the sidewalk and if they were listening to his advice to the small woman in front of him. "You'll find her, Maeve Conlon. I'm positive."

He walked away and as she waited for the light to change, she thought about what he had said.

"I'll find her," she said out loud to no one and everyone at once.

CHAPTER 47

Maeve was surprised by both how little and how much people told her when she started calling the group homes on the list. Maeve wasn't surprised to learn that Cal had called the places in the county with the smallest population—Hamilton County—but hadn't gotten any further. He got credit for looking but hadn't tried all that hard. She started with Dutchess because it was the county in which Mansfield had been located but it also had the largest number of group homes. No wonder Cal had chosen to start his search north of the town.

The first few calls yielded nothing in terms of real information; two of the places even hung up on her before she got out her initial inquiry. When she reached the sixth place on the list, she got a kindly woman with an accent that spoke to the life she had lived upstate, who sympathized with her plight but explained kindly that no group home director in their right mind would give her the information she needed, because they were bound by strict laws that protected their residents. Earlier that day, Chris Larsson had called and let her know that he had run up against the same brick wall when he had called a few names on the list.

Maeve knew the rules. She tried to appeal to the woman's softer side, something that Maeve knew she had; her voice, her inflection said it all. She wanted to help Maeve but couldn't.

"Those people have been missing a long time," the woman said. "It's like they vanished off the face of the earth."

"Yes, it is."

"I'm so sorry, Miss Conlon," she said before hanging up. "I'll say a prayer that you find your sister." Before she hung up, she said softly, "She's not here, honey. I've been here a long time. I don't think she ever was. Or your friend Winston."

Maeve's next call was to Doug, who was working. "Maeve, it's not a great time to talk," he said. He was out of breath. "I'm on my way to a call."

"I'll make it quick," she said.

"What do you want?"

"Regina Hartwell. Anything?"

"Nothing," he said, his panting getting louder and more furious. "No parking tickets, no arrests, nothing to suggest she's anything but an upstanding—"

And the phone went dead.

Maeve wondered if Poole had been with Doug, if he now knew about her loose blackmailing of his partner. She was getting nowhere and she was getting frustrated, two things that didn't bode well for her mental health.

In the basement, she went through Jack's things again, tearing through the boxes to see if there was anything else to indicate the existence of a sister, to point her in the right direction, but there was nothing. She could no longer go back to Buena del Sol, Stanley Cummerbund now living in Jack's apartment.

She called Jimmy Moriarty again, knowing that he wouldn't return her calls.

There was only one way to handle this and that was by going back to Rhineview. While the girls slept, she assembled all of the things she would likely need, her headlamp and shovel included. Her gun. She put everything in a bag next to her bed so that she would be ready to go when the alarm rang early the next morning.

She couldn't deal with Rebecca and the empty bank accounts right now; she had too much to do. She had to think. She had logged on to the school account to make sure the tuition was paid and up to date; paying tuition was Cal's responsibility and well, she knew how much he thought he had on his plate and how that could contribute to his dereliction of duties when it came to paying the bills that needed to be paid. But everything was fine.

Maybe she was going about this the wrong way; maybe she should widen her search. She got into her bed and dragged her laptop onto her knees and looked up any information she could find on the missing people, the dozen who had been lost when Mansfield closed. She searched through articles. The woman she had last spoken with was right: it was like they had vanished off the face of the earth.

There was a Facebook page started by one of the families, and on it, they asked for any leads, any sightings; photos of their missing relatives were on the banner at the top of the page. Maeve's sister wasn't in one of those photos, but was it possible that she had gone missing anyway? She guessed anything was possible. Maybe Jack hadn't included her in the group that was missing; he could be like that, keeping things quiet. Keeping a few secrets.

"Don't want to be a member of any club that would have me as a member," he would say, even though being a member of the New York City Police Department was like being a member of a club, the men (in those days) sticking together like glue, helping each other out, watching each others' backs.

Apparently, Margie hadn't gotten the memo on that one, if the stories about her fall from grace were to be believed.

So, two possibilities existed: Evelyn was one of those missing.

Or Jack had known where she was.

CHAPTER 48

It was Saturday, early morning. She had five days remaining to figure things out, the store opening again on Wednesday.

She focused, figuring out her next steps. Vacation—from the store, from the search—had reinvigorated Maeve. She had stopped at the hardware store and bought a thick, metal carabiner, all the better to hook the shovel that Jo had given her to a belt loop on her jeans. The headlamp was dangling around her neck and her gun was tucked in the pocket of her pink down coat.

She was ready.

She realized, on the drive up, that she felt better than she had in months. She pulled up to her hiding spot, sliding the Prius in and locking it, keeping herself under the cover of the trees as she jogged slowly but deliberately toward her destination. The Rambler was gone from the front of the house and it only took her a few minutes of good, old-fashioned reconnaissance to wander around the property and look in a few windows to ascertain that the house was empty. She stayed away from the barn today; the house was more interesting to her on this cold morning, especially since it seemed like no one was home. She knew that what she had planned next would constitute breaking and entering but she didn't care in the least. She had been lied to by so many people for so long that she didn't care.

If she got caught, she would lie her way out of it. The house had been on fire. She had broken in to make sure no one was trapped inside. Something like that, but maybe a little bit more artful in its detail, its telling.

She tested the back door and found that it was unlocked. She forgot; she was in the country now. Inside of her still beat the heart of a city girl, the daughter of a cop. She was supposed to lock her doors, everyone was. She remembered most of the time, and when she didn't, she could hear Jack's voice in her head telling her to be careful, to make sure that she was safe.

As she already knew, inside the house was as dilapidated as outside, and bad smells—a conglomeration of rotten food, dirty clothes, and filthy conditions in general—came together in a way that made her eyes water. It was hard to imagine a place that smelled worse than a couple of dead cats but Regina Hartwell's house did. Maeve stepped over a stack of newspapers, yellowing and old, and into the kitchen. Dishes were piled in the sink and the water dripped on plates that had crusted food on them. A box of rat poison sat next to a toaster oven encrusted with grime. It was like an episode of *Hoarders* come to life.

Maeve shivered in disgust.

If Regina Hartwell sold the place, or whatever happened to it after her death, it would be a teardown. Judging from the trees that outlined the property, there were several acres to be had here, maybe more if the line extended beyond the forest to the back of the place. There was no saving this place. Its time had come and gone. In its place would be gleaming new condos or a development with fake Tudors. That's the way things went now.

Maeve didn't know if she had the guts to go much farther into the space, afraid that the stuff that covered every flat surface would rise up and enclose her, suffocating her before she had a chance to escape. At the far corner of the kitchen were tanks; she recognized them as similar to those she had seen at Buena del Sol.

Oxygen tanks.

Mrs. Hartwell, if Maeve had to guess, had emphysema or what was now called COPD on the ads that touted relief from the symptoms. That breathing, the raspy voice, didn't come from anything but someone who had smoked themselves into a few steps short of lung cancer. She didn't know how to tell if the tanks were empty or full and didn't want to take the time to figure it out, so she carefully picked her way through the kitchen and into the living room where the smell of musty upholstery and cat pee hit her nose like a sack of hammers.

Thank god for turtlenecks. She unfolded the material at her neck and pulled it up over her nose, breathing in the scent of freshly laundered clothing and her body wash, hoping that it was enough to stave off the horrible odor that permeated the living area. How did anyone live here? she wondered as she made her way through the house. The living room faced the front of the house and offered a great view of the road beyond; Maeve would know if Mrs. Hartwell returned and would have ample time to make a getaway out the back of the house and into the woods. She'd find her way eventually back to her car. She felt better knowing that there was an escape route.

Her phone vibrated in her pocket, her home number coming up. "Mom, it's me." Rebecca. "Do we have any milk?"

"Rebecca, I can't talk right now," she said, thinking that in her elder daughter's case, that was a good thing. She had a lot to say and not a lot of time to say it, so the conversation was better put off for another day when Maeve didn't feel like killing someone, anyone. "And if there isn't any milk, you can walk to the deli and get some."

Her sigh let Maeve know just how put out she was. Rather than get into a battle royale over Maeve's absence and the lack of dairy products in the house, Maeve hung up.

Seconds later, the phone buzzed with a text. Chris Larsson. *I miss you.* She didn't take the time to text back immediately, hoping she wasn't breaking some code of dating etiquette in the twenty-first century.

She continued through the house, stepping gingerly. To her right, and behind a fireplace, was a small room with a window that faced the woods that encircled the premises, neater than the rest of the house, with a small desk and filing cabinet in it, a cushy desk chair. This room had been untouched by Mrs. Hartwell and her hoarding tendencies; it was clearly the domain of someone who was far more organized and who abided by stricter rules of cleanliness than the home's main resident, the only person who Maeve knew lived there. Maeve looked at the desk and through some of the papers on its surface. A home insurance policy. Term life information. A renewal for the Rambler's registration, a vehicle that had been on the road since 1967, a testament to American car-making in the last millennium.

Maeve opened the drawers of the desk, finding a collection of pens and pencils. Ah, so this is where Mrs. Hartwell's junk collecting came to roost, she thought. Maeve pocketed a couple of Sharpies; they always went missing from the store. She suspected if she checked Jo's desk drawers at the cottage, she'd find a stash of fresh pens in there, all purloined from The Comfort Zone. One desk drawer was stuck and Maeve yanked on it to pull it out completely, finding that a box with a hinged lid was the reason it wouldn't open.

She pulled out the box. In the distance, she heard the rumble of a car with a faulty muffler. The Rambler. Mrs. Hartwell was on her way back.

Maeve opened the box and looked inside. Underneath a holy card, one that had been taken from Martin Haggerty's wake, was a stack of social security cards. Maeve riffled through them quickly even though the one on the top, bearing the name Winston Alderson, made her gasp.

She counted them quickly. There were ten social security cards, all bearing different names.

But none bore the name of Aibhlinn Conlon.

CHAPTER 49

Above her, Maeve heard floorboards creak, but rather than stay to find out who was there and what they might do to an intruder, she shoved Winston Alderson's social security card into her back pocket, pushing the box back into the desk and slamming the drawer shut before she tore out of the house through the back door, knocking over a canister of oxygen before she hit the porch. Outside, she wondered why she only grabbed his card, why she panicked and didn't keep them all. His was the only name that was familiar to her, in her quick glance through the stack; his was the only one she really cared about, she decided. She steeled herself for the loud bang that would accompany the explosion that was sure to come if the oxygen canister was full, but none came. She ran across the backyard and took cover in the dense woods, hearing the car drive up to the parking pad out front and coming to a stop.

She rested behind a large fallen oak, the trunk providing cover for her shaking body. She lay down on the ground, flat, sure she couldn't be seen, and tried to slow her breath. She folded her hands on her chest and looked up at the sky. After she heard the back door slam again, Mrs. Hartwell using the kitchen entrance, there was no sound that came from the house, nothing to indicate that the woman was going to pick up her gun and stalk Maeve until she found her, shot her, and killed her. Maeve wondered if the oxygen canisters tipped over often, especially when they were empty, if that occurrence was her cover. She had waited too long inside the house, her curiosity at what was in the box and then what those social security cards might mean causing her to take a chance that she couldn't afford to take.

She murmured the names she could remember but found she could only come up with one additional name, the rest of the names, the letters that formed them, swimming in front of her eyes. Eileen Mackin. Damn it. There had been one more familiar name. She had to be the sister of Lorraine, the woman at the support group who Maeve liked but who had told her that her hunt was fruitless. Fruitless, huh? Maeve thought. Well, look at what I found, she thought, putting her hand to her pocket. She wished she had thought to take every card in the box, but she had panicked, which, given the circumstances, she had to believe was the appropriate response.

Still, she was disappointed in herself.

She sat there for so long, she might have fallen asleep; she wasn't sure. Time had a way of bending itself here, making it seem like hours had ticked by when it had only been a few minutes. She willed herself to move.

It seemed straightforward: head south in a straight line toward the car. But it turned out to be harder than she thought it would be, the light playing tricks, coming through the trees at odd angles, making it seem like she was walking the right way but instead taking her deeper into the woods. A cloud covered the sun and the nervousness started to form a tight band in her gut, forcing her to sit down and take stock of the situation.

She looked up at the sky. "There's the sun," she whispered to herself. She looked behind her but couldn't see the house anymore. "So that's west." She looked at her phone; even though there was no service out here in the woods, she knew the girls had downloaded a bunch of apps—many that she didn't need and were related to beauty and grooming—and wondered if there was a compass on there. She scrolled through the screens on her phone. There wasn't. But there was a flashlight app and she turned that on, surprised at how much light it threw on the ground in front of her. That would be far more helpful than the eyebrow-plucking chart that Rebecca had downloaded in a not-so-subtle hint to her mother about her wayward brows.

She walked for what seemed like an hour but was really fifteen minutes, according to her phone. And she was getting closer, she thought, because she could hear a door slam in the distance, not too far away. Her heart went from a dull pound to a racy pitter-patter but that was better; she was getting her sense of direction back and felt confident that she would be out before it got completely dark.

She was nearly in line with the house; she could tell by the break in the trees in the distance and the sound of the back door opening and closing. She trudged in what she hoped was the right direction.

"I'm almost there," she said, turning to make sure that her inner compass was correct. In the distance, like a mirage, she spied a row of crudely cut pieces of wood planted in the dirt and, abandoning her plan, she walked toward them even though she knew she was going in the wrong direction, the dread at this discovery like a delicate web descending over her from above.

She stopped and surveyed the line of what she now saw were crosses, all white, all roughly hewn and hammered together at one midpoint on each. Some had initials; others didn't. They were spaced apart, not unlike headstones at a cemetery.

It took her a minute to comprehend what she was looking at and to realize that she was backing away from them, not walking toward them. She backed into a large tree trunk, falling over and landing hard on her butt, wet seeping through her jeans and onto her underwear, reigniting the dull pain in her hip. Momentarily stunned, she sat there, staring at the crosses, finally getting up slowly and testing her legs.

She buried them here, she thought, unhooking the shovel from the carabiner at her waist. She started with the freshest grave, the one with the initials "E.M.," and started digging, fueled by the adrenaline streaming through her blood like a thick, energetic ocean of power. It had been warmer than usual, some days even reaching the high forties, and the ground was hard but not impossible to break. She pushed the little shovel into the packed dirt, knowing that this would take a long time and that it would eventually get dark, but she wanted proof of what had happened here so that she could tell everyone what she knew to be true: this would explain what had happened to those people all those years ago.

She dug until her back ached, and her stomach roiled, muffled cries coming out from behind her clenched teeth. She stopped when she got to a hand, white and frozen solid, polish on its nails, not a foot below the cold surface.

She took off, running out of the woods.

CHAPTER 50

Maeve knew that Mrs. Hartwell was in the house because she knew that the old woman relied solely on the Rambler for transportation. She went into the barn and found an old gas can, one with just enough gas to light a fire, along with some fireplace matches, the same brand as the ones that had been in Devon's mouth on Christmas Day. These, fortunately, weren't soaked in toddler saliva and worked just fine, Maeve found, as she doused the front seat of the car with gas, threw a match in, and watched from a distance as it started to burn.

You're trapped now, she thought as she watched a kaleidoscope of beautiful colors embed in the black smoke that rose from the car. She smiled at the beauty of the carnage, thinking that this might help subdue the buzzing, the impending murderous rage that was sure to come when she saw Regina Hartwell. Maybe this will help, she thought, as she stepped back.

Maybe this will be enough. Maybe this will make me feel better about what you've done and I won't feel like I have to go further.

She went around back and entered through the kitchen again, crossing through the trash-filled mudroom and across the threshold into the kitchen. Behind her, the car blew up with a satisfying crack, making Maeve smile. Her hand was thrust in her jacket pocket, Heather's old pink down coat from the eighth grade; the thought of her grazing her gun with her fingers while looking like a little snow queen was ludicrous and incongruous. She kept her hand there, ready to strike when necessary.

The time was coming. She could feel it.

She hadn't knocked, preferring the element of surprise, but she figured that the sound of the Rambler exploding announced her arrival just fine. The woman was sitting in the overloaded kitchen, her chair jammed between the table and the stove, a gas appliance, which she had lit so she could have a cigarette. Maeve wished she remembered even one thing about her junior-year chemistry class and if oxygen was flammable; if the woman's complete disregard for smoking in the room with two canisters—empty or not—of pure oxygen was an indication, the answer was probably no.

Mrs. Hartwell regarded her coolly. "You're that little snot that lived down the street. You're the one who wouldn't let my niece ride your precious pink bike," she said. "You lived by my brother and his wife. It took me a while, and some digging, but I finally figured it out. You were the one whose father spoiled you rotten."

Maeve stood by the door to the mudroom, her hands in her pockets.

"Conlon, right?"

She nodded.

"I remember you. Your parents, too." The old woman sneered at her, the sight of Maeve angering her in a way that Maeve didn't understand.

"You took my sister."

Regina Hartwell took a long drag off the cigarette, which precipitated a prolonged bout of coughing. One elbow on the table, one on the counter next to the stove, her legs were splayed, making her look relaxed and uninterested in their conversation. There was a stack of magazines, yellowed and old, by her elbow. Rock Hudson, young, tan, and fit, was on one, a testament to its age. "Took her where?"

"To Mansfield."

She started laughing, which only served to start the coughing again. "Yep. You got me. Took her to Mansfield. Best place for her at the time." The cigarette hung from her lips; Maeve noticed that around her neck was the tubing that she likely used when she was hooked up to the oxygen. "Your parents didn't know what to do. They begged me for help."

Maeve now knew why she thought of Dolores the first time she had seen this woman; Regina Hartwell was Dolores in thirty years, right down to the dead, beady eyes. Now that they were talking, Maeve heard a hint of a brogue.

"Where is she?" Maeve took her left hand out of her pocket and pointed to the woods. "Is she out there? In one of those graves?" she asked, the last words coming out in a hoarse whisper.

"Could be. Maybe not. How much is it worth to you?" the woman said, smiling. Her teeth were large and even, tobacco-stained, the eyeteeth a little longer than the front ones. An animal's teeth.

"You're playing this all wrong," Maeve said. "It's what it's worth to *you*. Because now that I'm here and I see what's going on, I'm going straight to the police."

"Go ahead," Regina said. "My son's on the local force. He knows a lot of Staties, too," she said, making Maeve wonder if that was how Regina had stayed under the radar all these years. "Probably best not to tell him that you blew up his mother's car."

Maeve wondered if he had already been called and was on his way.

The woman looked at her, waiting for Maeve to crack. You'll be waiting a long time, Maeve thought.

"You want to find your sister, though. You think I know something," Regina Hartwell said, her gaze something that Maeve didn't want to engage but had to.

"Of course you know something. Why else would Margie have sent me here?"

She shrugged, the ash from her cigarette falling onto the floor. "Good question. She is really messing up a good thing. Wish she had less of a conscience, hadn't taken Catholic school so seriously."

"If she had taken Catholic school seriously, she wouldn't have stolen my house key. Slashed the tires on my bike. Been involved here."

The old woman shrugged.

"'A good thing'?" Maeve asked, inching closer. "What could be good about what seems like six or eight dead people buried in your woods? People whose families are still looking for them? What do you mean 'a good thing'?"

She didn't respond to Maeve's question, dragging slowly on her cigarette; Maeve was sure that she would never get the smell of the cigarette or this house out of her skin, the fibers in her nose.

"Why didn't you kill me that day, in the barn?" Maeve asked, sure that this was the woman who had fired that shotgun blast the first time she had come here.

"I just wanted to scare you off, not kill you," she said. "But you don't scare off. I wish I had killed you." She arched an eyebrow. "Obviously. My sister-in-law always said that your father should have beat you more, told you who was boss. To get rid of that sharp mouth of yours."

Maeve held her gaze. "I was beaten. Every day. But not by my father. My father loved me, unlike your sister-in-law and her husband and their daughters. They never loved those girls. That's why they are the way they are now." She took a few steps, making her way farther into the kitchen, noticing the dotted Swiss curtains hanging from the kitchen window, an incongruous touch of whimsy in a house of horrors. "You took my sister and then you took those people from Mansfield."

"That's what you've got wrong," she said, fixing her rheumy eyes on Maeve. "Those people sent those kids willingly. Didn't want them back. That's why they were here."

"I don't believe you," Maeve said.

"Believe what you want." She pulled another cigarette from the pack and lit it from the flame on the stove. "They all had a proper Christian burial."

"Where you buried them is not a sanctioned cemetery. Not by any church, I would imagine," Maeve said. "Did you put holy cards in every grave?" She thought back to the cats in the garage, the holy card in the box.

Mrs. Hartwell opened her mouth, her lips pulling back from her teeth in a horrible facsimile of a smile. "Every last one. Pick up a holy card every time I go to church."

Maeve's eyes settled on the rat poison. "That?" she asked, pointing. "Is that how they died?"

"Natural causes. Every single one," the woman said, baring those teeth again in a sinister approximation of a smile. "You think you know. You think you know what happened. But you don't."

"Illuminate me," Maeve said.

"We were a family. I gave them a family. I took care of them. Sure, I needed help around here but what do you think would have happened to them after Mansfield?" She leaned in as close as she could to Maeve. "Huh? What do you think would have happened to them?"

"Did you know that there is a group that meets every week to talk about these people? To see if others have found the missing?"

Regina shrugged. "Think what you want. We were a family."

"And now they are all dead. All left in the woods," Maeve said. She didn't know what to believe but one thing she did know is that this wasn't a family. And Regina Hartwell had taken those people from their families.

In her boots, Maeve's toes had turned to ice. She thought back to the Monsignor at her local church and all of the hoops he had made her jump through—not to mention the carrot cake she had had to bestow upon him—to get him to bury Jack, someone the old priest hadn't seen within his church walls, Jack having been a communicant at the church at Buena del Sol. Technicalities. That cemetery in the woods was homemade and no one knew about it, except for maybe Michael Donner. She wondered what role, if any, he played in all of this. She pulled Winston's social security card from her back pocket. "And why this? The other ones?"

The woman's face darkened. "Where did you find that?"

Maeve stayed silent. The answer was obvious.

"You broke into my house."

"Door was open," Maeve said. "I smelled gas." That was her story and the one she would tell when she was asked how she came into possession of a social security card of a man who went missing from Mansfield and who was maybe buried in the woods in back of the house. "I was worried about you," she said, plastering a sick smile on her face. Here it goes, she thought. Here's where I start to lose it. And Rodney's not here to stop me. She pulled the gun from her pocket and pointed it at the woman.

"And the car? How will you explain that?" she asked, keeping her calm gaze on Maeve and the gun.

"Nothing to explain. Kids. Hooligans." She leveled the gun at the woman's face. "Really boring around these parts. Kids get into a lot of trouble." She took a step closer; she didn't want to miss when she finally pulled the trigger. "I'll probably bash in your mailbox on the way out just to make it look like an authentic teen job."

"Not if I tell them the truth."

Maeve smiled. "Tell who? Tell them what? And why start now?" She closed one eye, training her sights on the center of the woman's forehead. The woman wouldn't have time to tell anyone. She'd be dead and Maeve would have killed her. It was official: she was someone else now. "Where's my sister?"

"Not a clue," the woman said.

She has no soul, Maeve thought. The sight of the gun didn't even elicit a flinch. "You've got five seconds and then I'm going to kill you." Maeve knew it was a faulty gambit; she had used the five-second rule with the girls and had always failed. Using it with a hardened sociopath, someone who clearly had nothing left to lose, was going to result in failure. She felt it in her bones.

So, she would just kill her. The woman either didn't know, or wasn't going to tell Maeve where Evelyn had gone, if she was dead, so she served no purpose on this earth any longer, as far as Maeve was concerned.

To Maeve's right, a figure appeared in the door that led from the kitchen to the living room. A man, holding a kitten, was in the doorframe, crying copious tears. "I told you that if you kill the mama, the babies will die!" he said, holding the kitten in his hands forward, its lifeless head lolling to one side, as proof of his theory. "Now this one is dead!"

Regina looked at the man, clad in jeans and a white T-shirt, and threw a dismissive hand in his direction. She looked back at Maeve. "Big help around the house but really annoying when it comes to strays."

Maeve walked toward the man, his distress over the dead kitten leading to a high- pitched wail. She studied his face. "Winston?"

He looked at her, his face weathered, lined. Wet. "I'm not allowed to talk to strangers," he said.

Maeve wasn't sure what she was seeing, if she could trust herself. Her mind went back to that day in the barn. She looked from the old woman to the man, the cat lolling listlessly in his big, rough hand. "You buried those cats in the barn. Why?"

Mrs. Hartwell snorted. "That was Winston. He didn't want them to be outside. Like the others."

Maeve wasn't sure if she meant other stray animals or the people who were buried in the woods.

Regina Hartwell's shoulders slumped a bit. "I guess he can bury that one, too."

Maeve turned and looked at Mrs. Hartwell. "Here's what's going to happen. I'm going to take Winston and bring him somewhere safe." Maeve could only imagine what would happen when Winston's aging body gave out and his usefulness to the Hartwell house had come to an end. While she wanted to believe that the others had died natural deaths, like Regina claimed, she couldn't. "Winston, please wait for me by the front door."

"He won't go with you," Mrs. Hartwell said, sure of it. "He only listens to me."

Maeve turned to him. "I knew your mother, Winston. She loved you very much and wanted only the best for you."

He looked at her, confused. "My mama is dead."

She is now, Maeve thought, but she wondered how long ago he had been told that she had died. It had been years, if she had to guess. She looked at Mrs. Hartwell. "I'm going to take Winston somewhere safe, get him checked out. And then I'm going to come back with the police. And deal with you." The old woman had no car. She lived in the middle of nowhere. There was no way for her to leave. Maeve spied the woman's cell phone on the table and grabbed it, throwing it to the floor and crushing it with her boot.

Something changed on Regina Hartwell's face, something that indicated that she was done. Done with Maeve, done with Winston, done with the life that was leaving her every day, if the cough and the pallor and the oxygen canisters were any indication. She looked at Maeve as she turned the stove on again, all four burners, this time not igniting the flames. She grabbed a box of matches from the counter.

Maeve looked at Winston. "Run, Winston!" she said as the old woman attempted to light a match to throw onto the stove. Her hands were shaking, making it difficult to get the proper angle and force to get first one, and then the next four matches to light. Maeve didn't want to wait and see if the fifth one would be the charm, so she pushed Winston toward the front door, the dead kitten flying from his hands and onto a stack of newspapers. He was confused but he did what Maeve said. She ran past the piles in the living room to the room behind the fireplace and, needing something, anything, to prove the horrors this house had harbored, she grabbed the box of social security cards from the desk drawer, along with every file she could carry. She ran toward the front door, using her body to ram him out onto the porch and down the steps, ice having formed as the sun went down and the temperature dropped, the two of them rolling down the few short steps and onto the front lawn. Maeve dragged him up by the collar of his T-shirt and pulled him behind her, finally getting to the street. On the driving pad, the car was smoldering, most of the fire and flames having turned to black smoke, plumes curling up into the air and disappearing into the black night.

Good. She'd kill herself, Maeve thought. Now I don't have to do it. She was relieved at that thought.

The house blew up in spectacular fashion just as she reached the Prius with Francine Alderson's son in tow.

CHAPTER 51

Maeve called Cal while she was driving, her hands shaking. It took her four tries to say his contact information to her phone, her voice not sounding like her own. She put the phone on speaker because the Bluetooth wouldn't work at the same time as the radio, the music coming from her speakers seeming to calm down the man next to her. "You need to help me. I'll explain later," she said, as she drove like a bat out of hell away from the house, Winston in the passenger seat crying and repeating that he wasn't allowed to talk to strangers. Or drive in their cars. Or go anywhere without Regina. He was cold. He didn't know Maeve. She turned to him. "Do you like music, Winston?"

He nodded, shivering in his shirt sleeves. If she had to guess, he was a little older than she was, but the years of living in the Hartwell house had taken their toll. He looked like an old man, his hair long and unkempt, his teeth missing in a few places.

"What kind of music do you like?" she asked.

Cal was confused. "Who are you talking to?"

"Winston," she said, but that didn't really offer any indication of who the man was or why he was in the car. "Cal, find me the address of the nearest social services office, or child protective services or something like that. And then I need you to walk me through the directions."

Winston snuffled loudly. "I like music."

Maeve turned the radio up. The song that the girls had been sing-ing on New Year's Eve—the one that got stuck in her head and wouldn't let go—was playing. Maeve adjusted the heat so that it was blowing hot air directly at the shivering man.

"Cal, you're going to have to speak loudly because I've got music playing."

"I can hear it. And you're going to tell me what's going on, right?" he asked. "So I don't worry?"

"Nothing to worry about," she said. "Everything is fine." Next to her, Winston had warmed up a little bit but had listed to one side of the seat, his head resting on the window, singing a song different from the one on the radio, to himself. It was "London Bridge."

Cal worked the computer while Maeve drove into the town, pass-ing the fancy restaurants and shops, and finally, pulling over to get the information she needed. Before she went back to Cal, she turned to Winston. Her thoughts were jagged and disjointed, and when she started talking, she hardly made sense even to herself. "Winston, a girl. Maybe who looked like me. Was she there?" she asked. "Did you know someone named Evelyn?"

But she had lost Winston, alone with his thoughts, protecting himself from the conflict that he had seen in the house between Maeve and Regina, the carnage that ensued after they escaped.

"You're close," Cal said. "If you're in town, head toward County Road 214 and then hang a right. You should see a brick building on the right after a mile or two. It's the municipal building and houses the police station and a host of other offices, including social services for the county." Before he hung up, he asked her a question. "Do I want to know what you're doing?"

Same old Cal. In for a penny but not for a pound. "No. You don't."

She thanked him for his help and hung up. His directions had been very clear and she found the town's municipal building within minutes.

Winston had fallen asleep and Maeve shook him awake. "I miss Regina," he said, when he woke up. "Will she be here?"

She was the only person he had known for the past few decades, so he didn't know that he didn't have to miss her, that she had kept him from his mother. Maeve took his hand and led him into the building, walking down the long hall until she found a door with a sign etched into the glass indicating that she had found the social services arm of the municipality of Rhineview.

A pleasant-looking woman, chubby and bespectacled, sat at the reception desk. Behind her was an office, its door closed, where one of the social workers sat. "Can I help you?"

"Yes," Maeve said.

The woman finally focused on the duo in front of her, the petite woman with the wild look in her eyes and the disheveled ponytail and the slightly older man who was rocking in place, not wearing a coat, and somewhat disoriented. She stood.

"May we see the person in charge?" Maeve asked. "The head of social services or whoever is someone that can help me? And this gentleman?" Winston needed a doctor; Maeve was sure of that. Beyond that, she wasn't sure what to ask for on his behalf.

The woman looked alarmed. "Well, yes." As she said that, the door to the office behind her opened and a tall man came out, looking more than a little surprised to see Maeve and not hiding his shock at seeing Winston. The woman pointed to the man. "Mr. Donner here will be happy to help you."

Maeve backed away from the high desk that separated her from the two people who worked in the department. In her panic, she had forgotten about him and the fact that he worked in social services. But the look on his face—guilt mixed with confusion—let her know that this wasn't going to turn out well, that he had a hand in what had gone on at that house. It was written all over his face.

Donner looked concerned at her presence as well, at seeing Winston outside of his sister-in-law's house. Maeve could tell that underneath the calm façade, a panic was brewing and he was feeling trapped. His eyes darted from Maeve to Winston and back again, his receptionist looking at all three of them with confusion.

"Mr. Donner?" she said. "This woman . . ."

"Yes, Kathy. Thank you," he said. Maeve felt the seconds ticking off in her brain as she anticipated his next move. Would he play it cool and bring them into his office or would he dismiss her and the man she had brought in, unwilling or unable to help? Would he call the police and have her arrested? The gun felt hot in her pocket even though she knew it wasn't.

"This is a problem, Miss Conlon," he said. "If you'll excuse me, I need to see my director about how to handle this situation." He pushed open the half-door that separated the reception area from the office and walked out of the office at a pace that suggested to Maeve that he was leaving.

Maeve looked at the receptionist. "He's not coming back," she said.

"Of course he is," she said, the smile still on her face even though it was clear she was puzzled by her boss's behavior.

After twenty minutes, Maeve asked if they could see someone else. "He's not coming back," she said to the receptionist again.

Eventually, Maeve and Winston were led to the office of a less-twitchy social worker and then joined by a state police officer; Maeve had requested that the state police be called and the social worker had acquiesced, even though she wasn't sure why Maeve would have a preference. This officer was a woman and, along with the female social worker, she asked questions about how Maeve had come to gain custody of a man no one really knew had been missing. Maeve handed over the files she had gathered, the box of social security cards. After the social worker took Winston out of the office and down the hall to get him a coat from the piles in the lost-and-found, Maeve turned to the female officer, a no-nonsense woman named Detective Fahnestock.

"There are graves. With crosses."

"Where?" the woman asked, her eyes narrowing.

"Behind the house. In the woods." Maeve had been sitting on the edge of the chair across from the social worker's desk, every nerve ending on high alert. With the revelation of the graves, and the recollection of what they looked like, how they were spaced, she sank back into the chair.

"What's your connection to this, Ms. Conlon?" the detective asked.

She put a hand to her head and closed her eyes, reminding herself. She had almost forgotten what it was, the events of the past several hours, the past several days, clouding her thoughts. She recited the words that she had said a few times out loud but that she also said every night before she went to sleep.

"I had a sister. Her name was Aibhlinn," she said. "It means 'longed-for child.'"

The detective asked a question that Maeve hadn't considered until this very moment, and the thought of it, that she had overlooked this one important detail, made her sick to think about.

"Was there anyone else in the house?"

CHAPTER 52

Detective Fahnestock kept Maeve in the office while she sent a team of detectives from the state police to the house in the middle of nowhere and they confirmed what Maeve had told them: the car had been set on fire and was burned away, the house had blown up because of Regina Hartwell. There were graves in the woods.

The detective called Cal and he confirmed everything that Maeve had told them as well: she had a sister and she was looking for her.

"When will we know?" she asked the detective. "If there was anyone else in the house?"

The detective knew why she was asking but was honest with her. "These things take a long time, usually. I'm not sure. I'll work with the fire investigation team and see if we can't get an answer sooner rather than later."

"Do I need a lawyer?" Maeve asked. She had a lawyer but he was a bit of a sissy. She didn't tell the detective that.

The detective considered that question. "I don't think you do, Miss Conlon, but I also think I will have more questions for you." She had deep brown eyes framed by long black lashes and perfect eyebrows; maybe she had the app that helped you shape them just so? "I don't know why I believe you, but I do." She gave Maeve the

once-over. "Tell me your story one more time, please," she said, study-ing Maeve's face and her notes as Maeve recounted it one more time, looking for inconsistencies. There weren't any. When Maeve was done, the detective was silent for a few moments. "I guess if I had a missing sibling, I would stop at nothing to find her, too," she said finally.

Maeve had left out the more violent parts of the story and the fact that she was carrying an unlicensed gun; had she told the detective some of those additional details, the woman wouldn't have felt as sympathetic toward her. But Maeve didn't have to fake sincerity when a few tears spilled from her eyes. "Thank you."

When they were in the hallway, Maeve turned to the detective again. "What will happen to Winston?"

"We'll bring someone in from the state to be with him during questioning and then find a proper home for him." Detective Fahne-stock put a hand on Maeve's shoulder. "Don't worry. We'll make sure he's taken care of this time."

"There's one more thing," Maeve said, explaining about her new friends from the support group and how they got together to heal the wounds that were left by the idea of their missing relatives. "Will you tell them? Will someone tell them?"

The detective nodded. "We will."

She went back to the car and sat there for a few minutes, hunch-ing down low when a Rhineview police car drove by. She didn't know if it was Regina Hartwell's son or just some random local cop but the sight of the car made her more aware that she had to get out of this town as soon as possible. While she drove, she thought about what had happened. Just knowing that Eileen Mackin's card was in the box that Maeve turned over and that her dead body was now bur-ied in a shallow grave in the woods behind the burned-down Hart-well house filled her with sadness.

She banged the steering wheel, hard. Her hands ached but she

had to release some of what she was feeling. "Please, God. Please let her not have been in there," she said. "I can't take any more."

Her sadness eventually turned to a white-hot anger and she knew where she was headed next.

She didn't call Rodney Poole this time to let him know that she would be visiting Margie Haggerty in her office in the Bronx. She didn't want to be deterred from what she was going to do, which was get to the bottom of this once and for all.

She is really messing up a good thing.

Those were some of the last words Regina Hartwell had spoken before she had blown up her house and, with it, the evil that had resided there.

She had known everything all along. Maeve's suspicions about her old neighbor had been correct. She was rotten to the core, just like every other person who had lived in that house on her street. But why she had doled out information in little spoonfuls, making Maeve run around, making her feel the things she did, made Maeve rage.

So, while Detective Fahnestock and her staff combed the woods behind the Hartwell house looking for the white crosses posted on the shallow graves, the remains beneath the ground, Maeve drove, her hand intermittently caressing the gun that was in the pocket of her pink coat.

The IHOP lot was full so she drove around for a half hour looking for a spot. It was times like these that she gave thanks for her suburban life, the little parking pad at the side of her house that was so narrow that it forced her to squeeze in and out of her car, but it was hers nonetheless. That little strip allowed her to stow her car when the plows came by during snowstorms or when her neighbors had parties that required their guests to park on the street.

Four blocks over from Margie's office, she squeezed the Prius in between a huge van and a motorcycle, bumping the fenders of both

in the process, hoping the owners were far away and couldn't see her. She had hoped the walk to Margie's office would help her calm down, but with each step she took, the cold from her toes now spreading to her feet and ankles, she became more incensed.

Margie had played her. For what purpose, Maeve wasn't sure, but she had been played. Had she ever wanted to help Maeve find her sister, or was this just another sick, cruel game that Margie—the daughter of sick and cruel people herself—had concocted to make Maeve, who the sisters apparently harbored ill will toward, even all these years later, suffer more than she had? Their father had taken her mother's life and her father had died sick and broken, a widower for the better part of his adult life. Did they really need a pound of flesh from the only remaining Conlon on the planet?

She decided that they did. And that fueled her rage even more.

It was late and the other office on the floor was dark. Margie was still in her office but the front door was locked; Maeve could hear her talking on the phone. When she didn't answer Maeve's knock or maybe when she heard Maeve call her name, she stopped talking. Pretended she wasn't in there. Maeve took the gun out of her pocket and, protecting her hand with the sleeve of the pink coat, smashed the window that identified the office behind the door as MHK Law. She leaned in, found the deadbolt, and unlocked the door, letting herself in.

She looked around the room. "Margie, you've done so much with the place," she said, noticing that it was even more cluttered and messy since the last time she had been there, if that was possible. "Bad housekeeping runs in the family, I see."

Margie hung up the phone in her hand as Maeve came around the partition. "Was that Michael Donner?" she asked.

Margie stared back at her, her hands beneath the desk. "No, Maeve. This is a place of business," she said. "I talk to a lot of people throughout the day."

"Put your hands on the desk where I can see them, Margie," Maeve said, her gun in a safe place in her coat pocket, her finger on the trigger. She was ready.

Margie complied, and when she rested her hands on a stack of file folders, Maeve noticed that they were shaking again. When Maeve was around, they always seemed to be.

Maeve sat down across from her. "So, I've come up with a few theories on my drive down here. Tell me if I'm correct." She added an additional request. "And please don't lie to me, Margie, because I am so, so tired, and I've got this buzzing in my ears that usually means I do things that I normally wouldn't do." She smiled. "In your case, I can't even imagine what it might be, but trust me: neither of us wants to find out."

Margie licked her lips and scratched a space over her eyebrow until it turned bright red. "What do you want to know?"

"Everything," Maeve said. "Seems like your beloved aunt had taken some children from that home and kept them as prisoners in her house."

"They weren't prisoners," Margie said. "She took care of them."

"Tell yourself that, Margie, if it makes you feel any better, but they are all dead, with the exception of one." She watched Margie rub the spot over and over. "And if one of them is my sister, I'm not sure what I'm going to do," she said, and it was the truth.

Margie's face didn't give anything away, but if Maeve had to guess, Margie knew that they were dead.

Maeve continued. "She had their social security cards and a hook with a guy in social services. Her brother-in-law. That's all I can fig-ure out right now. Help me with the rest."

That brought a look of surprise to the woman's face.

"Yes. Michael Donner. I brought Winston in so that someone real and good could take care of him and you know what the guy did?" Maeve laughed out loud at the memory of the tall man in the blue suit leaving the office at the Rhineview municipal building. "He ran! Like a scared kid." Maeve inched closer on the chair. "So, the police are now at his house or his apartment or wherever he lives and they are getting evidence." She thought for a moment. "How did it work? She killed them and he pretended to check on them and let everyone know that they were still alive? She collected benefits?"

Margie didn't dispute that theory.

"He must have gotten a cut," Maeve said, thinking about how a plan like that might work. "They were in business together." Her mind drifted in a few different directions for a few minutes. "And where do you fit in, Margie?"

Margie had fallen mute, so Maeve pulled out the gun and pointed it at her.

"Stop it, Maeve," she said. "Stop." Her hands went to a space under her desk.

Maeve stood. "Margie, hands where I can see them," Maeve said. She sat back down, her bloodlust taking a backseat to a dull feeling that started in her stomach and rose to the back of her throat. "And me? Why did you help me?" she said, although the word "help" was a little generous in this case.

Margie shrugged, crying. "I wanted to help you find out if your sister was there. . . ."

"Was she ever?" Maeve asked, holding her breath.

"I don't know. But I thought that maybe I could help you find her. That maybe my aunt would help. She's a sociopath, Maeve," Margie said. "I know that now."

Maeve knew a thing or two about sociopaths. "I thought you hadn't seen her since you were little?"

"When Dolores told you about your sister, I tried to blackmail her into helping you. I wanted to make things right again." Margie held her hands out. "I'm not like those people. The people in my family."

"That is hard for me to believe, Margie." Maeve relaxed a little, taking in Margie's terrified face, her shaking hands. "You should have turned her in."

Margie looked surprised. "You don't turn against family."

And there it was, the root of all of the problems with the Haggertys. They didn't turn on family even when they knew that certain members were up to no good, making the lives of others a living hell. Before all of this had happened, Maeve had seen Margie, who had spoken ill of her own sister, something Maeve reminded her of now. "Why the family devotion all of a sudden? Especially to Dolores?"

"She's my sister. We've gotten closer since she became a widow."

"That's beautiful, Margie," Maeve said. She looked around the office. "You can't make this stuff up."

Margie fingered a stack of papers on her desk, avoiding Maeve's gaze. "I never meant to hurt you, for this to happen."

A sudden realization dawned on Maeve. "You are just really, really stupid," she said. What other explanation could there be for the woman sitting in front of her to hatch a plan like this? Maeve counted off the transgressions on the hand not holding the gun. "You withheld from me that I had a sister. You sent me to see your aunt, who you didn't tell me was a relative, to get information she was never going to give me." Maeve stood and walked around the office, the little space she could navigate, and gathered her thoughts. "You knew that she was awful. A 'sociopath.' This whole situation defies comprehension." She bit her lip, thinking. "I'm not entirely sure what I'm supposed to do with you, Margie."

In the front of the office, Maeve heard shoes crunching on the broken glass. Rodney Poole appeared around the partition, taking in Margie's terrified expression and Maeve's wild-eyed visage, the gun. "We need to leave, Maeve Conlon," he said, taking the gun from her hand. He looked at Margie. "This never happened," he said, waving a hand around the room. "She was never here."

Margie tried on a look of defiance that really didn't suit her; she was incapable, it seemed, of really having a backbone. "Or what?" she asked.

Poole studied her face. "Do we really need to get into that, Haggerty?" He put Maeve's gun in his pocket. "Let's put it this way: still a lot of cops on the force, around these parts, who would rather see you dead than help you one iota. That's just the way it is."

"Are you sure about that?" she asked, giving her stoic resolve one last try.

"I'm positive," he said. He mentioned a name that wasn't familiar to Maeve but which Margie seemed to know. "Just ask Ramona Ortiz. Oh, that's right, you can't. She's dead."

Margie's face turned in on itself, like an ice sculpture that was melting and then collapsed into a pool of water on the floor. "That wasn't my fault."

"I guess it wasn't," Rodney said, but the damage was done. "You ruined her life, she took her own. Seems to run in your family, that kind of behavior. Life has a funny way of coming full circle, though, doesn't it?" He took Maeve's hand and led her to the front of the office.

Out on the street, he reached into his pocket, and without anyone passing by being the wiser, he slid the gun from his coat pocket into hers. "This been discharged?" he asked.

"It's clean," she said.

"Good," he said. "Keep it that way. Unless you have no other choice."

CHAPTER 53

Maeve opened the store the following Wednesday, happy to be back in the routine of making scones, quiches, and cakes, channeling her sadness into creating beautiful things that people loved to eat. Jo's stream-of-consciousness monologues helped the days pass and she was grateful to hear more than she ever wanted to know about how one birthed a baby in the twenty-first century, her children having been born in the old twentieth century when epidurals and pain meds were still thought to be acceptable accompaniments to the painful process of delivering a child.

Jo was going to go "all natural," she said, adding "until it gets really painful."

Maeve had news for her: there was no area between "painful" and "really painful" when it came to childbirth. It all hurt, a lot, and all the time. Even after the baby was out, if her own daughters were any indication.

Jo was still determined to try every culinary item from the "Best of Westchester" issue of the local magazine, naming for Maeve all of the places they hadn't been. Maeve was exhausted just thinking about it.

Chris Larsson occupied the nights between her last trip to Rhine-

view and the opening of the store, his uncomplicated brand of wooing her just the salve she needed to heal her wounds, make her forget
the pain she had been witness to. She told him only what he needed to
know: that she had confronted Mrs. Hartwell, that the woman had
responded by blowing up her house. That she had found Winston.
That she knew now what happened to some of the Mansfield Missing.

"And your sister?" he asked one afternoon when they were in his
bed, soft sunlight coming in through the window, his long arms
wrapped around her body, his face in her hair.

"I don't know," she said. She still didn't know if anyone else had
been in the house, if other bones had been found, but she couldn't
admit any of that to him. It was too good, what they had. She wanted
it to last, if only for a little while.

She tried to hold on to the fact that Margie didn't think Evelyn
had ever lived there, but even if that was the case, the idea that she had
been responsible for an innocent person's death stayed with her.

Maeve scanned the papers and the Internet every day for the
stories related to what had happened up in Rhineview, her name
mysteriously missing from any mention of the investigation or
the missing man. She had asked Detective Fahnestock if that would
be possible, and apparently the woman had bent to Maeve's wishes,
a call from Chris probably helping secure her identity as "unidenti-
fied woman from downstate." She was grateful for the courtesies
cops showed each other, showed her as a cop's daughter.

A few days after she had seen what Regina Hartwell was capable of, saw her blow up her own house, Maeve was icing a cake when
Detective Fahnestock showed up at the bakery unannounced, a small
bag in her hand. Jo let her in, holding open the swinging door to the
kitchen and staying just long enough to hear that the detective wanted
a DNA sample from Maeve.

"I need a DNA sample from you, Miss Conlon."

Maeve put down the piping bag that she had been using to dot

florets around a chocolate cake, a beautiful, multi-layered concoc-
tion that would fetch close to thirty dollars. "What is it?"

The detective cut to the chase and didn't give Maeve a chance to
steel herself for the news that was going to shake her to her core.
"There were two sets of bones found in the rubble," she said. "The
medical examiner is looking at them now to determine who they
might belong to, if the person was even alive when the house
blew up."

"Female?"

"Hard to tell at this point," she said, pausing, "but most likely."

The next morning, she could still feel the scrape of the cotton
swab on the inside of her cheek, a reminder of her visit from the female detective. Of the news she brought. Maeve hadn't eaten a bite
since that moment, drinking only when she felt a dire thirst, her
parched throat reminding her that she was getting dehydrated.

Was there anyone else in the house? The detective's words rang
in her ears, every one an indictment of Maeve's impulsiveness, her
drive to make Regina Hartwell tell the truth.

That afternoon, after Maeve had sent Jo to the store to buy
butter, she asked both girls to come to the bakery and sat them down
in the kitchen area. They had been helping out that morning, though
Maeve hadn't uttered a word to either one of them. Finally, she found
her voice again and peppered them with questions. She had solved
one mystery; time to solve another. She left off the nice preamble,
going straight to the one question that she needed an answer to:
"Who was in my bedroom and why did a check for three grand go
missing?"

They were liars, both of them, and it was written all over their
faces. In the front of the store, the bell over the door rang and Maeve
went through to wait on the new customer.

"Get your story straight. I want the truth when I come back,"
she said before she left.

When she came back into the kitchen, they were still sitting there, looking as if they hadn't moved or spoken the whole time. "So?" she asked.

Rebecca was the mouthpiece. "We don't know, Mom."

"Where's the money from your accounts?" Maeve asked Rebecca. "And don't tell me you put it toward your tuition because I've already been on the account on the Web site and we're all paid up."

Rebecca wasn't a liar; she hadn't inherited the finely honed art of deception from her mother. "Fine," Rebecca said. "I spent it. I spent every last dime. I didn't eat in the dining hall, I partied, I treated my friends to dinner. We went to New York City. I rented a hotel room."

Heather looked at her, stunned. She was not used to seeing her sibling in the role of the less-than-perfect older sister.

"And shoes?" Maeve asked.

"Not too many, but yes, I bought some shoes," Rebecca said.

Maeve studied both of them, sitting quietly on the high stools that framed the butcher-block counter in the middle of the kitchen. Heather's hair was pulled back in a tight ponytail that she kept grabbing and smoothing with trembling hands.

Maeve looked down at her hands and saw the pulse in her wrist jumping out of her skin. After a few minutes, she looked at her daughters and gave Rebecca, her face pale and her own hands shaking, a hard look. But Maeve was honest; she was a bit out of her league on this one. "I don't know quite what to do right now, Rebecca, but I would like you to leave my sight, immediately."

The girls shared a look that Maeve couldn't decipher.

"Please go home."

Rebecca opened her mouth to speak.

Maeve held up a hand. "Please. Before I say or do something that I will regret."

Right at that moment Jo walked in the back door and put the butter in the refrigerator, chatting aimlessly about the store, who she saw, what a bitch the cashier had been to her, why she hated going on these runs for Maeve. She closed the refrigerator door and turned around, finally taking in the stunned faces of the Callahan girls and Maeve's own florid one. "What happened here?" she asked. "What did I miss?"

"Nothing," Maeve said. "Rebecca was just leaving."

Heather asked if she could go, too.

Maeve waved a hand in her direction. "Certainly. Go." As the door to the kitchen slammed behind them, Maeve called out, "Clean your rooms! Go to church! Feed some orphans! Stay out of trouble!"

Jo looked at her for an explanation.

"You don't want to know."

It was only minutes before closing when the bell over the door jingled for what would be the last time that day. She and Jo were deep into their closing routine, Maeve wiping the counters with a focused ferocity. When she was done, they gleamed. With the girls out of the store and wandering the streets of Farringville proclaiming the evilness that was their mother, most likely, she was happy to have an outlet for her stress.

"A little help, please?" the woman at the counter said.

Maeve turned at the sound of her voice, her words slurring and blurring together into one barely intelligible sentence. Maeve hoped she hadn't driven here herself.

"Hello, Dolores," she said, asking Jo to go into the kitchen. "What brings you here?"

"Where's my sister?" she said. Today, her auburn hair was freshly coiffed, her makeup artfully applied. It was only the crooked line of lipstick on her bottom lip that indicated that she was a little tipsy.

"Your sister?" Maeve asked. "Is she missing?"

Jo walked out briefly and tossed a bundle on the counter before returning to the kitchen. "Mail's here."

"Yes," Dolores said, leaning in. Maeve caught a whiff of something medicinal, vodka maybe, covered over by a strong breath mint. Oldest trick in the book, she thought.

"I don't know," Maeve said.

"Wasn't she helping you find your sister?" Dolores asked. Behind her, the clock clicked to four, and Maeve came out from behind the counter to turn the OPEN sign to CLOSED. No reason why her regular customers, the nice people who shopped here, needed to see this.

" 'Help,' Dolores, is a very loose term," Maeve said. "Listen, I'm closing. What do you want?"

Dolores surprised her by softening just enough to let a few tears spill from her eyes, the tears taking rivulets of black mascara along for the ride. "I miss her. I need my sister."

"That's rich, Dolores," Maeve said. "You want me to pity you for losing a sister." Maybe Margie, like Michael Donner, was in the wind, never to be seen again. "Forgive me, Dolores, if I don't feel a whit of sympathy for you," Maeve said, but deep down, if she had to admit it, she did feel a twinge of sadness for two lives that seemed to have seen hardly a moment of happiness. Those girls had never stood a chance in that household. Dolores had been right all along: Maeve had always thought she was better than them, what with her doting father and her cupcake making. She was never hit—at least by Jack— and he told her often that she was perfect. That he loved her. And that counted for a lot, made some of the hurt go away. She found herself welling up, thinking of what it must have been like to hear how fat and dumb, how useless, you were every single day of your life. It was almost worse than physical abuse.

Almost.

"I don't know what happened to Margie," Maeve said, softening her tone. "I'm sorry, Dolores. I hope you find her."

Seemed that Margie had been smart enough to hit the road. The jig was up, as Jack used to say, and the handwriting was on the wall. If she stayed around, she might be arrested and sent to jail for knowing what she knew and keeping it to herself. Her life, as she knew it, would be over and even though she hadn't been sent to jail for her role in the chain-of-custody case, or responsible for the other woman's suicide—someone she had brought down with her—this time, she'd be done for.

Hit the road. That was the answer. Where had she gone?

Not my problem, Maeve thought. Not my concern.

Dolores looked at her. "I've got no one, Maeve."

Welcome to the club.

"My husband is dead."

Good riddance.

"My kids never come around."

Wonder why?

"And now my sister has left. It's not fair!"

Life rarely is.

When she saw that she was getting nowhere, she turned. "I don't ever want to see you again, Maeve Conlon."

The feeling is mutual.

Dolores exited the store quickly, stepping out onto the sidewalk, not seeing the red car that zoomed into the parking lot, missing her by inches.

"Careful," Maeve said to the empty store. "Those red cars will get you every time. Ask your father when you see him in hell," she said, because it was a red car that had taken her mother's life.

She looked through the mail. Bills, flyers, magazines. And a postcard. She looked at the front; it was a photo of the White House. And on the back were three words.

I am sorry.

Margie Haggerty, it seemed, was heading south.

CHAPTER 54

That night, she followed Jimmy Moriarty from Buena del Sol to a rib place in town.

She got out of the car and walked across the parking lot, peering in the window and finding Moriarty sitting at the small bar in the front, drinking, oddly enough, a very pale glass of white wine. Sauvignon Blanc, if she had to guess.

She walked into the restaurant and was immediately accosted by the overzealous hostess, who she bypassed for a seat next to Jack's old friend. He stared straight ahead, even though he knew she was there.

"I bet your father never told you that he once saved my life," he said, taking a dainty sip of his wine. He motioned to the bartender to bring Maeve one, too. She settled onto a stool and stashed her bag at her feet.

"Saved your life? How, Jimmy? I didn't even know you knew each other before Buena del Sol. My father never mentioned that. You never mentioned it."

"He didn't remember sometimes. Sometimes he did."

"And you?" she asked.

"I guess it never came up, huh, Maeve?" he said. "How often have we really seen each other?"

Not a lot. But it was something that he should have told, she should have known. "So, how did he save your life?" she asked.

"Chasing a perp. It was bad in those days, back in the seventies. Streets were horrible," he said, his eyes not on her but looking down the barrel of the past. "Your father and I were together only once, on this thing. Didn't see him again until I moved into Buena del Sol."

She thanked the bartender for her wine, pushing the menu she was offered to the side.

"Perp had just sold a big bag of dope to an undercover but that guy couldn't reveal himself so we went in after him. Up eight flights of stairs. He made us on the fourth flight, I think." He looked over at Maeve. "You should look at the menu. The fried pickles . . ."

"I know," she said, holding up her hand. "They're delicious. And fattening."

He smiled. "Eat the fried pickles, Maeve. You've only got one life to live."

She wanted him to go back to the story. It took another glass of wine to get him started again. "We ended up on the eighth floor and the guy went out the door but I didn't see which one, so I ran the length of the hall and to the door at the far end when your father screamed my name."

Maeve had never heard this story so she didn't know how it ended or any of the intervening details.

"The door was to the fire escape. It was pitch black out. Someone had removed the floor grates so that anyone who ran out there would just fall through, all eight flights." He went back to looking straight ahead. "If your father hadn't called my name, I would have run out there, gone through the floor, broken every bone in my body. Probably would have died."

"How did he know?" Maeve asked. "That there was no floor?"

He turned back to her; she could see it in his eyes that all these years later, the entire story, though true, mystified him. "I don't know. And neither did he. He said he never even remembered calling my name."

She tilted her head; had she heard him right? "Well, that's impossible, Jimmy."

"I'm just telling you what happened."

It was another Jack story, burnished gold and only partially true through years of the embellishment of retelling.

"I was there, Maeve. It happened to me."

"So, Jack had ESP? What?" she asked. She was not really a believer when it came to things unexplained. There was always an explanation, always a reason.

"He said your mother told him," he said. "And she had been dead over a year at that point."

She had to bite her lip so that she wouldn't laugh. The guy was so intent on telling her this remarkable story, a story that he believed with all of his heart, that she couldn't disrespect it and him. Jesus, Jimmy. Do you really expect me to believe that? she thought but didn't ask.

"I don't expect you to believe me, Maeve," he said, seeming to read her mind.

"Why are you telling me this now?" she asked.

He chose his words carefully. "I just wanted you to know why I loved your dad like a brother."

They sipped their wine without talking, her rumbling stomach breaking the silence. She ordered a plate of ribs and some fried pickles. When it came, she pushed the plate toward him. "Here. I can't eat all of this."

"Sure you can," he said even as he helped himself to a rib and a pickle, putting them on the small plate the server had given them for sharing.

If she closed her eyes and imagined a time long ago, it was almost like sitting with Jack. But then, she'd open her eyes and see that she was just with another sad old guy who longed for his younger days, when he was on his own, when danger was a daily part of his life, and when he didn't have to answer to anyone at an assisted-living facility that sometimes treated its residents like children.

She noticed that even though they talked the entire time they ate, he never asked once about her sister, if she had found her. She found that strange and unsettling.

"Are you my sister's guardian, Jimmy?" she asked. It was worth a try. If Evelyn was alive, she had a guardian; she couldn't think of anyone Jack trusted more than Jimmy Moriarty.

"No, Maeve," he said sadly. "I do not have guardianship of anyone." He chuckled, to break the mood, relieve her of the pained look on her face. "I can barely take care of myself! Just ask Charlene Harrison."

She grabbed his arm, held on tight. "Jimmy, please. I've got nothing here, no one left besides my daughters."

"And they should be enough, Maeve." It was an admonishment, one she didn't take kindly to. "Take care of them. Love them. They'll be big soon and they'll go away."

"And that's why I need my sister."

"I don't know anything about a sister, Maeve," he said, but he couldn't look at her when he said it. He let out a rattling cough, one that seemed to start in his toes. Maeve asked the bartender for some water. She put her hand on his back to steady him. She had pushed him far enough.

"That's some cough, Jimmy."

"Yeah," he said. "Seeing the doctor tomorrow."

"Let me know what he says." She traced her finger around the bottom of her glass. "Did you give me that photo album, Jimmy?"

He considered his answer for a long time. "Yes, Maeve. I gave you that photo album."

"Thank you." She felt a sadness come over her, thinking that if she didn't get answers from him now, she might never. "She'd be in her fifties now. I wonder if she's short, like me." She went in for the kill. "I wonder if she's happy." I wonder if she's alive, she thought, but left that out.

His face gave nothing away.

She got up, threw some money on the bar for the drinks and their shared dinner and leaned in, giving him a hug. He smelled like Jack. He talked like Jack. He dressed like Jack. But he wasn't Jack and as hard as she tried to imagine that he was, she knew the truth.

He knew the truth as well, but it was a different truth.

She walked to the car, her purse weighted down by the gun, and allowed herself just one little sob before she got in and drove home.

CHAPTER 55

Cal showed up shortly after she got home with a lockset for the powder room door. It wasn't a moment too soon: Heather had been locked in there that morning and had almost broken her leg—according to her—jumping out the window over the toilet.

Maeve was still waiting to hear from Detective Fahnestock about the identity of the bones that had been found, if they had belonged to a female. The waiting was killing her. No amount of affection or comfort from Chris Larsson could take away the knot in her stomach, the pain in her heart.

Cal was fiddling with the lockset and the girls were now at Mickey's. After a prolonged protest about the lack of food in the house, Maeve had sent them to Mickey's with fifty dollars and a promise that they would bring her the change. It was walking distance; she had seen Rebecca's driving skills first hand and had not been impressed.

Cal knew the whole story and listened intently. "I hope it wasn't her, Maeve," he said.

Another massive understatement from her clueless ex. "Me, too, Cal."

Cal was wearing a tool belt, something almost as incongruous as the time Maeve had seen Gabriela wearing sweatpants. "A tool belt?" she asked. "Is this a job that requires multiple tools?"

Cal had never been the handy sort so Maeve was surprised he had any tools, let alone a tool belt. He studied the lockset and pulled out a long page of directions. She pulled out some cupcakes; he looked like he would need sustenance for the job. He fiddled with the pieces for a while and started to assemble the doorknob and its component parts. After a half hour, two cupcakes, and a prolonged spate of profanity, he instructed Maeve to go into the bathroom.

From her perch on the toilet seat, she continued her conversation with him. "So, not a dime to Rebecca this semester. She can eat in the dining hall and scrounge up old ChapSticks and use those before she gets another cent from either one of us."

"Uh-huh," Cal said, focused on his task.

"Twenty-five hundred dollars," she said, shaking her head.

"Yep." He clicked something into place. "Try it now."

The room was so small that she could sit on the closed toilet lid and touch the handle. She jiggled it, attempting to let herself out. "Doesn't work." She looked around the bathroom. She needed to give the girls a list of things they needed to do in her absence; she was tired of being the only person in the house who noticed when they were out of toilet paper and when they needed to clean out the shower drain upstairs. Two girls with long hair equaled lots of potential plumbing problems. She would leave a toothbrush beside the list; the grout around the sink was in desperate need of a cleaning and who better than her lazy daughters?

Beyond the bathroom door, she heard Cal grunting and groaning, the strain of replacing the doorknob far greater than she would have imagined. He called in through the opening in the door where the knob would go, one of the components holding the door closed and locked. "Maeve, sit tight. There's someone at the door."

When he returned to the kitchen, he was accompanied by

another man; Maeve immediately recognized his voice, the cadence that of someone from farther upstate than where she lived.

So Michael Donner wasn't missing, just biding his time until he could come visit Maeve and either tell her everything he knew or kill her.

Her money was on the latter.

"She's indisposed at the minute, Mr. Donner," Cal said. "Oh," he said, a little concern creeping into his voice. "Of course."

A chair scraped away from the kitchen table and Cal sat down, his back blocking the view she had from the powder room and, if she was on the same wavelength as her ex-husband, blocking her from harm.

"No need for that," Cal said. "Let me know what you need and I'll get it."

Maeve stood up in the bathroom, her bare feet making no sound on the tile floor. In a basket next to the sink were a variety of hair care products and appliances; she slid a travel curling iron into her front pocket. She got up on the toilet top and with one quick move-ment, opened the window above it, hoisting herself out as quickly as she could. Jo had been the champion gymnast in childhood, be-fore she had gotten so tall; Maeve was the clumsy little person with no coordination but no one would have known that by the way she silently threw herself out the window, onto the picnic table, and then to the ground. The girls had been locked in the bathroom so many times now that they had an escape route all planned: the picnic ta-ble was beneath the window, and although Maeve was several inches shorter than her daughters, she landed easily onto its surface, her feet hitting a stagnant puddle of cold water.

It was cold out and she wasn't wearing shoes. But she did two things before she entered the house again, as quietly and as stealth-ily as she could. First, she extracted the gun from beneath the seat of the Prius, the place she had returned it to after seeing Jimmy Moriarty. And then, she let the air out of the passenger-side tires of Donner's car, the same one she had seen a few weeks ago in Rhineview when they had met the first time. She would have loved to blow it up, the same way she had destroyed Regina Hartwell's old Rambler, but this was her neighborhood, her home. She wouldn't bring evil to the place she loved.

But she was a little worried at how much she was enjoying thinking about blowing things up.

She had lived in this house long enough to know which floorboards creaked, which were silent. How to open the screen door without giving anything away. How to hug the banister so that no one would ever hear you on the stairs. She loved that element of surprise.

Michael Donner was standing in the opening of the kitchen, his gun trained on Cal's trembling body. God bless the guy but her ex wasn't cut out for home repairs or this kind of violent confrontation. Fortunately, he had Maeve for that, but even she jumped a bit when Donner pointed his gun at Cal and fired.

Fortunately for Cal, Donner had terrible aim. It turned out to be a warning shot, even if he hadn't intended it to be.

While he did miss Cal, he did manage to hit the box of ornaments that were still sitting in the kitchen, despite Maeve's repeated requests to the girls that they put them away in the basement. She needed someone tall to do it, one of them, but her pleas had fallen on deaf ears. The box had sat there for the last several days, the policeman in the Santa hat, her favorite and a reminder of Jack, peeking out of the top. Michael Donner, with his terrible aim, had shattered that ornament, one that she had had since she was small and that reminded her of her father.

It was all she could do not to blow the guy's head off. She was behind him. He would never know what hit him. But she'd likely have to gut the kitchen when it was over; blood splatter was bad enough. But brain splatter was impossible to get out, if what she had seen on television was true.

Donner fired again, hitting the ceiling.

Maeve stuck her own gun in his back. "Drop the gun," she said. She only needed to say it once. The voice that came out of her throat sounded unnatural even to her but to Donner, it must have sounded like that of a demon. When he followed her first command, she ordered him to kick the gun toward Cal, who was bleeding from a wound over his eyebrow. The bullet had taken out a chunk of one-hundred-year-old plaster that had hit him square on the forehead. "Pick up the gun, Cal."

Cal did as he was told, holding the gun in one hand, a dish towel in the other pressed to his injury. He moved toward the back door and stayed there, his eyes trained on the much larger man and his ex-wife, someone he had never really seen before. Not like this anyway. She pushed Donner into a chair and slid the gun into the back of her pants pocket at the same time.

She grabbed the largest knife she had—a Wusthof seven-inch chef's knife—from the magnetic strip next to the stove and crawled up on the table, sitting cross-legged in front of Donner, who had a look on his face that told her that he may have stumbled across the one seemingly mild-mannered suburban mom with a murderous streak.

He'd be right.

"Why did you come here?"

"To talk," Donner said. "To explain."

"If you just came to talk, why'd you bring a gun?" Maeve asked, chuckling when it was clear that he didn't have an answer. "So, you came to threaten me or to kill me. Why?" He didn't have an answer to that either, so she tried another tack. She held the knife to his chin. "Where's my sister?"

"I don't know," he said. He turned his head slightly and the knife grazed him, drawing a thin line of blood. He looked to Cal for support. "I don't know."

Cal stood, as if in a trance, the gun dangling at his side.

She pushed the knife deeper into his chin, drawing more blood. "Where's my sister?"

"I don't know."

"Was she one of the other people in your sister-in-law's house?" Maeve asked.

"I have no idea."

She slapped him hard. "Was that my sister in that house? Little, blond, blue eyes?"

The slap jostled his memory. "I don't know."

"Who was there?" she asked. She raised her hand again. "Don't make me use this knife. Please," she said, the entreaty more to herself than to him.

His memory was suddenly sparked at the sight of the knife, her intention to use it telegraphed between the two of them. "It was someone else. Hispanic. Black hair. A woman. Not your sister," he said. "The woman had died. Jeannie. She was dead already. That's why I went to Regina's."

Maeve looked at him, incredulous. "To bury another body?"

He didn't answer.

Maeve adjusted her legs so she was more comfortable. "Want to know what my nickname was in culinary school?" When he didn't answer, she continued. "Guess," she said.

"I don't know."

She moved the knife and nicked his jawline. "Don't say that again." She stretched the arm not holding the knife. "Sweeney Todd. You know why?" When he didn't answer, she explained. "Because I was the best butcher in the class. Great with a fillet knife, too. Could clean and carve a pork shoulder, anything really, in under thirty seconds." She smiled at the memory. "Got an A in the class. Cal, did you know that?"

Behind her, Cal let out a little squeak to let her know that he didn't know that. "I'm calling 911, Maeve," Cal said, his voice, and his sense, returning to him.

She ignored him. "One last time. Where is my sister?" she asked, slowly and deliberately.

He answered in kind. "I don't know. I never did know. I never knew who those people really were."

She studied him. "You know how much blood there is in a human body?" she asked. She didn't know but was curious. Behind her, she heard Cal hang up the phone.

"No."

"Me either," she said. "I was just wondering what the cleanup will be like when I cut you open."

Cal vomited noisily into the sink. When he was done, he begged her to stop. "Please. Stop. The police will be here soon."

"Why did you come to the support group? To find out what we knew? What I knew? To find out if we were close?" Maeve asked.

His silence told her everything she needed to know.

Maeve waved the knife around in the space between her and Regina Hartwell's brother-in-law. "Coming here was a bad idea," she said. "No one threatens me or my family in my own home and gets away with it. No one comes to find out what I know and silence me," she said, guessing at his motive. She stared into his eyes, to see if there was any humanity there. "You kept those people isolated in a house far from civilization."

"Nobody wanted them," he said.

"Tell that to the people at the support group. The people you lied to," Maeve said. She felt a darkness grow inside of her, and the fear in the man's eyes grew to the point where if Maeve wasn't fueled by bloodred rage, she would have felt sorry for him. Laughed, even, at the roundness of his close-set eyes. In the distance, she heard sirens, so she got off the table and put the knife back on the magnetic holder, confident that Cal could keep the gun trained on him. "Jail is a better place for you than out there," she said to Donner's back, gesturing toward the outdoors. "Because I would find you. And I would kill you."

Cal was pressed up against the back door, not sure who he was more afraid of: the guy who had come to hurt his ex-wife or his ex-wife. By the look on his face, it was even.

"What did you do with Regina? Why did you have those people?" she asked.

"Money. We kept them alive with fake identities and got money. From the state. We used the social security numbers of people who had died at Mansfield toward the end, whose deaths hadn't been recorded. People who didn't have families. Weren't wanted. Regina needed help. The house was big. The yard, too."

"It couldn't have been that much that you were getting," Maeve said.

"It wasn't," he said. "But it was enough."

"And when you were done with them?"

"Some got sick."

"And the others? You killed them?"

"No!" he protested.

But that was all he said before a commotion erupted on the front porch, signaling that this part of her nightmare was now over.

Three officers entered through the front door, their guns drawn, Chris the first guy through the door. He wrinkled his nose when he got to the kitchen, Cal's upended dinner sitting in the sink. He didn't ask how the tall man sitting in the chair came to have a wound that looked like a slice along his chin.

"We're okay, Chris," she said, leaning against the counter nonchalantly.

"She threatened me! She has a gun!" Hartwell said. Blood dripped from the spot on his chin that she had cut.

Maeve pulled the curling iron out of her pants pocket. "You mean this?" she said. "Chris, get him out of here and I'll tell you what happened."

By the back door, Cal was on his knees, his hand holding the gun outstretched. "Someone please take this from me."

"And I think we need an ambulance," she said, pointing at Cal and the blood-soaked kitchen towel that was over his wound.

After the cops dragged him out, she gave Cal a glass of water and spoke to Larsson in the living room, telling him what she knew, what Donner had told her. "So nothing on your sister?" he asked.

"No," she said.

She thought about the past several weeks, about her father. She missed him now, more than ever, and wondered why before coming to the conclusion on her own. She had nothing left.

She looked at Chris. "I give up," she whispered.

CHAPTER 56

"Is that the last suitcase?" Maeve asked Rebecca, pushing the other things that had already been loaded into the Prius farther back into the hatch. The backseat was down, giving them some more room. Although Cal had volunteered to drive Rebecca back, Maeve had insisted. She and her oldest had a lot to talk about and the hour trip would give her the time she needed to have a very pointed conversation—okay, it was really a monologue—with Rebecca about fiscal responsibility.

The day was sunny but cold and in the harsh light Maeve could see that Rebecca's eyes were red and watery. Maeve knew why she had been crying: she had been caught. It was plain and simple. It had nothing to do with impending homesickness and it wasn't sadness over going back to school; she had told her mother several times that she couldn't wait to get back to Poughkeepsie, away from her mother and her rules. The tide was turning; it seemed that the freedom she had had at school had turned her into that recalcitrant teen that Maeve had been waiting to emerge since she had turned thirteen.

She was a late bloomer, it seemed.

"That's the last suitcase," Rebecca said, pulling a wadded-up tissue from her pocket and blowing her nose noisily.

"Did you say good-bye to your sister?" Maeve asked, checking her purse for her wallet, her keys. The night before, she had sat with Rebecca in the kitchen, supervising the numerous job applications that the girl had filled out: CVS, Boston Market, some retail stores at the Poughkeepsie mall. If she were going to beef up her accounts again and have money for those necessities like shampoo and school supplies, she'd need a job, something she never anticipated. The crying had started then and hadn't stopped since, it seemed. The blotches on her face were another hallmark of a night spent sobbing.

Maeve turned as Heather burst from the house, running down the front steps. "Wait," she called. Maeve expected a battle to ensue over Rebecca's absconding with one of Heather's shirts or Heather forgetting that she had borrowed five dollars from her sister.

As Maeve pushed the items closest to the edge into the trunk, she watched their heads come together, their whispering emotional and dramatic.

This burst of sisterly love warmed Maeve's heart, but that feeling was short-lived. There was a confession to be made, right here on the sidewalk, and one that Heather felt compelled to get off her chest thirty seconds before her sister left for school for another poverty-stricken semester.

"It was me," Heather said. "I took the check."

"What?" Maeve said. "The insurance check?"

Heather nodded. "Yes. That check."

Maeve was confused. Heather's bank accounts had never been as robust as her older sister's, the younger one being far less frugal and sensible about money overall. "How did you cash it?" Maeve ran through a variety of scenarios in her mind as to how that could have been accomplished but none of them made sense or seemed like plans that Heather could have pulled off herself.

"Tommy knew a check cashing place in Prideville."

Maeve saw red. She looked around the neighborhood, hoping that there was no one to witness what would surely be her last and final meltdown. Because she was going to kill one of them and then likely drop dead of a heart attack. "And they cashed it for you? How? Do I even want to know?" Heather must have forged her mother's signature. The check-cashing store had not asked for identification. It was all there on the girl's face.

Heather didn't respond. Apparently, it had been easy and Maeve didn't want to know.

"I took the money out of my account to repay you," Rebecca said, hoping that the flush that was rising in her mother's cheeks could be allayed by more news on this front. "I had to help her."

She was wrong; the flush in her mother's cheeks grew deeper, blotchier.

"Wait," Maeve said. "Back up. Do I want to know why you needed three thousand dollars?" She knew the answer to that question. It was "no." This is where the story is going to make me throw up, right on the street, Maeve thought. This is where it all falls apart and we all have to leave town.

Rebecca looked at Heather. "Do you want to tell her?"

Maeve pointed to the house. "Let's not do this out here. Let's go back inside." Before Rebecca could protest that they needed to leave for Poughkeepsie immediately and not one second later, Maeve shut her down. "School will be there whether we get there at four or five or even eight o'clock tonight. Or ever. Zip it."

The girls sat on one side of the kitchen table while Maeve stood. She needed to be ready to lunge at them if the spirit so moved her, knowing that what she was going to hear was going to make her very, very angry. There was no doubt in her mind.

Heather spilled it all at once. "Well, you know Tommy? Well, he had some stuff that he wanted to hide so I said we could hide it at the store and we put it in the flour but then when we went back it wasn't there." She looked down at the table. "Because you threw it out."

"Threw what out?" Maeve said.

"The stuff."

"What stuff?"

Rebecca filled in the blank. "The weed."

"It was in the flour," Heather said.

Maeve held on to the counter for support, her thoughts of lunging at both of them, of throttling them, gone. Weed. Pot. Marijuana. In her store. In her flour. She remembered the day well when she had accused Jo of not putting the top on the flour bin, but it had been Heather.

"Why?" was all she could get out.

"He couldn't keep it at home," Heather explained, as if this was an idea that should have crossed her mother's mind.

"So you put it in my store."

"It was his brother's," Heather said, the whole story coming out. "Tommy didn't want him to be dealing again, so he stole it and asked me to keep it somewhere safe."

Maeve put her head down. It was all too much.

"And we were coming back to get it. But you threw it out. And he had to pay for it. The stuff."

"If that's a hint of accusation I hear in your voice, Heather, I'm going to lose it." Her mind raced. "How tightly was that package wrapped?" she asked, her mind going through all of the possibilities. How Joan Weisman may have gotten a carrot cake with a dollop of weed in the center. How the DPW guys may have eaten marijuana-tainted scones. How everything she had made from that bin of flour may have included something the customers hadn't wanted.

How, if discovered, she was going to jail for the one thing she had had no hand in.

Heather tried to calm her. "It was wrapped really tight. It was in several layers of plastic, wrapped in tinfoil."

Maeve would have to take her word for it. So far, she hadn't heard of any hallucinogenic episodes around town after someone had shopped at The Comfort Zone. That kind of salacious news would have ended up in the blotter for sure. Maeve looked at Rebecca. "And the money?"

"She had to pay Tommy back because he had to pay . . . um, his brother's dealer . . . back," Rebecca said, her broad shoulders slumping in a way that suggested that she was happy that this was all out in the open and that her having to come up with a life—that of a baller who treated her friends to weekends in the city—that didn't suit her to cover her sister's misguided tracks, was a thing of the past. She let out a shaky, sobbed-filled sigh.

"Who's the dealer?" Maeve asked. When it was clear that both girls knew but didn't want to say, she asked again. "Who. Is. The. Dealer?"

"Some guy," Heather said. "I don't know."

"Is it Mr. DuClos?" she asked.

Heather shook her head. "Someone else. From Prideville."

"Is he the person that broke in?" she asked.

Heather's bottom lip was shaking so hard that Maeve was amazed she could speak. "Probably." She let out a pained sob. "I came back to get the stuff but it was gone. Tommy told them that it was gone from the bakery but they didn't believe him. So I had to help him get money. He owed them for that with interest."

"The Brantleys are one of the wealthiest families in town," Maeve said. "I think if you had thought this through just a little further, you could have come up with a better plan." She put her face in her hands, anything so that she didn't have to look at them. "The finger? And how did they get into my store?"

Rebecca paled a bit but answered for her sister. "Tommy's. I'm guessing it was a warning? To Heather?"

"Thank you, Nancy Drew," Maeve said. "How did they get into my store?" Her emotions went from sheer terror to white-hot anger and then back again. Sitting in front of her, her girls didn't seem to realize just how much danger they had put everyone in.

Heather took a deep breath before answering; that's how Maeve knew it was going to be a humdinger of an answer. "Tommy knew the code."

Before her mother could react, Rebecca took over the story and filled in the blanks. "Heather cashed the check before I came back from school. When she told me, I told her I would give her the money. From my school accounts. To pay you back."

Maeve did some quick math in her head. "I don't think you had enough money," she said to Rebecca. "Where did you get the total amount to repay me?" she asked.

The girls exchanged a look, not wanting to give up the one person they went great lengths to protect.

"Dad," Maeve said. "So you took all of the money you had and made up the difference by getting money from Dad. How much?"

"Five hundred dollars," Rebecca said.

"For what?" Maeve asked. "What did you tell him it was for?"

"Books. I told him it would be easier to use cash at the bookstore."

Maeve paced the length of the kitchen, her mind awhirl. "Where's Tommy now?" she asked. "Still at lacrosse camp?"

Heather shook her head. "He came back for a few days. I think he's leaving again."

"You think?" Maeve asked. She pointed at Rebecca. "Get in the car." She looked at Heather. "You, too."

Rebecca looked relieved and smiled at Heather.

"Oh, you're not going back to school," Maeve said. "You're going to Dad's."

When they got there, she let them loose. "You're on your own. And you'd better tell the whole story, and the whole truth. Because if you don't, there's no telling where this is going to go." She didn't want to go in for a number of reasons, the least of which being that Cal seemed terrified of her now after the night with Donner, more so than usual. Couldn't say that she blamed him.

They trudged up the walk to the Tudor like they were going to the chair, and once they were inside, Maeve drove off.

Maeve didn't know how it was going to end, but she didn't want to be along for the ride. "Siblings know." And apparently, protected each other. Here, this whole time, she had been thinking that they were ready to kill each other, when really, they had been negotiating and plotting and trying to figure out how to get Heather out of the mess she had gotten herself into.

She parked in front of the Brantleys' house, throwing the car so furiously into "park" that she was afraid she had broken the gearshift. The idea of what had transpired, the anger being replaced by white-hot fear, made her light-headed. It all made sense now, why Heather had stopped going out only to start again once her sister had come home, and ostensibly had settled the debt for Tommy, why she was in the store that day, a spoon in her hand covered with flour, the realization that Maeve had inadvertently disposed of precious goods probably making her tremble with fear. Maeve had spent her life keeping her girls far from danger, yet they insisted on finding danger, and the thought that she wouldn't be able to protect them forever made her feel more than impotent.

It made her feel weak. Useless.

She had lived through years of abuse and her only wish was that she could raise happy girls who had nary a care in the world. But,

Jack was saying to her, his voice drifting through her mind, people make their own choices. Screw up. Do the wrong thing.

That's life, he would have said.

He wasn't that cavalier, but he liked to put on a good front.

She could never trust them. She'd need to be more vigilant. She'd need to pay better attention.

"This is hard, Dad," she said in the cold confines of the little hybrid. "I wish you could help me."

But when he didn't answer, didn't have anything else left to say to her, she went to the front door, still clad in Heather's pink parka, and banged on the door, her fear and useless feeling being tamped down by the anger that had propelled her to come here. Tommy, looking like he had come straight from bed, answered the door. "I've got it!" he called behind him to the other residents of the house.

Tommy stood a little straighter when he saw her, either just because she was Heather's mother and she was at his house or because of the look on her face, the one that told him she was going to do the talking and when they were done, he wasn't going to do anything but nod in agreement. The screen door, him on one side, her on the other, afforded him some protection, but with the way she was feeling, it may not have been enough.

"Welcome back from lacrosse camp," Maeve said.

She wondered if he had the same look on his face when he told the dealer that his pot was gone.

"I'm going to say this once and you're going to follow through. Got it, Tommy?" she said.

He nodded.

"Stay away from Heather. Don't come to my house. Don't talk to her. Don't look at her. Don't text her or Facebook her or send her a Snapchat or Instagram or whatever else you punks use to communicate." She looked up the street. "I see you live in very close proximity to the police station." It was on the next street, practically in his backyard. "Keep that in mind as I watch every move you make, and chronicle every last detail of your life."

He tried to look dissolute, uninterested, but that was hard to pull off what with his left eyelid doing the salsa. Behind him, Maeve spied several suitcases, all lined up, waiting to go on a journey. With Tommy, hopefully.

"Nod so I know that you know what I'm saying here, Tommy," she said.

He nodded.

"What is it you kids say? 'I'm not playing'?"

He nodded again.

"Not only am I not playing, my hand is on speed dial to 911 so that if I see you within five feet of my daughter, I will call the cops and tell them that you stole three thousand dollars from me."

It all came together for him, in that instant. Heather's mother knew everything and no, she was not playing. She decided to go for broke. "Did you hit me over the head, Tommy, or was that some two-bit dealer who you owed money to?"

"I'm going away to school," he said, and the way his face caved in at the mention of the break-in, the assault, Maeve knew that it hadn't been him. "Tell Heather bye," he said.

She looked down the street in the direction of the police station and wondered what she should do. Go to Chris Larsson, dragging this kid by the hair, and making him tell everything he had done, compromising her own daughter's future?

He lifted his hand, the one with four fingers, and closed the front door.

And in that action, seeing his missing digit, Maeve let it go.

Maeve walked away from the house, the sudden urge to pee overtaking any other feeling she had in her body.

But it didn't seem like good form to ask Tommy Brantley, a kid whose life she had just threatened, if she could use his restroom.

CHAPTER 57

"You can take me, right?" Jo said, pulling her apron off and hanging it on the hook by the kitchen door.

Maeve was sure that they had had a conversation about where she was supposed to take Jo, but the day had been a blur and whatever it was, wherever it had been, was gone from her mind. It was two weeks after Michael Donner had invaded her personal space, her home, and had been carted away by the police. Jo had drunk in every juicy detail, Maeve leaving out the really juicy ones like the fact that she really had a gun in her pocket, not a travel curling iron. And that she had stopped short of slicing his throat open, not wanting Cal to be the witness to her depravity.

The day after it happened, Maeve asked Chris when he stopped in for his daily muffin if he had asked Michael Donner about Francine Alderson. Copping to that murder, he told Maeve, would have taken things to a whole new level. Donner denied any knowledge. "Nothing," he had said.

She remained convinced that it was Donner and him alone who had killed her friend, leaving her to die in the parking lot of the YMCA. He had been there that night. He had heard the conversations among the support group members, their recitations of the things they had done to find their relatives. He knew her name because Regina Hart-well had told him; she was sure of that. She asked Chris to find out what had happened to Winston and he obliged, giving her a little information confidentially.

"All I can tell you is that he's happy and safe," he said. "I can't tell you more than that. I don't really know a heck of a lot more, but just know that that's what I was told."

It wasn't enough, but it would have to be.

He started laughing, his mind on something else. He pulled the paper off his muffin, talk of death and dying not affecting his appe-tite at all. "You're going to see this in *The Day Timer,* so I can tell you, but a few weeks back, we got an anonymous tip from some-one to go to your landlord's house."

Maeve tried to act nonchalant, something she was getting better and better at doing. "Really?"

"Yeah," he said. "Lots of traffic at the house but we didn't find anything, had no just cause. But someone else came forth, not sure if it's the same person, and said that he was dealing."

She had been right.

"Want to know what?" he said, even though she thought the answer was obvious. She looked at him, waiting for the answer. "Medical marijuana."

"Really?" she said. "Isn't it legal? And I thought people who smoked pot were mellow."

Chris laughed louder. "I know! Not the people who grow it, though. It's still a cutthroat community because when it comes down to it, pot is pot. Lots of money to be made. He was growing pot in the basement." He grabbed a cookie from the sheet she had just taken out of the oven. "And tomatoes."

The tomato he had given her the month before had been quite delicious. Maeve put her arms around Chris's waist and looked up at him. "I'm not going to tell you how I know or why, but just keep an eye on Billy Brantley. He may not be as on the straight and narrow as you think." She left out the part about the finger's owner. When he opened his mouth to speak, she put her finger to his lips. "Not another word."

And that was where they left it, a kiss cutting off any further questions he might have had for her.

"Maeve?" Jo said, interrupting Maeve's daydream, taking some spray and cleaning the fronts of each cake case. "Café Americano?"

"Right," Maeve said, standing in front of the refrigerated case in the front of the store and taking a quick inventory of the beverages. "What do you need?"

"They got written up in 'Best of Westchester' for their hot chocolate. It sounds delicious. And I *need* it," she said, indicating that this was yet another item on the list of things that she craved incessantly and couldn't live without.

Maeve would be very happy when this baby was born, if only to end the cravings. Earlier today, it had been pizza. And now, hot chocolate. Who knew what tomorrow would bring? Chorizo had been replaced by capers and capers by tabouleh. Maeve wondered what was in this magical hot chocolate, but Doug had the car, the beautiful Ford Taurus, and Jo was without "wheels," as she called them. She had stopped riding her bike months ago and obviously couldn't ride all the way to Rye anyway, pregnant, in the snow.

Maeve, as was often the case, was "it."

Maeve hated driving across the county and avoided it like the plague. There was always traffic on 287. Sometimes, it was bumper to bumper. But Jo was the closest person she had to a sibling and likely always would be, and because of that, Maeve would have driven to Canada to get her what she wanted.

That, and Maeve could be guilted into doing just about everything. She blamed Catholic school.

On the ride over, Jo kept up a constant monologue, remarking on everything from the construction on 9A to the new entrance to the Taconic and how the lines overhead made the AM station that Maeve listened to for weather and traffic reports crackle with static. Did Maeve want to see the new Johnny Depp movie? Did she prefer the popcorn at the Hawthorne theater or at the Palisades Center? How come movie prices were so high anyway? How long did it take for a baby's umbilical cord to come off? And did you know that you could get practically new Dockers at Goodwill for like two bucks? Maeve had learned over the years that her participation in the conversation wasn't really necessary; she just needed to be there, to be the sponge that absorbed all of Jo's musings, from the mundane to the profound.

She knew her role. She was happy in it.

Maeve slowed as she approached the store, finding a parking spot on the street, rummaging around in the little holder in the car for a couple of quarters to feed the meter. She watched the café's clientele streaming in and out of the upscale coffee shop, feeling bedraggled in her baggy jeans and clogs, her shirt that smelled suspiciously of sour milk and some other unidentifiable odor. She wished she could be like one of those women she waited on at the store, or the women who seemed to frequent Café Americano, women who had disposable income, who didn't work, who vacationed with their friends because they needed a "break," from what Maeve wasn't sure. Yoga? Spinning? Pilates? Who knew? Instead, she was this woman, a woman with a friend who talked all the time and who sometimes felt as if she were still waiting for her life to start, even if she did have a successful business, a handsome guy to share a bottle of wine with, girls who were trying so hard to make her proud again.

A woman who had given up, just a little bit.

Maeve spied an area where she could sit and relax while Jo got this incredibly special hot chocolate. She asked if she could wait while Jo waited in line. "I'll be right here," she said, pointing to the surprisingly large seating area. Maybe Jo was right and this was the place to be.

"Do you want something? A coffee? Hot chocolate?" Jo asked.

"I'm good," she said, surprising both of them by giving Jo a hug. "Thanks."

Maeve took a seat by the window and looked out at the traffic going past on the road, letting her mind drift farther and farther away with each passing car.

It wasn't like her to throw in the towel ever, but she had nothing left. Would there come a time when a little burst of emotional energy would return and spark her brain, letting her renew a search she knew she had to resume?

Evelyn wasn't dead, like everyone said she was. Cal, more than anyone after hearing the story of the Hartwell/Haggerty deception, was more convinced than ever that if Aibhlinn "Evelyn" Conlon was alive and well, someone would have come forward to let Maeve know. But to Maeve, she was alive. And Maeve would find her. It was just a matter of when, not if. But she was so, so tired. She put her arm on the table and rested her head, her eyes growing heavy as around her, people sat, one woman surrounded by eco-friendly shopping bags, her purchases from the stores on the avenue.

The journey of one plastic bag. Maeve remembered seeing a video online and feeling guilty that sometimes her own eco-bags stayed in the trunk of the Prius for months on end. So this is how the world worked, apparently: people could follow the journey of one plastic grocery bag and even determine where it ended up but she couldn't find her sister, a living, breathing person. That seemed too hard to comprehend. She closed her eyes, the sounds of the coffee shop soothing her in a way that she wouldn't have thought possible, people placing complicated orders, voices all coming together into one gentle cacophony signifying the lives that were being lived all around her.

Everyone in her life had moved on, had lost interest in the search.

Cal had halfheartedly called a few more group homes, discovering that no one would give him any information, even if he did play the role of "lawyer." After all, it wasn't like Maeve knew her, he had said; did she really "miss" her or was she imagining a relationship that would never come to fruition? If she had had more energy after he had made that remark, she would have punched him in the forehead stitches.

Of course she missed her sister.

Rebecca was back to school, penniless and destined for an entire semester of eating in the dining hall. Heather was getting ready for the upcoming SAT exam. Jo was preparing for the baby. And Jimmy Moriarty, it seemed, didn't want to see Maeve anymore, so there was no one to talk to about the way she felt or to explore new paths for finding a woman she didn't know existed until two months earlier.

In her semi-conscious state, she thought about Jack. This coffee shop had become an unlikely but safe place to be alone with her thoughts, something that she couldn't really comprehend in her half-dozing mind, but it was what it was, as the girls would say. She thought about him, walking jauntily down the street, calling out to her when she was small, his mind still sharp in those days, his body still fit and cooperative. She would be waiting on the stoop. Lots to tell but not everything told. The day to rehash. Secrets to be kept.

She drifted in the sea of normal that enveloped her like a warm blanket. I am so, so tired, she thought again, not for the first time, probably not for the last. Bring her to me, Dad. Help me find her. Don't let her have lived in that house of horrors at any time in her life.

She wasn't sure how long she slept but when she sat up finally, her vision was cloudy, her head a dusty attic full of mental cobwebs, of disjointed dreams and unreliable memories. Jack. The day-old challah. French toast. Photos in an album, falling to the floor, Maeve's clumsy hands trying to put them back on the pages from which they had escaped.

"It's not challah," Jack had said in the dream. "It's rye."

He used to talk about Rye a lot when she was little, and she always assumed he meant bread, not the place in Westchester where she sat currently. "I'm going to see a friend in Rye," he used to say and when she got older, she assumed he was going to see a woman, because he had flowers and chocolates, always a few bottles of nail polish. Mimi Devereaux had had competition long before she had even come on the scene. Even though she and her father had both loved Claire Conlon so much, they both wished for Jack to find someone. Maeve wished for a new mother and Jack, a new wife. It was the unspoken betrayal to Claire's memory that both of them kept deep within their hearts, but it was there and they knew it. She had once heard him whisper to someone on the phone, "If I could just find someone to love as much as I loved Claire," and Maeve wondered why he hadn't wished for someone to love him as much as Claire had loved him. They had a different way of looking at things, she and her father.

She looked around but no one noticed the little woman who had fallen asleep in the coffee shop, everyone still content to go about their business, buying lattes and espressos and baked goods that she could have told them weren't as good as her own. Come to The Comfort Zone, she thought, and almost said out loud; I'll give you pastry memories to last a lifetime.

Behind her, she could hear Jo's voice, excited. High-pitched. She must have finally gotten her treasured hot chocolate, one that had taken an inordinately long time to prepare. Before she turned to find her friend, Maeve pulled a napkin from the holder on the sticky table. She had been crying in her sleep but hadn't realized it until now.

"Your eyes," she could hear Jo saying. "She has your eyes."

Maeve turned slowly, trying to find her friend in the throng of people who had assembled in front of her table. Jo burst through the crowd, using her belly to forge a path, one hand outstretched, the other trailing behind her. There was a lot of commotion and Maeve wondered if Jo was the thousandth customer that day; had she won an unlimited supply of hot chocolate? There was too much energy in the air, all coming toward Maeve in an emotion-filled whoosh, and it didn't make any sense.

Behind Jo was a little woman, older, with short hair cut in a sensible bob. Maeve's first thought was Sister Augustine from elementary school; although the woman had worn a habit when she was Maeve's second-grade teacher, Maeve had seen her years later and marveled at the fact that she had had hair all along under her habit. She had died a few years ago; hadn't Maeve heard that? It couldn't be Sister Augustine, then, but the nun's hair had looked just like that of the woman in front of her, neat and tidy, combed to perfection. The woman's blue eyes complemented her fair skin and her dull blond hair, a few thin strands of gray visible. She was wearing jeans.

She looked Irish, almost like a leprechaun, tiny, spirited, and happy.

Maeve wondered why these little details mattered to her; she wondered why she noticed.

Jo brought the woman to the table.

The tag on the woman's apron said EVELYN and Maeve prayed that she wasn't still asleep, that she was awake and seeing what she imagined: a woman, older and smaller, but who looked a lot like her.

"She has your eyes," Jo said softly as she took the woman by the hand to meet her sister.

CHAPTER 58

Maeve went through the red tape and the background checks to get access to the home where Evelyn lived. Whoever Evelyn's guardian was granted permission for her access to her sister, the place she had lived for many years.

In Rye.

She smiled at the thought of Jack, in her dream, telling her that it wasn't challah he had, but rye. Had he told her? Or had she known all along?

Siblings know.

In Rye. The coincidence was a benediction, a blessing.

It wasn't a girlfriend who Jack had gone to see when she was small; it was Evelyn. She liked to polish her nails, Maeve learned. She loved flowers and chocolate.

Maeve pulled up in front of the home, her trunk packed with cookies, cake, and some bread that she had made. Evelyn, not unlike her younger sister, had a sweet tooth and told Maeve in a recent phone call that she was "very happy" that she had a sister and that her sister knew how to make cookies. Today was Evelyn's birthday.

"My daddy died," she said that day in Café Americano, those words the first bond they would share.

"I know," Maeve had said.

She wondered how much Evelyn really knew or comprehended, if Jack had told her about Maeve, about how one day they may possibly meet? "My daddy loved cookies, too."

Just not my donuts, Maeve thought, and smiled.

"Do you know Jimmy?" Evelyn had asked. "He's my friend."

Yes, she knew Jimmy, and if she wasn't so overjoyed to see this little, happy person in front of her, she would find him and wring his neck. He had known all along and no cockamamie story about chasing perps and missing floor grates and Jack saving his life was going to get him out of this one.

In the end, she decided to e-mail him and tell him everything she knew. How Evelyn had found her, not the other way around. How she would forgive Jimmy in time for his devotion, albeit misguided, to his dead friend and his wishes, even though, in reality, she was still working on that and not sure it would ever happen. How she knew with almost one hundred percent certainty that he was Evelyn's guardian and that if he had just told her the truth, she wouldn't be mad. He hadn't responded.

Maeve had been told that four women lived in this lovely Victorian, all middle-aged, and three of them with jobs in the town, hired by people who loved Mr. and Mrs. Deckman, the couple who owned the house. The women were part of the community and the business owners who had hired them were happy to give the women jobs to fill their days. All had different developmental challenges but were all happily employed and taken care of. One of Evelyn's roommates also worked at the coffee shop and another at a deli in town. The last one, the oldest, was a little more infirmed and helped out at the house when she could, the irony and coincidence not lost on Maeve when she compared that situation to the one in Rhineview. Mr. and Mrs. Deckman were lovely people, whereas Regina Hartwell had been evil. That was the major difference.

Maeve couldn't believe the turn of events. Evelyn Conlon had been right under her nose all along. She just hadn't known.

Evelyn had been there a long time, had grown up in comfort and safety. When Maeve did the math, and it was sketchy, she had to assume that Jack had gotten Evelyn out of Mansfield long before the story on the television aired. He knew she wasn't safe and made sure to find her a new home. That mitigated her anger at his deception just a little bit. She still had to process just what he was thinking by never telling her about this sibling she never knew she had.

She sat in the parking lot. Evelyn, she could tell, was kind and happy. Unlike most other people Maeve knew, she always asked Maeve about her day first and then told Maeve about her own. She asked about the girls, Rebecca and Heather, and was truly interested in their well-being. She loved Jo. And she wanted to work at The Comfort Zone instead of Café Americano.

She wanted to live with Maeve.

In a lot of ways, she was a lot like Jack.

Maeve wasn't sure if they could work that out. The whole relationship required careful planning and baby steps, two concepts she wasn't sure Evelyn understood.

That day in the coffee shop, with people gawking at the sight of the two sisters' reunion, Maeve had touched her sister's cheek, not sure if she should, if Evelyn would be accepting of that.

"Your name means 'longed-for child,'" she had whispered, and Evelyn, in response, had said in a voice that exuded enthusiasm, "I know!"

Maeve thought of Jack and how, in the end, he had made sure that Evelyn had a good life, even if she wasn't in Maeve's. He didn't know that Maeve had longed for her sister and would never know that now she was here.

In the driveway at the side of the Victorian, a fine mist collecting on the windshield of the Prius, she watched as an older man, his profile flattened from an unknown number of nose breakings, lumbered toward his own car, a classic but sporty BMW. She had seen him go into the house with a gift bag, which she later learned held a new iPod filled with Evelyn's favorite songs—she loved Frank Sinatra—and multiple bottles of red nail polish.

"Jimmy Moriarty loves cars," Jack used to say. "Helped him when he did Auto Crime in the PD. Guy can tell you any year, any make, any model. He's amazing."

Maeve got out of the Prius and hurried across the long driveway. "Jimmy!" she called. He pretended not to hear her but it was too late; she had caught up to him and he was going to tell her everything he knew but especially, why he hadn't told her anything at all.

He sagged visibly. Whether it was under the weight of his heavy overcoat or the knowledge of his deception, she wasn't sure. "Maeve."

"You knew," she said, the lack of accusation in her voice surprising her. She hadn't expected to see him and this needed to be said. Out loud. He was an old man with not that much time left; that was clear from his sallow complexion, from the way his breath rattled out of his chest. He was sick. How she knew that for sure, she didn't know, but the once hale guy who used to shuttle her father around was weakening, almost before her eyes. "Jimmy, that was so cruel." Her voice broke on the last word. "You knew and you didn't tell me." She thought about what she had planned on doing, the mayhem she was prepared to unleash on Regina Hartwell. Jimmy Moriarty had no idea what she was capable of, how his deception could have wrought a chain reaction of violence and even death.

"I was going to tell you." He looked around. "Eventually." His mouth was set in a grim line. "I would have had to at some point soon."

They could have avoided so much had he only acted on his intention. "But you didn't." Do you know what I've been through? Do you know how much pain this has caused? She didn't say anything, though, because doing so would make him cry even harder than he was crying now and she didn't think she could take that. "Would you have told me before . . ." She paused. She didn't want to say it.

"Before I died?" he asked. Ironically, speaking those words seemed to calm him. "Yes." He reached out and grabbed her hands in his. They were rough, like Jack's used to be, with short, stubby fingers, a smattering of gray hair across the knuckles of his fingers. Working-man's hands. He squeezed her own small hands, her fingers. "I'm sorry, Maeve. I'll never be able to explain it to you. I'll never be able to tell you why I did this for him and have it make sense." He let go of one of her hands and reached into his pocket. "I don't know what to say to help you understand, but he thought he was doing the right thing." He looked over at the house. "Poor kid didn't get enough oxygen at birth or something like that. But she does well. She's happy."

He handed her a small jewel case with a DVD inside. Maeve took it and slid it into her pocket, not knowing what it was or why he had it on his person but knowing that she would find out soon enough. She wouldn't see him again; she knew that. There was nothing left to tell.

He looked off into the distance, over Maeve's head at the house. "He saved my life, your father did."

She knew that but wasn't sure why it meant that he had to lie.

"When I moved into that place, I thought it was the end for me. Old people. Lots of old people! And me." He chuckled at the mem-ory. "And then I find this old brother from the Job, a little wacky, kind of forgetful, but a guy who became my best friend in the world." He looked back at Maeve. "I didn't know I could have a new best friend at my age. We should have been best friends all along."

Her hair was wet and so were her cheeks, but it was only the rain.

"He asked me to never tell unless I knew I was going to die," he said. "He didn't want her to be a burden, something else for you to deal with. So, that's what I did. I lied."

Maeve closed her eyes and took a deep breath. "I'm not sure I'll ever understand that, Jimmy. I'm not sure I'll ever understand why you didn't tell me the day he died." A little ember, anger, flared in her chest. She was trying to forgive him, be true to her word, but it was hard.

"I was only respecting your father's wishes."

She got that. But he had waited an awfully long time after Jack's death to let the truth be known, and only because she had found out first.

He started to cry in earnest and her heart broke a little bit. She wrapped her arms around his broad, squat body and let him cry into her shoulder. Behind him, one of Evelyn's roommates was taking out the trash. She didn't know Maeve but she gave her a hearty wave that Maeve returned. Her smile said it all: she was happy here.

He finally pulled away and took out a handkerchief, blowing his nose loudly. "I'm so, so sorry, Maeve," he said. "I know the last few years have been hard on you."

You have no idea, she thought.

"Him, too," he said. The rain started falling harder, making it difficult to see him. "He was forgetting. He was forgetting her. He knew he should remember, but he couldn't. That's why he kept leaving."

Maeve brushed her wet hair from her eyes even though she was afraid to move, afraid to interrupt his train of thought. "Kept leaving? Buena del Sol?" she asked. It was one of his nightly jaunts to the outside world that had left Jack wandering around in the dark, only to be hit by a car and left even more broken than he had been before.

"Yes." Moriarty looked at her. "He was looking for her or something. He couldn't remember sometimes why he left. But wanted to say good-bye. To tell her he loved her."

She looked at this sad man in front of her, one who was so sick, who didn't have much time left.

A tear slipped down the old man's cheek. "He wanted to say good-bye before he forgot to."

CHAPTER 59

Maeve settled into the couch with a glass of wine so big that she was glad she was alone and that no one would ever know that she had poured almost half a bottle into this novelty goblet, which said, appropriately, *It's wine o'clock!* Heather was babysitting for Devon; it was "date night" for Cal and Gabriela, something that had never transpired with any kind of regularity during her marriage to Cal.

Cal, despite his serious "wound," as he called it—his oft-talked-about forehead stitches—claimed to have finally "fixed" the powder room doorknob even though she still got locked in there from time to time. The box of ornaments still sat in the kitchen and Heather still complained that there was never any food to eat. Life, as Maeve knew it, had returned to normal.

Heather had gotten a job and was paying her sister and her father back, week by week. She hated working at the local grocery store, particularly on Senior Day, but she wisely kept her mouth shut about her unhappiness.

And gave her mother the senior discount.

Tommy Brantley had gone away to a school far, far away in Plattsburgh, near the Canadian border where it was winter for nine months a year. Maeve hoped he was freezing his other nine fingers off.

Maeve hadn't seen Billy or DuClos and that's the way she liked it. She wondered who would take over the landlord duties now that DuClos was in the wind. Chris said that they were still looking for him but that he felt confident the odiferous building owner would surface again, dead or alive, his Mob connections in the hunt, too.

Because, as Chris said more than once when they talked about everything that had happened, a twinkle in his eyes, "Criminals are stupid. They always turn up."

Maeve turned on her laptop and slipped the DVD into the drive. In seconds, Jack's face filled the screen; his look of confusion, prevalent in his last days, was there but fainter, almost imperceptible. This had been a long time ago, obviously.

"Is this thing on?" he asked.

Jimmy Moriarty's Bronx-hewn accent was heard in the background. "Yeah! Start talkin'."

Jack turned toward the camera. "Hiya, Mavy. How's my beautiful girl?"

She burst into tears. She had cried more in the last few weeks than she had in her entire life.

"Don't cry, honey," he said. And then softly, he repeated, "Don't cry." He reached out toward the screen and Moriarty reprimanded him for almost smudging the lens. "Okay. If you're watching this," he said, "then I'm gone. But with the way things have been going," at this he paused and pointed to his head, "it's probably better this way."

Maeve looked up at the ceiling, trying to stem the tide of tears.

"So, I'm seventy-two years old . . ."

"Seventy-five!" Moriarty called from off-camera. So the recording had been made six years earlier.

"Seventy-five. And I hope I lived a little bit longer so I could be with you. You were . . . are . . . the best daughter a guy could have, Maeve. Sure, I hate it here . . ."

Moriarty chimed in. "Me, too!"

"But I know it's for the best. Some days are great and I remember everything but others . . ." He drifted off. "Anyway. I have some things to tell you."

She wondered why he waited until after he died to reveal his motivations.

"I bet you're wondering why I'm waiting to tell you this." He drew a hand across his eyes. "I don't think I ever want you to know but that's Jimmy's call after I go. I just didn't think that right now, the way I feel, I could look you in the eye and tell you the whole truth. It's a lot and it's painful." He drew in a shaky breath. "Turn it off, Jimmy."

When they came back, Jack was wearing a different shirt; it was another day. "I'm back. Let me tell you what happened." He tried to appear strong, make it seem like telling her this story was the most normal thing in the world. But his first admission—"she wasn't mine"—made his voice crack in a way that she wasn't sure that he could go on. "I loved your mother, Mavy. More than life itself. So that's why, even though she was pregnant with someone else's child, I married her."

Maeve stared at the television, wondering if she had heard him right.

"Because I couldn't live without her."

It was not easy having a developmentally challenged child back then, she imagined. Add to that that the child wasn't yours, belonged to someone else, and sending her away and then never speaking of her to your biological daughter may have seemed the only answer. She couldn't understand it, as hard as she tried, but it was what it was, as Jo often said. He didn't want her to know, to tarnish Claire Conlon's memory, so he kept the secret their entire lives, visiting the girl at the group home, having taken her out of Mansfield as soon as he had seen the first hint of impropriety at the place, the news story. That was her only guess.

"Time passed, Mavy, and I never told you. And then more time passed, and I was raising you alone, and there was this burden I never wanted you to share. Your sister. Your mother being pregnant when we married." He looked down at his hands. "I think you would have loved her, your sister, but I don't know. You might have treated her like she was the most special sister in the world. But there was never the right time. You had your own children. You got divorced. You had me to worry about." He looked at Jimmy, still off-camera. "It was never the right time," he said, as if to convince himself. "And something's been wrong with you lately. You're preoccupied. A little sad. It's not the right time now either."

She stared back at the screen.

"And I didn't want to see the look in your eyes that you probably have now. The look that says I did wrong by you and her."

Her reflection was etched around his face, backlit by the windows facing the porch. He was right: she did look disappointed. She did feel wronged.

"I hope you'll forgive me when you do find out, because when I'm gone and when Jimmy's gone, there is no one else." He looked down, contemplating a time when he and Moriarty wouldn't walk the halls of Buena del Sol. "You don't know her father, Maeve, and he didn't know he had a daughter, so don't worry about that." He looked back at the screen. "I hope you'll forgive me."

She did.

"It's different now, Maeve. I never wanted you to feel the burden of her," he said, repeating the words that Jimmy Moriarty had said to her in the parking lot.

But she wasn't a burden, she wanted to say.

She's a gift.

CHAPTER 60

When the sun shines and the air is clear, there is nothing better than sitting riverside and enjoying a barbecue. Mr. and Mrs. Deckman were on board when Maeve told them that she was going to rent the gazebo on the Saturday of Memorial Day weekend and host a little party for Evelyn and her roommates. Rebecca came home and Heather had cleared her active social schedule, neither protesting in the least when Maeve gave them a shopping list filled with items for the barbecue and making the holiday-weekend trek to Shoprite, where Heather now got a discount because she had been a part-time employee for over three months.

Jimmy Moriarty had passed away the month before and Maeve had wept in the back of the church in a way she hadn't when Jack died, her mind after her father's death too taken up with the store and pictures of a baby who belonged to her parents, trips to Goodwill. He was with Jack now; she was sure of that. And they were telling stories about their time on the Job, most of it made up, to other cops at whatever bar they had appropriated wherever they were.

Their time with Evelyn was still marked by a little confusion, some trepidation. Maeve sometimes wasn't sure what to say, how to act, but Evelyn made it easy. She was happy and chatty and told

Maeve everything about her day when they spoke. With each passing day and each joy-filled phone call, Maeve got more comfortable, putting the past—and Jack's secret—behind her. She had a sister.

Evelyn's social interactions were different than Maeve was used to, but she was kindhearted and loved seeing the girls, telling them about her latest adventures at Café Americano, and bringing them little gifts whenever Maeve brought her to the house for a short visit: the all-natural lip gloss that Heather liked, the body wash that Rebecca seemed to go through with alarming alacrity. The girls did her nails, every one a different color, her toes, too. They were becoming a family, one visit at a time.

Jo stood by the water's edge with the baby, a rotund little guy with a shock of black hair, strapped to her front. Unlike watching Devon in Cal's sling, Maeve enjoyed seeing the baby—John Stuart the final determination, or "Jack" for short—dangling from Jo's torso, his little feet kicking with delight whenever Maeve appeared.

If she didn't know better, she would think that the kid had a little bit of the real Jack, the old Jack, inside of him. No one should be that happy to see someone who wasn't his mother or father.

Chris Larsson manned the barbecue, stoking the coals. "Barbecue is man's work, Maeve," he said, laughing when she poked him in the side in protest. "You should know that."

She left him to it, walking back to the car to make a second trip with the cart that the Parks Department left for picnickers to transport larger items. Maeve had two cases of water in the trunk of the Prius, far more than she needed, but the amount the girls had bought. She opened the trunk of the car and hoisted both cases out, dropping the first with a loud thud onto the cart. When she had successfully loaded both on, praying that the worn tires of the cart would hold and not go flat on her, she slammed the hatch shut, surprised to find a man standing in front of her car.

"Maeve Conlon," he said, like he always did, using her full name.

"Rodney Poole." She held on to the cart, which seemed to have a mind of its own, not to mention bad alignment. "You turn up in the strangest places." She looked into the park; Chris was still messing with the coals and using what seemed like too much lighter fluid to light them. She hoped he stayed there. Explaining who Rodney was, what their connection was, would be too complicated.

"Gorgeous day for a picnic," he said.

"How did you know?"

He pointed at Doug, a long way away by a tree at the river's edge, rustling around in a very feminine diaper bag for something to soothe the baby.

"Right," she said.

"Lots of nastiness up in Rhineview this past winter." He stated this as if he were commenting on the weather.

The graves had been dug up, DNA testing was complete, and the people who had been members of the Mansfield Missing had been found and accounted for.

"You can say that again." In the distance, she saw the minivan that the group home used to transport its residents. He didn't give anything away and neither would she. "You appear at the oddest times, Poole," she remarked again, still a little mystified by his presence.

"Does it make you uncomfortable?" he asked. "Because I'll stop if it does."

Don't stop. "It's fine." She looked at the Deckman's minivan, pulling up into the handicapped spot not far from where she was stacking the water onto the cart.

"I just wanted to tell you that Michael Donner died last night."

She had vowed to forget that name forever but there it was again. "Good riddance."

"Inexplicably," he said, a smile on his lips, "he ended up in Sing Sing. No one knows what happened. Found him dead in his cell."

"Sing Sing, you say?" A tendril of fear traced her spine, landing in her solar plexus. Her mind went back to her conversation with Doug, about how his partner had a long-lost brother there, doing time. How much time, she didn't know. If he was still there, had been there for Donner's murder.

"Yes. Know anyone there?" he asked, turning and looking out at the water.

"No," she said. But you do, she thought. She looked at him, wondering. But he was the same Rodney, rumpled and kind, the man who kept her from doing the wrong thing at the wrong time, from going too far. Had he gone too far himself? And to what end?

"I hate to think of you hurting," he said.

"I'm not. I have a sister," she said. She didn't say another word lest she bring back that time when he told her what she had done, what he had figured out. How she had killed a man and never lost a night's sleep.

"Beautiful spot," Poole said.

"It is." She pointed to Evelyn, bursting from the front door. "I hear you've been through the same," she said, not sure she wanted to know. "Not knowing."

His mouth, almost smiling up until this point, went slack.

"I'm sorry," she said, busying herself with the water bottles, one case teetering dangerously to the side and threatening to fall into the parking lot. He walked over and helped her.

"We have a lot in common," he said, as if just discovering this for the first time. His arm brushed against hers as he righted the case of water. The sound of happy voices filled the space behind them.

"I know." She put both hands on the cart to see if she could push it herself. "Do you want to stay? Meet my sister and her roommates?"

His face got that sad look that she had seen once or twice before. "I'd better not. Conflict of interest and all."

That didn't really describe the situation but she let it go.

"There's my sister! There's my Maeve!" The little woman, shorter than Maeve but with her eyes—the shape and color—hugged Maeve from behind, taking her breath away. Maeve turned around and gave her sister a proper hug, one that wasn't quite so painful; when she looked for Poole, he was gone, and with him went the fear that she had felt in his presence, the thought of how he had closed another door for her, again leaving her consciousness at the sight of her sibling. Her sister.

"Are my nieces here?" Evelyn asked. Today, she was wearing jeans with a neat crease down the front and a tee shirt; all of the women who lived with the Deckmans wore the same shirt when they were out in public together. It was bright orange and could be seen from a distance.

"Yes," Maeve said. "They are. And Jo, and Doug, and little Jack. Everyone's here."

Evelyn looked up at her younger sister. "But not my daddy. He's not here."

Maeve took her sister's flushed cheeks in her hands, kissing her forehead.

But you are and I love you, she thought. You are my gift.